Ursula,
I enjoy
over the
enthusiasm you my
holiday ornament
contribution is fondly
remembered. Take Care
Carol

PAYBACK TIME

PAYBACK TIME

A Mystery

Carol Maranchuk

iUniverse, Inc.
New York Bloomington Shanghai

PAYBACK TIME
A Mystery

Copyright © 2008 by Carol Maranchuk

iUniverse books may be ordered through booksellers or by contacting:

iUniverse
1663 Liberty Drive
Bloomington, IN 47403
www.iuniverse.com
1-800-Authors (1-800-288-4677)

Because of the dynamic nature of the Internet, any Web addresses or links contained in this book may have changed since publication and may no longer be valid.

This is a work of fiction. All of the characters, names, incidents, organizations, and dialogue in this novel are either the products of the author's imagination or are used fictitiously.

ISBN: 978-0-595-48926-8 (pbk)
ISBN: 978-0-595-48982-4 (cloth)
ISBN: 978-0-595-60897-3 (ebk)

Printed in the United States of America

For Stephanie,
for being my friend

ACKNOWLEDGMENTS

I wish to thank several people for sharing with me their professional expertise as I wrote this mystery. First and foremost Corporal Marv Martens, a retired corporal of the Royal Canadian Mounted Police, Sheriff Lance Cranna, of the Edmonton law courts, Sharleen Maranchuk, paralegal, and Caroline Malo, a former jury member.

Most of all I want to thank Stephanie Sarafinchan, Cheryl Sarafinchan, and Georgina Fysh for their invaluable help with this book.

PROLOGUE

▼

I stare at the two inch knife scars zigzagging down my arms. A sudden shudder leaves my entire body trembling. Vibrating now, I hug myself tightly attempting to gain control, and ponder—not for the first time—how to escape these flashes from my past.

It is six in the morning and I am standing at the patio door of my home testing the lock and checking the security system for the third time in the past two minutes. Will I eventually shed this obsessive-compulsive behavior that has gradually gained control of my life?

I think about the person I was: a crown prosecutor with a successful rewarding career, a marriage to a wonderful man, great parents, and close personal friends. I had a life to be envied. How did an intelligent, sophisticated woman like me allow this to happen?

The howling wind draws my attention back to the patio window where I observe multicolored leaves forming patterns of mini tornadoes. These dance across the back yard to stop trapped against the east fence. Leaves still desperately cling to the branches of the trees only to eventually succumb to nature's forces. I feel myself being sucked in, twirling, spinning out of control as the events of my attack flash across my screen.

Heart pounding loudly, gasping for oxygen, my eyes lock on the scars again, and I feel panic. These irrational fears hurl me back to when I'm in the presence of evil. I can feel the knife slicing the skin on my arms and penetrating my back with brutal force.

Panting, nauseated, I scream out, "Someone help me, help me!" I feel arms encircle me from behind; bringing with them his touch of love and much needed reality. He whispers, "Ashley, I would take on your pain and fear if it were humanly possible."

CHAPTER 1

▼

Eighteen months earlier.

Feeling confident, I stroll into courtroom two hundred and sixty-four and head for my seat at the prosecutor's table. For years family and friends have questioned my choice: why a crown prosecutor and not a defense lawyer? Victim's rights are my top priority, and the main reason I prosecute rather than defend. The court system today is forgetting the victim. A victim of sexual assault is changed forever and in some cases ruined for life.

Little Karen was eleven, when she was grabbed off the street on the way home from school. Ernie Lott was charged with her abduction and sexual assault. If found guilty I estimate Lott will receive eight years and be eligible for parole in three. Karen, in the meantime, will probably continue experiencing her present nightmares for years to come. Further, it is likely she will encounter problems with relationships in later years.

The mere thought of defending the criminal individuals I face daily is bone chilling to me. Today, I will get justice for Karen Webster and her family. The jury has reached a final decision and I feel certain the verdict will be guilty on all counts.

Glancing around the courtroom I take in the beige walls, twelve short, and three long benches beyond the railing. The large elevated structure made of mahogany holds the bench, seat of the judge. The court clerk sits to the right of the judge's chair.

Facing this structure are two tables. One is for the defense and the other for the prosecutor. The tables are separated by a podium holding a microphone. To the left of the room are three shorter benches which will seat the twelve jurors.

The benches beyond the railing seat one hundred and twenty people. A combination of reporters, family, friends, and curious spectators are slowly filling the courtroom.

Three sheriffs employed by the provincial government are stationed throughout the courtroom. They are dressed in black pants and shirts with a blue trim. The sheriffs wear bullet proof vests and a side arm. The role of the sheriff is to provide security and protection. On more than one occasion I have been thankful for their presence.

A quick glance to my left reveals the defense table where Marty Kroll, the famous defense lawyer, and his entourage are seated. Marty leans into Ernie Lott. He is accused of kidnapping and sexually assaulting Karen Webster. Lott is listening intently, nodding, with an occasional glance in my direction. He is a tall, obese man. His eyes are small, hooded, and mean, and his mouth wears a permanent sneer. Ernie wears his hair long, and it is a tangled mess whether early in the morning or late afternoon. I know they provide shampoo to the prisoners, but Ernie must refuse to use it.

There is no love lost between Marty and I. In court, over the years, we have battled each other on many occasions with more wins credited to me. Recognizing and appreciating his professional abilities in a court of law is not equal to a personal respect or appreciation of this man. Rather his slick, swept back, black hair, well trimmed mustache, and fashionable, dark, Armani suits add to my impression of his sly and cunning attitude.

Marty has made his money on representing clients, who I consider to be the scum of the earth. The monsters he represents are not homeless men, but teachers, lawyers, oil company executives, and priests, who can afford Marty's price tags. Ernie Lott, for example, owns a trucking business in northern Alberta.

My team has spent a lot of time gathering evidence, interviewing witnesses, contacting and consulting with experts. We had discussed the crime scene with police officers, and listened to the gut wrenching testimony of the victim.

Yesterday, my closing statement appeared to be well received by the jury of five men and seven women. We have worked this case for months and the need for positive closure is immense. Logan Reid, a part of the troupe joined the prosecution team approximately two years later than I. He is tall with a medium build and deep set, hard, brown eyes. Logan's hair color is between a light auburn and red. His personality is aggressive and his mouth sarcastic. Logan's jokes are meant to injure, and he uses whatever tactics necessary in his attempt to reach the top as quickly as possible. I'm one of his stepping stones.

The jury deliberated for nine hours. Their verdict was reached at eleven this morning. Studying the jury members as they file into the courtroom reveals facial expressions of fatigue, but nothing more.

The court clerk announces Judge Brian MacIntosh. He commands attention with his six foot, four inch height, and two hundred pound frame. He has cool, blue eyes and bushy, black eyebrows. Some prosecutors dislike MacIntosh, but over the years I have found him to be as fair as he is strict. He sits down, and then his booming voice addresses the jury, "Have you reached a verdict?"

The foreman dressed in a simple, brown suit stands and replies, "Yes, we have, your Honor."

Judge MacIntosh asks Ernie Lott to stand and nods to the foreman.

"We the jury find the defendant, Ernie Lott, guilty as charged of kidnapping and sexual assault." This is announced by Mr. Simmons, the foreman. During this statement he doesn't make eye contact with Ernie Lott.

Feelings of joy and accomplishment rush in as I register Karen Webster's parents' cry, "Thank you God." What I observe in their eyes compensates for the late nights and hard work. Another monster is off the streets at least for a while.

During the reading of the verdict there is a blank expression on Ernie Lott's face. He then turns and looks at his lawyer, Marty Kroll, and I see fear in his eyes.

Outside the courtroom Marty Kroll brushes past me and whispers in a critical voice, "Next time." Due to the media frenzy I can't respond to his barb. It is going to be a long afternoon.

At 7:30 in the evening, after a hectic day, I head for my sanctuary.

My home is located on a quiet residential street close to a large city park. It has a two car attached garage which to me was the number one selling feature. There is a large front yard with flower gardens and shrubs. The back yard has a perfect array of ornamental trees, a fire pit, and two decks.

The kitchen is amazingly bright with maple cupboards and a huge central island. Every electrical appliance and kitchen gadget known to man is available. It makes cooking and baking enjoyable, easy, and delightful, particularly for me. I didn't inherit the excellent cooking abilities of my mom. An eight chair and table suite is part of the kitchen.

The dining room contains a sparkling chandelier overhanging a twelve chair dinner suite with matching china cabinet. Patio doors lead to a small deck holding the barbeque, and a brightly colored umbrella, table and deck chairs.

Next to the dining room is the great room where one wall holds the entertainment centre and fireplace. During the long, cold, winter months I love listening to the crackle of the fire as I settle down with a good book and a glass of red wine.

A white leather sectional faces in the direction of this wall. Three recliner chairs of various colors are placed around the room. There are patio doors leading to a large deck facing the back yard. Many after dinner parties have been held on this deck. In one wall of the great room an archway opens into a hallway.

Off the hallway are five rooms: the master bedroom which includes a full bathroom, two guest bedrooms, a main bathroom, and a combination computer and library room. My mom has accused me of spending far too much time in the computer room.

I am positive she and Dad would much prefer having me in the kitchen making meals for a husband. Although they would never voice this opinion out loud, I think my parents would love me to be happily married, and in the bedroom producing little grandchildren.

I have shared the comfort of my home with others through dinner parties, office gatherings, and neighborhood barbeques. Mom and Dad visit me regularly and often spend the night. My home suits my lifestyle perfectly and is a comfort to me.

CHAPTER 2

▼

Stretching, I check the alarm clock on my night table and realize that forty minutes of sleep is still available. Relaxing, I revisit my recurring conversations with Mom and Dad. My parents, Barry and Lucille Browne, are exceptional people. My dad is tall and a little on the heavy side; too much down home cooking. He has the deepest, dark blue, eyes imaginable, and a full head of blond hair which is graying at the temples.

My mom, Lucille, is a wonderful cook and baker. She is in addition the best mom a gal could want. While Dad is heavy, Mom is on the slim side. She has green eyes and red hair which she wears in a stylish cut. She loves clothes and jewelry, and on my Saturdays off we often spend the afternoon shopping.

Dad is currently sharing the principal position at the local high school in their home town. He is retiring soon and is now mentoring a teacher to take over when he leaves. Mom has her art work and charities. She has always maintained that her role in life has been to care for Dad and me. They are fantastic parents and I love them dearly.

Yesterday, they drove to the city to meet with me for dinner. We went to my favorite lobster restaurant, where I overate as usual. My dad pegged me early. "Your mom and I are concerned about your lack of a social life. All your time and energy is invested in your career. It leaves you alone many evenings."

Feeling hurt, I responded, "Law is like the medical profession. You can't turn it off at four-thirty and go home. Many of my evenings are spent at work, finding avenues to fight for the victims."

"We understand your commitment dear and have nothing but respect for your work. Our hope is that the work is not replacing a personal life."

This concern is voiced approximately every six months. Mom adds her concern, "Ashley, understand we love you and want only your happiness, but you are not getting any younger."

I'm thirty-two years old without a partner and appreciate my parents being anxious to become grandparents. I have had my share of relationships but nothing serious in the past two or three years.

Mom informs me, "Dad met this nice young man who started teaching at his school. He invited him for lunch last week. His name is Kevin Manguard. He is pleasant, good looking, single, and intelligent."

I think to myself, *Here we go again.* To prevent Mom moving from a normal conversation to an exaggerated fit I interrupt, "Mom, I'm fine. I date but am not involved with anyone seriously." I stop to consider the other crown prosecutors who are only interested in clawing out a respectable career. Prosecutors such as Logan Reid or some of the defense lawyers I have faced. Most defense lawyers force me to grind my teeth. I would not consider myself spending a life time with any one of them. I, too, wonder when I will meet Mom and Dad's future son-in-law.

Pacifying my parents I say, "I may be able to escape for a weekend in mid-May. Spend time with you and Dad." They smile at me and drop the subject.

My parents reside in a medium sized town approximately a one hour drive from the city. They have lived in the four bedroom house since their marriage. It was my home until I left for university. Being an only child, I feel a commitment and want to provide for them in their older years. From day one Mom and Dad have showered me with love and support. Financially, they saw me through law school. A generosity I would not soon forget.

The alarm clock sounds that my forty minutes have slipped by, and I quickly reach over to switch off the button. My first priority is coffee. This is followed by a quick run in a nearby park. I will then shower and dress for work. This is my daily routine.

CHAPTER 3

▼

The Law Courts building is located in the downtown area of the city of Edmonton. Twenty-five lengthy cement steps lead to the four storey structure. Everyone entering the building must pass through a security system, similar to the type found at airports.

Once inside, you can observe the glass sheets covering the front of the building and reaching to the ceiling. From there the glass curves to form a dome. Large, white pillars reach skyward to support the glass structure. The walls are painted off white, with grey and burgundy patterned rugs covering the floors. Burgundy cushioned seating is available throughout the building.

Arriving in my office I retrieve ten messages from my answering machine. One is from Jim Stromby, my boss, demanding my immediate presence in his office. A demand attendance usually signifies an assignment I will be reluctant to accept.

My office is small, measuring twelve by fourteen feet. The only window in the room overlooks a major downtown street. My computer desk with six drawers and a hutch is against one wall. There is a floor to ceiling book case and filing cabinets against the other. I have a few green plants and a picture of Mom and Dad in the room. My plants end up dying if my friend, Gail, doesn't attend to them. I didn't inherit my mom's green thumb either. A small table with three chairs stands left of the door.

I now leave my office and follow the spacious hallway to Jim's office. Jim Stromby, chief crown prosecutor, has maintained this position for the past seven years. He was a crown prosecutor prior to successfully applying for his present position. His large corner office is located at the end of the hallway. Four times the area of mine, he has two breath-taking views. One is of downtown and the other of the river valley. Knocking gently, I enter on command. Jim is sitting at his massive desk. His files are piled high and nearly obscure him from view.

Jim is of small stature with thinning, brown hair and hazel eyes. But his deep voice and aggressive demeanor demand attention. Today, he is dressed in a dark, blue suit, with a white, high collar shirt and matching dark, blue tie. He wears a Rolex and large, gold, cuff links.

"Good morning, Ashley, have a seat."

I wonder, not for the first time, why Jim bothers offering me a chair. I know from experience this will be approximately a one minute conversation. But I sit as instructed.

"Great work on the Karen Webster case. Caught a lot of media coverage. Good for your career."

"Thank you. But as you are aware, I'm more interested in putting these slime balls behind bars, than I am in advancing my career." He smiles at me. His expression conveys a message of caring.

"You become too involved in your cases. It's the one fault I find with you. You need to step back a little, before you burn out."

"I can't step back. When is our justice system going to wake up? We release repeat offenders time and time again. When interviewed, hundreds of pedophile offenders confessed that no amount of rehabilitation changed their sick minds, yet we keep discharging them back into the community."

"I know. The case I'm assigning you has many similarities to the Webster/Lott case."

I'm stunned. "I'm emotionally as well as physically exhausted. What about Reid? He hasn't prosecuted an alleged sexual assault case on his own in months. Even Shelly Galeno, though new to our team, has some experience in the area."

"The case requires your expertise. Reid is busy and his successes in this area are few. Logan basically rides your shirt tails and Galeno doesn't have sufficient experience. Contact sergeant Orlicky, from the Major Crime Unit, for information. Cheryl will forward any information from this office to you." Cheryl is Jim's executive secretary.

"Keep me informed," are his words of dismissal.

I stand quickly. My muscles are rigid and my teeth clenched. The meeting is over so I don't bother with a parting comment. It takes immense control not to slam his office door on my way out. I should be sainted.

Cheryl, who has been with Jim for the past seven years, smiles at me, "Have a great day Ashley."

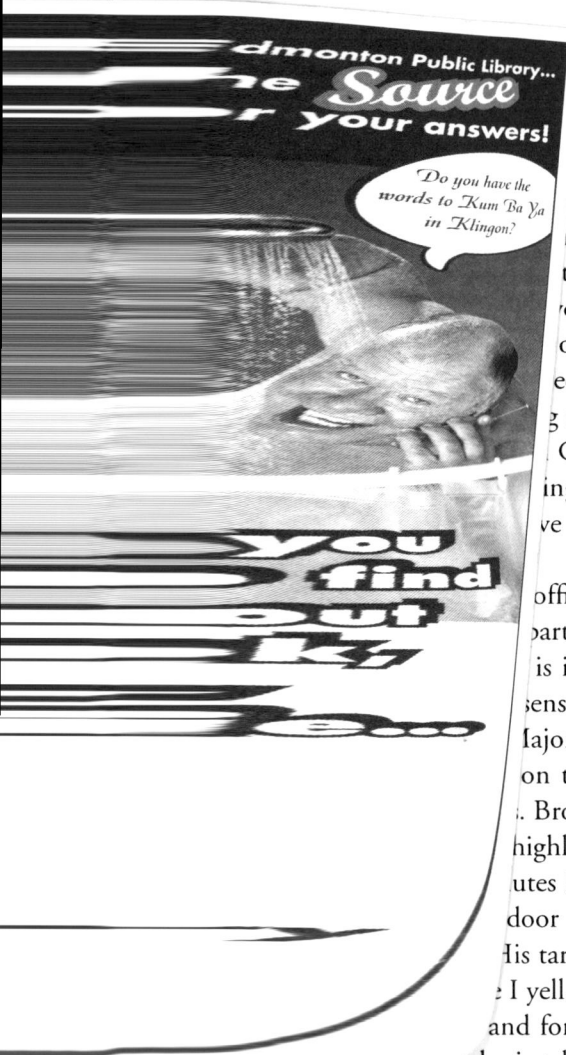

eeting but appreciate my anger is not the result
rn and mutter, "Same to you."

the Major Crime Unit and ask for Sergeant
oice message greeting is completed, I tell Sam
office at one-thirty the following afternoon. My
ed.

g the urge to cry. I'm exhausted and not prepared
Cheryl drops off the file, I do review the Kuzew
ing, I stretch, and glance in my mirror. Sky blue,
ve a wide, full lipped, mouth which is not smiling.

office secretaries, rings to announce the arrival of a
partment and adds a ray of sunshine to our other-
is in her mid-twenties, very attractive, with large,
ense of humor. Today she states, "Ms. Browne, a
lajor Crime Unit is here to see you." I hear her say,
on the right." Then to me she whispers, "What a
. Browne." We hang up.

highly of Sam, but he hasn't played a part in any of
utes late for our afternoon meeting. I'm a couple of
door when there is a pounding that could wake the
lis tardiness and pounding annoy the hell out of me,
I yell, "Come in."

and for a moment we stare. He stands there a second
icky is tall, very muscular, and much too handsome. He
wavy hair, deep set, green eyes, prominent cheek bones, a strong chin, and a radiant smile. He thrusts a hand forward with an, "I'm Sergeant Sam Orlicky."

For a second his stature, plus deep voice, take me by surprise and I continue to stare.

I finally extend my hand and say, "Hello, Ashley Browne."

"It's a pleasure to meet you." He holds my hand for an extended time so I pull it back. In response he smiles, then says, "We have a real sicko in Billie Chartrand. He kidnapped this eighteen-year-old, Sheila Kuzew, sexually assaulted her, tortured her, stabbed her, and left her for dead. A crop dusting farmer spotted her from his plane. She was on a side road on his farm. He notified the police immediately. General Investigation Section became involved and they in turn contacted us. The farmer was directly responsible for us capturing him so quickly. Otherwise, who knows?"

"It's so frightening, Sergeant Orlicky. Where are we growing these demented men? Why are they in such a rage?"

"Call me Sam, please. They are grown, as you say, everywhere in the world. Big cities, hamlets, you name it. I'm not a psychologist therefore I have no answer as to the rage. Speaking from experience, most of the ones I have talked to have abusive backgrounds as children. The more abuse suffered the greater the anger."

Sam pauses and a frown forms on his forehead, "Mind you, I do know individuals who were abused as children who grow to be upstanding citizens." He gives me a big smile.

"Do you have sufficient evidence in this case to take to a preliminary hearing?"

"We have opposed bail and Billie Chartrand has appeared before a Justice of the Peace. He was not released but sent back to the Remand Centre. Billie will appear before provincial court for the plea. We have positive identification by Sheila, through the use of photo line-up. We also have tire track photo matches. The bastard's body was completely shaved and he wore gloves and used a condom. Therefore, we suspect to find no deoxyribonucleic acid (DNA) from the sexual assault kit. But, we hope we got lucky when one of the Forensic Identification Section technicians, located two, long, blond hairs attached to the rug in the van's front passenger side. We are praying for a DNA match to Sheila Kuzew."

"Excellent. Any chance of locating the weapon used to torture and stab her as she attempted to escape?" With this question I can feel my anger.

"The constables have searched the crime scene, ditches along the farm road, and are currently doing the highway with no success. His two room rental was thoroughly searched by the constables, although I believe he did not have sufficient time to return to his room, before he was picked up. No sign of a knife in his van."

I ask, "Any explanation for the slash wounds covering the victim's arms?"

"No. She told us he kept screaming, "Mommy, how does it feel, bitch?" over and over. Is it true that Kroll is representing Billie?"

"Yes." Another round with Marty so soon is not what I hoped for. "How can Billie Chartrand afford Marty?"

"Don't know, but Chartrand must have bucks somewhere because Marty never does anything gratis. We are currently checking Chartrand's background. My investigators didn't uncover one shred of information on him. I trust them, but will give it a try myself tonight. Some of the criminals have become smarter over the years and do spend mega bucks covering their tracks. Was to meet my friend, Josh, for a few beers tonight, but I will dig into Chartrand's past instead. I'll be in touch as evidence is processed." A departing grin displays a row of bright, white, evenly spaced teeth. He adds, "I'm closing the door gently and quietly."

Instead of being annoyed, his parting comment and engaging grin leave me with a warm glow inside.

CHAPTER 4

▼

Saturday afternoon in mid-May finds me driving north for a visit with Mom and Dad. This is the weekend they want me to meet Kevin Manguard, Dad's new teacher. I feel cornered, at having to tolerate an evening with a complete stranger, when all I want is down time with my parents.

I arrive shortly before four in the afternoon. Mom already has the dinner of roast beef, roasted potatoes, squash, and cauliflower prepared for cooking. Salad is mixed and in the fridge. There is little left to assemble for this dinner.

I ask Mom, "Can I set the table?"

Mom smiles sweetly at me and replies, "Yes, thanks, but use the good china and crystal. Not often anymore do we entertain a guest for dinner. Our friends prefer to dine out rather than have guests over. We miss the visiting. Dad and I are so looking forward to this evening."

Dad exchanges a loving gaze with Mom, then turns to me and asks, "How is the job? Keeping our streets free from crime?"

"Dad, you know that would take a miracle. Gang wars alone, keep crime rates increasing."

Dad is passing me the plates and crystal from the china cabinet. He asks, "What are you working on now?"

"Another sexual assault case Dad. It's like an epidemic out there. I shudder at the notion of bringing a child into today's society."

Mom joins in, "Ashley, you and your family could move out here in later years to bring up a child. We so enjoy the peace and quiet."

I want to ask, Mom, where she thinks I would work? The door bell interrupts and Mom rushes to the front door. I hear fragments of conversation then Mom enters the dining room with a tall, fairly muscular male, with short, blond hair swept back from his face.

"Ashley, Kevin Manguard. Kevin, this is my daughter Ashley."

We extend our hands and shake. I notice the intense, dark brown eyes. Kevin holds my hand, "It is such a pleasure to meet you. Your mother speaks of you often and you are as pretty as your pictures."

Embarrassed, I mumble, "Thank you." Mom dispatches us into the living room, where Dad offers drinks.

I notice Kevin acts as if he has known my parents for years, rather than this being only the second time he has been to their home. Our dinner conversation consists of discussing the school system, crisis in the Middle East, and health care. Kevin is an interesting conversationalist and I am surprised that I'm enjoying myself.

The remainder of the evening is spent in the living room which is conducive to easy conversation, because Mom has placed comfortable cushioned chairs in a circular fashion. Politics and recent movies are the topics, but by now, I have noticed Kevin has not once referred to my career. He is very much dominating the conversation.

Kevin asks, "Has anyone seen the movie, Diamonds?"

I'm about to respond when he cuts me off with, "It was excellent. In fact, I would attend it again."

Dad turns to me and inquires, "Have you replied to Tim's wedding invitation?"

Before I can answer Kevin interrupts, "Talking about weddings my family keeps inquiring when my big day will be."

I'm becoming annoyed. At last Kevin stands and announces his departure. Walking him to the door I think to myself, *Thank goodness.* As he is leaving Kevin turns around and asks, "Can I call you? Maybe we can take in a movie?"

I hesitate a moment, then a "Sure" pops out of my mouth. Where did that come from? Do I like Kevin enough to accept a date or does my response have more to do with my parents?

"What is your phone number?" Kevin asks.

"It is 555–5341." It's too late now to change my mind.

He reaches into his jacket pocket and produces a little note pad with attached pen. Thinking, *What a convenient little tool,* I look up and catch Kevin staring intently at me.

"You are so beautiful Ashley." Kevin remarks to me in what he perceives as an enticing voice.

"Thank you. Goodnight, Kevin."

He stands there, perfectly silent, for what seems an hour then almost sings the words, "Good night."

My parents, especially Mom, are ecstatic about the events of the evening. I wonder, *Is it because she was in and out of the room all evening fetching snacks and did not observe Kevin's behavior?*

Mom asks, "Did Kevin ask you for a date?"

"Yes Mom. Or at least he asked for my phone number."

"That is wonderful. My word, look at the time. Barry, turn on the television; it's time for the evening news." I'm happy the subject of Kevin has been dropped.

The following morning driving back to the city, I have completely forgotten Kevin. Instead I concentrate on the upcoming interviews with witnesses for the Sheila Kuzew case.

The next evening the phone rings while I'm lying back with my sore feet elevated. It's Kevin, "Ashley would you like to take in a movie tomorrow night? We can take in an early one at six and enjoy a late dinner after."

I understand my hesitancy but still feel I owe Kevin a date. It's wrapped around my feelings for Mom and Dad.

I reply, "Thanks. I can't do an early movie because of prior work commitments. Let's see a nine o'clock movie and skip dinner."

"It sounds great. There's a movie I would like to see at nine. Pick you up tomorrow at say, eight o'clock?"

"I can meet you at whatever theatre you have chosen. Save you time." Quickly, I wonder, *Why have I suggested this alternative? Is it because I can drive home on my own without being forced into a good night kiss? Or is it the fact a movie has been chosen without consulting with me? How does he know I haven't seen the movie?*

My thoughts are interrupted by Kevin, "No need, I will pick you up. See you at eight tomorrow."

I stop him with, "Wait, you need my address."

"I already have it from your mom. Bye." He hangs up.

Annoyed with Mom for sharing my address without consulting me, I slowly hang up.

Next evening at eight sharp the doorbell rings. Opening the door I'm greeted by Kevin who places a quick kiss on my lips. Before I can move back, he hugs me close.

"Hi Ashley, it's great to see you. Oh, your hair smells perfect." He now has his face planted in my hair.

I want to ask, *Perfect for what?* Instead, as I push him away from me I say, "Thank you."

I wish I could ask him to leave. Instead, I lead him into the great room and offer him a glass of wine. I gesture toward the couch and take a seat on a recliner chair. We discuss his day at work and drive to the city. After fifteen minutes of this one-sided conversation, I inquire if it's time to leave. I'm uncomfortable.

The movie of his choice is a romantic drama. Surprise, surprise! In the darkened theatre Kevin places an arm around my shoulder and continually draws me up against him. It's uncomfortable, and I want to scream at him. Eventually, I ask him to stop. After my request not a word is spoken until we arrive at my home. Obviously he is angry and I couldn't care less.

As I open the car door I offer, "Thank you. The movie was enjoyable. Bye now."

"I will walk you to the door, Ashley." Kevin is busy reaching for his door handle.

"It's okay. I can see myself to the door. Thanks again."

"A gentleman never allows a lady to walk herself to the door in the dark. Never know what lurks in the darkness." For a moment I wonder if this is a threat.

Deciding against a reply, I quickly remove myself from his car and head toward my house. Kevin is beside me in seconds. At the front door I turn to say good night. With a thin lipped smile he asks, "What about tomorrow night, can you join me for Chinese food?"

Am I hearing right? At this point I want to be rid of him. "No Kevin, I'm working late tomorrow night. Good-bye."

"I will call you," he replies. Is he deaf? I move quickly as I can't wait to get behind a closed, locked door.

The evening episode is soon forgotten as I log onto my computer and immerse myself in my law books. For the Sheila Kuzew case, I require information dealing with certain law codes and old case results.

When I go to bed two hours later it is not Kevin I'm thinking of, but Sergeant Sam Orlicky.

The Kuzew case keeps me occupied with interviewing witnesses and consulting experts. I find myself speaking to Sergeant Sam Orlicky often. On a Thursday morning Sam arrives at my office to discuss an interview he had with Sheila Kuzew. After sharing the information, Sam, somewhat uncomfortable, looks at me and asks, "How do you spend your Friday nights?"

To this point all conversations with him have been centered on evidence connected to the case, but I'm certain we both feel the emotional undercurrent passing between us.

Attempting to keep the excitement from my voice, I answer, "If I have no exciting date, I spend it curled up on my sofa with a good book."

Sam places his hand on my upper arm and lowers his voice, "Can I call you some evening? Maybe we can take in a movie or a dinner?"

"Sure. Anytime."

He leans forward and kisses my cheek, then abruptly turns to the door. "See you later, Ashley."

I'm rooted to the spot and slowly place my hand over the area he kissed. I feel a twitch in my lower abdomen.

After this interaction, when face to face or during telephone interactions with him I feel happy and excited. No further reference is made to our personal feelings for each other. But I believe I'm in love!

Logan Reid notices the frequent meetings between Sam and me and decides to extract information. When questioning me about Sam's background he observes my facial expressions closely, for any reaction. I know what he is hoping to find and it takes willpower to refrain from slapping his face. Our last encounter ended with a typical comment from Logan, "He is certainly a handsome brute which must make your meetings more enticing."

Logan's visit to my office forces me to stay at work longer than usual. Following Reid's departure I take time to examine my feelings for Sam. Then realizing how late it is, I quickly pack my briefcase and drive home.

Many days have past since my movie venture with Kevin. I arrive home and notice my answering machine blinking. The first call is from my friend Gail White, requesting a girl chat, the other three messages come from Kevin. Playing back the messages from him I hear the following.

"Ashley, it's Kevin. Can we do dinner tomorrow night? Give me a call 1-780-555-7218."

I'm thinking, *Absolutely not. We can't go to dinner even if I was starving.*

Second message is, "Hi, it's me again. It is seven. Call me soon."

Highly unlikely, I think to myself. What is it going to take with this man?

By the third message he sounds annoyed, "Ashley, by now you should be home from work. Hope you're not out on some hot date. Call me, 1-780-555-7218."

He is annoyed. I am furious and have no intention of returning his calls.

My supper consisted of grabbing a fast soup and sandwich at work at six. I now have a glass of wine and prepare for bed. As usual, I am exhausted.

Two hours later the phone rings just as I am drifting off to sleep. Of course, it's Kevin. Answering, I attempt to keep my voice neutral, "Hello."

His voice sounds annoyed, "Hi it's me. It is about time. Your job demands are unusual. You probably heard my messages. How about going for dinner?"

Earlier, while preparing for bed I made a decision. If he called again I would meet him for dinner, and advise him that I didn't wish to hear from or see him again.

"I will meet you at the City Asian Restaurant on the corner of fifty-first and one hundred and eleventh street tomorrow evening at 8:30."

"I don't like the food there. There is a small Chinese restaurant near the CN tower that has great food."

"The City Asian Restaurant is where we will eat."

"Okay. I'll pick you up around eight."

"No, I will meet you there." Quickly, I hang up the phone.

The following day at work is another hectic one with interviews, and at eight in the evening I remember my dinner meeting with Kevin. I think of it as a meeting, rather than a date. As I leave work I say goodnight to a few other prosecutors who are grinding it out late.

I race from our office and into my car. Of course I hit every red light on the way. I swear many times that someone is following me with a remote control in their hand, and every time I near a traffic light, they flick it to red. I arrive at the restaurant at 8:28.

I glance in the rear view mirror, adjust a hair or two, and exit the car.

He is waiting at a secluded table. There is a half full decanter of red wine on the table. It appears Kevin has been waiting a while. I don't feel guilty as I did say eight-thirty and his earlier arrival is his problem. At present I'm not feeling charitable.

"Good evening Ashley, you are looking gorgeous as usual." Standing, he kisses my cheek before I can react. I ignore the kiss.

"Did you have time to study the menu?" I ask him.

"Yes, the dinner for two looks scrumptious."

"It sounds okay to me." I need sufficient time to advise him not to call me again. I am then out of here.

Until the meal arrives we discuss the restaurant and Chinese food which Kevin loves. The last time I ate was a breakfast of a two day old muffin and a glass of orange juice. When the food arrives, I attack it as I'm famished. Kevin begins pouring me another glass of wine, but I remind him that I'm driving.

His response has me grinding my teeth. "If you had agreed to my picking you up as suggested, there would not be a concern over wine consumption now. Next time, I pick you up."

The time has arrived, "There will be no next time. I will not be seeing you again."

"Why?" A pause, then, "Not fancy enough? Am I just a country hick teacher to you?" His voice is whiny.

"I have no special feelings for you, and besides I find you controlling and pushy. You are not my kind of guy."

"What do you mean by, "pushy?" I'm far from being that."

"One example, I suggested the restaurant tonight but you had trouble accepting me making a decision."

"Hey, I can back off. No problem." With this comment he raises both arms to shoulder level, and shoves his hands forward, as if pushing away from an obstacle.

"Absolutely not. It's not an option. No more dates or phone calls. I must leave now. Dinner is on me." With this response I grab the check, leave sufficient twenties, and practically run from the restaurant.

A mile from home I realize someone is following me. I desperately want to stop my vehicle, jump out, and throw a few punches in Kevin's direction. Instead, I pretend ignorance.

To prove to myself I'm not over reacting, I pull into a convenience store parking space. I observe the car which was following me and notice the brake lights come on as it drives by. I shudder.

I continue home and when parked I unlock the inside door connected to the kitchen. I turn on the light. Hurrying to the great room, but leaving it dark, I stand behind the curtain of the large front window. Pushing it aside slightly I peer into the street. I watch Kevin slowly drive by.

Tonight for the first time in years I have difficulty sleeping. Is it anger that keeps me awake or is it a premonition?

In the morning I telephone Mom to test if there will be any reference made to Kevin. Mom doesn't mention him.

I ask, "Mom, why did you give Kevin my home address?"

Sounding surprised Mom replies, "Why, Ashley, would I give him your address? Without your consent I would never divulge that kind of information. Is everything okay?"

"Things are fine." The lying bastard.

The following week I receive two more messages from him, begging me to reconsider. I ignore them. One day while having lunch with my friend Gail, Kevin entered the restaurant and stopped by our table. He joined us without an invitation. Gail was annoyed. She could tell I was not pleased with his intrusion.

His work day at school is completed at 4:30, which gives him time to rush into the city and occasionally follow me home, when I'm late leaving work. At times, I feel like pulling into a large department store parking lot, leaving my car, entering the store, leaving by another entrance, and taking a taxi home. Let him sit there for hours waiting for me. But, I don't have time for games.

The final insult takes place while shopping at the local grocery store. Kevin approaches me at the check out counter.

"Hi, small world, isn't it? Imagine running into you at a grocery store. Was in the neighborhood and decided to stop for some milk." With the comment he raises the milk carton to eye level, as if it's proof of his claim. He then glances at his watch and says, "Six, getting off work early?"

I am seethed, frustrated, angry, and speak before thinking. "Listen, if you don't cease calling, following me, and carrying out such stunts as riding up and down my work elevator, I promise you I will apply for a restraining order against you. Please stop this." Knowing I require more for an order doesn't prevent me from trying to frighten him.

Kevin glares for a second. He puts down the milk and before walking away says, "Fine, but you will be sorry. I love you and have loved you since seeing your picture at your parent's home. No one will ever love you as much." He abruptly turns and heads for the exit.

I'm hoping this will be my last contact with him. On the drive home I think no wonder he is single at thirty-two. Then I laugh when realizing who else is thirty-two and single.

When I arrive home I put away the groceries, grab a juice, and lie on the sofa in the great room. I spend a few seconds thinking about Kevin then my thoughts turn to Sam. I wonder what he is doing on a Friday evening and how nice it would be to go dancing tonight.

I wake at nine after experiencing a wonderful dream about Sam and me. While preparing a late dinner, I laugh, as I hope my dream tonight takes up where the last one left off.

CHAPTER 5

▼

On Sunday, I need release from my pent up energy so call my close friend, Gail White. I ask her to join me for an afternoon run. I suggest we follow this with a couple of glasses of wine and barbequed shrimp over wild rice and mushrooms for dinner. The shrimp and wild rice sell her.

We have shared a friendship for the past five years. Whereas, I am of medium height at five feet and six inches, slim build, with blond hair, and blue eyes; Gail is short, and stocky, with dark, curly hair and deep, brown eyes. She has been known to say, "If you want to call me anything call me Fluffy." Gail is a research assistant at the office and is super at her job. Five years ago during a Christmas party we both stepped back and watched the moves of Logan Reid. He was new to the team and he cornered every female present. During the party we discovered we had many things in common, including being an only child, single, not currently dating, and love of jogging. We made plans to get together the following Sunday to jog at the park located near my home. We have been friends ever since.

Gail arrives at 1:30 in the afternoon, dressed in her running clothes. I look at her and think how wonderful it is to have a steadfast friend. Not only is she helpful and dependable at work, but allows me to sound off in the evening when I'm annoyed with a service worker or someone I recently dated. She is my sounding board. The two of us have enjoyed short vacation breaks together, as well.

It is a beautiful day with the sun beating down and just the slightest of a breeze blowing. It's summer with temperatures hovering around twenty degrees centigrade. Running, we encounter tiny puddles of water on the path where rain from last night has not dried. Occasionally, a small animal darts across the path and scampers away. In some areas the dense tall trees throw a shadow across the path. Suddenly, I feel as if someone is following me. I quickly glance back. No one is there. It's probably my imagination. It is later in the afternoon so few other joggers are out. Most people are enjoying a picnic or visiting family. Half an hour later we turn and head for home. On arrival, the hour run feels invigorating, releasing the tension in my shoulders. The companionship warms my heart.

Four hours later, stomachs full, muscles relaxed, we sit in comfortable silence. Several moments later I turn to Gail and say, "I'm blessed to have you for a friend. You are so comfortable to be with, you're supportive, and I love your sense of humor."

"Thank you, my friend. Talk about humor, you are familiar with my mother jokes? Well I have a new one. Last week she bought a new stove, so I made arrangements to have it installed and the old one discarded. Two hours after the electrician arrives the deed is done, the man leaves and I am proud to have been able to help her. But just as the electrician is pulling out of the driveway Mom says, "Oh Gail, the stove doesn't have a night light; I have to have a night light; I can't keep this stove!" So guess what? We start over."

My abdomen is hurting from laughing. Gail often tells her mother stories with appropriate hand gestures. Her mother is much older than my mom. She is alone, as Gail's father passed away two years ago.

"Anyway, how are things going with Sam?"

Having shared my feelings about him, I reply, "Honestly, I think I love him. Isn't that ridiculous? He is so irritating at times, but when I'm not with him or haven't talked to him for a couple of days I miss him terribly. On Friday, I had a dream about him."

"What was the dream about? I hope it was something sinful."

"Actually, I discovered he's a dreamy kisser. In my dream it curled my toes and had me aching for more."

"May your dreams come true." Gail makes hand gestures as if a fortune teller.

"All kidding aside, I really do like him. There is something so soft and cuddly about Sam. I want to protect him if you can imagine."

"Well, he is certainly not clingy as that horrible Kevin, sticking to you like shit to a blanket. Sorry, but I disliked him immensely when he joined us for lunch that day. Is he still showing up unexpectedly while you are shopping or in the elevator at work?"

"He was, but the last time I read him the riot act. I informed him that I planned to apply for a restraining order if he didn't stop following me."

"My word, what was his response?" asks Gail.

"Oh things like, you'll be sorry; we could have been so good together; no one will ever love you as much as I. He then walks out of the store, gets into his vehicle, and drives away. Thankfully, I have not seen him since."

Gail shudders, "Thank God. I find him creepy."

"I think he was infatuated with me. He didn't know me long or well enough to feel love. Actually, I think he's harmless."

"Whatever, I'm just pleased he's gone. Speaking of gone I should move along. Morning comes too soon." She stands, finds her purse, and heads for the front door.

"Thanks for coming over. I enjoyed your company as usual."

We exchange good-byes and I watch Gail enter her car and drive away. This get together has elevated my spirit.

After she leaves I tidy then move to my computer room. I'm researching for the Billie Chartrand case. For some unknown reason he really bothers me, and I feel a shiver rolling down my spine. I recall my uneasiness in the park this afternoon and wonder why I didn't share this with Gail? Was it associated with Chartrand? I shrug it off, work for an hour, and head for bed.

I usually have no difficulty falling asleep, but tonight I lay awake thinking about Sam. I wonder if many women today ask men out on a date. Would he think me very forward if I called him at work and asked if he was interested in taking in a movie? I would never find the nerve to call.

Surprisingly, I fall asleep shortly after these thoughts and have a wonderful dream of Sam and me sailing off to sea. Highly unlikely.

CHAPTER 6

▼

The day has finally arrived. On Thursday, Billie Chartrand, answers to the charges of kidnapping, sexual assault, and attempted murder.

In courtroom two hundred and sixty-four is Marty Kroll, defense lawyer; Judge Tim Playden, the judge from hell; a court clerk; three sheriffs; five or six defense lawyers waiting their turn at pleas; and a few reporters and spectators. On a bench at the back of the courtroom sit Sheila Kuzew's parents and her older brother, Peter.

With a thin smile, Judge Playden requests that the sheriff bring in Billie Chartrand. He is tall and muscular, with a bald head, and the meanest looking eyes I have ever encountered. Evil is the only word that comes to mind. He is dressed in blue prison garb; his ankles are shackled and his wrists cuffed.

Judge Playden asks Marty Kroll if his client is ready to enter a plea.

Marty responds, "He is your Honor."

The court clerk reads the three charges and Billie replies, "Not guilty" to each charge. His face wears a sneer and his eyes appear blank, expressionless.

Marty informs the court, "The defendant has elected for a trial before a jury." This surprises no one as Chartrand has been proclaiming his innocence to anyone who will listen.

The court clerk announces, "Bail has been denied." When Billie Chartrand was arrested the police opposed bail. Within twenty-four hours a justice of the peace held a hearing in the cell block. Chartrand was not released by the justice of the peace but was remanded to a provincial court judge who denied bail.

We discuss the date for the preliminary hearing, which is held to determine whether there is sufficient evidence to send the case to trial. At Billie Chartrand's preliminary hearing, I will present evidence to bind him over for trial on the three stated charges.

The preliminary hearing is set to begin on Monday. At this point Marty turns to me, smiles and says, "See you at preliminary." The smile does not reach his eyes.

Chartrand, on the other hand, makes no attempt to hide his contempt. It chills me.

I spend the rest of the day and Friday going through my witness testimonies. I speak to Sheila Kuzew, the victim, three times, encouraging and supporting her for the upcoming preliminary hearing.

It is very difficult for a victim to speak about the attack in front of strangers, but even more punishing to be cross-examined. Marty Kroll is one of the best at attempting to degrade and discredit a witness and I dislike his approaches immensely.

On Saturday, my parents come in for a visit and shopping.

Mom asks, "Can we visit the place they call the common mall or something of that nature?"

"Sure Mom. Dad, are you coming with us?"

Dad laughs, "I'm not insane Ashley. Don't you remember the last time I almost killed us all and took three other people along? So no, you go ahead."

Dad is referring to the time he went through a stop sign and just squeaked by a car with three young people in it. We heard them yelling, "You old foggie, park it at home." This hurt Mom more than Dad. It is quite treacherous to drive the roads at the common mall if you come from a small community, and if you don't know where your store of interest is located.

Mom purchases paints for her rock art, a pair of shoes, a jacket, and a lovely, long, colorful, silk scarf for me. It's fun shopping with Mom, unlike my aunty from British Columbia who shops for hours and buys nothing.

On our return Dad decides to take us out for dinner. Oh, I love that man.

CHAPTER 7

▼

Monday morning I am up early. I dress quickly, skip my run, and arrive at my office two hours prior to the preliminary hearing for Billie Chartrand. All uncertainty has dissipated over night. I'm confident that following my presentation, Chartrand will be held over for trial.

In the courtroom, Judge Austin Holzzer, is presiding. He is a well respected judge both by prosecutors and defense lawyers. Judge Holzzer has white, wavy hair, gentle, pale blue eyes, and a kind, chubby face.

The courtroom is mainly filled with news reporters, but there are some spectators and again, Sheila's family is seated at the back of the courtroom. I smile encouragingly at them and receive the thumbs up sign from her brother, Peter. Sheila sits beside me as rigid as a board. I place a hand on top of hers and give it a gentle squeeze. I feel her start to relax. When the sheriff leads in Chartrand, I think she will run for cover, but she remains seated. She is my first witness and will leave after her testimony.

Marty Kroll is present as is Billie Chartrand. Judge Holzzer looks Marty's way and asks, "Mr. Kroll is your client ready?"

Marty stares at Billie for a second then states, "Yes, we are your Honor."

The judge turns to me and I say, "The people are ready, your Honor."

Judge Holzzer then continues by asking the defendant his name, reading out the charges, and asking Billie Chartrand if he understands the charges. He replies, "Yes" then turns and glares at me, his venomous eyes attempting to penetrate my being.

During the next week I present the accumulated evidence gathered by my team. We present the victim's testimony and the photo line-up, testimonies of the police officers involved, the physician and tire track matching. We refer to the hair strands that have been sent to the crime laboratory for deoxyribonucleic acid testing, but have not received the results as yet.

At the conclusion of the five days, indictments are returned on the counts of kidnapping, sexual assault, and attempted murder.

A date needs to be set for trial and Judge Holzzer addresses me, "How many days do you estimate for trial?"

"Six days," I reply.

When questioned, Marty answers, "Five days."

The trial is set to begin in two months. Marty Kroll makes no comment to me as he quickly leaves the court room.

I return to my office and receive a surprise visit from Pamela Fish. We became friends at law school. We look alike, so much that people often ask if we are sisters. Physically, we may be alike, but that is where the similarities end. Pamela is aggressive in nature, certainly more intelligent than I and would never consider working as a prosecutor. One of her favorite expressions in university was, "I entered law for the green."

She was born into a poor family and her dreams of becoming rich were certainly answered. Corporate law can be very rewarding financially. She drives a Porsche and owns a home worth four million dollars.

Pamela invites me out for a quick dinner since she is leaving the city on a business trip. I do have a few things to celebrate, so I accept.

Over dinner not referring to names, I relate to her my feelings about Billie Chartrand.

"He is definitely unlike anyone I have prosecuted. He makes no attempt to hide his negative feelings toward me, but rather wears them on his sleeve."

"Why do you think that?" She asks as she takes a sip of wine.

"It's the way he looks at me, very openly and with such hatred. He also sweeps his eyes up and down my body constantly. It's not in a complimentary but rather a degrading way."

"How creepy is that? Good thing he'll be in prison for a long time."

"I hope you're right. You know that expression, "You would hate to meet him down some back alley." Well, with this guy, I would hate to meet him anywhere." It relieves some of my stress to have a friend who understands where I'm coming from.

We spend some time discussing Pamela's love life, which changes every two or three months.

"So, tell me about this new guy in your life."

"He is wonderful. He is very kind, very handsome, and of course for me, very rich."

"What does he do for a living? And how is he in bed?"

"Corporate real estate is the name of his game, both here and in Calgary and I'm not telling."

"Good for you. As long as he is treating you well."

I wish her success on her trip and we go our separate ways.

When I finally arrive home, I quickly put together a light dinner of pasta salad with Melba toast. I take the dinner into the great room and turn on the television. Soon my mind is wandering until it settles on Sam. I'm really missing him and wish he would call, as promised.

After dinner I doze only to be awakened by the ringing phone. I hope it's Sam but it is Dad. He and Mom want to be at my opening remarks for the current trial. I inform him that the trial will begin in two months. Dad talks about his week at school and Mom's current charity and art project. We exchange our, "I love you," and say good-night.

I wander into the computer room. I grab the phone book and open it to the 'O's.' It does not take long to find S. Orlicky. I stare at the phone for five minutes and then think my behavior is no different than Kevin's. With this thought I slam the phone book shut, and storm to my bedroom. What is happening to me? I feel and am acting like I did when sixteen. Get a grip, Ashley.

I fall asleep quickly and dream not about Sam, but Kevin. I have a very restless sleep and feel exhausted in the morning.

CHAPTER 8

▼

I have two months to prepare for the Chartrand trial. There are scores of witnesses to further interview, Sheila Kuzew being the most crucial.

I did interview her and her family prior to the preliminary hearing, but not to the extent that is required now. The purpose of the current meeting is to connect with Sheila and her family, and establish my credibility with them.

The second meeting is restricted to Sheila and me. She needs to comprehend how critical her testimony is to the success of the trial. Initially, I appeal to her to communicate the details of the kidnapping only. We discuss this information including the fine details. I then adjourn the meeting. I certainly appreciate the difficulty and the impact this recall has for her.

As scheduled, four days later her parents escort her for the return visit. We spend two hours exploring the details of the sexual assault, beating, and torture. It is gut-wrenching. Individuals who have been sexually assaulted say that to discuss the traumatic event is like being assaulted over again. My heart wants me to charge to the Remand Centre, into Chartrand's cell and strangle him. I apprise her that one more meeting is required prior to trial. If she needs assistance, I advise and encourage her to telephone me at any time.

Following numerous attempts I manage to contact Mr. Dawson, the crop duster. When he arrives Mr. Dawson insists his wife must accompany him to the interview. In many circumstances this is an acceptable request and practice, but Mrs. Dawson has what I refer to as verbal diarrhea and dominates all conversations. It renders it impossible to keep Mr. Dawson on track. I sense defeat early and excuse them both.

I interview Corporal Scott Strand and the two constables Campbill and McKenzie, separately. I request that Logan Reid attend the meetings. He may learn a thing or two. All three police officers are professional and attentive. When the interviews are completed Logan immediately sneers my way, "I hear the male police officers enjoy being part of your court cases." He stares at my legs and continues, "Gossip is they love the long legs."

I am stunned by his ridiculous statement and rudeness. Rather than saying something I will later regret, I simply glare at him and utter, "Get out Logan." I slam the door on his butt. What a chauvinist.

My interview with Doctor Menka is short and meaningful for the prosecution. He is nearly as important to our case as the victim. As crucial as his testimony will be, his introduction of the ten photographs of Sheila after the attack, adds much credibility to our case. The saying, "A picture is worth a thousand words," is very appropriate here.

I will interview Constable Quinne a couple of days before trial. I did meet him on other occasions and know he presents well on the stand. I need only to advise, as to the types of question that will be asked.

My meeting with Corporal Hope Taylor is lengthy. We need to decide on the amount of and which evidence to include, in her summary of the taped interview with Sheila. Corporal Taylor is an intelligent police officer and I eventually leave the summary in her capable hands.

Corporal Quong's testimony contains the factual information. Once we discover which facts are true beyond a reasonable doubt, we then discuss the order in which I will extract this information from him. His importance to the trial is ranked highly and is most relevant to the prosecution's case.

The psychiatrist fails to appear for our two scheduled meetings, so eventually I do my interview over the phone. Logan Reid is responsible for calling the remainder of the witnesses to the stand. This includes two character witnesses for Sheila.

Following my interview of the psychiatrist, I sit back and think the effort necessary to obtain a guilty verdict would be worthwhile, if the justice system could throw away the key after the door slams shut behind criminals like Billie Chartrand.

Gail is standing by my door one morning, like a drill sergeant, when I arrive at work.

"For the past month or so I have seen a ton of people going in and out of your office, but never once have you come up for air. So today, meeting or not, you and I are going out for lunch."

"Okay, I agree with you. You decide where we go." I do feel a need for a break.

At noon she knocks on my door and we are off to lunch. She decides lunch will be at a soup and sandwich place near our building. It is a small place, very famous for its soups. Gail has called her close friend, the owner, and asked her to save us a table.

We are seated at a table at the window. Gail orders a chicken and Swiss cheese sandwich, and me a corned beef on rye. The soup of the day is beef barley, my favorite.

Gail opens the conversation with, "So, how is the preparation going for the trial?"

Gail has done some research for me regarding this trial.

"Things are moving along. I had difficulty with the psychiatrist, who I couldn't get in for an interview, and the man who first spotted the victim." This is managed between spoonfuls of soup. It's so tasty.

"What's his problem?"

"Well, he doesn't have a problem per se. It is his wife who controls him completely. I am afraid while on the stand he will call out, "Honey, now what was it I saw?" when I ask him a question on discovery."

Gail laughs, than shares another mother story, "Last Saturday I took Mom to the drugstore and while standing in line I ask her to get her money ready prior to reaching the lady at the cash register. Mom looks at me, questioning why she would do that. I tell her it is to prevent others behind us from waiting longer than necessary. She looks at me and says, "I pay my taxes too!" I have no reply. Now tell me, Ashley, what relevance does that have on my suggestion?"

Laughing I answer, "I have no idea. Your mom is such a nice lady and she loves you dearly."

"I know she does and I'm not laughing at her. I guess I appreciate the times we spend together and want to share them with you. I love Mom very much."

Our lunch hour is over quicker than I want it to be, but work calls.

CHAPTER 9

▼

It is Friday. Prepared for the Sheila Kuzew trial, I am keen to begin. I dislike having to wait. At this moment my top priority is to nail Billie Chartrand; to expose his evil, remove him from our streets, and erase the sneer from his face. Chartrand is one creepy customer.

My thoughts are interrupted by a gentle knock on the door. My surprise is twofold: one, the office secretaries usually notify staff about a visitor and two, not many visitors arrive late Friday afternoon. Colleagues usually phone first. I invite the person to enter with a cheerful, "Come in."

I'm surprised to see Sam standing in my doorway. In typical Sam fashion he announces, "Grab your coat. We're going for a slow dinner and some fast drinks. You are working much too hard."

"Sounds great, I'm famished," comes from my mouth. Why should this surprise me, as I have ached for this moment forever? I want to skip down the hallway, but manage to control my eagerness.

Approaching the elevator he asks, "Where would you like to dine? Do you have any favorite restaurants?"

"Yes, do you like lobster?" I ask shyly. I'm very pleased that he is consulting with me on choice of restaurant.

"Love it. Should we drive separate vehicles?" Sam asks. He smiles at me and I know I have fallen for this man.

"Sure, meet you there."

In an hour we are seated, enjoying salad and yummy cheese buns. I need to exercise caution, as I have a tendency to overindulge with the buns. This leaves little room for the main course. We both order the Fisherman's Feast, with a beer for Sam and glass of red wine for me.

We chat about politics, vacations taken, books read, and movies seen, but nothing personal. It is a comfortable atmosphere and I'm pleasantly shocked that two hours have passed. We observe the line of customers waiting for a table and decide to leave. I have offered, but Sam insists on picking up the tab. For a nightcap we decide to meet at a cozy bar near my home. Sam will follow in his new, black, Mustang G.T.

On route to the bar and realizing that the decision might be foolish, I decide to pull over, stop the car, and invite Sam to my home for a nightcap. He smiles, I melt, and we continue on our way. Because I parked in the garage and Sam on the driveway, I have a few moments to collect my thoughts before meeting him at the front door. The thoughts shared with my friend Gail, about loving this man, are real. People could label me easy, but at this point who cares?

Once seated comfortably, he on the couch and I on my recliner, we sip our wine and talk. To clarify, I talk. I share my life about my wonderful parents, good and bad times in law school, friends such as Gail and Pamela, and then by a slip of the tongue mention my problems with Kevin.

It was like I shot Sam. He is suddenly furious. "Has he been near you again? Is he still following you? If I catch the little bastard he will not be following you anymore; the prick's legs will be dangling from the end of his body."

"Whoa Sam, wait. It is fine now. I haven't seen Kevin in ages. Can you believe I threatened to get a restraining order against him?"

Sam is suddenly on his feet and rushing across the room. Taking my hand he draws me to my feet. My legs are like jelly, my heart bursting. Lowering his head he gently kisses me. Almost instantly the gentleness disappears as the kiss deepens, and I discover I am eagerly entering his mouth with my tongue, as my entire body is molded against his. We both move toward the couch at the same time. I can hardly wait to have his naked body next to mine.

"You are so beautiful, so beautiful and I have dreamed of this moment for many months, actually from the first time I laid eyes on you." His mouth wonders to my ear lobe and to the sensitive part of my neck. By now I am thrusting my breasts even nearer his mouth, wanting the sensation it will bring.

When his mouth covers my nipple over blouse and bra I desperately want to rip off my clothes. I love him so much. To gain composure, I push back gently and whisper, "I can not do this. It is not like me. Do you need a sip of wine?"

In a husky voice Sam says, "Later," and with shaky fingers starts unbuttoning my blouse. I can't stop him now. He is slowly, very slowly removing my blouse and is gazing longingly into my eyes. Is it love for me I see?

The blouse is off, than comes the bra. Sam looks fixedly at my breasts and groans, "God, oh God. Let me touch you." He lowers his head to my breast. It is so arousing. His other hand gently cups and massages the other breast.

Feeling so needy, so eager, I need to cry out, but instead move my hand under his sweater, onto his muscular chest and start massaging. My hand moves down his strong, muscular body. I feel his manliness, large and quivering. No words need to be spoken as we begin stripping the remainder of our clothes; tossing them about the room.

Sam suddenly interrupts the electrifying atmosphere and cries out, "Damn, damn, damn. I have no condoms."

In response, I squeal out, "Follow me. I have some in my night table, but have to warn you they may be two or three years old."

We gaze at each other across the bed and simultaneously say, "Who cares?" Grabbing the condom I tell Sam it is my job and slowly apply the condom. Sam is rigid, his every muscle tense as he pulls me up and gently lowers me onto the bed.

He follows, kissing my face and breasts. Finally reaching my womanhood, he touches me and I explode, calling out his name.

Sam moves up and kisses my mouth. I reach down, and urge his rock hard shaft into me. We reach a rhythm, so beautiful, climbing slowly to the top, and then erupting like a volcano. We are now screaming each other's name and I know I want to keep this man in me forever. I have never felt this sense of fulfillment with anyone else.

During the night we make gentle love often. When resting, Sam shares a bit of history with me. I hear that when he was twenty-one he joined the Royal Canadian Mounted Police and later attended the university in Saskatoon. Sam informs me he hasn't had many steady girlfriends. It's hard to believe, as he's so handsome, and considerate, with a wonderful sense of humor.

Tender by morning, I slide from the bed attempting to reach the kitchen without waking Sam. Mission accomplished, I quickly prepare coffee, and make toast and a mushroom cheese omelet. Wanting to surprise Sam with breakfast in bed, I am leaning over attempting to locate my carrying trays in a lower shelf, when I feel his hands on my rump. I chuckle, "Don't even think about it."

"About what?" he asks innocently.

"You know what. Besides, our bodies need replenishment, at least mine does. Set the table for us please. Dishes are in that cupboard, cutlery in this drawer. I will be right back."

Returning to the kitchen I note he has completed his duties and is patiently waiting. "Dig in," is all he says.

We attack breakfast and are sipping coffee when Sam breaks the silence, "I need to report to headquarters. I have an important meeting this afternoon and should stop at my apartment first for a quick shower and change of clothes. Although, I want your scent to stay with me forever." I smile at him.

After coffee, we dress, then stroll to the front door, neither of us wanting this separation. Sam appreciates how busy I will be with the up-coming trial. He reaches down, lifts my chin and gently kisses me. "Call you tonight, if it's not too late."

I don't respond. I can't, as begging him to stay is on the tip of my tongue. Instead, I wave as he drives away, then close the door, and flop on the coach to dream. Reliving the entire evening, night, and morning brings a smile to my face. I instantly fall asleep.

Late Sunday afternoon, I finally hear from Sam. He is apologetic, but his meeting ran late and then he received another demanding assignment. We talk for some time and he promises a visit to my office the following week.

I was hoping he would spend the evening with me, but obviously not. I'm disappointed and decide to take a jog in the park before dinner. Twenty minutes later I again feel like I'm being watched. This is ludicrous, because I can't think of any individual who would want to cause me harm, and if they did how would this person know I was out jogging very late on a Sunday afternoon. My routine consists of morning jogs. Billie Chartrand, after one week, has managed to spook me.

Monday is jury selection and I am looking forward to the start of this trial. A start means an end and hopefully a guilty verdict.

CHAPTER 10

▼

Jury selection is difficult in itself without going against Marty Kroll, the best defensive lawyer in the province.

The first potential jury member is Mr. Mack Geovani, a Caucasian of Italian descent, who drives an eighteen wheeler for a living. He is a tall, muscular man in his late forties. Marty desires a jury filled with male chauvinists; while my needs consist of having female jurors who will feel compassion for Sheila Kuzew. I want jurors who will feel her pain.

Following Marty's hour examination of Mr Geovani, it is my turn. I start with, "Mr. Geovani prior to today were you aware of Billie Chartrand, the defendant?"

"No," he answers.

I continue, "Do you watch television or read newspapers?"

Mr Geovani glances at the judge for a moment, "Not much. I don't read but sometimes I'll watch a comedy show on the television with my wife. When I'm on the road, I sleep in my truck, otherwise I'm driving."

"Does your truck have a radio?"

"Yes."

Although I know most truck drivers listen to their own music, I ask, "Do you listen to the radio?"

He pauses for a moment, "No, I listen to my CD's; I love country music."

I take another approach, "When on the road do you meet with other drivers at local bars?"

He replies, "No. Done that, been there. I spent too damn much money drinking. Now with the kids, I don't party on the road."

I have a positive feeling about Mr. Mack Geovani, a gut reaction that he may be a red neck Albertan, but one who has a lot of respect for women. I continue, "Mr Geovani, how many times have you been married?"

He smiles, "Once, just Helen."

"Describe your relationship with your wife."

"Well, we have been hitched for nineteen years. A long time but I still love that woman." he looks at me with pride.

"Does she work outside the home?" I will see where this question will lead me.

"No, I believe a woman's place is at home caring for the kids." With this comment he gazes down and stares at his hands, perhaps feeling he has insulted me. Rather, I am pleased to be observing an old fashioned honest man.

"During your teens how did you relate to your parents?" I want to know about his upbringing.

Mr. Geovani suddenly looks sad, "Dad and I did things together like fish, hunt, and go bowling. He died last year of a heart attack. Mom and I still see each other often."

I now know the reason for the sadness. "When you were in your teens, Mr. Geovani, did you argue with your mother on topics such as staying out late, doing your homework, and driving the family car?"

He replies, "Yeah, when I was sixteen we were always at each other, you know, yelling but Dad always stepped in."

Returning to the prosecutor's table I have selected our first jury member. Of course Marty has his own rationale for selecting Mr. Geovani.

By noon, Marty Kroll and I agree on two more jurors. Edward Wong, of Chinese descent, is a professor of history, and is employed by the local university; and Timothy Washington, a black man, is a massage therapist, married and a father of two boys.

Judge Holzzer adjourns court for lunch break. We reconvene at one o'clock.

Anna Bodiski is Caucasian, of Polish descent, a housewife with three grown daughters. She is in her mid-fifties, very attractive and appears somewhat nervous to be on the stand.

I start with, "How long have you been married Mrs. Bodiski?"

"Thirty-five years."

"Do you read the newspaper or watch the news on television?"

"I don't read the newspaper. My husband does and then summarizes it for me. I do watch the nightly news."

"Have you heard about Billie Chartrand prior to today?"

"Yes."

"Have you formed an opinion on this case?"

"No, I have not."

"How many daughters do you have Mrs. Bodiski?"

"Three."

"What ages are they?"

"One is thirty-three, and one is thirty and the other twenty-seven."

"If you knew someone who had been sexually assaulted, what would be your reaction?"

"I would feel compassion for them and want to offer my support."

"What would be your reaction to the perpetrator?"

"If guilty of a crime, my reaction would be for him or her to be punished."

"Do you believe in vigilantism?"

"No."

"What is your opinion of capital punishment, Mrs. Bodiski?"

"I am against capital punishment."

"When you stated that you would want the perpetrator punished, you meant by the justice system?"

"Yes."

"Thank you Mrs. Bodiski, no further questions."

I have selected the fourth jury member of the day.

Chris Wall, a married community health nurse is the father of a son and daughter. He presents well. Marty and I pass him quickly. Following a twenty minute afternoon break the last person on the stand is Cindy Thomas, Caucasian, of English descent, married, and an esthetic salon owner. She is questioned by Marty for half an hour. Mrs. Thomas has blond hair, bright blue eyes, and a permanent smile on her face.

It is now my time and I commence with, "How long have you owned and operated your salon Mrs. Thomas?"

"Just over ten years."

"Are your customers mostly male or female?"

"Female."

"Do you discuss news topic such as this alleged sexual assault with your customers?"

"No."

"What do you and your clients talk about Mrs. Thomas?"

She smiles at me and answers, "Fashion, hairstyles, celebrities, and the best bargains in the city."

"How long have you been married?"

"Fourteen years."

"Do you have children?"

"Yes."

"How old are your children?"

"I have a girl age thirteen and a boy age twelve."

"Do you and your husband discuss news items?"

"Yes."

"What news items in particular?"

"My husband is very interested in politics, so we discuss provincial and federal politicians, and also what is happening in the Middle East."

"Did you discuss the arrest of Billie Chartrand?"

"No."

"Have you heard of Billie Chartrand prior to today?"

"No."

"Do you believe in our justice system?"

"Yes."

"Explain why you believe in our justice system, Mrs. Thomas."

"It is better than the alternative."

"What alternative is that, Mrs. Thomas?"

"Verdicts being decided by government, not juries, or having no form of justice with utter chaos being the result."

"Thank you, Mrs. Thomas. No further questions."

I pass Mrs. Thomas. She is a bright lady. We have our sixth jury member.

Judge Holzzer adjourns court for the day.

On Tuesday morning our next prospective juror is Vincent Tate, a Caucasian owner of a massive cattle ranch. He swaggers, as he approaches the stand. Mr. Tate is a very muscular man, tall, with blondish hair, and blue eyes. My questioning follows Marty's and I am ready to excuse Mr. Tate when my assistant, Logan Reid, leans over and whispers, "Take him. I will explain later."

Judge Holzzer asks Marty Kroll first. He responds, "Your Honor the defense passes Mr. Tate."

The judge now turns to me, "Ms. Browne?"

I answer, "The people pass Mr. Tate." Logan later explains he caught a disgusted look pass over Tate's face, as he glanced at Chartrand. I hope Logan is correct in his assessment.

By three in the afternoon we have added four more jurors, consisting of Carolyn Fisher, an attractive, middle-aged woman, who works at a travel agency; Paul Bychuk, single, of Ukrainian descent, who is a licensed electrician; Afzal Hinraj, married, of East Indian descent, who owns a pawn shop; and Kim Meade, single, presently unemployed, and likely is the youngest member of the jury.

It takes the entire day for Marty and I to agree on the selection of these five jury members.

Judge Holzzer announces jury selection will resume the next day at nine in the morning.

Wednesday morning finds us back in court continuing with jury selection. We require one more juror and two alternates. Marty and I finally agree on Marilyn Whitney, married, mother of two, who is employed by the local college. She is our final juror. One alternate is a female, the other male.

Judge Holzzer ends the day by thanking the men and women of the selected jury. The court clerk swears in the jury, then Judge Holzzer announces that the trial commences on Monday, at nine, with opening statements. The gavel strikes, the clerk says, "All rise." Judge Holzzer leaves the bench.

I take a deep cleansing breath and organize my papers, then insert them into my briefcase. I turn to Logan Reid and tell him which areas I need him to research.

As Marty leaves he smiles in my direction and again it looks forced.

Sam calls me at work Friday afternoon at three and asks, "I know it's late to call but are you free tonight? I would like to take you out for dinner."

"Yes, I'm easy." I immediately feel like a fool. Why can I control a witness on the stand and still be such an idiot around this man.

There is silence, then Sam asks with a smile in his voice, "Can I pick you up at home at seven?"

"Sure. Should I dress casual?" I want to see Sam in a suit.

"Yes. If you want us to go formally, you'll have to teach me how to dress."

He arrives on time, and he looks so handsome wearing black jeans with a black and white designer golf shirt. The heck with a suit, when you look this great. We are out the door, in his Mustang before I can say hello.

"What is the rush? Do we have a reservation somewhere?"

"Honestly, do you really want to know?"

"Yes."

"I knew if I stayed with you in that house for more than sixty seconds, I would rip that lovely outfit you are wearing off you, and carry you to bed."

"You are joking right?" I look at him and his face is red with embarrassment.

"No, I'm not."

I instruct him, "Turn the car around."

"What did you say?" He glances over at me as if he doesn't believe what he heard.

"I said turn the car around, because I'm not hungry for food." How brazen I'm becoming with him.

Sam squeals his tires making a quick left turn. He looks at me once more and says, "Hang on." We make it back to my home in record time.

As we enter the house he is removing my top before I have time to close and lock the front door. I tell him to hold on. He informs me that he can't.

We spend most of Friday night making love. We do come up for air at four in the morning, and I run from bed to make us a quick sandwich.

Bringing it back to bed, I say to Sam, "You must eat this to regain some of the calories you wore off tonight."

"If you would let me, I would weigh ten pounds before leaving your side." He smiles at me and my heart skips a beat.

"Sam, you do have a way with words."

We eat the sandwiches and promptly fall asleep. So much for all the declarations.

We cook a breakfast together on Saturday morning. I'm so comfortable with him it feels like we have been together forever. I don't share my strong emotions with him, as I don't wish him to feel cornered.

He leaves for an afternoon rugby match and dinner with his male friends. I'm so in love.

Mom and Dad call me later in the evening and when I mention Sam, Mom almost passes out with excitement. I tell her not to panic, that Sam and I have had only one date, but she rambles on as if I haven't spoken. We spend a few moments discussing my anxiety about Monday morning's opening statement. Of course, they reassure me that I'm the best, and the presentation to the jury will be impressive as always. It's wonderful to have supportive parents.

CHAPTER 11

▼

Driving to the Law Courts building on Monday morning I am brimming with confidence. Last evening and this morning I have practiced my opening statement in front of the full length mirror in the bedroom. I sounded dynamic and my objective is to have every member of the jury understand and internalize the victim's suffering, and to deduce the defendant's despicable acts.

For opening day of the trial I have chosen a well tailored jacket and skirt of beige cotton, with a rich, deep, royal blue, silk blouse. Keeping the jewelry to a minimum, I complete the ensemble with a pair of comfortable beige pumps. I'm prepared to fight the devil.

Sam visited my office on three or four occasions in the past three weeks to discuss the trial, and to bring me up to date on any new evidence they have uncovered. This past weekend was wonderful, but Sam is extremely busy and this trial has certainly consumed me for the past month. Love is on the back burner for now.

The courtroom is jammed with spectators. Judge Holzzer has banned news media from this trial. Arriving at the prosecution table I notice Marty Kroll is not yet present for the defense. As is his style.

Marty prefers a grand entrance. Five minutes later he waltzes in, owning the courtroom with his presence. Dressed in the inevitable dark Armani suit, his hair slicked back, mustache trimmed, he is the epitome of a poster boy model. Elegant, intelligent, handsome, but I dislike him immensely.

When the jury files in the court clerk calls the court to order. We stand and Judge Holzzer takes the bench. He looks at me and proclaims, "Ms. Browne," and the trial of Billie Chartrand commences.

Approaching the jury I start, "Ladies and gentlemen of the jury," I pause, making eye contact with each member. "This is a case about control and dominance. Billie Chartrand" and I stare at him now and almost recoil at the hatred hidden behind his still form. This pause is giving the jury time to look in his direction, "hungered for complete control over Sheila Kuzew. He needed to dominate and force her to suffer incredible pain and humiliation. This was calculated cruelty on Billie Chartrand's part. The people will prove beyond a shadow of a doubt, that this man," I pivot and draw the jurors attention back to Chartrand, and I actually experience the contempt emerge from him and need to expose this to the jury as frequently as possible, "kidnapped Sheila Kuzew off the street, drove her to a secluded wooded area, tortured her by slashing her arms repeatedly with a knife, brutally sexually assaulted her, and then stabbed her in the back, missing her heart by a centimeter of her life."

I pause here to provide the jury with time to internalize what I have said. I continue, "He drove away in his van leaving Sheila there to die." I feel the darts from across the room.

Initially my glance lands a few inches above Billie's head, as I point in his direction. "We will prove that Billie Chartrand brutally, sexually assaulted Sheila Kuzew." These words are emphasized by raising my voice as I stare into the eyes of Mrs. Bodiski, one of the jury members. I see her flinch, and I notice the expression of distaste cross Vincent Tate's face.

I continue with, "The people will prove that Billie Chartrand attempted to lose the police by not stopping his van as ordered, because he was concerned about traces of evidence that may be found in the van. He was right to be frightened. You will hear and we will provide evidence that Sheila Kuzew was indeed in Billie Chartrand's van, because he kidnapped her off the street."

Making eye contact with Mr. Wong I state, "Billie Chartrand left Sheila Kuzew in the woods expecting her to die. He could not let her live, because she could identify him. She eventually did."

I pause for a few seconds to allow the jury members to put this last statement in their memory. I then continue, "Billie Chartrand did not count on the reserve and determination possessed by the victim. He heard the far-off sound of the plane, panicked, and left before confirming Sheila Kuzew was dead."

I then list for the jury members how we will prove all charges against Billie Chartrand.

I close with, "At the conclusion of the trial you will know, without a shadow of doubt, that the defendant, Billie Chartrand, kidnapped, sexually assaulted, and attempted to murder Sheila Kuzew." I make eye contact with each juror and walk slowly back to the prosecutor's table.

As I approach my chair I spot Sam, who I anticipated would be in court today for my opening statement. One of Sam's favorite expressions is, "Firing on all cylinders," and I was there this morning. I feel confident, proud of the energy and effort that resulted in a convincing presentation.

Not surprised to see my mom and dad as spectators, I'm shocked to observe Kevin sitting next to them. Trying to capture Mom's attention, I am instead drawn away by a waving and smiling Kevin. Abruptly turning and ignoring him I sit at the table and stare at my hands. My deepest desire is to choke him! What are Mom and Dad thinking? My thought is diverted by Judge Holzzer announcing our lunch break. We will resume at 1:30 in the afternoon.

I return to my office and quickly call Sheila.

"I believe the opening statement was very well received by the jury. I think your parents and brother will agree."

"I am happy you said I could miss today. I will have difficulty handling being stared at by all those people in the courtroom." I can hear the tremor in her voice.

"It's normal to feel upset. Tomorrow you will do fine. Just try to remember the confidence you had before this man entered your life. Focus on that thought, as I ask my questions."

"I am praying very hard for God to provide me with strength, to make it through this as well."

"And so he will. I'll see you tomorrow." We hang up.

I then retrieve my voice messages and answer a couple of urgent e-mails. I am furious. Due to Kevin's presence I had quickly informed my parents that I was not free to have lunch with them today. We settled on a late dinner this evening. They have a key to my home and will go there for a restful afternoon. As they left the courtroom I took note that Kevin remained behind, hoping to speak to me. I left without acknowledging him.

Sam departed as soon as I had completed my opening statements. I appreciate how busy he is.

We are back in court at 1:30. This case has weighed heavily on me because of the viciousness of the attack. It is now Marty's turn with the jury. He struts up to them and commences his opening statements.

I notice that Billie Chartrand is not observing Marty, but is instead looking about the courtroom. I wonder if he is expecting some family members to attend. Suddenly he whips his head in my direction and the look of hatred on his face nails me to my chair. I stop breathing for a moment, then take deep breaths, and slowly recover.

As predicted, Marty Kroll lists all the things he knows the prosecutors can not provide or prove. The list consists of a lack of Sheila Kuzew's fingerprints in Chartrand's van; no traces of semen in or on Sheila; no hair or other deoxyribo-nucleic acid evidence from Billie Chartrand discovered at the crime scene; and of course no trace of the weapon, the knife.

He proceeds, informing the jury that Billie Chartrand has no previous record of assault or sexual assault. No criminal record, not even a parking ticket.

As he speaks Marty gently looks at each juror almost whispering his opening statements, which forces many of the members of the jury to lean slightly forward to hear him. This is a smart move by Marty.

He questions the jury as to why a handsome man such as Billie Chartrand needs to kidnap a woman off the street, when it is evident he would encounter no problems attracting females? What would be Billie Chartrand's motive for this alleged attack?

During Marty's opening statement jury members Afzal Hinraj and Harvey Wall spend a great deal of time jotting notes on their paper. I don't take this action as a positive sign for the prosecution.

I now periodically glance at Billie Chartrand. He appears nervous to me. I wonder if there are countless other victims that have come in contact with him, but never survived to tell the tale.

It is four in the afternoon before Marty completes his presentation and Judge Holzzer adjourns court for the day.

I complete my necessary return phone calls and head for home to see my parents. I feel so badly that I wasn't honest with them, but don't wish to discuss my past relationship with Kevin. My feeling would be different if Dad didn't work with him.

Driving home I notice Kevin's car behind me. I decide to drive to the nearest police station and park in front of the building. I watch him drive by. What a loser.

Despite his antics my parents and I have a quiet, relaxing dinner before they leave. I'm so fortunate to have them.

After their departure I receive a phone call from Gail. We haven't seen much of each other. I inform her of Kevin following me part way home this afternoon.

"Did you go into the station and talk to someone there?"

"No, I didn't. I just watched him drive by then drove home."

"You should have reported the little shit head."

"Reported what? He didn't do anything. After all these years haven't you learned that charges only come after the criminal has done damage, not before?"

"You're right about that. Sorry, I lost my mind for a moment there." Gail sighs, and we say our good-byes.

I make it an early night and sleep soundly.

CHAPTER 12

▼

Anger boils inside me as I stare at her back. I think this rage will explode! She is so sanctimonious, yet not ever looking within herself. I have a great urge to hold a mirror in front of her; see filthy bitch take a look. Do you see a sexy slut with your long, blond hair, dressed in skin tight, fitting clothing? You are always flaunting your body in front of the jury members.

I am surprised you did not seek and accept twelve male jury members. You could then sit at the table knees crossed, skirt up to your crotch, and have all twelve men panting and eating out of your hand. You are nothing but a disgusting, filthy whore!

Do you honestly think you are superior, more intelligent, and worthier than me?

Will you beg for mercy, cry out with abandonment during torture, and whimper while your life seeps away? Someday Ashley, I promise you, I will discover the truthful answers to these questions.

I also promise your death will be a slow one, filled with endless torture, and excruciating pain. It will be payback time!

It may take years, but I am a patient man. I can afford to wait, to live on the thoughts of pain to be inflicted, and control to be enjoyed. You are evil and deserve to be punished.

I feel myself harden and stare at the judge for a few minutes to take my mind off Ashley, as she struts in front of the jury. There will be plenty of time later to plan for her torture and eventually her execution.

If events happen as planned, it may be sooner rather than later, that I come after you.

I took your abuse, now you will take mine!

CHAPTER 13

▼

The victim, Sheila Kuzew, is first to take the stand. The court clerk asks her to state her full name and then to spell her last name for the records. Sheila then takes the bible in her right hand and the court clerk states, "Do you swear that the evidence you shall give the court touching the matters in question, shall be the truth, the whole truth, and nothing but the truth, so help you God."

Sheila Kuzew replies, "Yes, I do."

I dislike placing her in this position. I did explain prior to this morning that it is necessary to lay down a strong foundation, on which to build this case.

After she is sworn in I start with, "Ms. Kuzew how old are you?"

"I turned eighteen on May seventh, two thousand and six." She replies with confidence.

I follow this question with a difficult one, which she knows I will ask, "Explain to the jury what happened on that Friday, May nineteen, two thousand and six."

Head cast down she mumbles, "I was walking south on one hundred and six street." Aware the jury members are having difficulty hearing Sheila, I interrupt immediately. The probable reason for the down cast head and meek voice is that the victim, in many sexual assault cases, feels tainted, and is still frightened of her attacker.

I encourage her with, "Ms. Kuzew, I know this is difficult, but you must speak louder to ensure everyone can hear you."

"I am sorry," responds Sheila, with a little more confidence.

"That is fine. Start again please." I smile at her encouragingly.

"I was walking south on one hundred and six street at approximately twelve-fifteen in the afternoon. I know the time because I had looked at my watch just moments before. A black van pulled up beside me. The man stared at me for a second then looked across the street, I assumed at house numbers. Another lost visitor was what I thought. There was a red traffic light up ahead, so I slowed my pace. It had been so warm when I left home that I threw on a pair of shorts, and now it was getting chilly, and I was anxious to get home."

She takes a deep breath and continues, "Just as the light turned green, I saw out of the corner of my eye, the man jump out of the driver's seat of the van. I couldn't move fast enough. He grabbed me from behind and shoved a foul smelling rag over my face, then dragged me toward his van. I remember kicking my feet, but could not scream because he had a gloved hand over my mouth." Sheila's eyes plead with me, but I nod and hope the look in my eyes will encourage her to go on.

Again I nod at her. "What happened once you were thrown into the van?"

"I remember feeling faint and nauseated. Then I just drifted away to sleep. The next thing I recall is the van kind of swaying and bumping up and down. It made me more nauseated."

"Where did you think you were?" I ask.

Marty Kroll interrupts, "Objection your Honor, the prosecutor is leading the witness."

"Overruled." Then Judge Holzzer looks at Sheila, "You can answer the question."

Sheila continues, "I thought we were on a country road filled with ruts. I had opened my eyelids slightly and could see no sign of buildings, or power poles. I could see an overcast sky, with the sun occasionally breaking through. I didn't know how long I had been unconscious. Approximately twenty minutes later the van stopped in this little clearing, and he pulled me out the passenger door."

"Ms. Kuzew, how did you know it was approximately twenty minutes?"

She answers, "I was starting to panic because I was frightened, so to gain some control I counted to sixty approximately twenty times."

"What happened next?"

Sheila shudders and continues, "He pulled me from the van. I looked into his face and was going to beg him not to hurt me, when he suddenly slapped me a few times across the face. I was petrified."

I ask, "Do you see this man in the courtroom?"

"Yes." Pointing at Billie Chartrand she states, "That's him." Her voice is starting to shake.

I turn to the jury and state, "Let the record show that Sheila Kuzew has identified Billie Chartrand, as her attacker."

I wait a few more seconds then ask, "What happened after he slapped your face?"

"He punched me in the stomach and breasts. I tried to shield myself and kept screaming at him to stop. He drew a switch blade knife from his back pocket; the blade was about six inches long. He waved the knife in my face and shouted, "If you don't shut up bitch I'll kill you right now." I was so scared, I wet my pants." She lowers her head, embarrassed.

At this point I want to slap Billie Chartrand, but I restrain myself and ask her, "What happened after this?"

"He knocked me to the ground and kicked me in the ribs. Then he jumped on my chest, grabbed my left arm and ran the switch blade knife through my skin." She starts to sob, her body is racked with emotion and she is having difficulty catching her breath. I pass her a box of tissue.

Judge Holzzer asks, "Can you continue or would you like a recess?"

"I would like a break."

Judge Holzzer announces a twenty minute recess and leaves the courtroom.

I spend fifteen minutes talking to Sheila, about the great job she is doing on the stand. We discuss briefly the remainder of her testimony. We both use the remaining five minutes for a bathroom break.

Once court is back in session, I ask, "What happened after he started slashing at your arm?"

Taking a deep breath, she composes herself and continues, "He kept cutting, slicing, first my left then on my right arm. As he held my arm up blood was running down, and I could feel it pooling on my neck and chest. I begged him to stop. He repeatedly shouted, "Does this hurt Mommy? Does this hurt Mommy?" The pain was so severe that after a while I was numb to it."

To give her a chance to catch her breath, I interrupt with, "What happened after the many slashes?"

"He yanked down my shorts and panties and sexually assaulted me while holding the knife to my throat. He was very violent, while calling me these awful, disgusting, names. At some point he stuck the handle of the knife in me. By then I was beyond screaming. After a while he looked at me, and yelled, "Roll over." I could not move, so he rolled me over and put his penis in my rectum."

At this time I ask, "Did you attempt to fight him?" This question breaks my heart, but needs to be asked.

"I tried to get up and it was then that I felt him brutally stabbing me in the back, not once, but twice. "No Mommy, you are dying right here," he whispered in my ear and then he was gone."

"How were you found Ms. Kuzew?" I look into her eyes to give her some of my energy.

"After he left I crawled back to the road by dragging myself with my whole body. It felt like miles, but it was only around thirty feet. But I was bleeding a lot and feeling very weak. I passed out. Apparently a crop duster, doing his field nearby, spotted me lying on the road and called nine, one, one."

"Ms. Kuzew, explain to the jury how this horrendous attack changed your life."

Sheila is silent for a few seconds. She then looks at the jury. "I can't concentrate at all. Before the attack I had applied to and was accepted at the university. Since the attack I have withdrawn."

"What other things are you suffering?" With a nod toward the jury I have encouraged Sheila to look in their direction.

"The doctor said I contacted a vaginal infection and I had to be on antibiotics for a while. Sometimes it still hurts but the doctor said it'll eventually heal." Sheila again lowers her head as if embarrassed.

"What other changes have you experienced since the attack?" I gently ask.

"Emotionally, I'm frightened all the time and can't stand being alone. Even now, months after the attack, I will not go out alone even during the day. During the night, I have ongoing nightmares, which wake me up screaming with my heart pounding. My mom is always running into my room to hold me, because I have been screaming."

I inquire, "Are you seeing anyone professionally for the nightmares?"

Sheila answers, "I am still seeing a female psychiatrist once a week. She told me the attack left me with post traumatic stress disorder and it will take time to get back to normal. Sometimes it takes years. But I just know, I'll never be normal again."

I look at the jury as I ask her, "Have you entertained thoughts of taking your life?"

"Yes, many times, but I haven't followed through because then he" she stops and stares at Billie Chartrand, "would have won. I hate him too much for that."

I ask, "Do you date Ms. Kuzew?"

"No, I was going with someone before the attack, but he didn't stick around after. Now I feel soiled, dirty; who would want me now?" Sheila pulls up her sweater sleeves and shows the jury the scars on her arms. "Look at these ugly things." She sobs.

This is an excellent place to stop. "Thank you. No further questions your Honor."

Judge Holzzer informs us we will break for lunch and resume at 1:30 this afternoon.

Although not a common practice for me I invite Sheila and her family to lunch at a neighborhood restaurant. I feel such compassion for her, as I know from experiences of other victims that she will never be the same. I encourage her to hold up her head during cross-examination by Marty Kroll. I also praise her for a job well done. Her family adds how proud they are of her.

At 1:30 Marty starts his cross-examination.

He begins with, "Is it correct Ms. Kuzew, that you stated in your taped testimony that you saw Mr. Chartrand's face when he passed by you in the van?"

"Yes," replies Sheila.

Marty continues, "Today you stated he was looking out his window across the street. Is this correct?"

"Yes."

"Explain to the jury how you observed his face when the defendant was looking left out the driver's window, and you were on the street on the right of the van, the passenger window." Marty is staring at Sheila as he asks for clarification.

"Well, I saw his face before he turned his head left."

"You said in your testimony that you saw his face for a split-second. Are you saying you remember a person's face in a split-second?" Marty emphasizes the word, split-second.

Sheila responds, "Yes."

"Were you ever facing the driver when in the van?" Marty stands directly in front of Sheila.

"No, but I could see—"

Marty interrupts Sheila and does not allow her to finish the sentence. "Answer yes or no. Were you facing the driver at any time while in the van?"

"No," replies Sheila.

Marty fires the next question at her, "Is it not true that if you were slumped in the seat as you claim, looking toward the roof of the van you could only see the jaw of the driver's face?"

"Yes." I can see Sheila is becoming angry. This pleases me.

"In the clearing where you were allegedly assaulted you claimed the man sat on your chest. Was the sun shining?" asks Marty.

"Yes." states Sheila, taking time to respond.

"You were lying on your back?" asks Marty, grinning at her. The bastard. Does he think this is funny?

I am also wondering where he is going with this line of questioning. She is taking her time answering.

Marty states, "Would you like me to repeat the question, Ms. Kuzew?"

"No," she replies and then continues, "Yes, I was lying on my back."

"Looking up into the sun?" Now I know where Marty is going.

"Yes, but I could—"

Marty interrupts her quickly and turns to Judge Holzzer. He's angry.

"Your honor, instruct Ms. Kuzew to respond with a yes or no response to my questions, unless otherwise requested. I want her last statement deleted from the records."

Judge Holzzer frowns at Sheila and warns her to answer the questions with a yes or no response, unless otherwise directed. He then turns to the court clerk and requests her last statement be erased from the record. The Judge then nods to Marty Kroll

Marty resumes with, "You were looking up into the sun?"

"Yes."

"Would you say the sun was bright?" asks Marty.

"Yes." Sheila says with a sigh.

For the next question Marty is actually peering at her through half closed eye lids. "Were you squinting as you looked up into the face of the alleged attacker?"

She looks at me, as if for support, then replies, "No."

"Were there shadows cast across the alleged attacker's face from the nearby trees?" asks Marty.

"No."

"Did you look at the alleged attacker's face?" I know Sheila is sick of hearing the word, "alleged."

"Yes!" replies Sheila in disgust.

In a puzzled voice Marty asks, "Are you saying a man is torturing you, the sun is shining in your eyes, you are frightened, and still you can plainly see the alleged attacker's face?"

She looks directly at Billie Chartrand and almost screams out, "Yes."

This does not please Marty. "Ms. Kuzew when is the last time you had your vision tested?"

I immediately jump in with an objection, that counsel is badgering the witness.

Judge Holzzer agrees. "Mr. Kroll, if this line of questioning is without a factual base, move on."

Marty responds, "Yes, your honor."

He then turns to her and asks, "You agree that while in the van you did not have a frontal view of the driver's face?"

"Yes."

A few jury members are frowning at this point. Marty quickly picks up on this and decides to let it go.

He looks at Judge Holzzer and announces, "No further questions, your Honor."

Day one of the trial is completed.

I walk quickly to my office to take care of my e-mails. When I get home I realize I'm exhausted. I change into my lounging pajamas and rest on my favorite recliner.

The phone rings approximately twenty minutes later. I pick up and my hopes are high that it's Sam.

"Hello."

"Hi. Don't hang up on me!" It's Kevin.

I clench my teeth and ask, "What do you want Kevin?"

"You! I love you!"

"Listen to me very carefully. I'm not interested in you, never have been, and never will. I'm hanging up. Don't call again." I gently place the receiver down, although I would love to slam it and break his ear drum.

Fifteen seconds later the phone rings again, but I ignore it. From the great room I can hear the answering machine in the kitchen pick up. I slowly leave my recliner and walk to the kitchen to play the message.

Kevin's message, "Ashley, you'll be sorry one day." I quickly punch the erase button. A moment is spent wondering if it was Kevin's presence I felt when running in the park. I don't need this harassment in my life.

CHAPTER 14

▼

The morning of day two of the trial Mr. Dawson is sworn in. He is dressed in clean, pressed, blue jeans and a plain, black, knit sweater. Mr. Dawson is forty-nine, but looks sixty.

I begin with, "What is your occupation Mr. Dawson?"

"I am a farmer." With this comment he smiles at the jury.

I ask, "Where is your farm located?"

"Approximately twenty-five kilometers north of the city," answers Mr. Dawson.

To clarify I inquire, "Of Edmonton?"

"Yes." He smiles at me.

"Do you have another occupation in addition to farming?"

"Yes, I have a crop dusting business." Mr. Dawson peers around the courtroom as if seeking out a revenue agent.

"Mr. Dawson, describe crop dusting for the jury."

He replies, "I fly my special plane at low altitudes over crop fields releasing chemicals that kill undesirable weeds."

I am thankful Mr. Dawson is on the stand, not his wife. Her description of crop dusting may have taken us into next year.

"Describe to the jury what you were doing on the afternoon in question."

He responds, "I was crop dusting my own field as I do every late spring."

"What did you observe while you were flying your plane over your field?"

Mr. Dawson takes a deep breath, "I had completed my south field and was about to head north for home when I spotted movement on this little dirt road leading to the field. It appeared like someone was dragging themselves; kind of crawling along the road. I turned the plane around, took another sweep lower to the ground this time. Sure enough, I could make out a lady lying on the road, blood on her back, only this time there was no movement."

I give Mr. Dawson a few seconds to collect himself. "What did you do next?"

Mr. Dawson replies, "I called nine, one, one. I told them about the woman and that I saw a black van leaving the area."

"After you reported this incident Mr. Dawson, what did you do?"

He sighs, "I flew home, landed and parked the plane, and ran to the house. Told the wife what I saw, and that I was taking the truck and heading to the south field. Anna, my wife, said, "I'm coming with you." We took off, driving fast!"

I wonder, *What is Mr. Dawson's definition of driving fast?* I say, "What did you do when you arrived at the road where you had observed the lady?"

"Nothing, as the police were there. They had cordoned off the road and wouldn't let anyone enter. I explained who we were and Constable McKenzie asked me to wait. He wanted a statement from me." He looks about the courtroom as if to emphasize his importance to this case.

"Did the police officer interview you, Mr. Dawson?"

"Yes, they spoke to me within ten minutes; shortly after the ambulance left."

"Thank you Mr. Dawson, no further questions."

Marty Kroll is immediately on his feet for cross-examination.

He approaches Mr. Dawson with an air of confidence, "Mr. Dawson, was it overcast in the afternoon of the day in question?"

"Yeah, there were a few clouds."

Marty asks, "Would you say it was mainly cloudy or sunny?"

Mr. Dawson pauses for a moment, then answers, "Cloudy."

"Were you able to see your field well enough to continue flying?" asks Marty.

Mr. Dawson appears fidgety to me and I wonder why. He responds, "At the time, yes."

"Mr. Dawson, did you call your wife from your cell phone just prior to reporting something on the road?"

"Yes." Mr. Dawson replies, almost whispering this word, while glancing in my direction.

Marty smiles at the jury. "Explain why this call was necessary."

Mr. Dawson, at this point, gazes down at his hands and lowering his voice says, "I told her I was bringing the plane in early because it looked like we may be in for a big storm, and I didn't want to be caught in it."

"Mr. Dawson, please repeat your statement. I could not hear you clearly."

He does as requested, although I certainly heard him clearly the first time. My assessment of Mr. Dawson is that he is angry.

Marty continues, "You stated earlier that you spotted a person on the road?"

"Yes."

"Did you see a vehicle parked anywhere near this person?" Marty is waving his arms to indicate an area.

"No," replies Mr. Dawson.

"It was overcast Mr. Dawson, and you were flying your plane dangerously low. Could you absolutely, without a shadow of a doubt, see a body on the gravel road?"

"Yes. It is dirt, not gravel."

Suddenly Marty is annoyed at the added statement, but instead of objecting he turns to the jury, then quickly spins back and is in Mr. Dawson's face.

"How did you know the body was that of a woman?" Marty spits out these words very rapidly.

"I saw her long, blond, hair!" Mr. Dawson places much emphasis on each word.

I would have loved to see the expression on Marty's face, at that response. Marty hesitates a moment then asks, "Mr. Dawson have you ever seen a male with long blond hair?"

"Yes." Mr. Dawson smiles at Marty.

But this cross-examination has damaged Marty's defense, because all jury members remember Sheila Kuzew's long, blond hair. Marty stops his examination with, "No further questions."

I ask Judge Holzzer if I can approach this witness with a further question. The judge nods.

"Mr. Dawson, when you called nine, one, one, did you report seeing a black van leaving the area?"

"Yes."

"No further questions, your Honor."

Judge Holzzer adjourns court for a twenty minute break. I require additional information for examining our next witness and send Logan Reid to our law library to get it. I scan my notes while he is gone. Logan is back in time.

Corporal Scott Strand is next on the witness stand. He is tall, very muscular, with a handsome face. He is sworn in and I approach him.

"Corporal, were you present when Sheila Kuzew was presented with a photo line-up?"

"Yes," he replies.

"Did you administer this procedure?"

"Yes," he states with confidence.

Smiling at the jury I say, "Describe to the jury the differences between the two line-up procedures.

Corporal Strand states, "Line-up procedures can be done with people or with pictures or photos. In both situations you want to match the physical characteristics of the accused, as closely as possible. We have been using the photo line-up more often in the city, because it is difficult to locate people off the street to volunteer their time to become part of this procedure."

"To clarify, which type of line-up procedure took place with Sheila Kuzew?"

While maintaining eye contact with the jury he states, "In this case, we decided to use a photo line-up. Sheila Kuzew was presented with a sheet containing pictures of five different individuals arranged across it. There were two rows, for a total of ten photos. Just the faces of these individuals were exposed. The men in this situation all had bald heads. Billie Chartrand's photo was included in the line-up."

"What did you do next corporal?"

"Sheila Kuzew was asked to point to her attacker's photo if it was present."

"What was her response?"

"She looked at each photo carefully and immediately after pointed a finger at the photo of Billie Chartrand."

"Corporal Strand, was there any hesitation on her part?"

"No," he replies.

"Do you see the individual in this court room that Sheila Kuzew picked out of the photo line-up?" I'm maintaining eye contract with a few jury members.

"Yes, the defendant." Corporal Strand points to Billie Chartrand.

I turn to Judge Holzzer and say, "Your honor, let the record show that Corporal Strand identified Billie Chartrand, the defendant." Judge Holzzer replies, "It is noted in the records."

"Corporal, did you in any way influence her decision?"

His response is a prompt, "No."

"What was Sheila Kuzew's response following the identification of Billie Chartrand?"

Raising his voice Corporal Strand answers, "She started to sob, than she cried out, "I will never forget that face as long as I live." Following her statement she started to shake."

"Corporal Strand, how many times have you prepared and administered a photo line-up to victims?"

The answer is delivered with confidence, "I performed the procedure approximately one hundred and fifty times."

"Thank you corporal. No further questions for this witness."

The cross-examination by Marty Kroll is short and sweet for him.

"Corporal Strand, what would you say is the percentage of wrongly identified suspects who go to trial via the photo line-up?"

"Approximately point zero, zero, one percent are wrongly identified."

"So, is there a possibility that Sheila Kuzew's identification of the defendant falls in that percentage?"

"She was very—"

Marty interrupts, "Just answer the question corporal. Is there a possibility of mistaken identification in this case?"

"Yes."

Judge Holzzer adjourns court for lunch.

During the lunch break Sam pays a surprise visit to my office, bringing with him two ham and cheese sandwiches and my favorite coffee. I could have kissed him and I did.

We sit at my small office table where he can maneuver his chair only one inch in any direction. Sam is not only a big man, but my office is very small.

He is currently working a murder case and tells me the first person the division is looking at is the victim's wife. We exchange opinions on what pushes a wife or husband to kill rather than leave their spouse. There appears to be an increase in spousal abuse and murder in society today.

Sam suggests we go for dinner this evening and as usual during trial I can rarely keep promises for my evening hours. We leave the plan as a maybe.

I will now present testimony about the investigation of the crime scene. Constable Ian Campbill is called to the stand and sworn in.

"Constable Campbill, when did you graduate from the Royal Canadian Mounted Police?"

"Five years ago."

"How many crime scenes have you secured?"

"I have secured approximately forty-five." He looks about the court room as if expecting someone to jump up and question this number.

I approach the witness stand and ask, "Constable Campbill, describe the events which occurred on the afternoon of Friday, May nineteen, two thousand and six?"

"My partner, Constable Jim McKenzie, and I heard a radio call requesting the nearest officers to check on a possible assault, on range road two hundred and forty just north of Edmonton. We were the closest marked unit to the location, so Jim and I responded to the call."

"What information were you given, Constable Campbill?"

"We were advised that a crop duster pilot had called nine, one, one, and reported an individual lying on this dirt road, half naked, and apparently injured. He had also spotted a black van leaving the vicinity."

"Explain to the court what you observed on arrival at range road two hundred and forty, the crime scene."

"A female was lying face down in the dirt with her right arm extended above her shoulder. There was a large amount of blood on the ground, covering her right arm and soaking the back of her pink T-shirt. The T-shirt had rips in it. Her left arm wasn't visible, as it was tucked under her body."

"What did you do next?"

"I touched her shoulder, leaned near her ear and told her I was a police officer. I asked her name. There was no response. I determined she was still alive by checking her carotid pulse on the side of her neck." He appears pleased that he is knowledgeable enough to have accomplished this assessment skill.

I ask, "Did you move her, Constable Campbill?"

"I gently shifted her head just a small amount, turning it to the right therefore making it easier to breathe. I didn't want to roll her over because had she chest wounds, bleeding might increase."

Constable Campbill takes a deep, cleansing, breath and is visibly upset. I ask, "How was she dressed?"

"She wore a pink T-shirt and was naked from the waist down." He looks down at his hands, as if embarrassed.

"What did you do as you waited for an ambulance?"

"I asked my partner, Jim McKenzie, to stay with her and watch for the ambulance, while I followed the traces of blood. I was careful not to compromise the crime scene."

"Where did the trail of blood lead you constable?"

He answers, "It led into a clearing where the trail stopped at a pool of blood in the grass and weeds."

"What happened next?"

Constable Campbill turns his head and stares at the jury. "I ran back to the road for crime scene tape. The ambulance had picked up the victim. Constable McKenzie was on the phone talking to someone about notifying all surrounding offices and their officers to be on the look out for a dusty black van, driven by a single male occupant. With a BOLF any suspicious individual would be detained for questioning. A BOLF stands for, be on the look out for."

"At this time did Constable Jim McKenzie share information with you?"

"Yes, Constable McKenzie informed me that the Forensic Identification Section was now involved. They would be sending a corporal over to the University Hospital to interview the victim. As is usual, the Forensic Identification Section would notify the General Investigation Section, because a serious crime had been committed. The case was eventually coordinated by Sam Orlicky from the General Investigation Section."

"No further questions constable. Thank you."

Marty has only one question. "Constable Campbill, in your search did you find a knife at the crime scene?"

"No."

"No further questions." Marty returns to the defense table.

I call Constable Jim McKenzie to the stand. He is sworn in by the court clerk.

"Constable McKenzie, when Constable Campbill left you with the victim, Sheila Kuzew, what did you do?"

He answers in a loud and clear voice while looking at the jury, "I approached the victim because she moaned, so I knelt close to her face and heard her whisper, "Black van." I asked if her attacker drove a black van and she said, "Yes," before passing out again."

I ask, "What happened then?"

"The ambulance came and rushed her to the University Hospital. After they left I ran to the marked unit and called the main office about a BOLF on any dusty black van. Dusty, because that is what we found when driving to the crime scene. Our marked unit was covered in dust. I didn't think the perpetrator would take time to wash his vehicle."

"Did you speak to, Mr. Dawson, the crop dusting pilot?"

"Yes. He arrived shortly after the ambulance, so I asked him to step back but not to leave, because I wanted to interview him."

"No further questions for this witness. Thank you."

Cross-examination by Marty Kroll starts with, "Constable McKenzie, describe the victim's position when you arrived."

"The victim was flat on her abdomen with her right arm stretched above her head."

"Was her face visible?"

"Not when we first arrived."

"Your honor, I would like Constable McKenzie's last response deleted from the records and a warning given to Constable McKenzie to respond only to what I ask."

Judge Holzzer responds, "Mr. Kroll, Constable McKenzie's last statement will be deleted from the records." The Judge glances at the court clerk and she nods. "Constable McKenzie, you know better, stick to the question asked."

"Constable, let me repeat the question. Was the victim's face visible when you arrived at range road two hundred and forty?"

"No."

"Are you certain she said, "A black van?""

"Yes," replies Constable McKenzie.

"Did she shout out this statement?" asks Marty.

"No."

"Did she whisper this statement?" Marty's face has a fake smile as he looks at Constable McKenzie.

"Yes." I can see that Jim is becoming leery of Marty Kroll.

"Did she in fact say, "A black man?" I look at Constable McKenzie and give him a reassuring smile.

"No."

"You are saying constable, that an individual lying face down, with a voice that is whispering, said, "A black van," not "A black man," without a shadow of a doubt?"

"Yes."

Marty steps away from the constable, stands near the jury and whispers, "A black man."

I hear him, but Jim McKenzie does not make out the words.

"Pardon me," says Constable McKenzie.

"No further questions," responds Marty.

Jumping to my feet I ask Judge Holzzer if I may approach the witness and he nods affirmatively.

"Constable McKenzie, how were you positioned when you heard the victim say, "A black van?""

"I was leaning over with my ear near her mouth."

"Thank you. No further questions."

Constable Jim McKenzie leaves the stand visibly shaken. I appreciate the emotional impact on witnesses testifying.

Judge Holzzer reminds the jury not to discuss the case and states we will reconvene at nine in the morning.

Another hectic day and I'm exhausted, but rush home to prepare a dinner for Sam and me. Stopping at my favorite meat and seafood shop, I pick up two beef tenderloins and fresh shrimp.

Sam wanted to dine out, but I think a dinner at home is more to my liking, at this time. A quiet dinner, wine, and an early night is what the doctor has ordered for the two of us.

I prepare spinach and mandarin salad, a shrimp sauce, and two potatoes for the barbeque. Setting the dining table I use my favorite china, crystal glasses, and linen napkins. A mild, scented, candle finishes the table. The supply of red wine is running low, and I take note of this. My parents always have a glass of red wine with dinner or in the evening. I'm carrying on the tradition. It's not difficult.

I take a shower and change into a two piece lingerie outfit made from white satin, with a blue and white sash. I feel beautiful and sensual. I can barely wait to see Sam's expression.

When the doorbell rings, I answer the door. He is stunned, but so am I, because Sam has in his arms at least two dozen, red, long stemmed roses. We laugh out loud.

I accept the roses from him. Sam states, "We are obviously staying in for dinner, and I am ecstatic about this decision." He grabs me in a big hug and almost crushes the roses. I take the flowers into the kitchen and place them in a crystal vase, which I then place on the dining room table.

Sam has followed me into the room. "What a nice table setting."

I'm happy he noticed my effort. "Thank you, for the compliment and the roses. Look how beautiful they are."

"Not nearly as beautiful as you are. Come here please."

I go to him slowly and he draws me near for a gentle kiss.

When we separate Sam says, "Am I barbequing tonight?"

"Yes, I made a sauce you can apply to the shrimp prior to barbequing and I like New York meat spice on my steak. If you would start the barbeque we can put the potatoes on now. Thanks."

In an hour, dinner is ready to be served. Sam and I are both famished, but we eat slowly under candle light, with the scent of fresh roses filling the room. I am so happy.

Our conversation is light and occasionally Sam reaches for my hand and brings it to his mouth for a sweet kiss. Near the end of dinner he says, "I don't know how I maintained my composure over dinner with you looking so beautiful and sexy."

I shock him for the second time this evening by taking his hand and saying, "Come with me Sam, the dishes can wait until tomorrow."

CHAPTER 15

▼

It is the third day of trial. The first witness today is Doctor Stanley Menka. On the stand he makes an impressive witness. Dr. Menka is dressed casually in grey pants and shirt, grey and burgundy, patterned tie, and a solid burgundy, V-neck sweater.

He is sworn in by the court clerk. Leading him through his resume I know this witness will be a crucial blow to the defense. The jurors are very attentive as Dr. Menka discusses his impressive resume, including being chief of emergency staff for the past ten years at the University Hospital.

"Dr. Menka, were you the attending physician at the University Hospital's emergency department the afternoon Sheila Kuzew was brought in via ambulance?"

"Yes." He replies.

"Were you the physician who performed the assessment, diagnoses, and ordered treatment for Sheila Kuzew?"

"Yes." He answers with self-assurance.

"What time did Sheila Kuzew arrive in hospital?"

Computer screens are provided for the witness, judge, court clerk, prosecutor, defense lawyer and jury. Dr. Menka now refers to his assessment record displayed on the computer screen.

"According to my records she arrived at 2:45 in the afternoon."

"Describe your physical assessment of Sheila Kuzew."

Dr. Menka takes a deep breath and answers, "The most critical issue when she arrived at emergency was the massive amount of blood she lost. From the card in her wallet we knew her blood type and an order for blood transfusion was placed immediately. She was also grouped and matched to ensure there would be no blood transfusion reaction."

I ask, "Where had Sheila Kuzew been injured to cause so much blood loss?"

Until now, Dr. Menka has maintained eye contact with the jury. He now stares at Billie Chartrand and answers, "She sustained two deep stab wounds to her back. The object making one of these wounds missed the major artery, which supplies the heart with blood by just one centimeter. The object had been plunged into her back for a depth of approximately ten centimeters or a little over four inches. If the major artery had been cut, Ms. Kuzew would have died."

"What other injuries were caused by the weapon used by the perpetrator?"

"In addition to the back injuries, there were eight separate slashes or cuts on her left arm, each measuring three centimeters or just short of one and a half inches in length, and a half centimeter in depth. There were nine similar slashes or cuts on her right arm." He continues to stare at Chartrand and is now wearing a look of disgust.

"Doctor Menka, how did you treat the wounds?"

"The seventeen cuts on her arms were cleansed and sutured with five stitches each. The two wounds on her back were also cleansed and sutured."

"Dr. Menka, what other physical injuries did Sheila Kuzew suffer?"

Dr. Menka turns in the direction of the jury and his voice is filled with compassion as he answers, "Sheila Kuzew had been brutally sexually assaulted. The sexual assault team had been notified and they took all necessary swabs. I then cleansed the pubic and vaginal area and had to suture, as the perineum had a four centimeter tear from the vagina to just left of the rectum."

I notice that a few jury members are staring at Billie Chartrand and he appears to be glaring back at them. Marty Kroll leans over and whispers something to him.

"Were there any other physical injuries?"

"Yes, her face, chest, and rib area were beginning to swell and bruise."

"What did your assessment reveal about these areas?"

"Ms. Kuzew had suffered a cracked cheek bone. I ordered a portable x-ray of the rib area; the results later showed she had suffered two cracked and one broken rib. She was fortunate the broken rib did not puncture her lung."

"Doctor Menka, what treatments did you order for and did Sheila Kuzew receive?"

"Initially she received two blood transfusions for all the blood lost. An intravenous was established to replace lost fluids and have an open line to deliver intravenous antibiotics. The antibiotics are preventative for such things as a resulting vaginal infection. Sheila Kuzew was given Demerol intramuscular, whenever necessary every four hours, to control pain, particularly to the ribs and surrounding tissue."

I ask Dr. Menka, "What other swabs were taken from her by the police officer?"

"Swabs were taken from under her fingernails, by a member of the Forensic Identification Section."

I pause and then ask, "Was Ms. Kuzew conscious while you were treating her?"

"Yes, although she was unconscious when arriving at emergency."

"What, if anything, did she say to you Doctor Menka?"

"She first observed her surroundings then called out for her mother. When I explained that it was necessary to suture her in her private area, her perineum, Ms. Kuzew looked at me and I saw pure terror in her eyes." I'm looking in the direction of the jury to bring their attention to Doctor Menka's description of Sheila.

"Objection your honor, that statement is a subjective observation by Doctor Menka." shouts Marty Kroll.

"Sustained. The last statement will be removed from the records," says Judge Holzzer. He looks at me and says, "Continue."

I take the same course, only reword my question. "Can you attach an emotional label to the look you observed in Sheila Kuzew's eyes?"

"Yes."

"What would the label be?"

"Petrified," remarks Doctor Menka, looking at me with a respect that wasn't visible before.

"Did she speak to you again?"

"Yes."

"When and what did she say?"

"When I started to inject the perineal area with freezing, prior to suturing, she cried out, "God, it hurts."

"Doctor Menka, were you present when Corporal Todd Metcall took photographs of the victim Sheila Kuzew?"

"Yes. The corporal asked if I would be present while he took photos both the day of the attack and three days later."

"Your honor, I ask that the ten photographs be a part of the evidence in this case and labeled exhibit number sixteen."

"So noted," responds Judge Holzzer. The photos are marked for identification and I make a motion to enter them into evidence.

I hand the originals to the clerk for evidence and then distribute copies to Doctor Menka, Marty Kroll, and Mr. Wong, a member of the jury. I observe Mr. Wong recoil as he stares at the top photo. There is nothing pleasant in any of the pictures.

"Doctor Menka, do you recognize these photographs?"

"Yes. They are the ones taken of Sheila Kuzew by Corporal Todd Metcall."

I turn to the jury and request they remove the remainder of the numbered photographs from the envelope.

"Doctor Menka, walk us through the photographs."

Dr. Menka describes each photo while looking at Billie Chartrand. "The first is a facial picture of Sheila Kuzew, taken three days following her admission to emergency. It shows the bruising to the face with a closed right eye, which is a dark purple color. There is swelling to the left check bone and swollen lips with four sutures to the corner of the lower lip. In addition, there is swelling to the right side of the forehead."

"Describe the remainder of the photographs."

He continues, "Pictures two, three, and four are of Sheila Kuzew's arms. Pictures two and three are of her left and right arms, with the gaping wounds prior to suturing, and photo four is of both arms after treatment. Photo five and six show the discoloration over the rib area, both right and left which probably came from a kick or blow of some sort. The seventh photo shows the frontal view of the same area. Sheila Kuzew suffered a broken rib. Pictures eight and nine are of the wounds inflicted to her back; number eight before and number nine after treatment. Photo ten is a full body shot with private areas covered. In this photograph you can see additional bruising and scratches to the lower extremities."

Marty Kroll makes no objection now, as he previously had objected to the submission of the photos as evidence, but was denied by Judge Holzzer. The three of us met on this issue prior to the start of trail. Marty does not want the jury spending any more time than needed on the gruesome photos.

"I have no further questions for this witness."

The Judge looks over at Marty. "No cross-examination," he says as Marty knows photos do not lie. He wants Doctor Menka off the stand quickly.

Judge Holzzer glances at the wall clock and asks Doctor Menka to step down from the stand. He then calls a twenty minute morning recess.

Grabbing a quick cup of coffee I spend ten minutes reviewing questions for our next witness. I also spend a few moments with Sheila and her family. To encourage them, I want to add a promise of a guilty outcome, but know from experience a jury's verdict can never be predicted.

When the sheriff escorts Billie Chartrand into the courtroom, Billie attempts to stop at our table. The sheriff nudges him forward, but not before he makes eye contact with me. I shrink from the loathing and hate in his eyes.

Late morning of the third day of trial, Constable Perry Quinne is sworn in. He is tall, muscular, with black hair, and kind brown eyes.

"Constable Quinne, how long have you been employed by the Royal Canadian Mounted Police?"

"I have been with them for seven years."

I approach the witness stand, "Constable Quinne, where is your host office located?"

"I work out of the Leduc host office, south of Edmonton."

"What happened on the afternoon of Sheila Kuzew's attack, constable?"

Constable Quinne states with assertiveness, "I was driving north on highway number two when a, be on the look out for, was radioed to all marked units in Edmonton and surrounding areas."

"What were you to watch for?"

"The BOLF was on a black, possibly dusty, van, driven by one occupant, a male."

I ask, "What happened next?"

He looks at the jury and answers, "I spotted a black van, somewhat dusty, heading south on highway number two."

"What did you do?"

"I crossed the median and pursued the black van. As I approached the van it picked up speed and was now traveling one hundred and forty kilometers an hour, in a one hundred and ten kilometer zone."

"What happened next?"

"I immediately put on the siren and the driver of the van accelerated and sped away from me."

"What happened then constable?"

Constable Quinne looks at Billie Chartrand and answers, "A chase ensued. At one point the speedometer reached one hundred and eighty kilometers an hour. I received a radio call from another marked unit coming from Leduc, hoping to assist by cutting the driver off. The driver of the van slowed to take the Leduc turn off, just as the other marked unit was coming down the highway, and the van suddenly tried to get back on the highway."

"What was the result constable?"

"The van started to skid and I was positive it would roll but it somehow stayed upright."

"What did you do when the van became stationary?"

"After the van settled we stopped, and jumped from our unit. We approached the van guns drawn. I was shouting for the occupant to get out of the vehicle, with arms raised."

"What were the constables in the other marked unit doing at this time?"

"They pulled to the right of our car and one officer knelt behind the passenger door, with the other behind the driver's door. Both had their guns drawn."

"What happened next?"

"The male suspect opened the van door and stepped out with his hands in the air."

"What was the driver's reaction as he stepped from the van?"

"If the driver had been armed I would have been dead—"

Marty Kroll jumps to his feet and yells, "Objection, your honor, the witness is speculating and I ask that his last statement be deleted from the records."

Judge Holzzer stares at Constable Quinne and announces, "Sustained." His voice hardens and he states, "Constable, you know better."

The constable quickly glances at the jury, then back at the judge and replies, "Yes, your honor."

I resume with, "What did you do after the man exited the van?"

The constable, who has been criticized by the judge in front of the jury, now appears less self-assured, "I handcuffed him and informed him of the Charter of Rights. Later, he would receive an advisement that he didn't have to speak a word to the police."

"What did you do next?" I walk to stand in front of Constable Quinne attempting to restore the confidence displayed earlier.

"I then maneuvered him into the back of my marked unit."

"What happened following your placement of the man into your marked unit?"

"My partner and I transported him to the Remand Centre in Edmonton."

"What happened to the van?"

"The van was treated as a crime scene. A constable was left at the scene to ensure no one approached it. I advised the constable not to touch it. The Forensic Identification Section was notified and would send someone to retrieve the van."

"Do you see the individual from the van, who you took to the Remand Centre, in the court room today?"

"Yes, the defendant Billie Chartrand." replies Constable Quinne.

"Point him out for the court." I request.

Constable Quinne points at Billie Chartrand, and I state, "Let the record show that Constable Quinne has pointed to the defendant, Billie Chartrand."

I add, "No further questions for this witness."

Judge Holzzer adjourns for lunch. We will resume court at 1:30 with the cross-examination of Constable Quinne.

Sam has agreed to meet me for a quick lunch at a small restaurant close to the Law Courts building. We order salads and discuss the activities of our day. Although Sam continues to be involved as the coordinator for the Billie Chartrand case, he has moved on to a double murder. He speculates that the couple's youngest son, who is a drug addict, might be the perpetrator. We discuss the case briefly and I update him on the Billie Chartrand trial. I'm hopeful that in five or six days we will have a guilty verdict.

Promising to keep in touch, Sam returns to work. As I make my way back to the Law Courts building I have a feeling I'm being watched, but it quickly vanishes. It is probably the result of my eye contact with Chartrand today, which scared me.

At one-thirty, Marty Kroll starts his cross-examination of Constable Quinne.

"Constable, do you know where range road two hundred and forty is located?"
"Yes."

"Do you know how many kilometers it is located from Edmonton?"

"No," replies Constable Quinne.

"It is twenty-five kilometers north of the city limits. Have you driven from the north to the south side of Edmonton?"

"Yes."

"Approximately how long did it take you to drive that distance?"

"Approximately one hour."

"How long would it take you to drive from the south outskirts of Edmonton, to the point where you spotted the black van?"

"Approximately fifteen minutes."

"Constable, then how long do you estimate it would take you to travel from range road two hundred and forty, where Sheila Kuzew was found, to the point where you saw the black van driving south on highway number two?" Marty has moved to stand beside the jury.

"It would depend on—"

"Constable, answer the question. How long do you estimate it would take you between the two points on a Friday afternoon?"

Constable Quinne thinks for a minute, then replies, "Approximately one and a half hours."

"At what time was Ms. Kuzew discovered?"

"At two in the afternoon." replies Constable Quinne, as he glances in my direction.

"At what time did you spot the black van?"

"At 3:15 in the afternoon."

Marty asks, "What is the difference between the two times?"

Constable Quinne takes a moment before answering, and then replies, "One hour and fifteen minutes."

Marty is trying to establish reasonable doubt and would love to declare a mistrial, due to the constable stopping Chartrand and the van without just cause. But Billie Chartrand made a big mistake, by traveling over the speed limit.

Marty continues, "Constable, did you touch the van at any time?"

"No."

"Who closed the van door?"

"The defendant, Billie Chartrand did."

"Constable, did you not state Billie exited the van with his hands in the air?"

"Yes."

"No further questions for this witness," states Marty as he returns to the defense table to seat himself beside Billie Chartrand.

I immediately speak to Judge Holzzer, "Redirect your honor." The judge nods in my direction.

"Constable, tell the court, who did close the van's door?"

"Billie Chartrand," replies Quinne with assertiveness, as he glances in the direction of the jury.

"How did he close the door with his hands in the air?"

"With his butt," answers Quinne.

"No further questions."

Marty requests to further cross-examine this witness. I am thinking, *Now what?* Judge Holzzer gives him permission.

"Constable Quinne, did the prosecutor, Ashley Browne, go over your testimony prior to appearing here in court today; to tell you what to say?"

I think, *You bastard, how dare you.* I want to rush over and slap his face.

"No."

"When did she have a discussion with you?"

"Two days ago."

"Were your responses rehearsed?"

"Absolutely not!" replies Constable Quinne in an angry voice.

"Did Ashley Browne coach you?"

"No."

"What did you and Ms. Browne talk about?"

"We talked about the types of questions that would be addressed."

"Thank you constable, no further questions."

When Constable Quinne is excused from the stand, he leaves the courtroom in anger.

I call Corporal Hope Taylor to the stand, as a prosecution witness. She has short, brown hair and a very attractive face. After she is sworn in, I begin with, "Corporal Taylor, what division of the Royal Canadian Mounted Police do you work for?"

"I work for the General Investigation Section."

"How long have you been in your current position?"

"Five years."

"Corporal Taylor, did you interview Sheila Kuzew in the hospital following her attack?"

"Yes."

"When did this interview take place?"

"When Sheila Kuzew was in stable condition, the physician, Dr. Menka, allowed me to proceed with the interview."

"What happened after you received this information?"

"I had a tape recorder with me and asked permission of Sheila Kuzew to tape the interview."

"What was her reply?"

"She replied in the affirmative."

I turn to the jury and advise them that the tape in its entirety has been allowed to be entered as evidence, as exhibit twenty-nine.

"Corporal Taylor, please summarize the tape recording between Sheila Kuzew and yourself."

She turns and speaks to the jury, "Sheila Kuzew was walking down one hundred and sixth street, at approximately 12:15 in the afternoon when a black van pulled up beside her. A man jumped out of the driver's seat and came rushing up behind her, while she was waiting for a red light to turn. He placed a foul smelling rag and his gloved hand over her mouth. He then proceeded to drag her to the front passenger seat of the van. Ms. Kuzew stated she went unconscious and upon awakening felt she was on a rutted country road. After some time, the van stopped and Ms. Kuzew, now conscious, was pulled out of the van."

Corporal Taylor pauses for a second, and continues with her testimony.

"Ms. Kuzew stated she was slapped, punched, knocked to the ground, and kicked in the ribs. The man then slashed her arms with a knife, roughly ripped her lower clothing off, and brutally sexually assaulted her. He then rolled Ms. Kuzew on her abdomen and was sodomizing her, when she attempted to raise her body. The man then brutally stabbed her twice in the back and left her there to die."

Marty shouts, "Objection your honor. I request the last statement be stricken from the record. It contains a statement about which the victim can not claim personal knowledge: the perpetrator's intentions."

Judge Holzzer stares at Corporal Taylor, "Did the victim state, "Left me there to die?"

"Yes," replies the corporal.

Judge Holzzer looks at Marty Kroll and states, "I am allowing the statement to stand as part of the record." The judge nods at me to continue.

"Corporal Taylor, was the rag which was placed over the victim's mouth further investigated?"

"Yes."

"What was the result?"

"We interviewed Ms. Kuzew and she stated it was a very abrasive smell. We took three different containers with abrasive smells and asked her to smell them."

"What was the result of your test?"

"She immediately picked out the ether container."

"Did you locate a rag or ether container?"

"No."

"No further questions. Thank you."

The first question from Marty is, "Corporal Taylor, did you at any point during your interactions with Sheila Kuzew refer to the baldness of the individual apprehended?"

"No."

"Did you discuss the color of his eyes or skin?"

"No."

"You're asking me to believe no conversation took place between Sheila Kuzew and you about the identity of the individual apprehended?"

"Only what the victim said," replies Corporal Taylor, as she looks in the direction of Billie Chartrand.

Marty decides to let her statement go and stares at the corporal until I see her lower her head. Marty's stare is very intimidating. He ends with, "No further questions."

Judge Holzzer adjourns court until Thursday morning at 9:30.

My feet ache from standing at the podium most of the day. I want to go home, but tomorrow's witnesses need my attention. It will be hours before my head has any chance of hitting a pillow.

Arriving at my office I realize how exhausting and emotionally upsetting this day has been. Listening to Doctor Menka's testimony forced me to focus on the pain and anguish experienced by the victim. The memory of her story of torture leaves me emotionally drained.

When the knock comes it shakes me from my daydream, and I'm almost unaware that it is at my door. I call, "Come in."

Logan waltzes in, closes the door and takes a seat. Wanting to be rid of him as quickly as possible I say, "What is it Logan? Can't it wait until tomorrow morning?"

"Hey lady, chill out. I just wanted to congratulate you on a job well done in court today. You were amazing."

I stare at him waiting for the sarcasm to surface. When he remains silent, I say, "Thank you Logan. But really I am exhausted and am on my way home."

"What's the big rush? You usually leave here late." He leers at me.

"Well, not today."

I stand up hoping to encourage him to leave.

Instead he stands, grabs me around the waist and yanks me tightly against him. I can feel his erection. He whispers, "Feel that, it's all for you. I haven't seen Sam here lately; you must be boiling hot!"

While he is talking, I desperately, furiously, try to shove him away.

"Logan, release me or you'll regret this move for the rest of your life."

He continues hanging on to me, so I take a big swing and slap him hard across the face. I see the shocked expression. He quickly drops his arms and looks at me with surprise.

I say through clenched teeth, "Logan, get the hell out of my office and if you ever touch me again, I will march down to Jim's office and charge you with sexual assault. You are a disgrace to your profession!"

Logan glares at me, "What about tomorrow? Want me in court?"

"Oh yes. You will report to me tomorrow morning, as usual, at the prosecutor's table. Embarrassed face and all, you will perform your duty."

Glaring at him, I open the door and literally shove him into the hallway and slam the door shut. I lock it. I should report him today but proving sexual harassment is very difficult. It is often referred to by others as a, "He said, she said," scenario. If I wasn't so involved with my current case, I believe my action would be to go after Logan.

When I finally arrive home, Sam surprises me by bringing over Italian take out. Sam and I sip wine, and enjoy the meal and each other. Around 10:30, I am falling asleep on the sofa while Sam holds me, so he suggests he will go home to his apartment.

Before he leaves, I relate the incident in my office.

"Sam, I had a run-in with Logan late this afternoon."

"Now what did the moron say?" Sam asks as he straightens his clothes and heads toward the front door.

"It's not so much what he said, but what he did."

Sam frowns at me and asks, "What do you mean?"

"He came to my office and during our conversation he grabbed me in a bear hug and would not let me go. I ended up slapping him, hard."

Sam explodes. I have never witnessed a man so angry.

"That bastard! That little prick! I will kill him! Trust me, when I'm through with him he will not be able to walk, much less touch you again!"

"Calm down. It's okay. I am fine. Look at me."

"Where does the bastard live because I'm going after him!"

"Please Sam, settle down. I wish I'd kept my mouth shut."

"Sorry. I'm fine. Just the thought of that asshole touching you got to me."

I finally calm him down. We kiss good night and I head straight to bed.

CHAPTER 16

▼

Sitting in my office I am excited as day four of the trial brings with it my last key witness. This witness, without a doubt, will tie Billie Chartrand to Sheila Kuzew.

As usual, I am at the prosecutor's table early. Ten minutes later I feel Logan slip into the chair next to me. To break the ice I say, "Good morning."

Logan does not respond, so I ignore him for now. When Judge Holzzer enters the courtroom I glance at Logan as we rise and nearly drop back down into my chair. The left side of his face is black and blue, with skin colored band aides here and there. His left eye is swollen shut and I see he is having difficulty standing straight.

Inside my head I am repeating the same phrase, "Oh my God, Sam, you didn't." But I know he did. I hate violence of any kind, but inwardly I smile.

When we are seated I turn to Logan and say, "What happened to you?"

He glares at me, "As if you don't know."

I respond, "I have no idea."

We stop our conversation as court begins; it is now 9:30. Corporal Sam Quong, an evidence technician from General Investigation Section is first to testify today. He is sworn in and I decide to go for gold early.

"Corporal Quong, were you the technician responsible for gathering evidence from the black van belonging to Billie Chartrand?"

"Yes."

"Where was the van located when this evidence was gathered?"

"The van had been brought into the police compound in Edmonton."

"What did you find in the van, if anything?"

"Two strands of long, blood hair." Corporal Quong looks at the jury members.

"Where did you find the strands of long, blond hair?"

"The strands were found on the carpet under the front passenger seat of the van."

I leave my position and walk to stand beside the jury. I ask, "Did you send the strands of blond hair to the crime lab for deoxyribonucleic acid testing?"

"Yes."

"Explain this test to the jury."

Corporal Quong looks at the jury and slowly delivers his description, "DNA stands for deoxyribonucleic acid. Our cells contain chromosomes which are made of strands of DNA and proteins. Coded information is found in the DNA strands. This coded information is used to determine the unique characteristics of the person."

"Did you receive the results back for the blond hairs sent to the laboratory?"

"Yes."

"What was the result?"

"The strands of long, blond hair found in Billie Chartrand's van belonged to the victim, Sheila Kuzew." Constable Quong, delivers this in a loud and clear voice.

An audible gasp could be heard in the courtroom.

"Your honor, I ask that this laboratory report be entered as evidence as exhibit number twenty-six."

"Your request is granted." Judge Holzzer declares.

"Corporal Quong, what are the chances that the strands of long, blond hair found in Billie Chartrand's van could belong to someone else?"

"Five billion to one," replies Corporal Quong.

Vincent Tate, one of the jury members is writing feverishly in his notebook.

"What else did you locate in the van belonging to Billie Chartrand?"

"In the glove compartment there were the usual insurance and registration papers, a flashlight, an unopened package of condoms, a roll of candy, and several provincial maps."

"Who was the van registered to?"

He glances at Billie Chartrand and answers, "The van was registered to the defendant, Billie Chartrand."

"Did you locate anything else in the van?"

"Yes. I found an empty, large, sports duffel bag behind the driver's seat."

"Corporal, did you take photographs at the crime scene?"

"Yes."

"What specifically did you photograph?"

"The photos were of tire tracks."

"Corporal, I will ask you to look at these photographs. Do you recognize them?"

"Yes. Those are my initials."

"What are they?"

"These are the photographs I took of tire tracks near the crime scene just off range road two hundred and forty."

"Did you take photographs of the tires on the van owned by Billie Chartrand?"

"Yes."

I hand Corporal Quong the remainder of the photographs. "Do you recognize these photos corporal?"

"Yes. They are photos taken of the van's tires."

"Your honor, I want to enter these into evidence as people's exhibit number thirty-three." Judge Holzzer nods to the court clerk.

Turning to Corporal Quong I request that he, along with everyone with computer screens look at them now. "Corporal, in front of you is a comparison of one of the tire prints found near the crime scene and the other a photo of the van's left rear tire. Is this statement correct?"

"Yes."

"What are the results of the comparison?"

"A perfect match was found."

"Thank you. No further questions for this witness."

Judge Holzzer calls a twenty minute recess. During this time I attempt to reach Sam, but he is not responding to his cell. When the answering machine comes on, I decide to hang up.

When returning to the prosecutor's table I suggest to Logan that he go home, take a couple of Tylenol and go to bed. He sneers at me, "You'd like that. No sign of the beating, no guilt felt. Well sorry, I'm staying right here."

"That's fine with me, Logan. I absolutely don't feel guilty." It's the truth because I'm not responsible for Sam's actions.

Judge Holzzer returns and court resumes. Marty Kroll is eager to cross-examine Corporal Quong.

"Corporal, did you check the van for finger prints?"

"Yes."

"Did you find any prints?"

"Yes."

"Who did the prints belong to?"

"Billie Chartrand and four unidentified prints were found in the van."

"In the van did you locate any prints belonging to Sheila Kuzew?"

"No."

"Did you find any traces of blood in the van?"

"No." All of Corporal Quong's responses are delivered with confidence. He has been on the stand, to testify, many times in his career.

"Are you telling me there was not one spot of blood located anywhere in the van? Not the door handle, not the steering wheel, or not the seat cover?"

"Yes."

"Who moved the van, corporal, from the highway to the police compound?"

"I did."

"How was it moved?"

"I had the van attached to a tow truck and the driver towed it to the city."

"Did anyone enter the van?"

"No."

"Corporal Quong, did you have an opportunity to examine the weapon used on Sheila Kuzew?"

"No."

"Explain to the jury why."

"The knife was never located."

"Did you exam Billie Chartrand's clothing?"

"Yes."

"Did you find any trace evidence proving contact between Billie Chartrand and Sheila Kuzew?"

"No."

"Corporal Quong, you said the photograph of a tire track at the crime scene was an exact match to the photograph of the van's left rear tire. Is this correct?"

"Yes."

This match was evident to everyone with a computer screen, so I wonder where Marty is going with this line of questioning.

"Where was the photograph of the tire track taken?"

"It was taken near the crime scene."

"Be more specific, corporal."

"The print was taken from range road two hundred and forty."

"How far from the clearing where the alleged attack took place?" asks Marty.

"One quarter of a kilometer."

"So, not near, say within yards of the clearing?"

"No."

"Could the van have turned around on the road and gone back to Edmonton without being anywhere near the actual clearing?"

"Possibly," says Corporal Quong.

I think Marty has to be joking.

"Yes or no? Could the van have turned around on range road two hundred and forty and therefore not have been close to the clearing?"

"Yes."

Marty states, "No further questions for this witness."

I stand, "Your honor I wish to question the witness." I'm happy because the information brought forward by Marty Kroll's cross-examination, now allows me to question Corporal Quong on Billie Chartrand's clothing. Judge Holzzer nods at me to proceed.

Sam, with his investigative talents, brought the following to my attention.

"Corporal Quong, when you interviewed Sheila Kuzew, what did she say Billie Chartrand was wearing?"

"She said Billie Chartrand was wearing blue jeans and a white T-shirt with a print of skull and bones across the front. This information is on the taped interview."

"When you interviewed Constable Quinn, who stopped the defendant, what did he say Billie Chartrand was wearing when arrested?"

"A long sleeved black T-shirt and beige pants."

"Thank you. No further questions."

I can feel the stunned silence in the courtroom. We knew that Chartrand was able to dispose of the knife, his gloves, the condom, and clothes between leaving the scene and being stopped on the highway. There were hundreds of dumpsters along the way. All he needed was a big green garbage bag to dispose of the clothes, and wet wipes to clean the blood off himself and his van. This could be accomplished while he was driving.

As for the ether and rag, my guess is he disposed of these prior to arriving at the clearing. Despite not producing the weapon, we have a strong enough case to get a conviction.

Judge Holzzer adjourns court for lunch. We will return at 1:30.

During lunch I return to my office and find Gail waiting for me. She is bubbling with excitement about the office gossip on Logan. Many reasons for the beating are flying around. Anything from being surprised by a husband coming home early, to Logan coming on to some male at a bar are being discussed.

Gail asks, "What is your opinion?"

I knew this was coming, yet I stand there for what seems an hour, not knowing how to respond. Do I lie to my best friend? I decide on telling her the truth, with a promise from her that she will never repeat what she is about to hear. When I complete the story, Gail sits down in a chair and just stares at me, stunned. She attempts to start a sentence but is lost for words. Finally, in typical Gail fashion she says, "Is Sam selling videos?"

She starts laughing, tears rolling down her cheeks. Gail stands and claps her hands together repeatedly, while singing, "That is awesome, that is awesome!" I calm Gail down, we hug and she leaves my office.

I return to court for the 1:30 start. I call to the stand Corporal Lindsay Smart from the Forensic Identification Section. Corporal Smart is in her late twenties, pretty, and has one of the brightest minds in the police force. She is often the first to interview a suspect, because she is very successful in obtaining necessary information.

After she is sworn in, I begin with, "Corporal Smart, when did you first meet the defendant Billie Chartrand?"

"I met him at five in the afternoon on Friday, May nineteenth, two thousand and six."

"What was the purpose of this meeting?"

"The goal was to obtain as much information as we could from the defendant."

She stares at Billie Chartrand and I can see her tense. Without looking at him I know he is glaring at her.

"What happened at the meeting?"

"I introduced myself and assured Billie Chartrand that he did not have to talk to the police. His response was, "I am familiar with the rules." I asked if he wished to call a lawyer and he responded, "I have called a lawyer." When I asked who, he just stared at me. I questioned him for one hour, but he did not answer any of my questions. He either stared up at the ceiling or whistled during my questioning."

"Did you meet with Billie Chartrand at any other time?"

"Yes, on two different occasions I attempted to have a conversation with the accused, but he ignored me." I thank the corporal and Marty doesn't cross-examine.

I ask Judge Holzzer if I can approach the bench. He nods his head and Marty Kroll joins us. I tell the judge and Marty that my next witness is not available until tomorrow morning. Explaining that I expected longer cross-examinations, I apologize for delaying the trial.

Judge Holzzer accepts the apology, but Marty just looks at me with distaste. We return to our tables and Judge Holzzer announces court is adjourned. We will resume tomorrow at nine in the morning.

I leave my office two hours later. On arrival at home, I put a chicken breast in the oven and cook some wild rice with mushrooms. Taking my meal into the great room, I turn on the television to my favorite news station and eat my dinner.

I'm about to call it a day when the phone rings. I pick up with a, "Hello."

A raspy voice says, "Ashley, check your windows. You never know what may be out there. Possibly death is calling on you."

I drop the phone and it bounces on the rug. I pick it up with shaky hands and press the receiver back to my ear, but the line is now dead.

I sit back down on the sofa and then suddenly jump up and run from room to room checking all windows and doors. I leave every light on. Back in the great room, I check the clock, see it is ten-fifteen and hurriedly dial my parent's phone number.

Mom answers, "Hi dear, how are you this evening?"

I realize right then that I can't share this call with them. It's probably a one time call and I will upset my parents unnecessarily.

"I'm fine Mom. This is just a brief call to see how you and Dad are feeling."

"We are okay. Are you okay is more important? Your voice sounds troubled."

"I'm in the midst of the Chartrand trial and it has taken a lot out of me. You are probably hearing exhaustion in my voice. I must get some sleep. Say hi to Dad. I love you both, so very much."

"I love you too. Get some sleep."

We hang up and I wonder if I should call Sam. Deciding against it, I check the windows and doors once more and go to my bedroom. I have shut off the rest of the lights in my home, but I keep the bedroom light on.

I lie in bed and wonder at the identity of my caller. The voice was definitely disguised and sounded raspy. It was certainly meant for me as the nutcase called me, "Ashley."

The message itself sounded so sinister. Something that Billie Chartrand would deliver. I attempt to place the call in the back of my mind.

I have a very restless sleep.

CHAPTER 17

▼

I feel tired when I awake. It has been some time since I have had such a restless sleep. I decide to miss my short run before breakfast.

My morning runs provide me with renewed energy and an emotional high, so I feel missing my run today has added to my feelings of fright. I have my breakfast and take my time showering and dressing for work.

At my office, I take care of the e-mails and prepare for my morning witness, Doctor Ursula Straus.

Doctor Straus is in her early sixties. She is short, slightly overweight, and has very kind blue eyes. I enjoyed the conversation we had on the telephone.

I'm in the courtroom early and am able to spend a few moments with the Kuzews. They are keeping up a good front, but the weariness is starting to show. I ask Sheila if she is sleeping and she answers, "Most of my shut eye takes place during the evening when my parents are still awake. When night arrives, I'm just too frightened. Even with the sleeping pills and a light on, I'm too terrified."

I wish Sheila and her family well and go to the prosecutor's table.

When I see Logan's face my reaction surprises me. I actually feel sorry for him. His face is distorted and has every color of the rainbow. I realize he can't be permitted to present testimony from the two friends of Sheila's, as was originally planned for this afternoon. I share my decision with him and he stands up and leaves the courtroom without a word.

I decide not to follow him because Judge Holzzer has arrived in court. We stand, court commences, and I call Doctor Ursula Straus to the stand.

"Doctor Straus, what is your profession?"

"I am a psychiatrist."

"From where did you graduate with a doctorate?"

"I trained in London, England, under Doctor William Smithers, the world renowned English psychiatrist."

"How many years have you been in practice?"

"It will be twenty-seven years this September."

"What are your accomplishments?"

"I am the dean of psychiatry at the university; I have written nine books which include psychiatric diagnosing, assessment and treatment. I had a private practice for fifteen years."

"Doctor Straus, did you have the opportunity to interview Sheila Kuzew?"

"Yes I did."

"How many meetings did you have with the victim?"

"A total of six meetings."

"What was the length of each meeting?"

"Approximately one hour per meeting for a total of six hours."

"During this time did you discuss with Sheila Kuzew all aspects of her alleged encounter with Billie Chartrand?"

"Yes."

"What is your opinion of the entire attack on Sheila?"

"My opinion is the attack was planned, from the time of kidnapping to the stabs in the back. The sexual assault and knife wounds on the arms were an intentional act."

This is my intent to prove an intentional criminal act, because it will carry more prison time.

"No further questions. Thank you."

Marty chooses not to cross-examine as he will call his own psychiatrist to testify next week.

I call Marlon Wright to the stand. Marlon is tall, very muscular, and extremely handsome. He is a neighbor and friend of Sheila Kuzew. After Marlon is sworn in, I approach and start with, "How old are you Mr. Wright?"

"I'm twenty."

"Where do you live?"

"I live next door to Sheila Kuzew."

"How long have you known her?"

"I have known her since we moved next door to her parent's home ten years ago."

"Describe your relationship with Sheila Kuzew."

"We are very good friends. When we were younger, ten, eleven, twelve, we played together every day after school. We drifted apart for a couple of years, then became close again when Sheila turned sixteen and me eighteen."

"Were you ever romantically involved with her?"

"No!" exclaims Marlon, as if the thought never entered his head or heart.

"What did you do together when she was sixteen to your eighteen years of age?"

"We went skiing with my parents in the winter and fishing with Sheila's mom and dad in the summer. I always looked out for her. She is very kind and considerate. She was a happy person with a wonderful sense of humor."

"Did she date a lot?"

"Last year she started going out on dates with a guy she met in high school. He was nice, but there was nothing really serious between them."

"Some male teenagers have labels for girls, such as easy lay. Did you ever hear this remark about Sheila?"

"Absolutely not," he replies. I have discussed this question with Sheila and she understood the need for it.

"Have you talked with her lately?"

Marlon turns and speaks directly to the jury, "I talked with her a few times. We went to a local restaurant two weeks ago and Sheila spent most of the evening with a blank look on her face. I had to repeat my statement or question three times, before I received a response. We also went to the mall together, but she asked to be taken home ten minutes after we got there. She kept peering around and grabbing my arm. I could tell she was very frightened."

"What do you do, Mr. Wright?"

"I'm a university student in civil engineering. Sheila had applied and was accepted for this fall, but she withdrew after the attack."

"Thank you. No further questions." Marlon has turned out to be an excellent character witness.

Judge Holzzer calls a twenty minute break. When we resume court, Marty Kroll is ready for the cross-examination.

He approaches Marlon Wright and asks, "You stated you played together with Ms. Kuzew when she was ten, eleven and twelve. Is this true?"

"Yes."

"What did you play?"

Marlon smiles as he recalls fond memories, "When she was ten she made me push her doll carriage and sometime have tea with the dolls and her. By eleven and twelve we played catch, tennis and went to movies together with either her mom or mine."

"Did you ever play doctor with Sheila?"

"Sorry, but I'm not familiar with that game."

"Did you pretend to be the doctor and have Sheila as your patient?"

"No." Marlon looks over at me and I interrupt, "Objection your honor. There has been no factual evidence presented to be used as a basis for this line of questioning."

Judge Holzzer ponders a minute and then asks Marty where he is going with this line of testimony. Marty has no appropriate response, therefore Judge Holzzer states, "Sustained."

Marty then asked, "When you were teenagers did you go to parties together?"

"Yes."

"Did you both attend parties every weekend?"

"No."

"Did you come home alone from the parties or was Ms. Kuzew with you?"

"She always came home with me. Her parents trusted me."

"Did she dress provocatively?"

I interrupt immediately and ask Judge Holzzer for a bench meeting. He agrees to my request and dismisses the jury from the court room. Marty and I approach the bench. I explain the rationale behind my request; to have Marty Kroll explain the relevance to this case of this line of questioning.

I ask, "Why is it a concern of anyone how Ms. Kuzew dresses?"

Judge Holzzer asks Marty to provide factual evidence to support his current enquiry. Because Marty is unable to provide this information, he is cautioned about this line of questioning by the judge.

We return to our respective tables. The jury is called back and Marty approaches the stand. He stands in front of Marlon Wright then turns and announces, "No further questions."

It is now nearing lunch time and Judge Holzzer adjourns until one-thirty.

I invite Sheila and her family to my office for fifteen minutes. We discuss how well Marlon did on the stand. Sheila tells me that Marlon was scared to appear but wanted to be of assistance to her. I share that Sheila's best friend, Rayanne Mullon, is our last witness this afternoon. I add we will rest our case this afternoon and that Marty Kroll will take over on Monday morning. I give each of them a hug of encouragement when they leave.

At 1:30, after being sworn in, Rayanne Mullon takes the stand. Rayanne is tall and slim, with facial features similar to a famous movie star.

"Ms. Mullon, how long have you known Sheila Kuzew?"

"Since kindergarten, when we were five years old."

"How old are you, now?"

"Eighteen."

"Have you been friends with Sheila Kuzew for the entire thirteen years?"

"Yes."

"What words would you use to describe her before the attack?"

Rayanne glances at the jury and then responds, "She was bubbly, happy, funny, generous, and smart."

"How would you describe her now?"

Rayanne looks down at her hands, then up at me. There are tears in her eyes when she answers, "Sheila is now withdrawn, as if detached from her surroundings. I feel as if she is a totally different person. She never wants to go out or talk on the phone. I know I have to be patient, but it's so hard to see her suffering this way. I wish I could help."

Although unusual in a court of law, I decide a little encouragement is called for. If Marty objects, so be it. "Rayanne, you are helping just by being there when Ms. Kuzew needs you. Continue to call and visit." I pause, "What else have you observed since the attack on your friend?"

"The biggest thing is her fear. She is afraid to go to the mall, or a movie, or out for food or a pop. She never leaves the house at night."

"Thank you, Ms. Mullon. No further questions."

Marty decides not to attempt to discredit this witness and announces, "No cross-examination". I inform Judge Holzzer and the jury that I have completed the people's case and that the prosecution rests.

Judge Holzzer adjourns court. Marty is on the podium Monday.

When I arrive home I decide to call Sam and fill him in on my phone call of last night. He doesn't respond to his home phone, so I call his cell. Sam answers on the second ring.

"Hi, I was about to call you. What's up?"

"What were you going to call me about?"

"I want to ask you out for dinner tomorrow night. Are you interested?"

"Of course I'm interested. I debated on whether to tell you this now, but I received a frightening phone call last night. I'm fine now, because it is light out."

"What? Can you hold on for another couple of hours? I'll come over after work. What happened? What did he say?"

Sam sounds rushed and I don't want to keep him.

"First, you don't need to come over and second, he used this raspy voice and said to check my doors and windows because death may come calling. What a bastard."

"Are you sure about my coming and staying with you? I can get one of the guys to cover for me here."

"No, you're not going to come running every time I'm frightened. I will see you tomorrow. What time are we going out?"

"I'll pick you up at six. See you then, Ashley." We hang up and I do the routine of checking all doors and windows.

CHAPTER 18

▼

It is Saturday and I'm applying the finishing touches to my makeup in preparations for my date with Sam. The phone rings. Hoping he isn't canceling due to job demands, I dash to the phone and pick up with, "Hello there." No response. "Hello." I repeat a few times. About to hang up, I hear a raspy voice, "Ashley, you can't run far enough. Death awaits you."

"What?" I shout.

"You heard right." The phone goes dead.

I'm mortified and start to tremble. I can't control my fear and run to check for locked doors and windows. I was hoping the first call would be the last. Should I call my parents or Sam?

I'm about to call him when my doorbell rings. I scream in fear. Totally freaked out, I approach the door cautiously, check the side panel window and am overwhelmed with relief when I see Sam. He's about to ring again when I open the door and literally fling myself into his arms.

"What's wrong? I thought I heard a scream. You're trembling."

"I just received another threatening phone call!" I explain the terrorizing way in which the caller's words were delivered.

"Let's sit down and talk about this. You could be mistaken. Maybe it was a wrong number?"

"No, he called me Ashley."

"Was his voice deep, higher pitched, loud, or soft?"

"It sounded muffled, also raspy. Like, "Ashley, you can't run." I hesitate between each word. "It sounded so threatening."

Sam is on his way to the kitchen when he asks, "Do you have any wine or would you prefer water?"

I realize my mouth feels very dry and could use a liquid. "There is a bottle of chardonnay in the fridge and the wine glasses are in the china cabinet. You will find the corkscrew in the top drawer, next to the stove."

Within minutes, I am holding a filled wine glass with trembling hands. Sam keeps chatting, his arm around me and gradually I relax and stop shaking. He refills my glass. I don't know if the warm feeling spreading throughout my body is from the closeness of Sam or from the wine.

"What type of security system do you have in your home?"

"I don't have a security system. Never saw the need."

"You are contacting a security company on Monday. Meanwhile, I'm not leaving you alone tonight."

"It's okay. There is no need to panic."

"Let me be the judge of that. I'm staying. Get used to it."

I'm becoming annoyed with Sam for controlling the situation and I walk away. His strong arms are suddenly around me, holding me close. "No, Ashley, I am staying." He gently turns me around and places a finger under my chin and lifts my head up to kiss me gently.

Before the kiss can deepen, I move away. I have been making my own decisions forever and find it difficult when someone attempts to make them for me. "I'm becoming hungry, let's order Chinese."

The food arrives and is delicious. We wolf down sweet and sour pork, ginger beef, and beef with mixed greens. We finish the wine and I feel a need to know Sam better.

"Where were you born, here in Edmonton?"

"No, actually I spent my younger years in Toronto. At age twenty-one I joined the Royal Canadian Mounted Police and moved to Regina, Saskatchewan. Later I attended the Saskatoon University. Think it was nineteen ninety-seven when I was transferred to Edmonton."

"You told me about the university, but you still haven't disclosed anything really personal."

Sam appears uncomfortable.

"What do you want to know, Ashley?"

"Well, you never mention your parents or any siblings."

"I'm an only child."

"Do you have any deep, dark secrets?"

"Actually, I don't."

It seems that Sam has chosen not to share his history with me. It hurts and my response is sharper than I intended.

"God, it's like pulling teeth. Forget it, I will stop prying. This isn't about being nosy, but about caring about you."

He is silent for a long time. Sam looks at me, almost with an apology in his expression, "Ashley, my home life was not great. Mom and Dad were alcoholics and often my dad was out of work. He would become angry and beat us. Frequently there was not enough food in the house. Mom tried in the beginning but eventually gave in and was oblivious to her surroundings. At eighteen I moved out. Mom passed away when I turned twenty. I attended her funeral and said good-bye to Dad. I haven't seen him since. I'm sure he is dead by now."

"Oh God, Sam, I'm so sorry. And I'm sorry for prying and forcing you to remember a painful past. My parents were excellent, and even after the many years I've spent prosecuting child abusers, I still find it difficult to understand a mother and father abusing their child."

His voice and facial features portray sadness. He responds, "I remember watching other kids' parents coming to the school and looking at their sons or daughters art work. I would lie to everyone and say my Dad was away on business. It hurt so much."

"What else do you remember?" I believe that discussing painful memories helps in relieving the pain, so I encourage Sam.

"Every Christmas our school would put on a concert and I would fib, and tell the teacher it wasn't possible for me to have a role in the play or sing in a choir because, as a family, we were going away at Christmas."

"You have such terrible childhood memories."

"It's okay. Let's go to bed. I can think of a few things to make my painful memories disappear."

Tonight our lovemaking is slow and gentle. In the morning I peer into Sam's face. He is sleeping, mouth slightly open with his arm encircling me. Watching his face, I reach down and stroke him. This gets his immediate attention. His eyes open and widen in surprise. I stare into the green pools and feel myself falling. It feels comforting, protecting, and loving. Sam groans and is all over me.

Two hours later we settle in the kitchen over pancakes. When stuffed, Sam thumbs through the yellow pages searching for a security company. He comments, "I'm not leaving you here alone at night until a top notch security system is installed." I smile, hoping all companies have a waiting list.

"Who do you think called you?"

"I have been reflecting on that this morning. At the top of my list is Logan."

"Why do you think Logan?"

"He is very angry at me right now, and I think he is capable of death threats."

"What about Kevin? Have you considered him?"

"Yes. One day while running in the park I felt as if someone was watching me. Possibly it could have been Kevin. He is belligerent, but I'm not really afraid of him."

"You're saying he's not aggressive or threatening?"

"Yes. Kevin is not threatening. Who do you think is making the calls to me?"

"My guess is that Billie Chartrand is responsible."

I stare at him and can't believe what he is suggesting, "But he's in a jail cell, and it's difficult to call from there this often."

"Not if you have plenty of money, which Chartrand must have to have Marty Kroll as his lawyer."

"And exactly how would he accomplish this phone situation?"

"He would purchase a stolen cell phone in prison or pay someone to call you. If you have the bucks, everything is available to you behind the walls."

"I know drugs are available, but cell phones? How do you know this is possible for inmates?"

"I have a friend, Kurt, who works in the system. You must meet him, a real wonderful character and friend."

We make it an early evening and Sam stays over. We make love.

On Monday morning at five, I watch him coming out of the bathroom. He has a towel wrapped around his waist. Water is sparkling in his dark, curly hair. I say, "You look good enough to eat."

"Don't tempt me. I'm worn out."

"Okay sweetheart, you dress and I will put on the coffee. Court begins at nine."

"Thanks. I love you."

The statement stops me in mid-stride. We haven't broached the subject of love. "What did you say?"

"I love you, Ashley. Come here. Forget breakfast. I need to make love to you right now."

I hungrily approach him and yank off the towel, pushing him back until the backs of his legs are touching the bed. I push, and then straddle him. "I love you too, Sam."

"Say it again."

"Sam, I love you, love you, love you, and think I have from the first day I saw you."

My words have joined the rhythm of our bodies.

Much later Sam turns to me and says, "Man, I hate to leave you but work calls. I have to stop by my apartment. Tonight I'm coming back to take up where we left off."

"Men are so predictable. Love them a few times and they become demanding."

"Ashley, it will be more than a few times if you don't stop this."

"Promises, promises, all I ever hear are promises."

He looks at me and we are back in bed.

Later Sam grins as he dresses quickly. I follow him out to the kitchen, where we exchange a quick kiss and then he is gone.

I sit at the table, nursing my coffee and replay this morning's exchange. Yes, I love Sam. He is kind, intelligent, humorous, protective, and a remarkable lover. Am I ready to commit if that is what he wants? His attack on Logan Reid has never been referred to by Sam, Logan or me. It is like it never happened. His anger at the time worries me.

Ten minutes later I realize I still have time for my run. A phone call is not going to confine me to my home.

CHAPTER 19

▼

I'm taking the elevator up to my office. Usually, I climb the stairs, but this morning I have more books and files than usual. When the door opens on the second floor I don't look up. I'm busy reading a memo I brought home on Friday, but didn't read. I smile, thinking, *What is more important, a memo or making love with Sam?* The elevator is packed and I feel people shifting around.

Wondering at the cause of the commotion, I look up to see Kevin standing in front of me. I whisper savagely, "What are you doing here?"

"I came up to see if you have a moment to see me. It's about your Dad and I thought you would want to know."

"What is wrong with my dad?" I feel a flip in my heart.

"Can I come to your office?"

When we leave the elevator I turn to him and say, "I have to be in court in fifteen minutes, so I can give you five. My office number is four hundred and twenty-two, and is on the right of the hallway. I will join you there in a second."

When Kevin turns right I turn left and head straight for Gail's office, hoping she is in early as usual. She is and I quickly explain the situation. I ask her to come to my office in four minutes and to say I'm needed for a short meeting.

I don't know who to trust. Maybe it was Kevin who called me at home the other day.

He is waiting for me and I open my office door and ask him to take a seat. I hate having him between me and the door, but there is nothing I can do about it now. He looks around my office and says, "Nice office here. I wanted to see where you worked. How are you?"

I'm experiencing difficulty controlling my angry, and ask through clenched teeth, "What about my dad? You said you had concerns you wanted to discuss."

"Hold on! Can we not have a wee conversation before you start jumping down my throat?"

"No Kevin, we can't have a wee conversation or anything else. Now, what do you have to say about my dad?"

"I have heard gossip at work that he is suffering from memory problems. Has your Mom said anything to you?"

"You have got to be joking. There is nothing wrong with my dad's memory. Now remember my warning to you and leave."

"I really miss you! I want you to come back to me." Kevin is actually crying.

"Stop this. We were never involved in a relationship. It's impossible to return to something that never was. Did you make up the information about my dad?"

I'm angry and want to shake him for scaring me.

"So what if I did. Would you have invited me in if I didn't express a concern about your dad?"

"No, you are correct. Don't pull a stunt like this again." I start walking toward the door and he steps in front of me. Just then Gail arrives.

"Ashley, you are needed at an emergency meeting for ten minutes before your court appearance." She glares at Kevin and pushes her way past him.

Kevin looks at her and says with contempt, "Don't worry friend, no need to lie, I was just leaving. Good-bye Ashley."

He turns and walks out the door.

"Gail, close and lock the damn door. I'm so glad you showed up when you did. I was about to leave my office and Kevin stepped in front of me. Crap those phone calls have me jumping at every little deviation from the norm." I have shared the nasty phone calls with Gail.

She says, "Don't tell Sam, or there will be children without a teacher for a couple of weeks." She leaves and I go to the courtroom.

This is day one for the defense. I have received a list of Marty's witnesses and I'm aware he doesn't have much. People like Billie Chartrand don't cultivate close relationships. They are loners who get gratification by feeding their dark souls with darker thoughts and by inflicting pain on the innocent. I believe there is no cure for sick minds like Billie Chartrand's.

Court convenes at nine. Marty's first witness is a private investigator. His name is Denis Brestow. Denis is sworn in by the court clerk and Marty starts off the morning.

"Are you a private investigator Mr. Brestow?"

"Yes."

"How long have you held a private investigator's license?"

"I've had this license for twenty-two years."

He smiles at the jury and folds his hands in front of him on the railing.

"Did you visit the clearing off range road two hundred and forty where the alleged attack took place?"

"Yes."

"Did you take someone with you?"

"Yes. My wife Kelly came to assist me."

"Is your wife the approximate height and weight of Ms. Kuzew?"

"Yes."

"Did you enact the scene as described by Sheila Kuzew?"

"Yes." Mr. Brestow looks at Chartrand and receives a sneer. He quickly glances down at his folded hands.

"What time of day did you enact the scene?"

"It was one in the afternoon."

"What did you and your wife do?"

"I first asked my wife to lay down on the ground in the same direction as was described by the victim. I straddled her across the chest, and asked her to describe my features as if I was not familiar to her."

"What were the results?"

"Kelly stated it was difficult to clearly make out my features because the trees were casting a shadow across my face."

"Thank you. No further questions."

I decide to gamble with this witness.

"Mr. Brestow, to your knowledge what date did the assault take place?"

"It took place on Friday, May nineteen, two thousand and six."

"What date did you and your wife, enact the attack?"

"We enacted the attack on Saturday, August five, two thousand and six."

"That is a difference of how many weeks?"

He thinks for a moment, "It's approximately an eleven week difference."

"Thank you, no further questions."

Everyone is aware that as the weeks pass, the shape and length of shadows change. Brestow's enactment results mean nothing to the outcome of the trial.

Marty's next witness is Doctor Bonnie Haverlow, a well known psychiatrist. She is in her early forties, with brown stylish hair, and an attractive face.

Marty leads her through her impressive resume and then asks, "Doctor Haverlow, are you familiar with the alleged sexual assault on Sheila Kuzew?"

"Yes."

"Did you meet with Billie Chartrand?"

"Yes."

"What took place during this meeting?"

"I administered two tests on Mr. Chartrand."

"What were the results?"

"The first examination taken by Mr. Chartrand was an intelligence quotient test. The results showed that he falls within the genius range."

"What were the results of the second test?"

"The second examination tests an individual's aggressiveness. The results showed that Mr. Chartrand does not have traits of aggressiveness."

"What conclusion did you draw from the test results and your interview with Mr. Chartrand?"

"He showed no signs of aggressiveness during the hour interview or from the test results."

"Are you aware that the accused has no prior criminal record?"

"Yes."

"In your professional opinion, after your interview with Billie Chartrand and knowing he has no prior record, is it likely for him to have committed such a heinous crime?"

"In my professional opinion, it is highly unlikely."

"Thank you, Doctor Haverlow. No further questions."

I stand and approach the stand. "Doctor Haverlow, how much time did you spend with Billie Chartrand?"

"Two hours."

"In two hours you managed to assess that Billie Chartrand showed no signs of aggressive behavior?"

"Yes."

"Would it be possible for an intelligent individual to hide signs and symptoms of aggressiveness?"

Doctor Haverlow pauses a split-second, then answers, "Over the short term they could."

"Hypothetically, if a person had a history of criminal activities would they more likely, in your professional opinion, be capable of committing such a heinous crime?"

"Yes."

"Thank you, Doctor Haverlow. No further questions."

A thorough search by the police and my office produced no criminal record on Billie Chartrand. Both Sam and I believe he used many aliases, but to date our efforts to prove prior criminal activity have been fruitless.

Marty calls a character witness to the stand. It is Linda Donbye, owner of the walk-up rooming house where Chartrand had rented two rooms.

She is sworn in. Mrs. Donbye smiles at the jury, places her hands on the railing in front of her and starts fingering her wedding rings. Her shoulders are squared, as if trying to portray an upstanding citizen. Marty approaches the stand.

"Mrs. Donbye, how long have you known Mr. Chartrand?"

"I have known him for ten months."

"How did you meet Mr. Chartrand?"

"He came to my rooming house to rent one of my two room suites."

"Was he pleasant?"

"Yes."

She smiles at Chartrand and he leers at her which causes Mrs. Donbye to step back in the witness stand.

"Was he clean and appropriately dressed?"

"Yes."

"In any of your conversation with Mr. Chartrand has he been rude?"

"No." Mrs. Donbye is now avoiding eye contact with Billie Chartrand.

"Has he paid his rent on time each month?"

"Yes."

"Did he ever entertain or have wild parties in his rooms?"

"No."

"Do you like Mr. Chartrand?"

"Yes." But the jury and I catch a slight hesitation in her response.

"Will you continue to rent to him?"

"Yes."

"No further questions. Thank you." Marty returns to the defense table.

I approach the stand. "Mrs. Donbye, did you have conversations with Billie Chartrand other than those concerning his monthly rent?"

"No."

"Did you at any time socialize with him?"

Mrs. Donbye looks down at her hands. "No," she replies.

"For what length of time was Billie Chartrand in your presence, when he paid his rent?"

"Usually about two minutes." She looks down at her hands again.

I can't refer to Billie as Mister Chartrand; rather I have a great desire to address him as Billie the Butcher.

"Did he pay in cash or by check, Mrs. Donbye?"

"He always paid in cash."

Surprise! Checks can be traced.

"Did you find this odd?"

"No. I prefer it."

"Thank you. No further questions."

The judge adjourns court for lunch. We are to return at one-thirty.

I'm looking forward to lunch today because Gail is bringing us a soup and salad and we will have an hour get together to further update. The first thing Gail asks, after we discuss the Kevin episode, is if I have heard from Logan.

I reply, "I sent him home from court last week, because he looked battered. I couldn't have him facing witnesses looking the way he did."

"Did he say anything to you, threaten you?" she asks.

"No, in fact I received no response. He just up and left the court room. Has Jim said anything about his absence or have you heard anything? I have been too busy with the Chartrand case to pay much attention to office politics and gossip."

Gail answers between bites of her sandwich, "Cheryl doesn't confide much, but did share with me that Jim talked to Logan on the phone for almost an hour. Other than that, I have heard nothing."

"Well, Jim knows I can get through this case without any assistance from Logan."

Everyone in our office wonders why I allow Logan to assist me.

"What about Sam? Are things working out between you two?"

"Let me be the first to tell you, we are madly in love. I guess you could say Sam has basically moved in, although he still goes to his apartment regularly. We are happy and are good together. It scares me a little."

"Don't let it scare you. Just give me plenty of time to purchase a bridesmaid's dress. You know, pretty, does not come in large sizes. Seriously Ashley, I hear very nice things about him, around the office."

"Yes, he is awesome. There is one more thing I want to tell you before I have to get back. I received another threatening phone call. It scared the hell out of me and Sam is ordering a top notch security system for my home."

"My word, what did the caller say?" Gail's eyes are huge and she is holding onto her cup with white fingers and knuckles. I reach across the table and place my hand on her arm. "Sorry to scare you. I am fine. I will get the security system and Sam sleeps over. You saw Logan, so you know I should be relatively safe with Sam."

Gail chuckles, then her face becomes serious, "Just be careful friend. Do you have any idea who is responsible for the calls?"

"Sam and I think it is Chartrand, my current psychopath defendant. He is one scary customer, Gail. I can hardly wait for this trial to be completed and the sicko sent to prison for twenty-five years. Anyway, I have to go. Thanks for the lunch and I'll see you soon."

Gail hugs me and repeats, "Be careful, friend."

I clean up the table, answer two e-mails and head back to the court room. The phone call still remains in the back of my mind.

In the afternoon Marty's witness is a waitress in a chain restaurant where Chartrand often ate his dinners. Marty is really scraping the bottom of the barrel with this witness. I decide not to cross-examine her. At three, following her testimony, Judge Holzzer adjourns for the day.

When I arrive at my office one of my voice mail messages is from Sam, letting me know the security system has been ordered. He adds that it is a top of the line system. He says that he is paying for the installation. I don't know how I feel about that. He informs me the installers will be at my home today at six. I glance at my watch. It is four. I have plenty of time. I must remember to give Sam a key to my home. This will be a first for me but a relationship is all about trust.

I arrive home at 5:30 and decide to heat a piece of left over lasagna for dinner. Before I have completed my meal the doorbell rings. It is two men from the Edmonton alarm security system. They say it will take approximately three and a half hours to complete the installation. I wish Sam was here to talk to them.

I'm happy when he arrives at 6:15. He's not hungry, because he grabbed two cheese burgers at five-thirty. I feel exhausted and ask Sam to have the installers do my bedroom windows first, thereby allowing me to have a rest.

Mission accomplished, I can't wait to rest my weary feet and promptly lay down without changing from my work clothes. This is something I rarely do.

According to my bedroom clock it is three in the morning when I awake. I feel so much better. I go in search of Sam and find him asleep on the couch.

A quick change and I'm in the kitchen filling a water glass when he joins me. He can't wait to explain the entire security system and I just want to get back to bed. We compromise and Sam relays the minimum information I require to exit and enter, without having the police charging my house.

We return to my bedroom and almost instantly are asleep. At six the alarm rings and we have a quick shower and breakfast. A long kiss and we depart.

This is the final day for witnesses. On Wednesday Marty and I will present our closing statements.

Marty has two more witnesses. The first is an occasional drinking buddy of Chartrand's, who swears that Billie Chartrand is the nicest friend in the world. On cross-examination, it doesn't take long to discover the witness is an unemployed drunk. He is easily discredited. No, this psychopath doesn't have many, if any, friends.

The final witness for the defense is a young gas jockey who thinks he filled a black van driven by a bald man on the Friday in question. The time of the fill was at one in the afternoon, which would make it impossible for Billie Chartrand to have been Sheila Kuzew's attacker. It takes me only three minutes to discredit his testimony.

Marty informs Judge Holzzer that the defense rests. The judge adjourns court with the announcement that closing statements will be heard tomorrow at nine.

Marty doesn't glance in my direction, but Billie keeps glaring at me as the sheriff leads him out of the courtroom. I have two more days to tolerate that creepy psychopath.

It's a lovely, warm, summer evening when I arrive home and I decide to weed my flower garden. There is something healing in gardening. It decreases the anxiety and stress of the day. I am pulling the weeds around a rose bush when I hear the telephone. Hoping it is Sam, I decide to run inside and answer. Glancing down at call display I don't recognize the phone number.

Picking up, I say, "Hello." I hear a few heavy breaths and I'm about to hang up when a raspy voice replies, "Hello Ashley. Were you in the shower? Better get dressed, because I'm sending one of my buddies over to check you out."

With anger, I spit out, "You can't frighten me, you bastard."

His gravelly retort sounds deadly, "No? I'll do that and much more. I'll control you completely. Death for you follows." He breaks the connection.

The garden's beauty is now secondary and I stay put behind locked doors.

When Sam arrives he holds me close, while I explain the frightening phone call.

"His voice holds such hatred for me that it actually feels like he's choking me. If he keeps this up he will totally control me."

"No, he will not. You are too strong to allow someone to dominate you."

"You don't understand. Every time the phone rings, I feel this overwhelming fear."

Sam continues to hold me, and once I have settled he tells me stolen cell phones are a dime a dozen in jail. He adds, "You can purchase anything behind bars, from cigarettes to cocaine."

I discuss with Sam the possibility of applying for an unlisted phone number. He hesitates, not agreeing with this idea. He makes me aware that if the caller can't reach me by phone, his attempts to reach me could escalate to a dangerous level, such as coming to the home.

In my situation, because Chartrand is behind bars, he could indeed have a buddy pay me a visit. The thought sends chills down my spine.

Periodically, during my career I have been threatened by men and women whom I have prosecuted. The threats for the most part were delivered in the courtroom. On three occasions, I used the services of the sheriffs for protection.

One man, Taylor Comdstalk, a parolee, did approach me on the law court steps with an, "I am back," comment, but I didn't hear from him again. The incident was over two years ago and I doubt my caller is Taylor. Chartrand is at the top of my list.

I now want to question others as to whether in their careers, they have met someone who they knew from the start would eventually have a negative impact on their life? Maybe it was a student, a peer, a boss, or a service worker who made life miserable for them? I felt this way about Chartrand from the first time I saw him. It's in his eyes, which are devoid of any kindness.

I know deep down that this is far from over. Sam has advised me to ignore the calls, when I don't recognize the phone number. I have to share my approach to phone calls with Sam.

"I have been ignoring the solicitor's calls for years. If they become too bothersome, I relieve some steam by picking up the phone and starting to talk very rapidly, non stop, for five, sometimes ten minutes, before I hear the line go dead. They can't manage to get one word in. I'm positive the individual on the other end of the line takes me off their list or labels me the crazy lady. What do you think?"

Sam laughs. He places an arm over my shoulder and we walk toward the bedroom. We both know it's a serious situation, but for now, there is absolutely nothing we can do.

CHAPTER 20

▼

It is time for the closing statements and as is common for me in this situation, I feel slightly nauseated. I place pressure on myself because this is my last chance to influence the jury toward a guilty verdict.

Approaching the jury, I make eye contact with each member. "Ladies and gentlemen of the jury, the people have proven beyond a shadow of a doubt that the defendant," and I stop to point, "Billie Chartrand, kidnapped, sexually assaulted, and attempted to murder Sheila Kuzew. The deoxyribonucleic acid hair evidence has placed Sheila Kuzew in Billie Chartrand's van. Ms. Kuzew, in this courtroom, identified Billie Chartrand as her attacker. Sheila Kuzew also selected Billy Chartrand from a photo line-up."

I pause for a moment, "She informed the constable first on the scene that the perpetrator was driving a black van. A black van was later stopped with Billie Chartrand driving it. He drugged and kidnapped an innocent eighteen year old walking on our own city streets in broad daylight. He felt no mercy, as he savagely sliced away at the arms of Sheila Kuzew. After causing horrendous pain, he sexually assaulted her."

I take a deep breath and continue, "This was not sufficient to satisfy the evil in Billie Chartrand. He then stabbed her twice in the back and left her there, ladies and gentlemen, to die."

The air feels warm and humid and my mouth is dry. Before going on, I sip some water. I then continue, "Sheila Kuzew was so filled with terror she made no further attempt to fight him off. She suffered in silence." I go on for one hour with the results of the attack on Sheila physically and emotionally. I conclude with, "Help Sheila Kuzew speak out by finding Billie Chartrand guilty as charged of kidnapping, sexual assault, and attempted murder. I ask no mercy be shown to Billie Chartrand." I look at each jury member and slowly return to the prosecutor's table.

Judge Holzzer decides on an early lunch. He adjourns court and advises everyone we will convene at 12:30.

I hurry to the cafeteria and grab an egg and ham salad and an orange juice. Taking the food back to the office, I eat while going through my e-mail.

I feel someone's presence and whirl around in my chair to face Logan standing in my doorway. He asks, "Can I come in?"

"Sure, just keep the door open please."

A look crosses his face, but I'm unable to read it. Was it hurt, anger, or hate?

Logan sits at my table and says, "I'm thankful you did not divulge the reason for my distorted face. My career is important to me." I am beginning to realize that Logan isn't here to apologize for his behavior, but to save his reputation and career. He continues, "We work together so we need to be civil to each other. Do you want me back in court this afternoon?"

I desperately want to say, "I never want to see your face again," but instead respond, "No, it's not necessary."

"Jim called me into his office for a chat." He stops, looking at me.

After thirty seconds of awkward silence I ask, "What did you chat about?"

"Initially, I assumed you had gone to Jim to officially complain about me, but he made no reference to my battered face."

Logan stops and glares at me. This time my decision is not to pick up the conversation, although I'm interested in what Jim said to him.

Finally he states, "Jim requested that I be more available to you during demanding trials."

I stand and this time he looks at me with an expression of loathing and walks out.

Yes, I can understand his dislike of me. It's a demotion. And to add salt to the wound, he now must work with me.

I return to court in time for the 12:30 start.

Marty Kroll spends one hour and a half attempting to convince the jurors that Billie Chartrand is innocent of all charges.

He expresses empathy for Sheila and her family and then launches into informing the jury of facts the prosecutors didn't present. Facts such as where is the knife, where are blood traces of Sheila Kuzew on Billie Chartrand and/or the van, and where is the evidence of his presence at the crime scene? He points out that no evidence is found at the scene connecting Billie Chartrand to the alleged attack.

Marty then speaks to Chartrand's clean record, no previous arrests, not even a parking ticket. He concludes with a demand for a not guilty verdict.

No mention is made of the lack of character witnesses for Chartrand. Who is this man? I desperately want to know, so I can understand who I'm up against.

The judge announces that the jury will be sequestered until a verdict is reached. Court is adjourned.

It's two in the afternoon. The waiting game begins.

It is a long evening waiting for tomorrow to arrive. From past experiences, I find the longer the jury is out, the more possibility of a not guilty verdict. If the jury comes to a decision in seven or eight hours, it is likely a guilty verdict. I'm hoping by two tomorrow afternoon the trial is history.

Sam and I spend an hour reviewing the security system. He is like a child in a toy store. Do men ever grow up? He is diligently showing me every fine detail of the system. I want to say, "Teach me only the necessities."

Finally I say, "I appreciate all you have done for me, including having the security installed, but do I need to know so much detail?"

Sam looks hurt. "I'm sorry. We can stop now."

"Don't be angry. Allow me to express how I feel about things. I do appreciate your knowledge, but to me it's not an area of interest. Yes, I want the protection but not the little details."

Sam smiles at me and says, "You are right. I did get carried away. Come here, I want to tell you something."

I walk over to him, he hugs me close and whispers in my ear, "When you want me to go shopping with you for clothing, will you mind if I say no, for I'm truly only interested in the final product."

I punch him playfully on the arm. Everything is fine between us.

With the tour completed, I call my parents.

My mom answers.

"How are you and Dad doing?"

"We are fine. You sound more rested today. I can assess your state of mind by your voice." Mom laughs.

I laugh as well and then ask, "Is Dad having any problems?"

"No," she replies. Mom makes no mention of a memory problem but I needed to check anyway.

Mom says, "Just a minute. Barry, it is Ashley, and she wants to talk to you."

Dad comes on the phone and spends fifteen minutes describing all the activities he plans for retirement. We hang up with a promise to get together soon. I make no mention of the frightening phone calls or Kevin's visit to my office.

I decide not to mention his visit, to Sam either. To me Kevin is annoying but never menacing, so I don't share this information for now.

We retire early and sleep soundly.

When I arrive at my office, I keep busy by organizing the complete file on Chartrand. I need to sort through hundreds of sheets of information gathered over the past two months. I return reference books used for the trial to our main library. As I walk down the hallways I receive many well wishes from other prosecutors for a guilty verdict. It makes me feel part of the larger team. Except for Logan, I have a great working relationship with the other prosecutors and support staff.

Every time the phone rings, my heart skips a beat. Will the jury ever reach a decision?

It rings at 1:30 and my prayer is answered. The call is from the judge's chamber letting me know the jury has reached a verdict. I quickly call the Kuzew family, to tell them court resumes at 3:30.

I clear up a few important calls and hurry to the courtroom, praying all the way. I take note that Sheila and her family have arrived and for the first time they sit near the front, just behind the prosecutor's table.

As Chartrand is led into the courtroom I can feel Sheila's angst. The jurors are next. Not one jury member looks in Billie Chartrand's direction. We all stand as Judge Holzzer is announced. When everyone is seated, he asks the jury foreman Vincent Tate if a verdict has been reached. Mr. Tate answers, "Yes your honor."

Judge Holzzer turns to Billie Chartrand and asks him to stand. Then he turns to Vincent Tate and nods.

Mr. Tate speaks, "We, the jury, find the defendant Billie Chartrand guilty as charged of kidnapping, sexual assault, and attempted murder."

I give Vincent Tate all the credit in the world, because he has the courage to look at Billie Chartrand, while delivering the verdict.

Billie on hearing the verdict turns, winks at Sheila, then leers at me. He points an index finger at me and mouths "Bang." I feel sick. He has managed in two seconds to eliminate any vindication Sheila, her family and I were hoping for. I want to slap him.

Judge Holzzer announces that the sentencing of Billie Chartrand will take place tomorrow at nine in the morning. He then adjourns court.

I'm overwhelmed with the amount of media attention when I leave the courtroom. Prior to departure I informed Mr. and Mrs. Kuzew to take Sheila quickly out the back door to their car and not to stop to respond to any questions.

I chose to spare them the ten microphones currently being shoved in my face. They were grateful. I attempt to answer one question out of every five fired in my direction.

I notice Marty leaving the courtroom, but this time he doesn't stop to make a comment. He is ignored by the media. They are only interested in winners. Eventually, I'm able to escape.

The next morning Billie Chartrand is sentenced to eight years in prison, with no chance of parole for four years.

I invite Sheila and her family to my office. I relate to them that Chartrand will probably be incarcerated in Prince Albert, Saskatchewan, the nearest maximum federal penitentiary. I encourage Sheila and her family to continue with victim counseling. After an hour we say our good-byes.

I am happy with the guilty verdict, but not the length of sentence. I am saddened with thoughts of Sheila's future.

Will she improve sufficiently to one day register at university? Is marriage in her future, or will she have difficulty with long term relationships? Will she ever walk down a street alone, with a feeling of confidence? Does her future hold a life of drug abuse? There are numerous questions with no answers. Sheila is now a statistic. Billie Chartrand will be on the streets in four years to repeat his crime.

At home, I make a light dinner and call a couple of friends. I'm very tired tonight, which is usual for me following a demanding trial.

I fall asleep quickly, but do not sleep soundly.

CHAPTER 21

▼

Morning brings clear skies and warm sunshine. The guilty verdict still feels grand this morning. Occasionally there is justice for the victim. The terror experienced and pain endured by Sheila Kuzew deserved more, but we have to settle for the eight year sentence.

I decide to take a couple of days of vacation, one for myself and the other to visit my parents. When I'm involved in a demanding trial, they often feel ignored.

The first day, I spend at home just catching up on doing laundry, purchasing groceries, and doing some gardening. It is fun grocery shopping for two. It has been a rather lonely experience shopping only for me. I have often put it off in favor of a quick take out or home delivered meal.

As I shop now, I remember Sam referring to items he loves, such as grape and nut cereals and the ones he abhors, such as pot pies and it brings a smile to my face. In addition to steak, rib roast and chicken, I splurge on yummy chocolate ice cream treats, something I rarely did before Sam.

I have a house keeper who comes in every week, which leaves me more free time to pamper myself. I let Sam know that occasionally I need time for me.

Today, I have an appointment for my hair and a manicure. Because it is long I get my hair trimmed every month to keep it tidy and free of split ends. The stylist treats it with a special conditioner which brings out the volume and luster of my hair. Pamela was to meet me for the manicure, but had to leave the city again on a business trip.

In the evening I call Gail. She is gushing, "I met this great guy at my aunt Martha's daughter's wedding on Saturday."

I laugh, "I assume that means she's your cousin."

"Don't tease, I am serious."

It must be important because Gail rarely tells me to be serious. "Sorry. Tell me about him. I didn't know your cousin was getting married."

"Yes, she met this fellow last November and nine months later she's married."

Gail takes a deep breath and continues, "This guy is just perfect for me. His name is Randy and he is, I guess, between thirty and thirty-five."

"What does he look like?"

Gail sighs and says, "He has the most beautiful blue eyes I have ever seen. His hair is light brown and cut short. Like me, Randy is overweight and his height is about five feet, ten inches. I think I'm in love."

"Slow down." I laugh but then think about my love for Sam. I ask, "What does the love of your life do?"

"He's a manager at a local auto body shop and loves to build race cars. Of course, he races them as well."

"Did he say he would call?" I ask with my fingers crossed because I want Gail to find love and have her picket fence.

"Yes and he already asked me out for this Saturday evening."

I'm hoping things work out for her. Although Gail goes out fairly often; she hasn't had a serious relationship in some time.

The following day I drive to my parents early, arriving around ten. We have a great day together. Mom is so excited about Sam. They joined us for dinner one evening, but then he was paged to go to work. Dad didn't get time to check him out. One of my Dad's favorite expressions when it comes to men in my life is, "Ashley, I have to check him out."

Today, I say to Dad, although I know it will not prevent his interrogation, "Sam, is a wonderful, kind, and generous person. I like him a lot. He had a very difficult childhood."

Dad asks, "How is that?"

"He grew up in an abusive home. His parents were alcoholics and his Dad beat him and his mother often."

Mom exclaims, "Oh my heavens. The pain that the poor boy suffered gives me a heart ache."

With a stern look on his face, Dad asks, "Where are his parents now?"

"His mother passed away approximately twelve years ago and he has no idea whether his father is alive or dead."

"Are you sure he's the kind of man to be interested in?"

Dad is staring at me with the look, which used to quiet me in my teens. But it's not keeping me quiet today.

"Dad you know the saying, "You can pick your friends, but not your family," well it applies here." I'm getting upset with Dad, and Mom senses this and immediately steps in.

"Come on you two, we need some fresh air."

Mom needs me to appreciate her garden, although most has been removed. She packs boxes of potatoes, carrots, cucumbers, and tomatoes for me. Dad carries them to the car.

At seven, we say our good-byes.

Dad comes to me and places a hand on my shoulder. "Sorry honey, I trust your ability to assess a person's character. If you like this fellow, then so will I. I love you Ashley."

I head back to the city.

On the highway I think a red sports car is following me, but when I reach the city just before the major avenue where I turn left, the red car keeps going straight. Calm down Ashley, I tell myself.

My phone is ringing when I arrive home. I dash into the kitchen grabbing the phone, but not bothering to shut, much less lock, the door. It may be my parents confirming my safe arrival at home. This is our routine.

Breathless, I answer, "Hi".

The reply is chilling, "Ashley, is the heavy breathing for me? I'll allow you to live for one more day, or maybe one week, or five minutes from now."

It's the same raspy voice. I scream, "Who the hell is this?" into a dead phone.

Glancing up, I see the wide open door and fly to slam and lock it. I sit at the kitchen table attempting to recall the exact words used. Should I telephone Sam or just ignore the call for now? What can Sam achieve at this point? I make a decision to ignore the call when the phone rings. I scream, but see by call display that this time it is my parents.

Mom asks, "Are you okay? You sounded weird when you answered."

"Yes Mom, I'm fine. I was in the garage when the phone rang and I had to dash from there." We chat about my visit.

Mom says, "Dad feels badly about his comment on Sam and his family."

"I know. He apologized to me before I left." We hang up.

I stand against the kitchen counter for a moment contemplating my next move. With some trepidation, I wander from room to room checking doors, windows, and the security system. I will absolutely not allow myself to peer under my bed.

It is getting late, but I call Sam at his apartment. He answers on the third ring.

"I'm sorry to be a colossal pain, but I just received another call and I'm scared shitless. Can you come over right now?" I want to weep like a baby but control myself.

"Absolutely, I'll be right there. Make sure you don't open the door for anyone but me. I mean that, no one." He hangs up and I go to the great room and sit in front of the large window to watch for him. I'm too scared to return to my car and retrieve the vegetables from my mom. In addition to scared, I'm angry. I feel like a fool. First, I tell Sam I need some space and now I'm begging him to come over.

He arrives ten minutes later. Sam must have broken a few speed limits. As he approaches the front door I open it and start sobbing. He reaches me in a split-second and holds me close. I feel so safe now and hang on to him tightly. He gently pushes me away and says, "Honey, you are going to squeeze me to death. What did the asshole say this time around?"

"He told me he is going to kill me, but basically he hasn't decided when. I just arrived home from my visit with Mom and Dad. In fact, the phone was ringing and I ran into the house to pick up."

Sam asks, "I wish we knew for sure who is doing this. They are transferring Chartrand to Saskatchewan, right?"

"Yes. I am sick of this idiot terrorizing me and forcing his will on me from a distance. I want him to come and face me right now. Of course, I need you by my side."

He laughs and I join in. He says, "I would love nothing more than two minutes alone with the sick bastard doing this to you."

"Do you think the calls will stop when he is transferred to Saskatchewan?"

"Chances are they will, but cell phones will still be available to him." Sam places a hand on each side of my face and says, "Sorry, but I will not lie to you. I love you too much and you have to appreciate the danger in order to protect yourself."

We go to the car and bring in the vegetables. He has never seen home grown vegetables that have not been thoroughly cleaned and placed on display in a supermarket. I clean a carrot for him and within seconds it is gone. At my suggestion he makes himself a tomato and cucumber sandwich. Within seconds it is gone and he is making another.

I ask him to stay the night, as the fear remains with me. He doesn't have a problem with that and we retire to bed. Sam and I make love and for a while the fear vanishes. I sleep well.

CHAPTER 22

▼

I am in my office making the final notations in a file when I receive a phone call. It's Jim Stromby, the chief crown prosecutor, requesting I immediately come to his office. Please not a new case, another assignment so soon. I just completed the Kuzew case last week.

I enter Jim's office and see the expression on his face. I know something is terribly wrong. My first reaction is that something has happened to Mom or Dad or both.

"What is it?" I ask with a tremor in my voice.

"I just received word that Billie Chartrand has escaped. They were transferring him from the Remand Centre to the federal penitentiary in Prince Albert, Saskatchewan when he overpowered the two guards, killing one and seriously injuring the other. The police have a BOLF posted across Canada."

I think, *The psychopath has escaped.* Jim knows about the calls and now states, "You are white as a sheet. Come sit down. I heard about his gestures toward you in the court room. If you want I can request police protection for you to and from work. Due to staffing problems in the police department, I know that twenty-four hour surveillance is not available."

I want to scream. I want to be placed in a cage with twenty-four hour police protection until this animal is caught. But I know it's not possible. I'm so frightened, that thinking about driving home tonight is too terrifying to entertain.

I yell, "He's a monster. An evil, evil, man and I'm petrified right now."

Jim is standing by my chair with his hand on my shoulder, "I'll drive you home. Take a few days off."

"Thank you for the offer, Jim, but I will call Sam Orlicky and have him pick me up."

Jim looks at me and raises an eyebrow. I explain, "Sam and I are what you could call an item. I like him."

"That is marvelous. He's a fine man. Now back to Billie Chartrand. With all police forces on the lookout for this criminal, I estimate we'll have him back behind bars in hours. Remember, if you need the time, take it."

Thanking Stromby, I head straight to the bathroom where I throw up, for what seems like hours. I'm thankful no one enters. Finally, I am able to return to my office.

I jump when the phone rings. The call is from Marty Kroll who congratulates me on the victory. Then he refers to the escape of Billie Chartrand.

He asks, "You're not afraid are you?"

I reply, "Of course not." He thinks this is funny? I thank him and hang up. No, I'm not afraid, I am petrified.

Logan Reid stops at my office late in the afternoon.

His first comment is, "Man I'm delighted that Chartrand doesn't hate me. You ended up doing me a favor. Imagine the slime ball roaming the streets of our city. Capital punishment is what the justice system requires. You take care of yourself. No walking the streets alone at night. And if you need an escort to your car, just ask me." He grins and exits. I have gone mad.

I chase him down the hallway, "Logan, I wanted you to know that just before they took Chartrand out of court, I gave him the news that you, Logan Reid, were responsible for organizing all the information which is sending him away." Now I feel better.

Two other male prosecutors who have heard about Billie's escape stop at my office and offer to walk me to my car or drive me home. I thank them and let them know Sam Orlicky will see me home.

Sam finally arrives in my office at 5:30 and wants to drive me home, but I refuse. I tell him he can follow me, but he's not to become my private chauffeur.

I say, "It is no different than after the phone calls. I can't run and hide forever."

"I understand, but short term, like the present, I'm going to protect you."

"Sam, I want my car at home. Tonight, follow me, okay?"

"Absolutely, I will follow you. Okay, let's go."

"Not quite. I need to gather a few things and I must make one phone call."

The call is to Sheila and her parents to make sure they are safe. The police are there when I call. I spend five minutes talking to Sheila, trying to reassure her, when inside I'm vibrating with terror.

Sam takes my briefcase and we find my car in the underground parking lot. I drive Sam to his car and he follows me.

Once home, he goes step by step over the security system. I promise him I will keep my cell phone on and with me whenever I leave the house. Although, not legal for Canadian citizens to carry it, he provides me with a can of pepper spray. People can purchase bear spray, which is similar to pepper spray but not as potent. Sam asks that I keep it with me in my purse always.

"You know, he's probably down in Mexico by now. Why in the world would he stay around here to be captured?"

"Yeah, you are right." But I can tell by his facial expression he's not buying it; deep down neither do I.

"I don't want to live in fear. I have such a vivid imagination that it took me years before I would shower after seeing that old film, Psycho. A friend convinced me to watch it with him. He liked all the old films."

Sam searches my face, "Some friend. Should we discuss him or was this years ago?" I nod my head and he continues, "I picked up two steaks before meeting you at the office. You get them ready and I will fire up the barbeque. Hey look, you don't have to become paranoid, just be careful."

We share a wonderful dinner followed by Sam holding me tight in his arms as we watch the news. There is a segment on Chartrand's escape, with a picture of the officer he killed.

I say to Sam, "Look at the people he has affected. There is Sheila, her brother, parents, the dead officer and his wife and family members, the officer wounded and his significant other, the many police officers out there now looking for him, and me. I actually feel sick to my stomach when I think about him. He is just evil."

"I agree with you."

"This is the problem as I see it. Everyone sits in their cocoons not affected by the news of the day. They read about a sexual assault in the paper and thirty seconds later the paper is in the trash, the story forgotten."

"What would you like to see happen?"

Enthusiastically, I say to Sam as I have to others, "I want people to take notice and make noise. Go to their Members of Parliament and demand stiffer sentences. Look at Chartrand. He received eight years but would have been out in three or four. It's ridiculous."

"I know it's ludicrous. We notified Sheila and her parents and sent over a constable for this evening and night."

"Yes, I called her. Imagine her terror, Sam."

"I hope he will be caught or killed quickly."

"I hate myself but I hope it's the latter."

Sam agrees. "Let's get an early night. It really helps lower the anxiety and we are both experiencing a hand full of it lately."

"Before we retire, I want to give you this key for my house and a check for the installation of the security system."

"Thank you for showing your trust in me. I will keep the key, but here is your check." Sam rips it up and hands it to me.

"My mom taught me to accept gifts graciously, so thank you. Now let's retire to bed so I can thank you properly."

We make love and Sam then holds me tightly in his arms. He says, "Talk to me about it."

"You are getting to know me. I'm very tense and am having difficulty concentrating on things other then Chartrand. His evil touched me in court and I'm terrified. I will be honest with you. I have never faced anyone like him. There have been some demented minds, but not one of them touches his." I shudder.

Sam comments, "In our office we have discussed him, and can't believe there is no evidence of his existence prior to his arrest for Sheila's kidnapping. How has he lived?"

"I don't know. They must catch him soon, before I have a heart attack. My heart feels like it is in my mouth just by talking about that asshole."

"Try for some rest. I will hold you close and protect you."

CHAPTER 23

▼

In the morning, Sam wakes me with breakfast in bed. He cooked a cheese omelet and added slices of Mom's tomatoes with a piece of toast. The glass of orange juice is chilled.

I gaze at him and say, "I love you so much. This breakfast is precious because you prepared it. Come Sam, join me."

"Be right back. Mine is in the kitchen waiting."

He is back in seconds and we sit in bed enjoying the food and each other. This being in love is the best experience in the world. It's not just the love making, but the sharing which warms my heart.

We dress and leave, with Sam following me in his car. I have convinced him that it is safe for me to drive during daylight hours. It is highly unlikely that killing me in a drive by shooting will satisfy Chartrand. He will want to take a more active part in my death. Something slow and well planned would satisfy his needs.

There are many people leaving their vehicles and heading for the stairs and elevator. It feels safe and I join the others to climb the five flights. The climbing is a great workout, especially since I have had to give up my morning jogs. It's too dangerous with the calls I have received and now with Chartrand on the loose.

I have a meeting this morning with a Corporal Sherry Sparks, who is working on a possible incest case involving a prominent citizen in the community. She arrives at nine-thirty as planned.

Corporal Sparks is tall and slim with green eyes and platinum hair. She looks more like a retired model, than a corporal in the police force. Initially, Sherry is very officious and I suggest that she relax.

Corporal Sparks replies, "I am relaxed Ms. Browne. My angst is probably due to my overwhelming desire to be successful in charging Mr. Clossete for the sexual abuse of his daughter."

Sherry sits perched on the chair, her body tense and her face determined.

Attempting to relax her, I say, "What you mean is you desperately want to nail his ass to the ground? By the way my name is Ashley, not Ms. Browne. This partnership will work better if I call you Sherry."

Sherry relaxes and grins, "Yes, I want to nail him. The daughter, Maggie, is ten years old and apparently told the school nurse that she is frightened of becoming pregnant. When the nurse asked her what she meant the little girl told her that she had seen a movie on television, that showed people doing what she and her daddy do, and the lady on television became pregnant."

"Wow. That makes me nauseous and so very sad."

"Can you believe our sick society?"

I share with Sherry my thoughts on dealing with the scum of the earth, "I see it every day. As you know the main reason why people suffer from burn out is that they take their work to heart, as I think you do. Be careful. Burnout is the result. I know, because I have been there."

"You're right, but it's extremely difficult to shut off my feelings when it comes to children being abused."

"I agree with you."

Sherry asks me, "What do you suggest I do in this situation?"

"What do you have for me? Did you speak to the ten-year-old?"

"I did, but she refuses to say anything about her relationship with her father. He obviously got to her."

"It's critical to approach children slowly and not to push."

"Yes, I know. So I've spoken to her only twice."

"What role does the mother play in this family?"

Sherry's expression is sad as she answers, "When I spoke to the mother, she said it was ridiculous to even suggest that her husband would abuse their daughter. In any case, the mother will not testify against her husband."

"What is your opinion of the mother?"

"I find Mrs. Clossete repulsive because I believe she stays in the relationship for the prestige and financial perks and agrees to sacrifice her daughter for these gains."

"Jesus, it's a sick world. Did you confront Mr. Clossete?"

Sherry is angry and her voice becomes louder, "Yes, on two different occasions, but he told me to screw off or to talk to his lawyer. He told me he pays him enough."

"Let me guess, Sherry. Is it Marty Kroll?"

"Yes, it is as a matter of fact. So what do you think?"

I hate to be the bearer of bad news, but I say, "I need more evidence if we're going to bring him to trial. Right now we only have the nurse. It is not sufficient evidence to lay charges. We need the mother or Maggie. Keep digging. Maybe you will think of another angle. If I was in your position, I would work the mother. Once you have her, the child will be available to you."

"Thank you so much. I'll keep in touch."

When she leaves, for the first time in my career, I wonder if I can remain in this position. Every day, our society appears to become sicker. Or is it because I face it daily? My present situation is a prime example of what is out there, living among our so called normal citizens, waiting to pounce. Sam was telling me last night that a telephone company was making pornography available on cell phones.

I would love to help Sherry bring Clossete down, but we need cooperation from his wife. Right now, money is where her loyalty lies.

If I were to stop a hundred mothers on the street and give them the Clossete scenario, a hundred percent of them would say they would further investigate a claim of their husband abusing their child. But the facts are that three or four of them would be lying. Lying because of love, money, and the most common being fear.

At lunch, I venture down to Gail's office, but she is busy researching for one of the prosecutors going to trial next week. I leave, promising to bring her back a sandwich from the cafeteria. When I return we spend ten minutes together and between bites Gail shares with me that she is visiting her Mom this evening.

I spend the remainder of the day doing research of my own. I'm attempting to locate precedence of a trial in the past, based solely on the hearsay of one witness. As I thought, it doesn't look promising.

An idea does come to me and I call Corporal Sparks.

"This is Corporal Sparks speaking. How can I help you?"

"Sherry, this is Ashley. I have an idea. Find out if the child has been taken to a physician recently and if she receives yearly checkups. If she does, the physician may get permission from the mother to examine her. There will be signs if she has been sexually abused."

"That's a great idea. I assume I will require a judge's ruling to allow me to approach the physician?"

"You will. Run it by your supervisor. To obtain the physician's name, I suggest you return to the school and talk to the nurse who originally contacted you about this situation."

"Thank you so much, Ashley."

"You are welcome. Keep in touch."

At five o'clock, one of the male prosecutors walks me to my car. I thank him, but feel totally ridiculous. The fear stays with me as I drive home. It's difficult to drag my eyes away from the rear view mirror.

Five minutes after leaving the office, I glance in my mirror and see a red sports car following me. I change lanes and the car follows. I know there is a gas station a couple of blocks in front of me and I plan to pull into it and see what the red car will do. In the meantime, I call Sam.

"Sam, do not panic, but I think I'm being followed. It's a red sports car similar to a corvette, being driven by one occupant."

Speaking rapidly, Sam asks, "Where are you, near home?"

"No, I pulled into a gas station." I give him the address.

His voice sounding almost panicky, Sam says, "Stay right there. I'll be there in five minutes. If you are afraid, lock your car and go into the station."

Attempting to calm him, I reply, "I'm fine. I don't see the red car now, but I remember seeing it before. We will talk about it when you arrive."

Sam actually shows up in three minutes. He has the siren going and I hear him in the distance. As he turns into the gas station he shuts it off. I pull up to his car and roll down my window, "Sam, I am fine. Follow me."

When we arrive home we sit at the kitchen table with a drink and discuss the car.

Sam starts with, "Did you switch lanes as you drove?"

"I did and the car followed my moves."

"How about your speed, did you vary it?"

"Just like you told me to, but whoever it was matched my speed."

"You said you've seen this car before?"

"Well, I can't be positive, but when I came back from my parent's home I spotted a similar car which I thought might be following me."

Sam is upset with me. He asks, "Why didn't you tell me this?"

"It was the time of Kevin and I thought it might be him."

"Okay, I want to take this information down."

He retrieves what I call his, "little black book," and returns to the table to fire away his fifty questions.

"The color you said was red?"

"Yes. On both occasions it was the same color."

"It was a solid red, no other color of trim that you noticed?"

"No. It appeared to be a solid red."

"Was the car small, medium or large in size?"

"It was small and close to the ground like a sports car."

"Do you have any idea as to the make of the car?"

"I think it was a corvette because it had a long front, but I can't be sure."

"Was it a convertible?"

"No, it appeared to have a solid roof. Although I was frightened so it was difficult to concentrate."

A better word to describe my state of mind was to tell Sam I was petrified, but I decide against it.

"Was there only one person in the car?"

"I could only see one occupant."

Sam will attempt to find the owner by running the information into the computer system. I would not be surprised to discover that the owner turns out to be Kevin.

Once I am settled, Sam leaves. He is going to a friend's bachelor party. He offered to stay with me, but I pushed him into attending. Whoever is tormenting me, will not have the added satisfaction of interfering in all aspects of Sam's life. He is on call until midnight, so will not be doing too much drinking until then.

I check the security system, and tonight, turn out my bedroom light before I lay down. In ten minutes I get up and switch on the light. Finally, sleep.

C H A P T E R 24

▼

I am patiently waiting for her. This will be so easy. Almost too easy, therefore I assume not as much fun.

The clothes in the closet hold a woman's scent. It is pleasant and I take a deep breathe. Fifteen minutes later I wonder, should I step out for a while?

I take another look at the room and notice her pictures. Looks like one of Mom and Dad? No doubt they will be devastated.

Maybe I should lie on her bed; looks inviting. Nice white spread with fluffy pillows. I decide to stay hidden, as I know we will use it later. Red will soon stain the white.

Suddenly, I am drawn out of my daydream by the faint sound of a car motor. It runs for another ten seconds and then fades. Shortly, I hear a door slam, then silence.

Singing, I can hear her singing. She is happy to be home, no doubt. The happiness will not last long. It takes another five minutes before she wonders into the bedroom and flicks on the light. I watch her through the closet door, which I have left opened a few centimeters.

She takes her time removing her outer garments and jewelry. Then she grabs her housecoat from the end of the bed, puts it on, and leaves the room. I can hear the water running in the bathroom.

Two minutes later she is back in the bedroom and picks up her work clothes.

Eventually she makes her way across the room and opens the closet door.

She cries out, "Oh my God! What are you doing here?"

I smile at her. But I can see it, smell it, and almost touch it. It is in her eyes. She knows. Fear, it fills my senses.

Her scream pierces the room when she sees the knife. I am in control.

CHAPTER 25

▼

It is 4:22 on Tuesday morning, when the phone rings.

I answer, feeling confused, "Hello."

It's Sam. He slept in his apartment last night. "I'm coming right over."

"What is wrong?" I ask groggily.

"Put on the coffee, I'll be right there." He hangs up.

It is something catastrophic otherwise he would not call at this hour. I pray Chartrand has been apprehended and nothing has happened to Sheila. Please God, let her be safe.

I quickly throw on a pair of jeans and a T-shirt and run a brush through my hair. I glance in the mirror, thinking that I don't look my best. I rush to the kitchen.

The coffee is perking when he arrives fifteen minutes later. His face is somber and I am afraid to ask. I offer him a coffee and he leads me into the great room. He guides me to the sofa. We sit, and he puts an arm around me.

"What is it?" I ask, but don't want an answer.

His face is sorrowful and his voice gloomy, "I just came from assessing a crime scene. This is so hard, so very hard, but your friend Gail has been murdered. It happened sometime between six and ten-thirty last night."

I jump up and stare at him in disbelief. My voice is shaky, "Oh my God, that can't be. I just talked to her yesterday at noon. Please tell me you are wrong, anything else. Please Sam."

I look into his eyes and at the moment feel something inside of me changing forever. I will never be the same Ashley Browne.

"What about Sheila?" I say in a panic. "Have you sent someone to her house?"

"That was one of the first things we did. I also sent a marked car over here to watch your house."

Gail's death hits me like a blow to my stomach. "This is my fault!"

He quickly interrupts, "No, it is not, it is—"

"I know it's that fucking bastard, Billie Chartrand. He killed her to get back at me. My God, she is dead, dead, and I am to blame. If she hadn't been my friend, Gail would be alive."

Sam grabs me and holds me tight. I can't cry, I'm stunned, frozen in time. I push him away, and start pacing.

"Gail's poor Mom will be devastated. Is someone with her mother? She lives alone."

"Yes Ashley, someone is with her. It's because of her mother that Gail was discovered so quickly. Apparently she called her mother at six last evening, saying she was bringing chicken over for dinner at seven. Seven came, than eight o'clock, but Gail didn't show. Mrs. White called Gail's home numerous times and there was no answer. She also tried Gail's cell phone."

Sam takes a drink of coffee and continues. "Apparently by 9:30 she was in a panic and called police. She explained that she didn't drive and begged the police to check Gail's house. A patrol car arrived at Gail's at 10:15. Her car was in the garage. A constable called Mrs. White and asked if she had a key to her daughter's home. Mrs. White screamed for them to break down the door and enter Gail's house. Constable Johnson found Gail in her bedroom."

Sam stops and assesses my face. He gestures for me to join him on the sofa. I slowly sit down beside him.

"Continue Sam. I'll eventually hear, so tell me now."

Sam takes both my hands in his. "She was severely beaten, tortured, and sexually assaulted, and stabbed in the back. From the amount of blood I would say he didn't miss the heart this time."

"Oh God, I can't accept this."

I leap up and start my pacing.

"I'm so sorry. And I have to agree with you. Unless we have a copycat killer, the same bastard who committed Gail's murder, also was responsible for Sheila Kuzew's attempted murder. The madman somehow got into Gail's home without breaking into it."

"No evidence of forced entry?" I ask quietly.

"We have nothing so far. He left the back door unlocked. The patrol constables are still there, but I needed to tell you myself prior to the media having it splashed across every screen in the country. I must get back. Do you want to call one of your friends or your parents to come stay with you?"

"No. I'm going to call Gail's mother and offer to spend time with her. She must be suffering."

"Mrs. White's physician offered her a sleeping pill prescription and her sister was notified and is on her way there."

"I can't imagine the pain that woman is going through right now. To lose your only child has to be devastating."

Sam glances at his watch.

"Its five-thirty, but I hate to leave you alone."

"You go back to work. I will be fine. In a couple of hours I'll call Gail's mother and ask if she needs company. I can help her with funeral arrangements. Shit! How can I frigging think Gail and funeral arrangements in the same thought? It's crazy Sam."

I'm so angry, yet so frightened. I want to find Chartrand and beat him to within a breath of death.

"I know. Keep the doors locked, security on, and the pepper spray with you. Remember the cell phone when you leave. I asked for a twenty-four hour patrol car for outside your home, but I was turned down. They agreed to the initial eight hour car and then hourly patrols."

"Thanks Sam." I walk him to the door and we kiss. I check the lock and then the security system.

Refilling my coffee cup I venture into the great room, sit in my favorite chair and break down. The tears pour from my soul and I can't stop. I think about Gail's kindness, humor, smile, and helpfulness to everyone. I remember her giving a five dollar bill to a homeless person and I asked her why. She responded that the five dollars bought her nothing of importance, yet the five dollars would buy the man a lot. She didn't care if he spent the money on a cheap wine. She was such a ray of sunshine and everyone loved her. The tears eventually stop. I feel completely drained.

Slowly the anger builds until I'm ready to explode. I have never truly understood the old adage or expression, "Anger can kill." Now I do. If Billie Chartrand was in front of me now I feel I could kill. I feel rage, a new emotion for me. I want to pound on something and never stop. I spend an hour talking to Gail, as if she were here.

At nine, I call Gail's mom and offer to assist her. She is relieved to hear from me and we make arrangements. She invites me for lunch.

Arriving at Mrs. White's place, I see Gail's aunt Martha has arrived. Martha is the only family member living in the city. They have a younger brother in Hope, British Columbia. I ask Martha about her daughter's recent marriage and I remember how happy Gail was with the new fellow she met.

After lunch Mrs. White brings out paper and pen and the three of us discuss funeral arrangements. It takes hours, because we have many crying episodes. I share my opinion of who murdered Gail and what my role is in her murder. There is complete silence and as Gail's mom leaves her chair to come to me, I rise. We hug and then she says, "Ashley, Gail loved you like the sister she never had and would never wish for me to blame you for her death. I don't, please believe me."

"Thank you Mrs. White. Thank you." And we both cry for what seems an eternity. It's difficult to stop.

By five in the afternoon we have finalized the plans. I tell Mrs. White that I will return tomorrow. I offer to notify the necessary people such as the minister, funeral home, florist, and Gail's other friends, and people from work.

Martha must leave and because she does, Mrs. White insists I spend the night.

"Ashley, I have an extra new tooth brush you can use, stay please."

I tell her I'll stay and ask to use the phone. I call Sam and ask him to stop by my place to pick up my toiletries and night gown. Sam is very pleased with the arrangement because he feels I will be safe at Mrs. White's home. I then call Mom and Dad who insist on coming tomorrow to stay with me. I will have to fill them in on my recent telephone calls. A task to which, I don't look forward.

Mrs. White and I have dinner which we have difficulty swallowing. Sam arrives shortly after eight with my required articles. He spends a few minutes with Mrs. White asking her some relevant questions.

After Sam leaves, Mrs. White and I retire to her living room and talk far into the night. It helps relieve some of the pain.

I'm unable to sleep. I lie in the guest bed and stare at the ceiling. This was Gail's room until she moved out at the age of twenty-one.

Finally, I give in and turn on the lights. I take in the pictures around the room. A photo of Gail at about age ten, fishing with her father; one of Gail graduating high school, gazing into the face of the tall, slim, handsome, young man beside her; another of Gail with her parents when she graduated from university.

I jump when I realize someone is in the doorway. It's Gail's Mom and she says, "I can't sleep either. It's like I'm in a nightmare and can't wake up. What am I to do? I'm feeling so lost."

I go to her and hug her tight. "I'm so sorry. I can't imagine your pain. It is hard enough for me to think I will never see her smiling face again. We have to talk about her. Phone me any time. We'll also manage to go out for lunch and dinner. I will do everything in my power to help you."

She attempts a smile, "Thank you. You were her best friend. Gail loved going on short trips skiing or hiking with you. She said you have an awesome sense of humor."

"Thanks. I meant what I said. If you ever need anything remember me. I'm just a phone call away."

"It will be difficult without her."

"Who is the handsome man in this photo?" I want her to talk more about Gail to relieve even a tiny amount of pain.

"He's Barry Townstain. They went out together from age fifteen to nineteen. I'm not sure why they broke up, but Gail insisted it was because Barry wanted to get married and she was more interested in learning and university life."

"Actually that can happen when one person in a relationship attends university and the other doesn't. I assume Barry didn't?"

"You assume right."

I wonder if Gail shared her recent heart throb with her mother. "Did Gail talk to you about the fellow she met at your niece's wedding?"

"Oh, she did. She was so excited about Randy. In fact, the night they met the two danced all evening. Her face just shone."

"I'm sure it did."

"We had better try sleeping again. You eyes are slamming shut, Ashley, and I think the sleeping pill is finally working. I loved her so much. She was my life."

"I know you did. She was such a complete, wonderful person. And yes, you're right, we need to sleep."

Early the next morning I contact the appropriate businesses, the minister, Gail's friends, and my office.

I call Jim directly and am thankful he is in his office.

"Jim Stromby."

"Jim, this is Ashley. I'm sure you have been notified about Gail."

"Yes and I'm shocked. Why would someone want to murder Gail of all people? How are you doing?"

"I believe Sam will be discussing that with you. As for me, I'm in a state of shock. Jim, I need a week and a half vacation. Can you get someone to handle my case load?"

"Yes, take the time. Arrangements have been made to cover for you."

"Thank you for your support." We hang up.

The phone rings shortly afterwards and Mrs. White informs me her brother is coming to spend some time with her and that Martha is on her way over to take Mrs. White out to shop for groceries.

On the way home Wednesday afternoon from Mrs. White's, I feel terribly depressed. The funeral will be held the following Wednesday. We are into September and a few leaves are turning color. It's a month of brilliant colors to look forward to, not a time to be burying a friend.

Sam has promised Gail's body will be released from the coroner's office by then. He suggested a closed coffin.

My parents arrive at six and we have a quick light dinner followed by hours of discussion. I tell them about the threatening phone calls I have received. I explain Billie Chartrand's role in all of this. I talk about his escape and Gail's murder. My parents are upset and very frightened for me. I show them the security system Sam ordered and Dad is very impressed.

Mom says, "I like Sam more and more. He seems very protective of you."

"He is. This system is top notch and should protect me. He also gave me something similar to bear spray."

"Excellent dear," says Mom. "Neither of which, I hope you'll ever have to use."

Sam has agreed to return to his apartment during Mom's and Dad's visit. I am thankful I have my own attached bathroom, because many of Sam's things are in it. Yes, I'm thirty-two but my parents are so old-fashioned. When they leave Dad will probably say to Mom, "Do you think she is sleeping with Sam." And Mom will reply, "Of course she is, but don't let her know we know." Someday soon I will talk about Sam's and my arrangement, but not now.

Wednesday arrives quickly. As requested, my parents and I sit with the White family. The entire office is present. They too loved Gail. I offered and paid for the flowers in church. There are arrangements of roses, lilies and carnations of every color. These are the flowers Gail loved.

Gail's mom asked me to do the eulogy and I accepted. I now stand in front of everyone and talk about my friend. It is difficult to hold back the tears, as I speak about her warmth, her kindness, her helpfulness, her love of humanity. Gail touched many lives. Her sense of humor was amazing and she always had a good word for everyone she faced. I talk about how her life was taken too soon. She wanted to be married, to have the picket fence with the three point two children. Gail wanted love and to give her mother who she loved a grandchild to spoil. At the end of my talk, everyone, including me, is crying.

I notice Marty Kroll is in church and after the service he approaches me. He says, "That sick bastard deserves the death penalty." For once, I agree with him.

I stop to speak to Jim, who again reinforces the need for me to take some time. I thank him and move on. I feel I'm in a fog but do notice Logan's presence. I choose to ignore him.

At the graveside I wait until everyone has left. I look around and notice a nearby maple tree which I know Gail would love. I promise her I will not rest until this monster is caught and brought to justice. I want him to rot in jail for the rest of his life.

Walking toward my parent's car I see someone leaning into Dad's window talking to him. As I approach I recognize Kevin. He lifts his head, "Ashley, I'm so sorry about your friend."

I want to tell the little weasel to leave me alone, but because my parents are present I say a polite, "Thank you." I quickly get into the car and we drive away. Kevin is not mentioned as we drive home.

Mom and Dad leave the next day. Although I love them, I'm glad to have the space. I have also missed Sam, his presence in my home and in my bed.

It is back to work on Monday. How will I cope knowing Gail will never return to her office? I will miss our lunches, her quick jokes, and emotional support. These thoughts leave me feeling so lonely.

Sam, where are you? I need your love right now.

CHAPTER 26

▼

Monday morning arrives and I lay in bed beside Sam not wanting to move, much less go into work. I force myself out of bed and make breakfast. We eat in silence, our thoughts troubled.

Sam follows me to the office. We wave as we separate and I drive into the underground parking lot.

I reach my office and it somehow appears different to me. How can this be? I sit at my desk, looking out the window for an extended time. I can't concentrate and I lose track of time. This continues in spite of the abundance of work that has accumulated in my eight day absence.

Eventually, I go through my e-mails but have difficulty responding. I walk down the hallway to Gail's office. Jim has not disturbed it but left the office as it was when she went home on the day of her murder.

Wanda, an office secretary approaches me as I stand in the doorway. Wanda is slim, in her early forties, with blond hair and an age defying, pretty face. She has two grown sons and looks young enough to be their sister.

She timidly says, "Ms. Browne, Mr. Stromby requested that I watch for you this morning and ask if you would pack up Gail's personal items and take them to her mother."

Wanda has tears rolling down her face. I give her a hug and ask, "Wanda, would you locate a box for me?"

"I left one on her file cabinet. If you need help just call me. By the way the eulogy you gave at the funeral was so touching."

"Thank you. I loved her." I enter her office, find the box and start packing. There are personal items: a picture of her parents, one of the two of us skiing at a provincial resort, a soap stone carving she purchased up north in the Yukon, an artificial flower arrangement made by her Mom, and several green potted plants.

I call Wanda and ask her to bring a trolley. When it arrives, I pack the box and add it along with the green plants to the trolley and roll all of it to my office. I call Gail's mom and ask if I can keep a lovely fern, as well as the picture of the two of us skiing. Mrs. White is more than pleased to have me keep them. I tell her Sam and I will drop the rest of the plants and the box at her home this evening.

I look around my office and place the fern on my computer hutch and the photo next to my phone. I sit back looking at them both. Staring at the picture I feel more relaxed, as if Gail is somehow with me. I settle down to the volumes of paperwork.

Things do stabilize, both at work and home. Jim decides to grant me some slack and allows me time to complete projects. At home Sam has essentially moved in although he still maintains his apartment. We are enjoying each other in our new roles.

Today, prior to ending my workday, I make a few calls needed to close a file. Grabbing my briefcase I head for the parking lot and my car. I look at my watch as I enter the underground lot and realize it is later then I thought. Few vehicles remain. Why didn't I ask Sam to meet me?

The place is essentially deserted. It is dimly lit and my heels echo as they hit the cement. I can hear my quickened pace, along with the increased beating of my heart.

Ten seconds later I sense I'm not alone. I quickly look to my right and see a shadow of a man by a blue van. He is stationary, staring at me from beneath a dark baseball cap. I start to run, listening intently for any movement behind me. I am petrified. I fumble for my keys, hindered by my heavy briefcase. In my panic I run faster. Sensing that the man following is gaining on me, I stumble slightly, than run full out. I hear distorted laughter.

This spurs me on. I locate the keys, push the wireless button, yank the door open, throw myself into the vehicle, and almost simultaneously hit the door lock. I start the car, throw it in reverse, then drive and squeal out of the parking lot. My eyes are darting to the rearview mirror and I almost slam into a cement pillar. Turning the steering wheel sharply, I straighten the vehicle and make the turn. I am now on street level.

I am shaking and can barely control the car. My heart is in my throat and my breathing is erratic.

I don't notice anyone following, but none-the-less I study the rearview mirror. After an eternity, I arrive home. Shaking, I use my automatic garage door opener, enter and close the door. Only then do I take a huge breath to control the terror.

I sit there. My heart is pounding as though trying to escape my chest and it is many minutes before I gather enough courage to leave the car. I turn on every light as I walk through the house checking inside closets, under beds, and behind shower doors. Suddenly, I realize how bizarre my behavior. If the shadow man was indeed laying in wait at the parking lot, then he can hardly be in my home now. I tell myself that I was successful in getting away and am now safely home.

I dial Sam's cell. On the second ring he answers, "Hi beautiful."

"Someone was waiting for me in the parking lot." My voice is still trembling and the fear is overpowering.

"What? Are you okay? What happened?"

"Take a deep breath Sam. I'm okay. I was walking toward my car in the underground parking lot, when I caught a glimpse of a man in shadows watching me. He then gave chase and was chuckling. I am home safe, Sam."

Sam, speaking rapidly says, "I'm sending over a patrol car immediately and I'll be there shortly. I want to check the scene."

"He will be long gone. If he had intentions to harm me, I doubt he'll have left behind any evidence."

"Ashley, I'm pissed at you. I told you to always get someone to walk you down. I'm furious. You must listen to me because we are dealing with a madman here. A madman, don't you understand?"

"I know, Sam, I know."

Sounding calmer, he asks, "Was there anyone at work who could have escorted you to the car?"

"Yes, but honestly I didn't think of it. You would think I would have because I was thinking of Gail all day. The dirty bastard Sam, I could kill him."

"Check the security system. Keep the phone close. I'll be there in about an hour."

One hour later Sam is home. We discuss the parking lot episode over dinner. Sam did visit the area to assess the scene, but he didn't find anything. I knew it was a senseless visit, but can understand why he had to try. Chartrand is too crafty to leave behind evidence.

While we are lying in bed later, Sam can sense my troubled thoughts.

"Ashley, you are restless. If you talk to me, it will help you to relax and sleep."

I sigh deeply and ask, "What does he have in store for me? He could have brought me down today, but didn't. I can't believe that he was actually laughing at me, the demented bastard."

"We know he's a sick asshole. Just look what happened to Sheila and Gail. I would love to be alone with him in an alley and discover how funny he thinks things are then."

"I would give my life's savings to see that. I'm so afraid that I continually jump out of my skin at the slightest noise. He is playing a game and when he tires of it, he will kill me."

"I plan on catching the bastard long before then."

"I hope you do." A shiver passes through my body when I remember the chase.

"He is clever, and we need to remember that. "Never underestimate your enemy," is what they say."

"I'll not."

"Just think about today for example. If he wore a balaclava instead of a baseball cap, he would stand out in a crowd. The cap pulled low to hide his features serves the same purpose and he can mingle undetected with the masses."

"You are right. I speculate that if someone drove into the underground parking lot, he pretended to be getting into a car and that when someone was leaving, he could make as if he was coming to the building."

"Now, you're thinking like a cop. Keep it up."

"I will try. But I'm so afraid and it eats away at my energy and my confidence. I am sick of it!"

"I wish more than anything that I could make you feel safe, be safe again. I vow to you, that I will do everything in my power to make that happen."

"I love you."

"Come here." Sam tightens his arms around me and rubs my back. I finally drift off.

CHAPTER 27

▼

Power. Complete control. Ashley's fear was a scent that left me hard. There was no doubt I could have caught her. But that is for the future. As long as I feel safe, I will play the game. I enjoy the hunt.

I loved the way she panicked and almost fell flat, face first. Had the bitch fallen, I would have walked away. I adore her weaknesses and want to continue with this scheme. This game is safe.

Driving out of the underground parking lot I head for the red light district. Ashley is one hell of an aphrodisiac. Anyone will do; age, color, does not matter to me. The first will satisfy my needs.

I spot her, swinging her hips like that Ashley whore. The slut is alone on the street, and I contemplate driving out to the country and killing her, but I must not deviate from my plans for Ashley.

I stop beside the whore and pay her. She enters the car and I drive away. I growl, "Bitch, no small talk, just do your job."

I drop her off ten blocks away. I want to tell her how fortunate she is that she is not laying on her back in some field, staring up at the sky, eyes wide, totally blank, totally dead. My cap still shades my face.

Ashley, Ashley, we are eventually going to celebrate my intelligence, not my stupidity.

I desperately want to drive to her house right now, enter, and have loads of fun, but I must control these urges. It could lead to my capture, when I have spent time and money setting up these perfect crimes.

Grinning, I drive home to replay the parking lot scene.

CHAPTER 28

▼

I'm gradually becoming accustomed to Gail's absence. For therapy, I shut my door for a couple of minutes each day. I talk to her picture about my visit with her Mom and anything new in my life or at work. It makes office life bearable, and I noticed I need to do this less each day.

I have a meeting at ten this morning with Sheila Kuzew and her parents. I know how frightened she remains especially with Chartrand on the loose. She was to have started university this month. It must be a sad and unnerving time for her.

When they arrive, I guide them to the small conference room Wanda booked when they called to set up this meeting. My office is too small for the four of us. I offer them coffee and juice to help them relax. Mrs. and Mr. Kuzew accept the coffee and Sheila the juice.

Once seated and comfortable I look at Sheila's drawn face and ask, "How are you doing? Any improvement since we last spoke?"

She looks down at her hands and starts to sob, "I'm exhausted and am constantly crying. The sleeping pills no longer help."

My heart goes out to her and I ask, "When did you last see your physician?"

"I saw him just last week. When I told the doctor that my fears and nightmares keep me from sleeping he said I should put the past behind me and the sooner the better."

"You can't be serious." I glance at Mrs. Kuzew and she seems as upset with this response as I am.

"Yes, I am."

"Allow me to refer you to a wonderful physician who specializes in victim services. I have been referring my victims and their families to her for years. Her name is Doctor Joanne Turner and you will love her. She is in her late forties with a kind, motherly face. The most important fact is she will be supportive and understanding. It's not as simple as putting your past behind you. I'm certain your psychiatrist has shared that you must face the past and deal with it before you can be happy in the future. It's a lengthy process that can't be rushed."

"I know, that is why I was shocked when my doctor said that to me."

Sheila reaches for a tissue I offered her.

Mrs. Kuzew asks, "Why didn't you share this with me, Sheila?"

"Mom, you have so much on your plate right now, I didn't want to add one more thing."

Mr. Kuzew, who has been sitting silently, asks, "What news do you have of the animal that did this to my baby?"

"The police are answering approximately two hundred tips a day and are following up each and every one. So far not even a flicker."

Mrs. Kuzew speaks, "The reason we came to see you is because I want to sell the house and move to the west coast or Ontario. There are too many bad memories here for Sheila, and we are all frightened with Chartrand on the prowl." She is now crying softly.

"Sheila, how do you feel about moving away?"

Sheila looks at her parents before responding, "I don't want to move. Each of us has friends here and we would be leaving everything that is familiar to us. Yet, a part of me is afraid to stay because of Chartrand."

"I can't guarantee your safety. No one can. But I don't believe he will come after you. He is motivated by challenges. In his mind you no longer pose a challenge. To be up front with you, he is more interested in me."

Sheila exclaims, "Oh my God! Why is he after you? Is it because of the guilty verdict?"

"Yes. I also think he may have been involved with the death of my friend, Gail White." I can't keep the anger from my voice.

"We were so shocked when we read about her murder. So you think Billie Chartrand killed her?" Mrs. Kuzew asks me.

I decide to be honest with them. "Possibly he did. I believe whoever killed her did so to get back at me. It was either that or a random act. There was no robbery involved. My opinion, and it is only an opinion, is that whoever killed Gail did so to hurt me."

"We are so sorry to hear that. I'm sure many people have already told you none of this is your fault." says Mrs. Kuzew.

Mr. Kuzew asks, "What is your opinion about us moving? Be honest with us."

"Start with the positive reasons for staying. They include: friends of the family; the relationship built between Sheila and her psychiatrist; and Sheila has graduated from high school, therefore when she is well again she will be just another face at university. She will not be referred to as, "The girl who was sexually assaulted." The other pro is that Sheila will not have to carry the guilt of being the one responsible for uprooting the family."

The parents look at Sheila and her Mom says, "Would you feel guilty? I never thought of this. We were making a decision to help you cope and because we are so frightened."

"Mom and Dad, Ashley is right. I would feel guilty. Not only am I uprooting you but Peter as well."

Peter is Sheila's older brother and has been very supportive throughout this ordeal. Obviously he would move with them.

Mr. Kuzew stands and extends his hand to me. "It was my suggestion we come to see you. You are very bright and because you aren't a member of our family you can look at this objectively. We thank you Ashley, for being honest with us. Our family will hold off a sale and move for now."

Mrs. Kuzew, Sheila and I hug. "Come to my office and I'll give you Doctor Turner's phone number. Try her once and see what you think."

When the Kuzew family leaves, I understand that I went out on a limb with a promise, but it doesn't make me feel edgy. I believe that in life we sometimes have to make decisions that affect others. For me these decisions have had mainly positive results.

I want to go for a jog during lunch but know it's impossible. Maybe one of the male prosecutors can join me for ten minutes, because I suddenly feel a great need for some fresh air. I know if an environmentalist heard me say fresh air and city in the same breath, he or she would probably laugh. I put on the jogging shoes I always keep in my office and go looking for someone to accompany me.

I stop at Paul Strychuk's office and ask if he would mind joining me for a walk. The office gossip is that Paul works out a lot. He tells me he is more than willing, any time. Paul is one of the prosecutors who walked me to my car at the end of the day.

I remind him, "Of course, you know there's some danger involved in being with me."

Paul puffs out his chest and says, "Yes, I'm aware of Chartrand. I would like nothing better than having the psycho approach me. By the way how is your man, Sam?"

I'm happy he has referred to Sam. Although I heard Paul is dating a very attractive lady from the local television station, I don't want him to question my motives behind the jogging request.

"Thank you for asking. Sam is fine; very busy like you and I. Guess you could say we have a good thing going." Looking at Paul I smile and think, *I like this man*.

Outside, I take a deep breath and we start jogging. We run to the famous river valley, which is approximately fifteen minutes from our office building. The ten minute walk lengthens to an hour. The weather is gorgeous and I enjoy the view.

As we part company Paul reminds me that he is available to escort me to my car anytime. I thank him and return to my office.

The day slips by and when I arrive home without incident my thoughts turn to the evening ahead. Sam has purchased tickets for the dinner theatre.

I prepare a lightly scented bubble bath and immerse myself in it for some time. I feel so refreshed after my day, that I sing while applying my makeup and brushing my long hair. My choice of garment for tonight is a low cut front and back red designer dress that even to me makes for a stunning appearance. I add a diamond and ruby necklace around my long neck. It was a graduation gift from my parents. With one last look in the mirror I'm off to the kitchen.

When I hear his car door slam I rush to greet him at the door.

His first words are, "My heavens you are gorgeous. Every male there will want to change places with me."

"You know, I believe you are right. By the way I didn't know how late you would be, so I laid out your change of clothes."

He leaves the room to shower and change. I go to the liquor cabinet to pour each of us a glass of merlot. When Sam walks into the room forty-five minutes later, I'm stunned.

"My word, Sam, look at you. Speaking about gorgeous I will have to bat away the females wanting to steal you from me. Seriously, this is the first time I have seen you in a suit and it definitely works. Here's to our union, our love." I pass him the wine glass and we drink to our relationship.

As we leave the house I see Sam stiffen and scan around. I make no mention of my observation as we drive away. I will not allow anything to spoil this romantic night.

CHAPTER 29

▼

One day in the last week of September, Sam arrives home with a demeanor that screams with frustration. I sense his agitation and suggest that he needs some tender loving care.

"Go take a long, hot bath. While you do that, I'll prepare stuffed pork chops for the oven. And when you're out of the bath I will massage your neck and shoulders."

"Thank you. You're one in a million."

Later, I straddle him and start the massage. I get many, "ahs," so my therapy must be working. When my hands tire I direct him to the sofa and gently cover him with a satin comforter.

"Sleep my love. I will wake you when dinner is ready."

I sit in the dining room and look through the patio windows at the colorful leaves covering my back yard. Autumn can be so pretty and I find myself day dreaming about a little girl or boy jumping into piles of leaves that Sam and I have raked.

I almost burn dinner with my day dreaming of children. I wake Sam and we eat in silence. Finally he says, "Thank you for the rub down. I slept like a baby and still would if you hadn't awakened me."

After dinner we clean the kitchen and retire to the great room. Following a few minutes of small talk I ask him, "What is bothering you? You seem so frustrated today."

Sam looks at me. He nods and says, "Nothing is going right in my efforts to track your stalker. First, none of the other cameras in the underground parking lot picked up on anything. He had taken out the one camera that covered the area where he was standing. The others gave us nothing."

"What about finger prints?"

He shakes his head and I can hear the frustration in his voice. "I had the technicians lift some prints from the parking lot door and elevator to see if we could place him in the area. The results were negative."

"When you think about it would Chartrand be able to fit in the surroundings enough to remain undetected by the guards?"

"I think so, but would he bother? Has he changed his appearance? Maybe he is wearing a wig, grown a beard, or added horn rimmed glasses. We have discussed the use of the baseball cap. Would you recognize him with that disguise?"

"If I saw his eyes absolutely I would recognize him. No one who looked into those pools of hatred would ever forget them. Although no, I don't think I would recognize him from a distance."

Sam is silent for a moment, "The man's height in the underground parking lot was similar to Chartrand's?"

"Yes, his stature was comparable. As I ran, petrified, it was difficult to get any impression of the man other than his stature."

"I have exhausted options for gathering evidence in or near the underground parking lot. As you know I stuck information sheets in the elevator and on the stairs asking for anyone who may have noticed a male loitering in the area. I included the date and police phone number. So far we haven't received one call."

Sam pours himself another glass of wine. "In the investigation into Gail's murder, all the fingerprints lifted have been accounted for, with the exception of one smudged print."

"And nothing else was found?"

"The hair recovered from the bed sheet has produced the deoxyribonucleic acid needed, but it is not a match to Chartrand. Does it even have a bearing on this case? I don't have that answer."

"Could the hair have been picked up elsewhere?"

"Yes, the bed sheets looked new so the hair could have been there prior to purchase. It also could have fallen off an article of clothing. Just think about sitting in a chair previously occupied by a cat and you will appreciate what we have to battle every day in eliminating evidence."

Although I know the answer to this because Gail shared everything with me, I ask, "Did your staff locate anyone who thought Gail may have been seeing someone romantically? Like someone who is married or with a criminal past, for example?"

"We interviewed her mom, all her friends, acquaintances, and coworkers, but no one heard of any man in Gail's life other than the one mentioned by you. Randy, of course has an airtight alibi."

"You said there were no signs of robbery?" I recognize that Sam needs to talk. He feels he has failed Gail's mom and me.

"I had Gail's mom go through the house and she did it meticulously. In her opinion, there was nothing missing including a wallet holding a fifty dollar bill. Do you want some wine?"

"No thanks. Help yourself."

"I will. I need it tonight because I feel this huge cloud hanging over my head."

"Is it possible the two incidents aren't connected? Maybe Chartrand murdered Gail and the person in the underground parking lot was Logan or Kevin."

"Anything is possible. But my money is still on Chartrand for both. Where is the psycho?"

He sighs and continues, "We have followed up literally five hundred tips and have nothing to show for them. I know he is intelligent, but to hide for this long is unbelievable. Especially with a Canada-wide warrant issued for him."

"Yes, I agree. Where do you think he is?"

"I don't think he is hiding per se. I believe he has changed his appearance, and with money he would be able to purchase alias identification papers."

"I agree with you. He must have money otherwise how could he afford Marty Kroll, the most expensive defense lawyer in the city? How he is getting it is anyone's guess."

"There is a possibility he is renting in another city and commuting here to carry out his crimes."

"We must remember what Doctor Haverlow said on the stand. Chartrand is extremely intelligent."

"I'll vouch for that. Look at the Kuzew case. Without the hair we found in the van, the bastard probably would have gotten off."

"I agree, one has to have a few neurons firing to commit such a crime and not leave any incriminating evidence at the crime scene."

"We didn't miss anything, Ashley. I personally checked the scene as well."

"I know. Come it's time to get some sleep." As we lay in bed, I hold him for a change.

CHAPTER 30

▼

Six weeks have passed since Gail's murder and the police are no closer to finding her killer or Billie Chartrand. Sam still believes they are the same person. He has spent many off hours trying to locate some history on Billie Chartrand, but without success.

It is like he was born at age thirty-four in Edmonton. No background and no evidence of his existence. I miss Gail so much I ache. Often I spend ten or fifteen minutes on the phone with her mother. Last Saturday we had lunch. It is difficult to keep reporting to her that there is no further progress in solving her daughter's murder. Chartrand appears to have vanished into thin air.

Today, I receive a call from Jim Stromby requesting a meeting at four-fifteen. He has an earlier business meeting away from his office with the mayor and chief of police.

I arrive at the appointed time and Cheryl asks me to take a seat. She states Jim should be in shortly.

The phone rings and ten seconds later she says, "That was the boss. He will be thirty minutes late."

Sam insists on dropping me off and picking me up at work. Using Cheryl's phone I call him now to tell him I'll be late, but I get no answer. I leave a message and I wonder, not for the first time, if this commitment is what is needed in my life?

At times the relationship between Sam and me seems a tad suffocating. Like today, I feel silly checking in, like a school child. Possibly, I have become too independent over the years. I may love my freedom but I believe I love Sam more.

Cheryl is starting to fidget. I'm sure she wants to go home, but is too professional to leave me alone. I suggest that I retrieve some work from my office and then come back and wait for Jim alone. This brings a smile to her face. There really is no need for her to wait with me. I leave and return with work to occupy my time. We say our good nights.

Finally at 6:30 Jim arrives. He is apologetic, but as he explains who says, "No," to the mayor? Feeling he owes me, Jim relates a modest amount of information from this meeting. He tells me plans are in the making to submit a proposal to the premier for more funding. This money is to be used to increase staffing for police services and the prosecution office.

Jim then gets to the point of our meeting. "A suspected serial rapist was caught this morning and I'm assigning the case to you. The chief of police also wants you on this one, because it will be a huge case. I'll give you Galeno, to assist when required."

Shelly Galeno is our newest recruit. She is someone I want to work with, because her beliefs appear to be similar to mine.

"What is the chief's interest in this case?"

Jim ignores my question and responds, "We need you on this one."

He looks at his watch. "It is getting late. We can discuss the details tomorrow. Sorry again for keeping you."

"It's okay. Do you mind if I use your phone?"

"No. Go ahead and use it. Actually I will leave you to it. Mind switching off the lights and locking the door when you leave?"

"No. Good night."

I reach Sam immediately. He is downstairs waiting in the car. I tell him I will be right down, that I just need to return my files to my office.

I switch off Jim's lights and close and lock the door.

In the hallway only the dim night lights are on and there are shadows everywhere. I see movement and swiftly turn, but it is only a blind panel moving from the air flow generated by the air conditioner. It is eerie. All staff members have left the office for the day. The silence is deafening. I can hear myself breathing and my heart pounding. I now rush down the hallway, as if chased. I feel ridiculous, but can't stop the fear.

Come on, Ashley, it's your place of work. Grow up.

Easy to think, but it is not the hustle and bustle of a normal work day with someone around to assist me. This is frightening and I tell myself to hurry and get the hell out of here.

Still, I am cautious as I approach my office. Of course my door is closed and the lights are off. The custodial personnel perform this function every evening.

I open the door keeping half my body in the hallway. I reach around the door frame for the light switch. I touch flesh. The flesh moves and I realize someone has their hand over my light switch! For one terrifying second I freeze and then scream, one long, continual, high pitched scream!

Then I run. I run down the hallway and through the central office. I crash through the double doors into the main hallway. Do I take the elevator or the stairs? Which may save my life, the elevator or the stairs? Quick, Ashley, quick; do something. Oh my God, no matter what my decision, I am going to die.

Dropping my briefcase and kicking off my heel, I head for the stairs. My heart is pounding in my chest, and my feet are pounding on the steps. My lungs are gasping for oxygen and my right hand is clinging to the hand railing, as I fly down the stairs. Please I want to live.

From above, I hear the stair exit door open. A raspy voice shouts, "Run Ashley, run to your death!"

I know there are three security guards on duty. They are probably all on the main floor. Reaching the main door, I shove it open and scream. Two guards come running.

One guard asks, "What's wrong Ms. Browne? You look like you saw a ghost. First take a deep breath."

Gasping between rugged breaths, I attempt to speak. "In my office, there was a man in my office with the lights off."

"Is he still there?"

I attempt another deep breath and find it difficult to gain the oxygen I need. I'm still in a panic. "I don't know if he's still there. He had his hand over my light switch."

"Did he hurt you?" asks the other guard.

I then come to my senses and direct them. "Check all exits now and don't touch any doors, because of possible fingerprints."

I rush past them. I tear outside in my stocking feet shouting for Sam. He needs only to see me sailing down the steps to know that something is dreadfully wrong. He leaves the car's flashers on and runs to meet me.

"He was in my office, my office. The bastard was in my office." I am gasping for air and feeling dizzy.

Sam gently shakes me. "Take a breath, slow down. Listen to me. Take a deep breath, Ashley."

I stop for a moment. "He may still be in the building."

"Go to the car and lock the door." He grabs my arm and starts guiding me toward the car.

I shake off his hand, look at him and shout, "Are you crazy? I'm going with you."

Sam looks at my feet. "You don't even have shoes on."

"I don't care. I'm coming with you."

Sam and I argue as we quickly mount the steps to the main door. He bangs hard and a third guard approaches. Sam flashes his badge and points to me. The guard recognizes me and opens the door. We quickly explain the situation. The guard joins us in the elevator and Sam calls work. He requests a technician to come immediately to the Law Courts building to dust for fingerprints.

When we reach my floor I see my briefcase where I flung it, but can locate only one shoe. Sam instructs the guard to stay with me and leaves to search my office, the washrooms, supply room, and other offices that are not locked in our department.

He finds no sign of the perpetrator or my missing shoe. The bastard has taken my shoe as a souvenir. Sam reminds me to keep the remaining shoe as possible evidence. Of course we may need it, but I am not processing information at this time. I'm still caught up in the fear.

The guard and I wait for the technician, while Sam checks the main and back stairway. Sam sends another guard to the underground parking lot. An hour later Sam returns with the technician, who dusts my office, doors, and the large door handle leading to the stair wells. When we finally leave, I am too wired to be exhausted. Sam thanks the guards and we drive home.

I ask myself if my life will ever be normal again. Once home, I dash to the bathroom and I obsessively wash my hands. I can't stop. Sam finally enters the bathroom and shuts off the taps.

"You're going to peel off your skin. Stop this!" he shouts, as I slap his hand away from the taps.

"I touched him. I want to kill him. Teach me how to use a gun. Tomorrow we buy me a gun and go to the shooting range. I'm going to blow his fucking brains out Sam. I swear it."

Sam places his hands on my shoulders and urges me to leave the bathroom. "Come and have a drink of scotch. Not wine, but straight scotch on the rocks."

I shout, "I don't want a drink, I want a gun!"

I am not a scotch fan, but this time it tastes and feels good going down. Sam pours me another and he encourages me to drink it while I vent. I do just that, three times in a row. I haven't eaten since noon and it is one-thirty in the morning, so I'm soon slurring my words.

"Sammy, spour, spour me another dlink."

Sam takes the glass from my hand. "I advise you to stop drinking. Here, let me make you comfortable on the sofa."

"I wanna scots." I feel tired and stretch out on the sofa.

Sam covers me with a quilt. "Great idea, I'll be right back with a sandwich."

When I awake at five in the morning, its like five armies have marched through my mouth. My head feels like a dozen hammers are banging at intervals.

I pry open my eyes and recall the horror of touching that malicious flesh. A shudder travels the length of my body. I suddenly feel nauseous and don't know if it's caused by the alcohol or the terror I remember.

Sam is asleep in a recliner across the room and I marvel at what a great man I have found. He must sense me stirring, because his eyes open and he's up and by my side.

"How are you feeling darling?"

"Honestly? Like shit. But I will survive. Sorry about my language and behavior last night."

"It's okay. I've heard worse. What can I get you? Would you like me to make breakfast?"

"For now, I just need some strong coffee and dry toast."

He brews and brings me a mug of steaming black, strong coffee. It tastes so good. I nibble at the toast.

After a few minutes Sam asks, "What did you sense when you touched him? Did you feel any sense of the man? Did you see anything?"

I know it's his training, but suddenly I'm angry. I shout, "Sam, shut your eyes and pretend you are reaching into a darkened room for a wall switch. Instead, you find a human hand. You are alone. No on is around. Be honest, what are your emotions? What is your reaction?"

Sam thinks for a moment than replies, "Fear."

"It's exactly what I felt last night. I saw nothing, heard nothing, and smelled nothing. I felt nothing, but this fear. No sense of anything. Just fear. That is what he wants and I sure am providing him with the ultimate high." I take a deep breath. Sam doesn't respond to my outburst.

"Again, he could have killed me right then and there, but chose not to. Eventually he will become bored with this sick game. You know that Sam. You also know we can't let him win."

No further mention is made of purchasing a gun and shooting practice.

Sam finally states, "Yes, I know all about fear. Let's go and get some breakfast. Are you going in today?"

"Yes, I think he will be watching our building today. He will want to assess whether or not he is controlling my life. So I want to show him, I'm stronger than he thinks. Especially after three scotch on the rocks." I laugh.

Sam grins and we are off to get breakfast. He does most of the cooking. I suggest a high fat, greasy meal. He fries bacon and eggs and spreads a pound of butter on each slice of toast.

He places my breakfast in front of me and says, "Just as you ordered my dear. It is full of calories, fat, and cholesterol."

His plate is over flowing with food.

"I notice you are digging in as well. Good for you. I remember when I was in university and if I suffered from a hangover, I wanted a greasy cheeseburger and fat full fries for breakfast. At that time I skipped a class or two, but today I am a responsible adult and must go into work. Is that not sad?"

"It is, but you will survive. Let's jump into the shower together and save some water for the city."

"I certainly believe your rationale. I need to be at work early to bring everyone up to speed."

We take longer than needed in the shower and have to dress quickly. I feel a little better after the breakfast, shower, and Sam.

CHAPTER 31

▼

The office is buzzing with the events of last night. Accomplishing any work is impossible, because everyone is dropping by my office to see how I am surviving the ordeal.

The one person I don't wish to see is Logan. Like a bad penny, he drops in. He begins with, "I heard what happened and it is dreadful. Are you okay? I'm so sorry."

He pauses and I wonder at such a supportive statement from Logan. But my positive thought is interrupted by, "You know, you dedicate too much time and effort to this job. If you had left the office at a reasonable hour like the rest of us, this horrible incident wouldn't have happened."

I glare at him and decide against responding. For the first time I think that he really is cold. He returns my glare with a grin and leaves. I had glanced at his hands and I speculate about the possibility of him being my stalker.

The technician has left fingerprint powder over most surfaces in my office. A cleaning staff member is notified to clean the area. When she arrives I move to our law library.

I no longer have Gail, my friend and sounding board. She is gone forever. Suddenly, I feel so sad.

Concern for my safety is expressed by everyone, particularly Jim. When I arrive for our scheduled meeting he apologizes profusely for keeping me late last night.

"I feel responsible. I should have called Cheryl earlier and cancelled our meeting. I'm so sorry."

"No apology is required. This psycho will come after me any time. Here at work, at home, or on the streets, it will not matter to him, as long as I die."

I contemplate to myself how long can I keep up this façade? I may appear calm, cool, and collected, but inside I'm petrified and beginning to withdraw.

We move to the topic of the serial rapist. The individual coordinating this case from General Investigation Section is not Sam, but Sergeant Edward Marlot. The individual charged is Max Jakubitz. He's twenty-nine and married with two children. He made a huge mistake when attacking middle-aged Leona Spenar in her home. He didn't do his homework in this case and had no idea the woman's husband, Bill, was asleep in the family room in the basement.

The police feel he fits the composite made by two victims. Both victims had ripped aside their attacker's balaclava and glimpsed his face. I leave the office with Jakubitz's file and Jim's best wishes for my safety.

It's back to work, fighting for the victim and prison time for the perpetrator.

I call Sergeant Edward Marlot and set a meeting for Monday morning. I then thumb through the information on Max Jakubitz.

Jakubitz, of Ukrainian descent, moved to Canada in nineteen hundred and eight-six with his parents and eight siblings. He was nine years old and didn't speak a word of English.

His father, Andrew, was a brute of a man who picked on Max because of his small stature. His mother, Natallia, didn't attempt to prevent the brutality because she too suffered from the beatings. Jakubitz married at age eighteen to get away from his father. His two children ages seven and ten are treated well by their father. His wife, Victoria, refuses to believe her husband would, "be with another woman," much less sexually assault one.

Max Jakubitz has worked as a garbage collector for the past six years. My theory is that his job would give him ample opportunity to scout the houses on his route, for women at home. This attempted sexual assault took place at noon, probably during his lunch hour.

His choice of weapon was a knife, the Swiss army type. There was no evidence he actually used the knife to cause physical pain. It was there to cause fear and give him a sense of control.

Sam calls an hour later and tells me he is on his way to pick me up. I am pleased the work day is done.

At home, I lie on the sofa and promptly fall asleep. I jerk awake by the start of a nightmare and see Sam across the room staring at me. He appears angry.

"You know, Ashley, you could have prevented what happened last night by warning me you were alone on your floor."

I instantly am awake and furious. I can't believe what Sam just said to me. I sit up. My body is rigid.

"What?" I need to hear his accusation once more.

"You knew I was outside your building. Why didn't you call my cell? You could have left and had a guard escort you to your office."

"Are you joking? You are blaming me? What a bunch of bullshit. The psychopath is out to kill me and it's my fault?"

"Just hold it Ashley. That is not what I said. I meant—"

I immediately interrupt him, "Yes, you did. How in the hell was I to know everyone had gone home. When I picked up my files and returned to Jim's office there were people around."

"When you went into the hallway after calling me from Jim's office and found a dimly lit hallway, you could have called me back. I was parked outside. Christ, Ashley, when are you going to realize this lunatic means business? How many more conversations do we need to have about his intentions?"

"I will not allow him to control my life any more than I will allow you to. I need some freedom."

"When will you start listening to me? You also made a bone head move when you went to the underground parking lot on your own. It's like your saying, "Here I am Chartrand, yours for the taking." I know you are not stupid."

"This is great. Maybe I should lie down and die. My tormentor will be spared the honor of taking my life." I gulp, hoping to prevent myself from breaking down.

Sam screams, "Stop being ridiculous."

"What do you know about the fear I'm living with right now?" I stop, remembering his childhood. I should apologize, but I'm too angry.

"Just because you have lived the good life, doesn't make you immune to the injustices of the world."

"I will not apologize for being fortunate enough to be brought into the world to decent parents. I have worked hard to purchase my own home and get to where I am today. Not everything was given to me."

"Yes, Ashley, I'm aware that this is your house." Sam has placed emphasis on the word your.

"Exactly what is it you're implying?"

"Everything is, "Mine" with you, as in my house, my television, my barbeque, and my bedroom. Well you know what, Ashley? You can keep your possessions, but I'm not going to become one of them."

"Great. Get your things out of my bathroom, and my bedroom, and don't forget your socks in my dresser."

Sam stands and responds, "No problem. But you should be careful for what you ask for in life. You may get it."

"Are you threatening me; you son of a bitch! Who the hell do you think you are? I have managed before you and I will do it again without you."

Shouting, he responds, "I am not a possession to be discarded, just as you throw away your slightly used towel."

I yell at him, "What makes you think, you conceited bastard, that I would want you as a possession?"

"Fuck off, Ashley!"

Sam storms from the room. Five minutes later I hear the front door slam. I had thought he would not leave. Looking out the front window I see his struggle. In one arm he has his clothes and in the other his shaver, electric tooth brush, and brush. Men, I'll never understand them. He can't be bothered to get a bag, but instead would drag his underwear across the lawn.

I am fuming. Not only am I infuriated at the reference to my possessions, but the audacity of him to say that my terrifying experiences were somehow my fault. I go to the bar and pour myself a large glass of red wine.

After ten minutes or so, I walk to my bedroom. The first thing I notice is the house key on my pillow. I sit down on the bed and think about all the negative things about Sam and find they are little annoyances. There is nothing major. Now that my anger has abated; I feel very lonely.

Lying on my side of the bed I grab Sam's pillow and hug it close. He is right. I am very possessive of my things and my position in this house. I have always slept on the right side of the bed and never once asked Sam what he preferred.

I recollect the many times I used the word, my, in sentences. I want to tell Sam the word was automatically used because I have never shared my home with anyone before. My angry response is directed more at the present situation, including Logan's remarks, than at Sam.

The next thing I realize it is one in the morning and I am still wearing my work clothes. It hits me like an ice cold glass of water in the face, Sam is gone. I snap on the lamp beside my bed and look around. The door to my walk-in closet has been left open and I can see the empty space where Sam had a few clothes hanging. Does it really matter that the door has been left open? Will it make a difference in one hundred years? I remember telling Sam to close my closet when he repeatedly left it open. Did he leave it open tonight as a reminder?

The stress of the last few hours has left me nauseous and I go to the bathroom to brush my teeth and remove my makeup. Taking off my suit I hang it in the closet and put on a robe. I leave the bedroom with the closet door left ajar.

In the kitchen I look into the fridge and the first thing I see is the large jar of Dijon mustard, which I purchased for Sam. He loves it. I use the left over ham to make a sandwich and I carry it to the great room. It is difficult to swallow, because I have a lump in my throat. My heart actually hurts and I'm trying desperately not to break down.

Sam has been gone for five hours, during three of which I dozed off, and yet it feels like he has been gone for days. I miss him; I love him; and I want him back. It's now 1:30 and I wonder if he's sleeping.

I put my plate in the dishwasher and look at the phone on the kitchen counter. Putting my hand on the receiver I pick it up, but do not dial. Instead, I run to the bathroom and have a shower. Since my stalker, I'm scared to do this simple act without someone in the house. For Sam, I realize I will do anything. After the shower I put on a sexy negligee and cover it with a bathrobe. I grab my long, winter coat and dash to my car.

As I drive to Sam's apartment I hope he is at home and will invite me in. There is a possibility that he went directly to a local cop bar. Now I ponder if I have made a wise decision. Before I can change my mind, Sam's apartment block looms in front of me.

I leave the car hoping no one is in the lobby or elevator. I take out the key Sam gave me and open the front door. At the time Sam gave me his key, I thought it would never be put to use. I accepted the key to please him.

I realize now that our relationship has been all about me. We have spent time as a couple with my friends, but never his. I recall him asking if I would be interested in meeting Bill and Cheryl, close friends of his. Apparently Bill is a president of an oil company in Edmonton and his wife is a manager at a bank. Somehow it was never convenient to meet with them or with any of his single friends.

I reach the fourth floor and am not sure whether to turn left or right. I have never been to Sam's apartment. Guessing, I turn right and see four hundred and twenty-six. I take a deep breath and knock gently on the door.

Within seconds, Sam yanks the door open. His face is angry; he wears the same clothes; and he holds a beer. When he sees me his face immediately softens and I see such love in his eyes that it almost brings me to my knees. We stand there, Sam in the apartment and me in the hallway and stare at each other. I move first, step inside, and close the door.

Staring into his eyes I groan and say, "Sam, I'm so sorry. Please forgive me. I want you to come home, our home."

He gathers me in his arms and holds me close, "I love you so much Ashley. It actually hurts. I have been sitting in front of your picture, missing you so much, while trying to forget you by socking back the beer."

I take in Sam's apartment. With the exception of the empty beer cans stacked neatly by my photo, it is well kept and clean. "I need a tour of your place, but first there is a greater need. Look what I brought you."

I open my coat and robe and provocatively remove them. I stand in front of him in only the sheer negligee. Sam's eyes are popping and he grabs me a little roughly and plants his mouth on mine. He whispers, "Everywhere. I want to make love to you everywhere. This means in the living room, kitchen, and bed-room. Oh, I love you, love you."

I laugh out loud and whisper, "It's now 2:30. Shut up, we don't have much time."

He picks me up and lays me on the sofa and with a chuckle says, "This first time will not take long; I'm so ready."

We do manage a couple of rooms and I get my tour. He has a picture of either the two of us or me in every room. In the kitchen there is a photo of us that he asked a stranger to take, while we walked along the ravine. In the living room, Sam has placed a picture I gave him of my graduation. Teasing him now I say the photo does not have my present wrinkles. He says, "My dear Ashley, even if you had the wrinkles; you would be beautiful to me."

In the bathroom on a little corner stand is a small picture of us in the back yard. In the bedroom is a picture of me which Sam obviously had enlarged. It was taken in front of the fireplace. He had asked me to give him a sexy smile.

"Come, we are going home, our home." We go into his bedroom and bath-room and pack the necessary toiletries and clothing. I empty one of his drawers of socks and briefs.

We arrive home at five. There is time for one more round of lovemaking. We can't keep our hands off each other. Totally exhausted, we fall asleep quickly.

We awake at eleven and Sam's arms are snuggly around me.

Sam explains, "I'm sorry too. It's just that I was angry at myself for being unable to protect you twenty-four/seven and for not being able to help with your fear."

I reply, "I understand and I do need to take more responsibility for my safety. It's just so difficult being controlled by fear."

"I am afraid for you. This man is very dangerous."

"I'm sorry for my comments about the fear."

Sam looks away embarrassed. "I did know fear. It was my constant companion when my dad was around."

"I know that Sam, because you told me. I was an ass to say what I did."

"It's okay."

"I did follow your advice about escorts. At lunch I asked one of the male prosecutors to jog with me."

"Which prosecutor did you ask?"

"I don't know if you'll recognize the name, Paul Strychuk."

"Shit, why did it have to be that guy? I know who he is because I worked a case with him. He is not only very intelligent, but what you females would call a, "Handsome stud." Don't you know a stooped, bald headed, sixty year old prosecutor, who has a vision problem?"

"Not that can run." I tease.

"I don't want you to depend only on Paul."

"Why Sam, I believe you are jealous." I rub my hand down his thigh.

"Yes, I believe I am."

"Listen to and believe me; I only have eyes for you. I love you, love you, love you."

We finally get out of bed at noon. Heading for the kitchen I have plans to make us French toast with slices of oranges, pears, peaches, and melons as a side. Sam is taking a shower.

He joins me in the kitchen and cheerfully asks, "What would you like to do today? The day is yours."

"Spend time with you. I would love to go out and visit the art gallery and have dinner at the new steak restaurant downtown. Call them for a reservation. Even though it's late we could get lucky. I will clean up here."

Sam returns in five minutes, "We are fortunate. We have a table for two at eight o'clock. A touch late, but all they had available."

"I'm so pleased. It will take me two minutes to throw on my jeans and shirt. We can do the groceries then I will bath and get ready for the gallery and dinner."

We are home by 2:30 with the groceries and while I bath, Sam puts them away. We both dress, Sam in a beautiful dark grey suit with a light, grey shirt and grey and burgundy tie. I wear a simply styled, off shoulder, light blue dress with a matching shawl.

Sam is lost in the art gallery but shows his interest by asking many questions. He tells me in his youth he was not exposed to art, opera, or live theatre, and it's difficult for him to gain an appreciation of it now. He is giving it a great try. I will in the future, attend a race car event with him, as it is his love. He shared this interest with me last night. We have promised each other to work on our relationship and make it happen.

Between the gallery and dinner we stop in a downtown bar to pass the hour wait. We arrive at the restaurant and are seated immediately. Sam orders a New York steak, medium rare and I order a filet mignon, medium rare. We share some stuffed mushrooms, my favorite. The food is scrumptious, the service excellent, and the company gorgeous.

We arrive home and fall into bed. We are relaxed, blissfully happy, and totally exhausted.

On Sunday, we lounge around enjoying each other's company. I talk about my upcoming case and Sam tells me a few things about Edward Marlot. I'm meeting him at work tomorrow. Sam and Edward have been friends for years. He is older than Sam. Edward is more of a father figure.

Sam says, "I have nice memories of weekends spent with Edward. We fished in the summer and attended hockey games in the winter."

"He sounds like a wonderful man."

"Edward and I partnered for four years until I was moved to management. He's the best there is on the force."

"I can hardly wait to meet him."

The day passes quickly and we retire early.

I remind him that we've accepted my parents' dinner invitation for Friday evening.

Sam says, "Wow, only five more days before I get to enjoy a homemade pie."

My mom never told me the old expression of, "The best way to a man's heart is through his stomach," I wonder why. She probably knew I would grow up to be more of a professional, than a stay at home and cook up a storm person.

I love Sam and cuddle up to him and sleep soundly.

CHAPTER 32

▼

As is our routine Sam drops me at work. I dash up the Law Courts building steps and become aware of people beside me heading into the building. Even with Sam watching from his car, I feel the penetrating fear. I tell myself not to be afraid, but it's like attempting to stop the flow of water from a cracked dam. It decreases somewhat as I pass through security, but heightens as I look around for a familiar face with whom to share an elevator.

Marty Kroll strolls through the lobby and I ask, "Marty, are you going to the fourth floor?"

"Yes, as a matter of fact. What's wrong, Ashley? You look frightened."

"No, I'm okay. Just thought I would be polite and hold the elevator for you."

"Your good Monday deed; how thoughtful of you." He smiles at me.

Not until the elevator door closes do I realize I'm trapped inside with someone I don't like. Glancing down at his hand, I get a shocked feeling of alarm. What have I done? I immediately look up and catch Marty staring at me, with a challenging expression on his face.

He then leers, not smiles, at me and says, "What?"

The door opens. I take a gulp of air and reply, "Oh, nothing. Have a great day."

As I exit the elevator I'm feeling less threatened. We go our separate ways.

I spend the next hour preparing for my meeting with the sergeant.

Sergeant Edward Marlot arrives at the appointed time. He is of medium height, slightly overweight, and balding, with a handsome face. I would guess him to be in his fifties. He is wearing blue jeans, a blue and white sports shirt, and a black leather jacket. Sam informed me yesterday afternoon that Edward is a hard worker. He is a man who plays by the rules, and tends to be very blunt when speaking. I'm looking forward to working with him.

Entering my office Edward extends his hand. He looks into my eyes and says in this loud, deep, voice, "Sam is one lucky man and don't give me any of that chauvinist bullshit." He wears a grin.

I stare at him shocked. I say, "No, but let's talk sexual harassment. Apparently the formal introductions are over Edward. Have a seat."

"Thanks. Let's do get started. Max Jakubitz has been in the system for years. Not because of him, but his father Andrew. Have you seen the social worker's report?"

"Yes. It appears Max suffered terrible abuse as a child. This continued to the time he was a teen. It blows my mind every time I get involved in these types of cases."

"Yes, it's upsetting to me too, no matter how long I have been in this job." He looks at me and shakes his head.

"Why haven't they received the necessary help? Where are Social Services to help these abused children?"

"Same old answer. There is not enough staff and too many dysfunctional families. The government needs to pour more money into the department of social services."

"Well, we both know help is now available to support children in abusive situations, but many of them like Max go on to bring pain to others. They should instead, be getting help for their own pain and suffering. In turn either their children or spouse suffer, or as in Max's situation, a complete stranger takes the brunt of their deep anger."

"I imagine you are like us and encounter these cases all the time. This is the evidence and information I have for you. Jakubitz was caught in the act by the husband of the intended victim. As is stated in the write-up, Jakubitz is not a big man. Unfortunately for him, Spenar, is a large man and he thrashed Max badly. When the officer arrived at the Spenar home, Jakubitz was unconscious and not going anywhere."

"How far into the act was Jakubitz when the husband intervened?"

"When Jakubitz entered the house he approached Leona from behind, and placed a hand over her mouth so she was unable to scream. He held a knife to her throat and ordered her into the bedroom. Jakubitz then told her to strip off her clothes. As he removed his hand Leona screamed and woke her husband in the basement. He came running."

Edward takes a breath then continues, "It is essentially an open and shut case with the Spenars. But, and they say, "There is always a, but," right? Anyway, for the past three years we have been chasing a serial sexual assault individual. Maybe we can prove Max is our culprit."

"Do you have evidence tying Jakubitz to either of the two victims? The two who pulled aside their assailant's balaclava, after he sexually assaulted them?"

"We took specimens from Jakubitz in an attempt to tie him to April Smith's assault of a year ago. April Smith immediately notified police after the sexual assault, and we obtained a semen sample from the bed sheets. She is one of the females that saw a portion of his face. Yesterday she picked him out in a photo line-up. I think the DNA sample taken from April's bedroom will be a match to Jakubitz's DNA."

"Did these other two assaults take place around noon in the same area of the city?"

Edward smiles at me, "Sam told me you were bright. Yes, they did occur between twelve and one in the afternoon."

"What evidence do you have from the other victim?"

"The other victim decided initially that she was not reporting the attack. Therefore, she had a shower; disposed of the clothes she was wearing, as well as the sheets; and scrubbed everything he had touched. A week later she called us, but all evidence was gone by then. We showed her a photo line-up and she picked Jakubitz, but no other evidence ties him to her attack."

I ask, "Have you spoken to his wife, Victoria?"

"Yes. She emphatically stated that her husband is very gentle with the entire family and doesn't believe him capable of such acts."

I comment, "He could very well be a gentle man at home. One who takes his anger out on a stranger. Has he made any type of statement since his arrest?"

"He hasn't said much. He hired a lawyer immediately."

"Before the lawyer's arrival what did he say?"

"He claimed that he was invited into the home by Leona and that suddenly her husband was all over him. Can you believe that? Jakubitz wants to charge Mr. Spenar with assault."

I laugh, "We have an eye witness, so we can do a preliminary hearing quickly. On a scale of one to ten, where do you place his DNA matching the specimen you took from April?"

"I place it as a ten for matching Max's DNA. We do have someone else with a DNA sample from an attack that occurred three years ago. But when we tracked her down, she refused to be involved. She has since married and no longer wants the matter pursued.

"So your opinion is that Jakubitz was responsible?"

"I think he was her attacker and she his first victim. Her name is Irene Tolerno. Her maiden name was Remdall."

"Leave her phone number with me and I'll call her. It would be beneficial to have her as a witness. More jail time for Jakubitz, if we are able to prove a serial sexual attacker."

"Okay, I'll wait to hear from you."

Edward stands; we shake hands; and I think, *Nice man.*

As soon as Edward leaves I call Irene Tolerno. In a gentle voice she answers on the first ring.

"Is this Irene Tolerno, maiden name Remdall?"

There is a long silence then she says, "Who is this please?"

"This is Ashley Browne, a crown prosecutor and I would like to talk to you about what happened three years ago."

"I told the cops the other day to leave me alone. I'm not interested in pursuing this now. I have recently married and my husband doesn't know about the attack." There is anger in her voice.

"I understand your trepidation Mrs. Tolerno. The situation is awkward to say the least. Would you consider coming in to meet with me just for a few minutes this week? I just want to talk to you. I'm willing to come to your home as well."

She answers quickly, "Don't even think about coming here. I was on my way out when you called, so I can stop by your office. Let me say right now, I'm not going to change my mind. What is your address?"

I give her my phone number and address along with parking directions. We hang up. Almost immediately my phone rings and I think its Irene calling back to cancel.

It's Sam. "How is your day?"

"It's busy and depressing. I met your friend Edward. He's a nice man. You described him perfectly. Is there anything exciting going on in your life?"

"Just wanting to let you know I may be a half hour late tonight. If everyone leaves at four-thirty take a cab home. I absolutely don't want you in the office alone."

"Okay. I have one unexpected meeting today at 1:30. Thank you for calling. See you later."

Irene is at my door at 1:20. She wears a frightened yet angry look. Irene is a slim woman of medium height, with long brown hair, and blue eyes. Irene appears to be around twenty-three to twenty-five, which would make her approximately twenty when attacked.

"Mrs. Tolerno, I can't tell you how grateful I am that you came. Please, let me take your jacket and do have a seat. Can I get you anything?"

Irene perches on the end of the chair, and says, "There is no need to take off my jacket. I'm not staying long."

"Please Mrs. Tolerno, sit back and relax. I'm not going to hurt you or railroad you into testifying, if you choose not to. I want to bring you up to date."

Suddenly she raves, "Where were all of you when that son of a bitch raped me? I notified the police. They took their specimens and did their interviews. I was willing to testify at the time. Hell, I would have killed the little bastard if the police would have caught him. But they didn't and now everyone wants me involved. It's not going to happen."

I slowly raise my hands and make a downward motion to calm her. I say, "You are right Mrs. Tolerno, the police didn't catch him then. I understand your anger. But we believe we have your attacker in custody now. We would appreciate your help."

She takes a long shaky breath and continues, "I'm now married and I didn't tell my husband about the rape. And I have no plans to do so now. When I think about it, I feel dirty and also somehow responsible. And if I feel that way, how could I expect my husband to accept me if he knew?"

This comment angers me. It's a common statement coming from the victim. "You were not responsible."

"That's how I feel."

"Did you receive counseling after the attack?"

"No. My parents just wanted to bury the whole incident, especially after the police couldn't find my attacker."

Deciding to clarify a few details, I ask, "Was the perpetrator or what you call your attacker a small man?"

"Yes. He was just this little weasel. If he didn't have the knife at my throat; I would have fought the little shit and won."

"To give you a heads up, we have arrested a man caught in the act of sexual assault by the victim's husband. Another woman was attacked last year and we had collected DNA evidence at that time. We are hoping that the specimen collected a year ago, will match the DNA of the accused. She also picked him out of a photo line-up. In both situations the man was short and used a knife to threaten."

"Then why do you need me to testify?"

"Because I believe you were the first victim, and that the evidence collected in your case will also implicate the accused. The more people we have who testify at trial, the better chance we have of getting a long prison term."

"I'm sorry Ms. Browne, but I have not changed my mind. As I indicated, I can't risk my husband and our relationship over this."

"I understand, and again I thank you for coming."

As she walks out the door I say, "Mrs. Tolerno, if you ever change your mind call me please."

"I will."

Alone now, I hypothesize Sam's reaction if he were to discover I had been sexually assaulted and had not told him. I sympathize with Irene that she must hide her past from her husband. It must be horrible to carry such a dark secret and not share it with your spouse.

At five Sam calls. He is parked downstairs and waiting for me. I know there are still employees on my floor, so he'll have no need to chastise me for being alone.

When we arrive home Sam says, "Rest. I will prepare dinner tonight."

I leave to tend to my routine of putting on lounging pajamas, washing my face and selecting what I will wear the next day. I then turn on the television and promptly fall asleep on the sofa.

Sam wakes me with a gentle kiss.

"Thank you. Something smells so delicious. What did you prepare for us this evening?"

He looks extremely proud and grabs my hand, "Come and see. I think you are going to enjoy this."

In the dining room the table glows in candlelight. Two dinners of chicken cordon bleu, baby carrots, and scalloped potatoes wait for us.

"Oh Sam, it looks wonderful."

"I hope it tastes as good as it looks. I checked with one of my female peers as to what she thought would be an impressive meal to cook for my special girl friend. She was so helpful she even wrote out the recipes for me. I bought the chicken before picking you up this afternoon."

"Just how old was this helpful female?" I grin at him jokingly and he smiles.

"Twenty-six or seven and shaped like a model."

"It's okay then. Models are just too skinny these days and I know you prefer someone with a few more curves. Like me, right Sam?" I lightly jab him.

"Actually, her name is Roxanne and she is very pretty. She's of medium height, with brown hair and eyes, but she is married with two small boys."

"Very interesting that you should remember to include she was married. Her husband is fortunate to have those fabulous meals."

"And you are right to know I prefer your lovely curves."

We dig in and it is definitely scrumptious. After dinner I offer to clean up while Sam has a shower.

Pamela calls and we catch up on bits of news. She invites Sam and me over for a late dinner on Friday, but I have to decline because we have accepted Mom and Dad's invitation. We say good-bye and promise to be in touch soon.

Sam and I spend the rest of the evening sipping wine and discussing our relationship and how to improve our communication. The fact that we are madly in love with each other is not questioned.

At ten just as we are preparing for bed the phone rings. I pick up in the bedroom.

The raspy voice says, "Did the hand scare you Ashley? I wanted to see you sweat. I have your shoe ready for delivery. Your time is near. What happened in your office is mild, compared to what I have in store for you."

I am frantically motioning to Sam and pointing to the phone. He grabs it from me and shouts, "Who is this?" The line is dead and Sam stares at it with an angry look.

He turns to me and asks, "What did he say?"

I walk to him to be held and whisper, "He referred to his hand on the light switch and that he is ready to deliver my shoe soon. He said the office incident is mild compared to what he has planned for me. The statement, "The time is near," is what scares the shit out of me. I'm so frightened and frustrated. Damn it, we need to find him, be it Chartrand or whomever it is doing these horrible things to me. Oh yes, he also said he wanted to see me sweat."

Sam holds me tightly, "I know sweetheart. No one wants that more than I. Right now I am fighting for a task force on this. It is difficult to put a great effort into Gail's murder and locating your stalker, when they keep loading me up with other cases. Instead of going after the stalker I'm sitting back attempting to protect you from harm. As we discussed, I can't be with you twenty-four/seven."

"I'll do my best to think safety first, but it's difficult, and I find myself withdrawing from situations needlessly."

"What do you mean by that?"

"Even tonight when Pamela called, in the back of mind I was thinking, *Do not expose another friend, to this twisted madman.* Even if we weren't invited to my parents I don't know if I would want us to draw attention to Pamela's home."

"I understand what you're saying, but I very much doubt if he would go after another friend. I believe he killed Gail to get your complete attention."

"Think about what you just said. I may agree with you, but can you wrap your brain around a mind that would eliminate a human to grab someone's attention. How sick is this?"

"It is definitely sick, but its how a psycho thinks."

"I don't want to discuss this further. I feel nauseated."

"I agree. And I'm exhausted."

We go to bed, but I can't sleep. I hear Sam's gentle breathing beside me and think about selling this house, about the two of use moving to another province or country. I fall asleep with that thought finally relaxing me.

CHAPTER 33

▼

During the week I am busy with the Jakubitz case. Darryl Black, the arresting officer, comes to my office for a meeting, and we discuss his role in the capture.

Darryl arrives promptly at 9:30 and extends his hand in greeting, "Hello Ms. Browne, I am Constable Darryl Black."

"Make yourself comfortable. Have a seat." Constable Black is tall, with a handsome face, blond hair, and blue eyes.

When he appears settled I ask, "What did you observe when you arrived at the scene?"

"The perpetrator, Max Jakubitz was unconscious on the bedroom floor from a second punch delivered by the victim's husband, Bill Spenar. This second punch probably resulted in Jakubitz hitting his head on a sharp object; when he was knocked to the floor."

"Where was Mrs. Spenar when you arrived?"

"She was sitting at the kitchen table."

"Did you notice what she was wearing when you interviewed her?"

Constable Black looks up at the ceiling. He is trying to picture the interview. "Mrs. Spenar wore a blue, terry cloth housecoat."

"Who answered the door when you rang?"

"Mr. Spenar answered the door and immediately led me to Max Jakubitz."

"What was your course of action?"

"After taking his pulse rate I immediately called an ambulance and radioed for backup because someone needed to accompany him to the hospital."

We discuss his interview with Mr. and Mrs. Spenar and later with Max Jakubitz. I request an additional meeting prior to trial.

The Spenars come in together, but I interview them separately. When Leona Spenar comes into my office, I'm facing a very attractive middle-aged woman. She is wearing a matching, blue skirt and jacket, with a white blouse. She has brown hair and eyes. I ask her to have a seat and to put her at ease I ask, "Can I call you Leona? I'm Ashley."

"Absolutely, I dislike formality."

"Do you have any family, Leona?"

"Yes, I did have three daughters but one passed away a few years ago. One of my daughters lives in a northern community with her husband, and the other lives in Victoria, British Columbia."

"I am sorry for your loss."

Mrs. Spenar looks at me with sadness in her eyes and says, "Thank you."

"How long have you been married to Mr. Spenar?"

"We just celebrated our twenty-ninth wedding anniversary."

"Congratulations. This conversation may upset you, but I need to ask these questions"

"I understand. The policeman told me you are the one who is going to prosecute Max Jakubitz. I will do whatever necessary to put him away."

"Explain what happened on the day of the attack."

Speaking softly Leona says, "I was making lunch for my husband and me. A man came up behind me."

"I need to interrupt for a second. When you are on the witness stand you must be very specific. For example, you need to indicate at what time of the day this occurred and exactly where were you standing. This will help establish credibility. You also must speak louder; with authority. Do you understand?"

"Yes. It was 12:10 and I was standing at the kitchen counter making lunch for my husband and me. My back was to the kitchen door."

I dislike interrupting, but it's necessary for trial. "Where was your husband? Remember to state this."

"My husband was asleep downstairs in the family room. Suddenly, there was this man behind me with a knife pressed at my throat. He said, "Scream and you're dead." I just froze."

"What happened then Leona?"

"The man ordered me into the bedroom. His hand was over my mouth and he screamed at me to remove my clothes. I was scared." At this point, she is close to tears.

"Did you think he might kill you?"

"Yes, because he still had the knife pressed against my throat."

"You must say that in your testimony."

"Okay. For some reason he removed his hand and I gathered my nerve and just screamed as hard as I could."

"What was his reaction?"

"He grabbed me roughly and told me to, "Shut the fuck up." That's when my husband showed up."

"What did your husband do when he arrived in the bedroom?"

"He grabbed the attacker from behind by both arms and just lifted him off his feet. My husband is a big man and the attacker was small. Bill hit him once knocking him to the floor, and then picked him up and hit him again. This time when the attacker fell, he hit his head on our dresser and it knocked him out. The whole time my husband was swearing at the attacker, and yelling at me to notify the police."

"You will do very well on the stand. During the trial I will ask if you see the man who attacked you in the courtroom. I want you to point him out, if he is present. Do you understand?"

"Yes, I'll do that. I'm not afraid to face him. Maybe I would feel differently if he actually had been allowed to complete his attack."

"Thank you Leona. I will talk to your husband now and will meet with both of you one more time before trial. As I explained on the phone you will testify soon at the preliminary hearing." We shake hands and say good-bye.

Bill Spenar is indeed a striking man. He is approximately six feet and two hundred pounds. We shake hands and mine is lost in his. He has brown hair and eyes.

I question him about the one-sided fight and he verifies the description given by his wife. I then ask him, "I didn't pose this question to your wife, but I will ask you. Why was your back door unlocked in your home?"

He looks down at the floor for a moment and then says, "I told Leona you would ask us this question and I thank you for leaving it to me. It is something we argue about. I'm the one who left the door open. Number one, I was at home and number two, I was raised on a farm where we never locked any doors, be it the house, car, truck, barn, nothing. My wife, on the other hand, was born in the city and wants everything locked up tight, including the house. I guess you could say the attack was my fault."

"No. It was not your fault. Please don't feel guilty. The attack is to be blamed on Max Jakubitz. He is responsible. Thank you for coming in Bill. I will see both of you one more time before trial. You will be testifying at the preliminary hearing."

"Thank you. We appreciate your help."

As he leaves I think what a nice couple the Spenars are, which leads me to think of Sam. I look forward to my evenings now and wish Gail was here, so I could share my happiness with her.

On Thursday afternoon I have a meeting with April Smith, the girl who was sexually assaulted a year ago. April is very young, probably twenty-one or two. She is slightly overweight, has tight, black, curly hair and dark brown eyes. Today she is dressed in blue jeans and a T-shirt. She carries her jacket on her arm.

"Have a seat Ms. Smith. Do you mind if I call you April?"

"Not at all, I prefer it."

"Excellent. If you feel nervous take a few deep breaths, blow out slowly and relax." I watch as April follows my instructions.

I start with, "Are you working or are you going to university?"

"I'm enrolled in the pharmacist program at university."

"Do you live at home with your parents or are you at the university dorms?"

"I live at home with Mom and Dad. I would love to get an apartment with my friend, but it's too expensive."

"I'm going to take you through the assault because it's necessary for preliminary and hopefully for trial. I have interviewed many women who have been sexually assaulted and they have said that talking about it is often like being assaulted again. I want you to know that I'm sorry to put you through this."

"You're right. The first time in particular; it was so difficult to explain everything to the cops."

"Share with me what you were doing the day of the attack and the approximate time it took place."

"The attack took place on a Wednesday at 12:20 in the afternoon. My parents were at work and I was sitting at the living room table doing an assignment. Wednesday was a great day, because I only had one class early in the morning

April takes a deep breath and says, "I had just let the cat out and didn't lock the door because the dumb cat always goes out for a minute or two and then wants back in. Anyway, in the position I was sitting I didn't see the bastard, until he was right behind me and by then it was too late."

"How tall was this man and did he have a weapon?"

She shudders, "He was a small man with a big knife and I was sure I would die."

I take April through the sexual assault supporting her as we go along. Two hours later I thank her very much for agreeing to testify. She appears emotionally strong and I think she will hold her own during cross-examination.

I still haven't heard from Irene Tolerno and doubt she will help us and thus herself by testifying. I can't imagine what it would be like to hide such a secret forever.

It's getting late and I can hardly wait to rush home. I need down time. Packing a small case, for our visit to Mom and Dad's tomorrow afternoon, is also on the agenda.

When we arrive home Sam and I choose a light dinner in anticipation of the large meal at my parent's place tomorrow. After dinner, Sam convinces me to watch a hockey game and we then make it an early night.

Saturday late afternoon we leave for my parent's home. I have not seen them in a while and am looking forward to this visit. Mom and I often chat on the phone, but it's not the same. She will have prepared a feast.

Mom has set a lovely table and she serves mixed nut and spinach salad, prime rib roast, mashed potatoes, gravy, cauliflower with cheese, fried mushrooms and onions in cream, and fresh cheese buns. Dessert is home made blueberry pie and ice cream. Sam is in his glory. He eats heartily and of course Mom is pleased.

At dinner we discuss Dad's current problem with one of the teenage boys at school. The student age fifteen has been threatening one of the teachers. Sam gives Dad advice on the law, which enhances his plan of action. Mom informs us that she was nominated for and won a regional election for president of the "Help the Needy" club. This club sells pastries, pickles, and vegetables in the summer, and knitting, scarves, quilts, and stone paintings in the winter, to make money for the less fortunate. They also gather mitts, gloves, and toques to give to the homeless in the winter months. She refers to her friend, Jane, who resides on a nearby farm, and is very generous with her time and baking goods. Sam and I update them on Gail's murder investigation. There is not much to say. We don't share with them the recent threats, such as the work incident or threatening telephone calls.

As we are tidying Mom tells me she has spoken to Dad about dropping further interrogation of Sam. He has been in Sam's company and likes him. Dad had commented to Mom, "He will make an excellent son-in-law."

After dinner, we join the men in the living room and Dad pours us a drink. When everyone is seated, Sam suddenly drops to one knee in front of me. He opens a small, blue, velvet box and says, "Ashley, will you marry me?"

I look at Sam and then my parents. Mom and Dad are as surprised as me.

"Yes." I gulp air, "Yes."

Mom and Dad are out of their chairs congratulating us and hugging each other. Sam then asks their permission to marry me. Dad replies without hesitation, "Of course son, of course." Mom is so excited she can't answer. She keeps repeating, "Oh my, oh my, oh my." The four of us end up in a huddle.

Sam places the ring on my finger and it fits perfectly. It's a huge marquis diamond and Mom and I admire it. Placing my hand in front of a lamp, I move it around and watch the wonderful light radiating from the diamond. I say, "Oh Sam, it is so beautiful. I will love you forever." Sam says, "I love you," and kisses me gently on the lips. Mom and Dad sigh together.

Mom immediately wants to discuss wedding plans and says to Sam and me, "When will you marry? We could set the date right now."

"Mom, sixty seconds ago I didn't know Sam would ask me to marry him. Now you want a wedding date. Are you serious?"

She looks serious and replies, "Yes, I am serious. There are so many things to plan and places to book."

"You didn't ask Sam where he would want the wedding to be held."

"Oh Sam, you would want Ashley to marry in her home town; would you not?"

I interrupt, "Mom."

Sam answers, "I think it sounds wonderful to hold the wedding here, but I agree with Ashley. The two of us need time to discuss dates."

"I'm sorry you two, but the excitement got the best of me." Mom smiles at us and we silently understand.

It is one in the morning when we decide to go to bed. Mom shows Sam his bedroom, which leaves no doubt as to whether we sleep together. I slowly make my way to my old bedroom.

The following morning after an excellent breakfast of bacon, eggs, hash browns, and toast, we leave for the city. We have given my parents a great event to plan for and fill their days.

The week following our visit to my parents I'm extremely busy preparing for the Jakubitz preliminary hearing this coming Friday. I have interviews with the police members involved in April Smith's assault. I meet with the technicians who collected evidence and have many telephone conversations with Sergeant Edward Marlot, Sam's buddy.

I talk to the Spenars on the phone and they appear ready to testify. Shelly Galeno has been a great help to me in preparing for preliminary. She has contacted friends of April Smith's and interviewed them as character witnesses. She did the same for Mr. and Mrs. Spenar.

She has interviewed the physician and psychiatrist who cared for April Smith following the sexual attack, and will question them on the witness stand. I'm so thankful to Jim for Shelly's assistance.

It is Wednesday evening and I call Pamela to relate my good news about Sam's and my engagement. She says, "I'm so thrilled for you, Ashley."

I spend fifteen minutes just describing the ring. I tell her how Sam proposed and she thinks that Sam is terrific and old fashioned. I agree with her. I relate how everyone in the office kept interrupting me on Monday to see the rock. I'm thrilled.

Pamela asks, "Does that include Logan?" She is aware of his behavior in the past few months.

"No it doesn't. I haven't seen him lately."

She promises to meet me for lunch tomorrow.

On Thursday morning Shelly and I meet for three hours to review all the information we have compiled, and the order in which we will present it. She will contact everyone to ensure they know their scheduled time to testify. I share with her how disappointed I am that Irene Tolerno didn't call back with a decision to testify. I guess I wanted her to speak the truth; for her sake as much as for ours.

Pamela arrives at noon and because I'm pressed for time, we escape to the cafeteria downstairs. She keeps looking at and admiring my ring.

"I'm so happy for you. What a striking couple you two make. Have you set a date?"

"We haven't even discussed a wedding. There seems to be no time. After my parents you'll be the first person to be notified of the date. How are things going for you?"

"I'm doing what I wished for during university, making tons of money. Maybe I am coming to realize that money is not everything in life. The men I meet in my job are mostly business tycoons who want a little on the side. They are definitely not interested in permanent relationships. I have come to realize that, I too, want a lasting commitment."

We are interrupted by Marty Kroll. "Lovely ladies, mind if I join you for a few moments? I have ten minutes before my next meeting."

Pamela says, "By all means Marty, have a seat. How are you keeping? I haven't seen you at any of your usual hangouts recently. Find yourself a new gal? Who is keeping you entertained at home?"

Marty looks at me, "Your friend here just loves to fire the questions, but gives no time for a response. How are you Ashley? The word is you are being harassed by a former client of mine. Is this true?"

Pamela interrupts, "Never mind that. Ashley is engaged." I look up then and catch something flash across Marty's face. Was it annoyance, frustration or anger? It vanishes as quickly as it came. I can't be sure if it was real or imagined.

Marty states, "I guess congratulations are in order. I wish you the best." He checks his watch and announces, "I must leave for my meeting. Nice talking to you ladies."

As soon as Marty is far enough away from the table I comment to Pamela, "He didn't answer any of your questions."

"Just like a lawyer." She laughs. "He is such a handsome devil, but everyone in high places comment that he's very much a loner. You don't like him, right?"

"He's a brilliant lawyer, but there is no love lost between us. Anyway, I must return to my office to finish preparing for the preliminary hearing."

"I'll talk to you soon. Time passes too quickly. Three quarters of an hour gone just like that." Pamela snaps her fingers.

We hug and go our separate ways.

Sam picks me up after work, and because we don't feel like cooking we stop at a local family restaurant for an Italian dinner. The food is good. We eat quickly and leave a generous tip.

Both of us are exhausted and too tired to get into marriage suggestions tonight. Tomorrow is a big day for me with the beginning of Jakubitz's preliminary hearing. I believe it will take four days to present. This means we should complete on Wednesday next week.

The next day I arrive at my office early and Shelly is already there waiting for me. She is very eager, bright, and helpful. We work well together and when this trial is over, I must remember to inform Jim of her excellent contribution.

We rest our case four days later. It is Wednesday. Indictments are returned on the counts of sexual assault on April Smith and attempted sexual assault on Leona Spenar.

A trial date is set for Max Jukubitz.

The letter arrives a few days later. I open up the envelope and read, "You Will Die Slowly." The words are centered on one sheet of eight by eleven, white paper. They are formed from letters cut from newspaper and taped onto the sheet.

Realizing it will need to be dusted for prints, I drop the letter on the kitchen table and lower my body onto a kitchen chair. I stare out the window without registering the time of day, the weather conditions, or my whereabouts.

Closing my eyes I see the page containing the threat and I start to tremble. My teeth feel like they are rattling around in my mouth, and my skin is covered in perspiration. Every article of my clothing adheres to my body. My thoughts turn to Gail's murder and I feel nauseated.

Who is doing this to me? Is it Chartrand? Whoever it is, he has finally brought me to my knees. I am scared and so petrified. I am so petrified that I can't find the momentum to push out of the chair. I need to call Sam or the police, or drive to the police station.

I appreciate how busy the police force is and I know the best option is to drive the evidence to the station. My cognitive functioning returns eventually and I am able to calm myself. I need a cup of coffee to provide stability. Attempting to stand, I place a hand on the table to provide support. A rush of dizziness over-takes me and I remind myself to breathe. I take a few deep breaths and fill my lungs with air. When I feel steady on my feet, I walk toward the coffee pot and fill a large cup.

The coffee steadies me and I use tongs to place the sheet of paper and envelope into an oversized envelope. I seriously doubt my tormentor would forget to wear gloves, but he may have licked the envelope.

I finally decide to call Sam on his cell to get advice. He had to work late tonight, so I caught a ride home with a co-worker. Sam answers with concern in his voice, as ordinarily I don't call just to chat.

"Is everything okay?" He asks.

"I received a threatening letter in the mail today. Stupidly, I had my hands all over it. Should I drive it to the station or will you take care of it tomorrow?"

"Don't leave the house. I'll take care of it. What does it say?"

"It says, "You will die slowly." I'm very frightened and will be more than happy to stay put."

"Hang in there. I'll be home in about an hour. Check the security system and don't open the door to anyone. I'll look at the note when I get home." Sam says good-bye and we hang up.

Walking through the house I feel restless. Feeling caged in; I want to run. It has been a month since I had my morning jog. Sam works out but dislikes jogging. Occasionally he will go with me, but I don't want to pester him. Tonight, I spend time with the exercise ball to rid myself of this pent up frustration.

As promised, Sam is home in just under an hour. I can tell he is stressed. We have dinner and discuss the letter.

Sam first looks at the message on the paper and comments, "It's similar to the one telephone call. I hate to say this Ashley, but the message means torture."

"And torture means Chartrand." I feel sick.

"You're probably right."

"Who else would make a reference to cruelty?" I ask Sam.

"I don't know, but I promise you I'll do everything within my power to protect you."

He looks at the tape used to attach the newspaper letters to the paper. He comments, "This tape is the common stuff every drugstore, grocery store, and office supply shop sells. There will not be a lead there."

"That's what I thought As usual he gives us absolutely nothing."

"Our only hope is DNA if he licked the envelope. We'll search newspapers to determine which paper was used to cut out the lettering."

"If you get DNA Sam it will certainly tell us if we're after Chartrand."

"I certainly hope we get DNA results, because at least we'll know if this slime ball is responsible for terrorizing you."

"I feel myself shrinking. It's the weirdest thing. Like if I become really tiny then no one will be able to find and/or hurt me."

"You probably need to talk to someone in the health care system about your feelings. Have you thought about it?"

Why did I open my mouth? "I'm fine. Just a little tired."

We go to bed early and I fall asleep in Sam's arms. It is a restless night for me.

CHAPTER 34

▼

Mom and Dad call once or twice a week, insisting Sam and I set a date for the wedding. They are anxious to begin planning. Sam and I finally settle on an April wedding. There are numerous areas to plan for; therefore April should provide plenty of time and opportunity to meet the deadlines. Mom and Dad want a large wedding, whereas Sam and I would prefer a few friends and family. Mom and Dad win. It was not much of a contest.

It saddens and depresses me that Gail will not be here. We promised the maid of honor role at each other's wedding. I have recently invited Pamela to be my maid of honor. I left her a message and am waiting for a return call. She may be away on one of her business trips.

Sam has asked his best friend, Josh Drummond, to be his best man. Sam has no family to speak of and I feel badly for him. Mom told him the last time we were together, that he now has parents who love him. He is the son they never had. Feelings are certainly mutual. Sam often tells me how fortunate I am to be in such a loving, supporting, relationship with my parents.

Mom is busy booking the church, hall, food, and flowers, and compiling a guest list. According to her direction Dad is responsible for ordering the wine, cocktails, a bartender, and music, including booking a live orchestra for the dance and a four piece live string orchestra for the wedding ceremony and the reception. They have also insisted on paying for the entire wedding. Mom's statement, "We only have one daughter," ended our argument.

My parents expect three hundred guests. My list, combining work and outside friends, number sixty. Sam has twenty. My parents have lived in their town since birth and so the remaining two hundred and twenty guests are a combination of local people and family members. Dad comes from a large family of eight.

It has been a few weeks since I received the threatening letter, and I can now have thoughts other than protecting myself from my tormentor. Of course, the envelope contained no saliva and no DNA, and the fingerprints on the letter and envelope were badly smudged and of no use. A partial print was lifted from my light switch at work, but no other significant prints were found. The partial did not match anyone in the fingerprint bank.

Both Sam and I are extremely busy at work and the days are flying by. Chartrand is no longer the first thing that enters my mind when waking. Pamela calls one evening and accepts the invitation to be my maid of honor.

Shelly and I have spent the past few weeks preparing for trial. Max Jakubitz's defense attorney is Dawne Atcheson. She is in her late forties, with brown hair, and an attractive face. She is overweight but wears stylish clothes which suit her frame. She is one of a few criminal lawyers who I respect. Dawne is bright and has won her share of cases. I contacted her earlier in this case to discuss a plea bargain, but her client Jakubitz continues to maintain that Leona invited him into the Spenar home.

I encourage Shelly to do jury selection. I'm there to lend a helping hand if required. She chooses an outstanding jury consisting of seven females and five males.

It is time to have a meeting with Jim to update him on the Jakubitz trial. The chief of police is for some reason interested in this case. It's probably due to the mayor's run for the city re-election.

Jim's executive secretary answers my e-mail requesting a meeting and advises me that he has a cancellation at two. If I'm brief, she can fit me in for a fifteen minute meeting. I accept the two o'clock time slot.

At two I enter Jim's office with a hand full of notes. In addition to a verbal report, Jim likes a written summary of what has taken place in a trial preparation.

"Have a seat. What can I do for you today?"

"I'm here to update you on the Max Jakubitz case."

"Wonderful. I was wondering if things were running smoothly."

"As you know Jakubitz was caught in the act by the victim's husband. The husband hit him twice. The second punch resulted in the perpetrator hitting his head on a piece of furniture." I laugh, "He wants to sue the husband."

"Of course he would. And it doesn't surprise me anymore than prisoners screaming for steak four times a week; or the choice to use cocaine in prison; or having their girlfriend sleep with them every night. Totally ludicrous, but they don't see it that way."

"I heard about the federal penitentiary riot just outside Winnipeg. Some of your examples were the cause of the riot."

"Do you believe that Jakubitz is the serial sexual assaulter the police have been chasing for the past three years?"

"Yes I do."

"On what do you base your opinion?"

"First, all the attacks took place between twelve and one o'clock when he took his lunch hour. Second, they happened within the same area of the city that Jakubitz serviced. Third, he fits the profiler's description. Fourth, we received the DNA from Jakubitz's specimens and they match those found after April Smith's sexual assault. Fifth, Smith picked him in a photo line-up. She was attacked one year ago."

"What is the significance of the time and area of the attacks?"

"We have witnesses, coworkers of his who will testify that Jakubitz took his lunch hours between twelve and one o'clock but never ate with them. They will testify that they called his home on four or five different occasions, asking for him at the lunch hour and his wife always said he was at work. The fellows he worked with thought he was having an affair, but never followed him. The place of attack is significant, because the attacks were all on victims whose homes were on Jakubitz's garbage route."

"Great work."

"Thank you." I take a moment then continue, "There is another victim, but she refuses to testify. She may have been his first victim."

"If you couldn't convince her to testify, no one can. How is Shelly working out?"

I smile at Jim, "She is one of the reasons I requested this meeting. We have a diamond in our midst. Shelly is extremely bright, has great initiative, and is quick thinking on her feet. In jury selection, I could not have improved on her line of questioning. She's a keeper."

"It's wonderful to hear. I assume with your engagement there will be a wedding soon, then a child or two. I may require someone to replace you eventually, right?" Jim chuckles.

"You are not getting me to commit to this job through pregnancy and the raising of children so stop the threat of replacing me." I can laugh because I know how much Jim depends on me.

"Okay, I'm joking, but you can appreciate how much of a crap shoot it is when you hire someone. Take Logan, for example."

"No, you take him. I'm through spoon feeding him, Jim, and I want to state emphatically that I don't wish to work a single case with him in the future."

"Do you have reason for laying an official complaint against him?" He is looking at me intently.

There is silence for thirty seconds. I didn't prepare myself for this question. I say, "No."

Jim peers at me and I can tell he knows something unusual has taken place between Logan and I, but he drops the subject. He appears disappointed in me.

Instead of referring to Logan, Jim states, "Thank you for the update on Jakubitz and, of course, Shelly. I am grateful that you took her under your wing. Are you doing okay? Have there been more recent threats?"

"I received a threatening letter a few weeks ago. No evidence was obtained from the letter or envelope. Sam is doing a grand job protecting me."

"Keep safe Ashley. Thanks again."

On the way back I stop at Shelly's office and ask her to join me. Once we are seated with the door closed I state, "I had a meeting with Jim just now to discuss Jakubitz's trial, and to sing your praises. I believe you are performing extremely well on this case and told Jim I expect great things from you in the future."

Shelly's face flushes and she stares at me, remaining silent for a long minute. Finally she says, "Thank you. I am stunned, but very appreciative. I thank you, not only for the compliment but for passing your evaluation to Mr. Stromby. In fact I am so happy, that, well—do you have any windows at home that need washing?" We both laugh and Shelly goes back to her office.

Sam is waiting for me at 5:30. When I'm settled in my seat he turns to me and asks, "Would you mind if we join Josh for a drink at the boys' local watering hole?"

"Sure, I'm okay with that. But if you prefer to meet your friends for a drink, I don't mind if you drop me off at home first."

"Actually, Josh wants to meet you." I haven't spent much time in the company of Sam's friends.

"I would enjoy the company of a couple of men and I could use a glass of wine about now. There was a grand opportunity to report Logan today and I didn't take it."

"Has he been bothering you?" Sam's voice has become hard.

"No. In fact I haven't seen him in awhile. I did share with Jim that I never want an assignment with him in the future."

"That is excellent, Ashley. Here we are."

The bar is dimly lit but clean and looks like it could seat approximately one hundred people. I don't see another female in the place. As soon as Sam and I enter, there are five to six men who turn our way and stare at me. I see admiration in their eyes. Sam's face lights up and he appears very proud.

Taking my arm he leads me to a table where a very muscular man is seated. Josh has blond hair, cut short and blue eyes. He has a four inch scar running from just below his left eye to the jaw.

"Ashley, this is my buddy, Josh Drummond. Josh, this is the love of my life, my fiancée, Ashley Browne."

Josh grins at me and shakes my hand, "A pleasure to meet you, Ashley. I now understand why we haven't seen Sam in here for months. In fact, I had to search out another drinking buddy."

Josh laughs and I decide I like this friend of his. I ask him, "How long have you known him?"

"It has been at least five years, right Sam?"

"Yes. I came here one night and Josh needed a pool partner and I volunteered. The rest, as they say, "Is history." A great friend is Josh."

"I understand you are the best man at our wedding. Mom and Dad extend an invitation to you to stay overnight at their home."

Josh is about to respond when Sam interrupts with, "Josh, Ashley's mom is the best cook in the world. Her homemade pies are exquisite. Say yes to the invitation."

Josh looks at me and replies, "Yes, I accept the invitation. Please thank your parents for me."

We discuss the wedding. When we finish our drinks we say good-bye and leave for our respective homes.

I ask Sam, "I didn't notice a wedding ring on his finger. Does Josh have a girl-friend?"

"No, he recently broke an engagement after a two year relationship." He sounds sad for his friend.

"What happened?"

"His girlfriend wanted him to quit the force and do something else with his life. She really wanted him to register in the law program at the university."

"Are you serious?"

"Oh yes. They fought about it often. Finally Josh gave her the choice; either drop the suggestion of him leaving the job he loves, or take a hike. She decided on the hike."

I place my hand on Sam's arm, "How horrible for him. Obviously she didn't love him very much."

"The sad part is that he still loves her."

"I worry about you, as well, but I would never ask you to give up your career. I'm pleased that much of your time at work is in management, but I worry when you're out in the field. I can't imagine what it must be like to send your constable husband out every day into our ever increasing criminal world."

"I guess that is why many marriages end in divorce. I would guess that half the cops in my unit are divorced or separated."

"Do the women not understand the danger before they enter the relationship?"

"Initially they are wrapped up in the uniform and side arm. The muscular physique of the men probably plays a role as well. Most cops are tall and well built."

"I know. I just need to look and feel my man." At this I rub his bicep.

Sam says, "Stop that or I will stop this car right now for a little down in the car loving."

I laugh, "Later Sam."

We stop at the local video store to pick up a film I have wanted to see. We have dinner in front of the television watching our movie. Both are great.

CHAPTER 35

▼

The Jakubitz trial looms large and there is much media hype. Shelly and I are amazed to read headlines like, "Serial Rapist's Trial to Begin," and "Mayor Promising to Decrease Crime." Under the headlines the mayor is referring to Jakubitz's capture as if the police were directly responsible for him being caught.

My initial reaction to the chief of police's interest in this case is correct. He is a strong supporter of the mayor who is running for re-election. Politics is one of the reasons I wouldn't want Jim's position.

The trial begins tomorrow and Shelly and I are eager to get started. We are prepared. Jim calls to wish me luck, which is unusual because he doesn't customarily call before trial. Obviously the call is one of those, "Get a guilty verdict, or I will have the chief of police and the mayor on my back," warnings.

This evening Sam and I have an early dinner and watch one of our favorite programs on television. We are on the way to bed when the phone rings. I don't recognize the number on caller identification, although this doesn't mean it will be him. I quickly ask Sam if I should answer it and he nods.

I answer with conviction.

The raspy voice is there, "Ashley, he can't be there twenty-four/seven. Watch your back." The line goes dead.

Sam is studying me. "It was him, wasn't it? What did he say?"

"The asshole warned me to watch my back. He also said that you couldn't be with me twenty-four/seven."

"I should have answered instead of you."

"I'm not sure that would make any difference. Do you think he was calling to upset me before trial?"

"If it's Chartrand what difference would it make to him?"

"I don't know, but I did manage to get a guilty verdict against him. That bastard, he wants me waiting for a bullet or a knife in my back. Christ, when is this going to stop?"

Sam reaches for my hand, "I don't know. I keep thinking of ways to catch him. Like a phone tap is probably useless, because he's using a different cell phone each time. They're probably stolen and he's discarding them after each use. But I will have a technician over to tap our phone. One never knows. Come on, get some sleep. You have a big day tomorrow."

Sam sleeps soundly, but I just lie there staring at the ceiling as the hours crawl by. The last time I look at the alarm clock it reads 3:30.

It goes off at six and I feel terrible. Not a nice way to feel for my opening statement.

When I arrive at my office, Shelly has the information needed for the trial stacked in order of our schedule. What an angel she has been to this case. We take some time to discuss approaches to witnesses scheduled for tomorrow. We then leave for the courtroom. I share the latest telephone call with her.

Shelly looks professional in a lovely rose colored, wool suit, and a white blouse. I wear a navy and beige striped suit with a matching beige blouse. Our shoes and jewelry coordinate with our outfits. I notice Shelly's briefcase is tattered.

I present my opening statement, promising the jury that we will prove Max Jakubitz sexually assaulted April Smith and attempted to do the same to Leona Spenar. I explain that her husband prevented the complete sexual attack

During the next four days Shelly and I present our evidence to the jury members.

On day one, I establish Jakubitz's work routine by calling his boss and then three coworkers to the stand to testify to his absence at lunch hours.

On day two, I get testimony from April Smith as well as the police and technicians who worked her case. Through DNA evidence they link Jakubitz to her attack.

On the morning of day three, Shelly calls to the stand the workers who provided health services to Smith after the attack. The physician and psychiatrist give a grand testimony, under Shelly's guidance. In the afternoon she calls character witnesses for Smith. She has done a fantastic job in preparing everyone. I couldn't have improved on her presentation.

On day four, I call Leona Spenar to the stand first, followed by her husband. I have warned the sheriffs to keep an eye on Bill Spenar, because I know he still harbors a lot of anger against Jakubitz. As I approach him on the stand, I glance over at Jakubitz and realize what a difference there is in size. Looking at them both it is obvious only one punch was needed to stop Jakubitz.

Following my examination of Mr. Spenar it is lunch break, which I take up in my office. I am on the phone when I suddenly become aware of someone in the hallway looking into my office. Turning my chair, I lock eyes with Logan. He quickly walks away and I have shivers going down my spine. What the hell was that about? It bothers me and I recall the telephone call of four nights ago.

In the afternoon Shelly assumes control of the testimony from friends of Leona and Bill Spenar. They swear to the couple's integrity, honesty, and compassion.

We rest our case at 3:30.

For the next two days the defense takes command of the court and attempts to prove that in both the Smith and the Spenar situations the alleged victims invited Jakubitz into their homes. She admits sexual intercourse took place between him and April Smith but maintains it was consensual. Assault allegations were made by Ms. Smith only after the sexual encounter.

The defense also claims that Leona Spenar invited Max Jakubitz into her home to have sex with him and screamed, "sexual assault" after her husband's unexpected return home. Dawne has a weak case and she knows it. On cross-examination I rapidly destroy the testimonies of her witnesses.

On the seventh day of trial, Dawne and I present our closing statements to the jury. Shelly and I feel a guilty verdict is in the bag. I do tell Shelly to be careful in what she promises a victim, because it's impossible to predict a jury's decision.

The next day at 1:30 in the afternoon a verdict is reached in our favor. Jakubitz is found guilty on all counts. Shelly and I are disappointed in the sentencing. He is sentenced to five years, and will probably be eligible for parole in two.

I congratulate Shelly on a job well done. April Smith and Mr. and Mrs. Spenar thank us. They too are disappointed in the sentencing. When we exit the courtroom the news media are in a frenzy. We are kept busy for an hour. I later tell Shelly, this is the prize we receive for winning.

Three months have passed since Gail's murder and I continue to find it difficult to accept. At this time of the year it had become our tradition to shop together for the staff. We would purchase inexpensive, appropriate gifts for most of our coworkers. Gail took pleasure wrapping and distributing each gift. The staff appeared to appreciate her efforts. Gail signed the gifts from, "Ms. Claus," meaning me, and the "Elffette," referring to her. I miss her deeply.

With Chartrand roaming the streets it's difficult to feel confident enough to shop on my own. The threatening letter in early November and the telephone call didn't add to my sense of freedom. Last week Sam's technician came to the house to set the phone tap. We haven't received further calls from my stalker.

One day at lunch, fed up with the restrictions imposed by this villain, I venture out to a nearby jewelry shop to select a pair of gold cuff links for Sam as a Christmas gift. Two minutes later I notice Logan Reid examining some watches. I didn't notice his presence, when I entered the shop. Instead of ignoring him, I stroll over and ask in a friendly manner if he is purchasing a watch for himself.

Logan pivots and leans into me and says, "I do fancy a watch. Unfortunately, I haven't acquired or demanded the big bucks at work like someone I know." He laughs like it's a colossal joke.

Not certain how to react to his comment, I don't. Instead, I exit the store without my intended purchase. Why do I make the effort with him? Later, I wonder what he spends all his money on.

On the weekend Sam and I visit a large mall to shop for Christmas. It's a wicked decision and a foolish mistake on our part. We do manage to purchase a large screen, high definition, plasma television for Mom and Dad. The store will deliver it to our home, for a fee of course.

Christmas celebrations are at our house this year and Dad will find a way to get the television home, even if he has to carry it on his back. Sam tells me a friend of his, Ken, has a truck and would be pleased to deliver the television for a case of beer.

Sam and I decide to escape the mob at the mall and head home. We promise to continue our shopping on Monday and Tuesday evening. I need to purchase gifts for Pamela, Joan, Fred, Cora, Shelly, Gail's mother, and of course Sam. Joan is a high school friend who resides in the city with her husband Fred and one and a half year old daughter, Cora.

Sam wants to purchase gifts for his friends Bill, Cheryl, and Josh.

On Monday evening I find a lovely gold bracelet and matching drop earrings for Pamela. I have them gift wrapped. She will be pleased with this gift because she loves jewelry.

For Cora, Sam and I purchase a play tent. On the side of the box is written, easy assembly, in large print. I later discover easy for this company is spelled difficult. Four hours later, with welts on my arms and legs, from the easily flexible insert rods that constantly pop out and slap me at random, I scream for Sam. I've had it with the easy assembly.

Sam is in the computer/library room undertaking a gigantic research project for work. He laughs at me, but then suddenly stops when he sees the expression on my face. Sam manages to complete the assembly.

For Joan and Fred we purchase dinner theatre tickets. Joan loves to attend live theatre.

On Tuesday evening I buy a soft, pale rose housecoat for Gail's mom. She did share with me that in her home she is often chilly in the mornings. I'm aware that the elderly will decrease the thermostat at night.

For Shelly, I splurge and purchase an expensive burgundy leather briefcase. Her favorite color is burgundy and I noticed her carrying a tattered briefcase. Shelly put herself through law school and has huge bank loans. Purchasing a new briefcase wouldn't be at the top of her priority list.

On Thursday at noon I return to the jewelry store. I spotted on my last visit a gold medallion on a thick gold chain. It is ideal for Sam. I will add it to the gold cuff links. I join the line to the cash register with my service person waiting for me with my selections. There is an elderly lady in front of me, who is having difficulty with her credit cards. She finally gives them a debit, which is also declined. I notice the sales person is trying to remain calm. I'm prepared to skip the purchases for the second time, when the person makes a decision that the silver pin she was about to buy, is not for her after all. By this time the sales person's face is crimson. Sam is fortunate he will receive the medallion and cuff links at Christmas.

Sam's shopping has resulted in a gold lighter for Josh, who smokes, and a lovely crystal vase for Cheryl and Bill. He tells me their home is beautiful.

A week prior to Christmas, Sam and I invited Gail's mom, Pamela, Joan, Fred and daughter Cora, and as well as Josh, and Cheryl and Bill for a late dinner. It's an enjoyable evening with talk of art, travel, movies, books, cars, and kids. We take turns playing with Cora and her toys. It's the first time I have seen Sam with a child and it is wonderful to watch.

Bill and Cheryl are warm and friendly. Bill is of medium height, with a great build and a very handsome face. Cheryl is slim with brown hair and eyes. She has a lovely dimple in her chin which is not something one often sees in a female. It adds to her beauty. Both are dressed stylishly. Extremely intelligent, Bill and Cheryl entertain us with their travel stories.

I ask them, "Where in the world did you meet Sam?"

Bill answers, "A disgruntled employee who had been fired came into our building waving a gun. He fired it and injured one of the employees and escaped. One of Sam's men apprehended him on the outskirts of the city. As the president of the company, Sam and I had a few meetings about the incident and we clicked."

Cheryl adds, "Bill kept referring to this police sergeant he met, so I asked him to invite the man for dinner. We've had many a great time since then."

Josh also shares a tale or two about Sam when he was running wild.

When everyone departs Sam turns to me and shares, "Before you I never knew how wonderful it is to be a couple. Take tonight, for example: having people over for dinner and enjoying relaxing conversations with friends. Before you, my life consisted of bars and wild parties. I much prefer this lifestyle. I love this and you."

It is a perfect ending to a perfect evening.

The next morning Sam and I look over our gifts we received last night. Gail's mom gave us her homemade, matching, knitted, blue toques and scarves. Sam comments he has never received a gift before that was made specifically for him. From Pamela, Sam and I received a gift certificate for dinner for two at an expensive restaurant recently built in the city. Little Cora and her parents bought us a set of cocktail glasses which match my crystal. Josh brought us four very expensive bottles of red wine and Bill and Cheryl, a beautiful, large, white, linen, table cloth with twelve striped blue and white napkins.

On Christmas Eve, Mom and Dad arrive loaded down with presents, baking, and a lovely tree. A week earlier Sam inquired about the lack of a Christmas tree, and I told him that our family's tradition is to decorate a tree as a family on Christmas Eve. We sing carols and enjoy eggnog.

Tonight, I take out the decorations while Mom makes the eggnog and Sam and Dad stabilize the tree. It is heart warming to watch Sam as he joins in the festivities by singing and hanging garland and ornaments. Happy experiences he missed as a child. My heart goes out to him. We retire early. All of us are looking forward to tomorrow.

On Christmas morning we arise early. Mom has cooked strawberry pancakes and bacon for breakfast. We eat heartily then move to the great room. Sam is like a small child, grinning from ear to ear. We had wrapped a gigantic red bow and ribbon around the big screen television and placed it on a dolly Sam borrowed from his friend, Ken.

We now push it from our bedroom into the great room. When we wheel it in absolute glee is expressed by Mom and Dad. It is worth every penny we spent. They are beyond grateful; like small children with their first tricycles.

Sam loves the cuff links and medallion which he asks me to place around his neck. It looks wonderful on him and he keeps touching it as if to ensure that it is still there. He is not accustomed to wearing jewelry. I know he will never remove this piece, because I had it engraved "Love Forever Ashley," on the back.

Mom and Dad's couple gift to us are tickets to a concert by our favorite group. They have, in addition, bought Sam an electric razor and a stylish black leather jacket. To me they give a very fashionable, lined, black, leather coat, which fits perfectly and looks absolutely stunning.

Sam is overwhelmed at their generosity. I observe tears in his eyes.

He is nervous as I open his gift. It is a delicate gold chain which holds an oblong gold tablet with inserts of two large diamonds. On the back are the words, "Forever Yours Sam." I am deeply touched. It brings tears of joy to my eyes.

In front of my parents I stand and say, "I love you Sam."

What a wonderful Christmas this has been.

The day after Christmas, Sam calls his friend, Ken, to ask if he would consider delivering a large screen television, to a town approximately an hour away from the city. Ken agrees and comes to pick up Sam and the television.

Ken is in his mid thirties, handsome with black hair, and hazel eyes. He works for the postal system and has been Sam's buddy since his arrival in Edmonton. I'm finding Sam has many great friends.

Mom and Dad follow the boys in their car. They are so excited and previously asked Sam if he can set it up for them. Sam's friend, Ken, is very familiar with electronics, and offers to do that in exchange for a slice of the pie, which Sam is always raving about.

When Sam arrives home he says to me, "Thank you for the best Christmas I have ever experienced. I will remember it forever. It has erased all the horrible memories I carried around for years. Today they are gone."

I smile at him and say, "I assume Mom fed you and Ken." When he nods I continue, "Let's go lie down in bed for a while and rest."

Sam laughs out loud and says, "You have such a way with words."

Two hours later we leave our bed. I fix a light snack and we start watching the evening news. The phone rings and it is Mom. "Ashley, we just received a weird phone call."

My heart starts to pound rapidly and I almost drop the phone. Sam is staring at me with raised eyebrows. I ask, "What do you mean by a weird call?"

"Well, the phone rang once and I said, "Hello," and the person hung up. It rang immediately after I hung up and when I answered the person said, "Is Ashley there?" I asked the caller who he was and he hung up again."

Oh my God, my worst nightmare is happening. I'm dizzy and feel like throwing up. I remember to breathe to get oxygen into my lungs and the dizziness disappears. I ask, "What did he sound like? Was his voice deep, high pitched, loud, soft, or raspy?" Please Mom, do not say raspy. I am now praying to myself.

"The voice did not sound like any of those you mentioned. It actually sounded very normal to me. To tell you the truth, I thought it sounded like Kevin, but I can't be sure."

"Mom, the voice was not raspy?"

"No, it was not. Don't worry about us dear. We have never shared this with you because of your attitude toward guns in the home, but Dad does have a rifle. He knows how to use it and can protect both of us."

"Oh Mom, I hope this is just a coincidence and Kevin is attempting to talk to me before the wedding. If anything else appears out of the ordinary please call us immediately. I mean that."

"I will. Good night."

When I hang up I shriek, "I can't take this any longer! You catch that bloody bastard soon, Sam, or you will have to admit me to Ponoka's psychiatric hospital. I'm not joking. Someone phoned Mom."

"Come here and sit beside me." I stumble towards him and Sam catches and picks me up and gently lays me down on the sofa.

"Take a few deep breaths and then relax. I'm going to massage your feet and hopefully you will relax and sleep."

I look at him as if he's crazy. "I can't sleep at a time like this. Do you know what this might mean?"

"Yes, I do know what it means. What exactly did the caller say?"

"He asked for me. Mom thinks it might have been Kevin."

"Was the voice raspy, because if it wasn't then I would think it would not be your tormentor?"

"No, it wasn't. What difference would that make for crap sake?"

"You are upset so are not thinking clearly. If it was your tormentor, he would have spoken in a raspy voice to send you spinning out of control."

"You're so bright. Thank you." I start to relax.

Sam rubs my feet, and surprisingly, I sleep.

CHAPTER 36

▼

New Years Eve has come and gone. Sam and I celebrated the evening with Bill and Cheryl at the Petroleum Club. We danced the night away. This couple is very entertaining and a delight to be with.

Today is Saturday and a very relaxing one for me. Sam and I spent the afternoon together, but this evening he is attending what he calls a card game session at one of his friend's home. He will spend the night at his apartment. I wonder how much drinking takes place at one of these sessions.

I'm in my favorite arm chair, feet up, listening to a Celine Dion song and reading my favorite author. I glance at my watch and see it's ten o'clock. I decide to continue reading in bed, as soon as I complete this chapter. Counting, I have another six pages to go.

The lights abruptly go out. The stereo system goes silent. My first thought is of my tormentor, and I panic. I jump from the chair and run toward the front door. I stop suddenly, realizing that if this is him he's smiling at my reaction. It's also black and I can't see.

I'm petrified, but risk a fumbling crawl to the kitchen in search of a flashlight. Candles are placed throughout my home, but I'm terrified of leaving a light on as the psycho may be peering in the window. I finally locate the flashlight and crawl across the room. I sit with my back pressed against the kitchen cupboard. My heart is racing.

I don't move, and am not conscious of time. Fully aware of the total darkness, I attempt to control my ragged breathing, which if I'm not careful will render me unconscious from hyperventilating.

My objective is to listen intently for any unusual sound, any movement or breathing. I hear a ticking type sound near the kitchen door. Perspiration starts rolling down my face and back. Sitting perfectly still I hold the flashlight tightly in my right hand. I can use it as a club if needed. I eventually realize the ticking is my wall clock, hanging just right of the kitchen door. I'm so frightened my mind is starting to play tricks on me.

My cognitive functioning is slowly returning, and I register the fact that the phone is on the counter just above my head. I inch up slowly and grasp it and slide back to the floor. Elated with this accomplishment I shine the flashlight on the phone and dial 911. I then place the receiver to my ear. Nothing happens. There is no ring, no sound, and no dial tone. Fumbling, I try again. I can't believe this is happening and realize I'm dead. If he doesn't kill me, I'll die from a heart attack.

I crawl to the great room to feel for and test that phone. It too has no dial tone. I'm now in shock. What do I do? Where, the hell is this madman, and what is he doing? Who will help me now? Is he in the house? How do I prevent him from killing me? Think, Ashley, think.

First, control your breathing. Deep breathes, Ashley. You can do this. I keep telling myself to repeat the deep breathing procedure until I'm able to think clearly. I recall my cell phone is in my purse, which is sitting on the night stand in the bedroom. I am saved, you demented asshole. I'm elated.

Crawling in the direction of our bedroom, I slam my head into the corner of an end table. Wanting to cry out from the pain, I choke back the scream. He may be in the house. I must be silent. I lie flat on the floor where dizziness and nausea overtake me. I stay perfectly still, attempting to control the urge to vomit.

Sometime later I reach my purse, only to discover my cell phone is missing. How did that animal get into my office and when? We are warned to lock our purses in a cabinet drawer, but often when busy I just stick it on top of one of my file cabinets. It's too late to scold myself. I find it difficult to believe he has planned this so perfectly. He will kill me today. Impossibly, my fear accelerates.

I need a weapon because I'll not leave this world without a fight. I crawl back to the kitchen, pausing every so often to listen. The only sound I hear is the rapid beating of my heart. I retrieve a butcher knife and return to the bedroom. I close and lock the door, then haul an arm chair over to prop against it.

I walk slowly over to the window and push aside the drape a fraction of an inch. I peer into the black, back yard. I see no movement. I notice lights on in the neighbor's house and neighborhood. Clearly, the power problems are limited to my home, and this confirms that the psycho is out there terrorizing me.

I sit on the floor and face the door. I lean against the foot of our bed and hold tightly to the knife in my right hand and the flashlight in the other. Occasionally, I flick on the flashlight and light up the door, to see if someone is turning the knob. In my panic, I forgot to check the security system. It may save my life tonight.

I think about Sam and how devastated he will be if my stalker does get into the house. I have at this point given into the fear and wear it as a second skin. If this was the first threat, I know I would feel differently. But months of this have rendered me helpless. I hope I will be brave and not beg for mercy.

I realize the house is getting cold because the power is off. I grab a quilt and wrap myself in it. We haven't had any snow in the past few weeks and all the roads are clear, but the air is still cold. For hours I sit staring into the darkness, until eventually, I fall asleep.

Stiffness and the cold air wake me, and for a moment I wonder what has happened. It comes rushing back to me like a slap in the face. It is remarkable how daylight gives one courage and comfort. I manage to lift myself off the floor and I peer outside the window. I'm about to push aside the chair and open the bedroom door, when I hear a panicked voice calling my name. It is Sam.

I quickly remove the chair and unlock the door. Sam is moving down the hallway, but stops suddenly when he observes the swaying knife in my hand. He exclaims, "What the hell is going on?"

"Chartrand was here last night! He shut off the electricity and cut the phone line! It's dead. My cell is missing too. I have never been so afraid! I have been sitting in my bedroom waiting for him!"

"Was he in the house? Did you see him?" He gently removes the knife from my shaking hand and his arms encircle me.

"No, but I'm positive it was him. We have to do something. I can't take this!" I start to cry.

"I'm so sorry I wasn't here." He holds me tighter.

When my sobbing stops Sam studies my face then asks, "What happened here?" as he gently rubs a finger over my forehead.

"I banged my head into the corner of a side table while crawling on the floor in total darkness. Don't ask why I was crawling." To myself I now think the reason I chose to crawl was to remain as invisible as possible. Chartrand may have been peering into any window.

"I will search the house now Ashley, then check outdoors. Meanwhile, use my cell and notify the police. It's freezing in here and we must get the electricity turned on soon before your water pipes freeze."

I ring the police station and file a report. I'm told someone will be right there. Ten minutes later a marked car with two officers arrives and I am interviewed by Constable Sharleen Lesyshen. The other officer, Michelle Smith, follows Sam outside.

I ask Constable Lesyshen to follow me into the kitchen, where we can use the kitchen table for the interview. She is in her late thirties, has long, brown hair rolled up into a bun, and kind eyes. I apologize about not having coffee, which is impossible to make without the electricity.

"Would you like a juice instead? I'm having an orange juice."

"Not right now. Thank you Ms. Brown. At what time did the lights go off in the house?"

"Approximately ten minutes after ten last evening. I was reading and had just glanced at my watch a few minutes prior."

"When did you check your phone?" Sharleen Lesyshen is writing my responses in her black, note book.

"Approximately ten minutes later, when I had crawled to the kitchen." Sharleeen stares at me, so I decide to clarify.

"You see constable, I have been terrorized for many months and I think my stalker was responsible for last night. I was afraid to walk upright and give him a bigger target."

"I'm so sorry. Did you see or hear anything?"

"No, I didn't hear or catch any glimpses of the man responsible. I shudder to think what would have happened if I had."

"Do you own a cell phone?"

"Yes I do, but someone took it from my purse. I believe it was taken while I was at work."

"You work where?" She knows but must ask, so I give her the address and phone number.

"Is there anything more you can share with us?"

Suddenly I'm angry, "Yes, catch the bastard before he kills me."

Sharleen looks at me with sympathy in her eyes and replies, "I'm sure Sergeant Orlicky is trying. Thank you Ms. Browne." She leaves to join her partner outside.

I'm now angry with myself for snipping off like that. But I am so sick of this fear and just want to scream forever.

After they leave Sam comes in and reports that no foot prints are visible. He expresses doubt that the crime technicians, who are on their way over, will locate any fingerprints. He notifies the phone and electrical companies and requests emergency services. The house is getting colder by the minute.

By early Sunday evening the phone company has repaired the cut phone line and the electrician has replaced the outdoor electrical panel box. The house is back to normal. I'm not. Will I ever be?

Sam and I discuss how bold the attacker is to have actually approached my house and steal my cell phone from my office. Either it's Chartrand in disguise or it's someone from my office. The police officers are going door to door interviewing the neighbors. They later report nothing unusual had been noticed.

I question Sam. "Do you think the psycho was in my yard for any length of time watching me?"

"No, I don't. It would be too dangerous for him to do that. But he may have observed your property with night binoculars, from a convenient spot in the park. I sent an officer to walk the outer perimeter of the park that faces this direction. Did you hear anything?"

"Yes, every damn creak in this place. But no other sounds. I was reading and listening to some music when the power went off, leaving me in total darkness. Panic took over. During the many hours I was awake in my bedroom, I came to the conclusion that this type of terror is driven by hatred. This hatred is directed entirely at me, not my family or you, thank God. Sam, who do you think hates me to this extent?"

He replies, "Chartrand is still my educated guess."

"Yes, of all the demented minds I helped place behind bars, none were as evil as that man."

Sam replies, "Kevin needs further scrutiny, but my bet is still on Chartrand. Anyway, let's catch some shut eye. I need just a couple of hours."

A police officer later returns and reports that he has located a spot in the park where my home is visible. The grass in the area was trampled, as if someone had stood there for some time. Sam inquires as to whether the officer marked off the area with crime scene tape and receives an affirmative. Sam calls for a technician to visit the designated area.

During the week, I'm plagued by nightmares; one in which Chartrand is peering in my bedroom window. His face is massive and fills the entire window area. These red eyes are rimmed with black circles and emit shots of light rays, which burn any object on contract.

Sam shakes me awake and holds me tightly. He whispers soothing words to me. My fear lessens. The words help when I'm awake, but as soon as sleep overtakes me, so do the nightmares.

Mid-week, Sam insists I see my physician for a light sleeping pill, because I have averaged two hours of sleep per night. Work has been unproductive and I'm abrupt with everyone. The sleeping pill helps somewhat and I'm now sleeping approximately four hours a night.

On the way home from work on a Thursday, Sam asks if I would mind if he invited a few friends over to play cards one evening. I reply, "Of course not. Imagine having a group of handsome men in our home." I'm happy for him and know having friends over will boost his spirits.

"On second thought, cancel that request." We both laugh.

It is Friday and tonight is Sam's card evening. He has purchased enough beer to feed an army and approximately twenty bags of chips, nachos, and cheese twists. I slice a variety of cheese, meat, and add crackers.

I have met Josh, Bill, and Ken previously. Although Sam has spoken of him often, I have never met Kurt. Kurt Morse works at an Edmonton penitentiary. He is single, but has a girlfriend. Kurt is of medium height, muscular, and handsome. He has the nicest smile. All the men arrive by taxi, so I anticipate a late night. At least they'll not be drinking and driving.

The guys are playing poker using chips for their betting. I don't know if they later exchange the colored chips for money. Nor do I want it clarified, because gambling of this nature is illegal if money exchanges hands.

I spend the evening reading my book in the great room and am about to head for bed when Sam and Kurt come into the room. Sam states, "The other fellows have taken their taxi home. I asked Kurt to stay for a little while, so the two of you can get to know each other a bit."

Kurt comments. "From what Sam has told me about you, I think he is one lucky fellow."

"Thank you Kurt. You are a charmer. If we are dishing out compliments then let me inform you that Sam thinks you are wonderful. A great friend and a comedian, he tells me."

"Well, actually the more drinks I have the funnier I am to everyone but my mother."

He smiles at me. He is like a teddy bear.

"I can empathize with her. I understand you work within our prison system."

"Yes, I do. To be honest lately I find it difficult to leave home and report for duty. I feel squeezed dry of emotion by the inmates and wonder how much longer I can hang in. I'm older than Sam, but still have a hell of a long way to retirement."

"You are probably suffering from burn out. I'm there as well. People who don't work closely with the scum of the earth like you and I, may not understand what it is like."

"You are right. It scares me when I see one of these rapists or child molesters being discharged back into our communities, because I know there is a good chance I will see them again. And every time they return they have left a trail of mentally and physically broken bodies behind them."

"I can see it in your eyes Kurt, the sadness is there. I, at least, can replenish my soul with the positive feedback I receive from my victims after a guilty verdict is reached."

"Yes, I hear you get your fair share of them. Keep up the great work. I have enjoyed our conversation and hope we can have others. Sam, can I use your phone to call a cab?"

"Yes. Come over any time and bring your girlfriend."

"I will. Nice meeting you, Ashley."

After Kurt leaves Sam and I talk about the evening. He appears happy and I'm glad for him, because I have been a bear lately. It is after one in the morning when our heads hit the pillow.

CHAPTER 37

▼

The ringing of the phone drags me from a deep sleep. I lift the receiver and whisper, "Hello."

"Hi, it's Pamela. Sorry if I woke you. I arrived back from a short trip to Vancouver yesterday. I'm thinking a shopping spree would be ideal for today. Rays are out and wind is down. There is nothing but blue, blue, sky. We can attack a shopping center and look for honeymoon outfits and such. Then we can follow it up with your favorite, a lobster dinner."

"What time is it? My body didn't meet the bed until two this morning and I feel wasted."

"It's nine." She chuckles, than says, "You should allow that man of yours some sleep at night."

A smidgen of guilt washes over me for a split second. I have slept seven hours. The guilt soon vanishes, when I recall that the last time I slept a solid seven hours was approximately three months ago.

I answer Pamela with, "Okay girl you're on. Give me two hours to shower, grab a light breakfast, and drive to the shopping center. I'll meet you at the south east door at eleven. Keep your cell phone on in case I get tied up with an emergency. This sounds like fun."

"Great. See you at eleven."

Sam left early this morning for work. We stayed up late last night talking after the boys left. Sam was not very energetic when he had to wake up at seven this morning. He told me he would be late coming home this evening as well, so Pamela's suggestion for today is a good one.

Following my shower, with the bathroom door bolted, and a quick breakfast, I choose a long sleeved, cotton, white blouse with a pair of grey, lined, wool slacks. With the air conditioning I find the shopping centers cool on most winter days. A quick glance in my full length mirror and I'm out the door.

I call Sam from my cell phone. He is working on a Saturday; because an increase in violent crime in our city and surrounding area has increased his case load. He doesn't respond, so I leave a message. I'm worried about him suffering burn out; because he has been working many Saturdays of late.

The drive from home to the center takes half an hour. I check my rear view mirror often, but can't make out anyone following me. I have seven minutes to spare but, Pamela, dressed smartly in a black, pant suit and white blouse, is waiting. We exchange greetings and hug and we are off.

The afternoon passes pleasantly. This girl sharing thing is just what the doctor ordered. We have hit every lingerie shop and Pamela insists I purchase two outfits. We have also spotted a perfect dress for me to wear the day following the wedding. I buy it without hesitation.

The wedding gown shopping and selection is being saved for mother and daughter. Since I was a small girl, Mom has talked to me about the fun we would have shopping for a gown for my wedding.

Pamela buys red, skin tight, swim trunks for Sam to wear on our honeymoon. She says, "It's my wedding present to him." This gift doesn't surprise me. It's typical Pamela.

Later we are in a large department store and because I haven't seen Pamela in some time; I start looking for her. I glance quickly to my right and notice a man abruptly turn his face away from me. He is wearing a dark baseball cap low, shadowing his facial features. He moves briskly to the department store exit into the major hallway in the shopping center. Soon, he is lost in the crowd.

An eerie feeling washes over me, as I recall this same image from two other stores we shopped at today. I can't shake the feeling that he has been following me.

Suddenly, I feel the fear and desperately look around for my friend. I feel alone and vulnerable.

A few minutes later we find each other and it's a unanimous decision that dinner is calling. We are exhausted.

I decide not to mention my stalker to her at this time. We are in the midst of the late afternoon shoppers, and I know she will freak out and start shouting about killing the bastard. The last thing I need in my life right now is a scene in one of the largest shopping centers in the world.

We drag our packages to our respective vehicles, and proceed to the south side lobster restaurant. I keep checking the rear view mirror to see if I'm being followed.

We arrive safely at the restaurant and order the Lobster Feast. We dig in with pleasure. After dinner we both are stuffed and tired. I decide it's an appropriate time to mention the man in the department store.

"Don't panic and make a scene, but when we were in the last department store I believe my stalker was there. When I noticed him he immediately left the store, and I lost sight of him in the crowd."

"What?" exclaims Pamela, "And you didn't say anything to me. He could have run you off the road."

I reach across the table and cover her hand with mine. I say, "Keep it down or we'll get thrown out of here."

"Did you see his face?" she asks shocked.

"No. He wore a baseball cap pulled low over his face. It was just like in the underground parking lot."

"That scene scares me. I know you and what your work has exposed you to over the years. If you have a feeling about what happened today, go with it. Man, I wish he'd been there when we met up in the store. I would have killed the little slug for you."

"That is the point. He isn't little."

"I think you should call Sam." She is reaching for her cell phone.

"I am not calling him. He is behind with his cases and is in the field today. He is not able to provide protection for me. It's different when he's at home."

"How big is this jerk?"

"He is approximately the same size as Sam. Many people fit into the same height and weight. Including a few you know like Logan Reid, Marty Kroll, Marshall Pickten, and Paul Strychuk. Of course, Billie Chartrand fits the size as well. The other man you don't know is a jerk named Kevin Manguard, who has been following me around. There are thousands of men who can fit."

"You said the man who chased you in the underground parking lot wore a cap as well. Obviously it's the same person as today."

"Yes, the shape of the man in the parking lot was exactly the same shape as the one this afternoon."

"That is scary, Ashley."

She is staring at me with a frightened look on her face.

"I'm sure everything is fine. It's just my over active brain making mountains out of mole hills."

"Okay, but I am following you home and no argument. It's the end of this story."

"I accept and thank you." I grab the check as it's on me today. I leave a generous tip and we make for our vehicles.

There has been a change in the weather. The wind is gusting and light snow is falling. I'm frightened and appreciate Pamela's offer.

"I will wait until the light comes on in the house," Pamela whispers as she heads for her car. I want to ask why she is whispering, but decide to drop it. She may have a point.

The drive home is uneventful and once in the house I turn on a few lights and wave from the living room window. My purchases of the day consist of a red, wool blazer, a lovely blue, silk dress to wear on our honeymoon in the Bahamas, two negligees, a pair of runners, a set of satin sheets, and a couple of crystal brandy snifters. Sam occasionally enjoys a brandy.

It takes fifteen minutes to put away my purchases. I lie down on the sofa with a glass of wine in front of me. I'm full from dinner and tense from my encounter in the department store. I need rest and relaxation. I drink half my wine and promptly fall asleep.

A noise jerks me awake. Was that a knock on my patio window? Or was I dreaming? The drapes are open on the patio doors.

Did I lock the patio door? Shit, I don't remember checking the security. It's very dark out.

I lay perfectly still, for what seems like an eternity. My nerves are shot and I'm shaking like a leaf. I slowly turn my head to peer into the darkness. I seem to be rooted to the sofa. My heart is pounding in my ears

I think about being a prisoner in my home; afraid to move. It's not sufficient that he has confined me to staying home, but now I am frightened here as well. Slowly my anger builds and I jump up from the sofa, and head to the patio doors.

I shut off the security system and yank the doors open. I shout into the darkness, "You bastard! You twisted freak! Come out of hiding. Face me like a man, not a yellow, striped skunk lurking in the darkness!"

I take a deep breath and continue, "You are a coward, a demented freak, a monster, and a misfit! I hope you rot in hell!"

There is nothing, no sound except the wind whistling through the trees. It's spooky. I realize I have lost it. Quickly, I slam the doors, lock them, and put on the security. I glance into the darkness before nearly ripping the drape cords from their mooring.

Furious, I'm just furious and I kick an ottoman and hurt my toe. I refuse to be frightened in my own home. There have been unexplained creaks and the like in my house in the past, which I have ignored. Since the asshole cut my telephone line and shut off the electricity, I find myself reacting to every sound. I now tell myself to let it rest but the anger remains. So does my fear

There is a dim light on in the great room, so whoever was out there could have been watching me sleep. The perverted bastard was peering in my windows. The thought makes my skin crawl. I want to strangle the lunatic and find I'm holding my breath again.

Sam arrives home shortly after ten and I share my two stories with him. He first rants about being out in public on my own. I remind him that I wasn't alone.

He ventures outside and does an initial assessment. When he returns his voice is filled with concern.

"There are fresh prints in the snow leading to the back gate. I need my camera and a tape measure." He grabs his camera and I hand him the tape measure. He switches on the patio spot lights, takes photographs of the shoe imprints, and then measures the left and right imprints. Sam can't wait for the experts to take photos, because it has started to snow heavily.

On his return he says, "I will check again tomorrow in the daylight."

"Were the shoe imprints large?"

"I would estimate a size eleven."

I don't share with Sam my opening of the patio doors and ranting into the darkness. It was a very foolish and dangerous thing to do. Now that some of the anger has gone I fully realize what I did.

"What exactly did the noise sound like?"

"I was sleeping at the time, but I think it was a knock on the glass."

"It means he was standing by the door and wanting you to be aware of his presence. It's all about fear with him."

"He is getting closer, isn't he?"

"Yes, he is. Please be careful no matter where you are."

Sam walks to me and gently kisses my lips. I grab and hold onto him. He makes me feel strong.

We retire to the bedroom and he wants to see my purchases. I inform him that he can't until the honeymoon. I add, "If I model a negligee you'll not leave it on me anyway. Am I not desirable without it?"

Sam laughs. "You always are to me."

Tonight we don't make love. He holds me tightly and I feel safe in the comfort of his arms until sleep comes.

CHAPTER 38

▼

What a bitch she is. I call her every disgusting name and term I can think of. She wants a man? One day soon she will see and know how big a man I actually am. Won't she be surprised?

How dare she call me a twisted freak and a misfit? Oh, she will suffer for her mouth, while I slash away at her body. At the end I may just place my hands around her neck and squeeze. She was looking so innocent, asleep on the couch. Proves you never judge a book by its cover. Now that is hilarious.

I should have kidnapped her tonight, but I still love this game too much. Allowing her to relax; to be in a threat free environment then yanking her chain. My planning is without flaw, it is excellent.

They will not catch me. I am brighter, smarter, shrewder, and quicker on the uptake. This is so much fun.

I want to smell her fear up close, see her sweat before I execute the grand finale. Or I may just kill her the next time. There are so many options and I lay in bed at night thinking about them all.

I appreciate her anger. I know where she is coming from. I lived that fear and feel the same anger toward her. We have more in common than she thinks. Yes, soon it will be payback time.

That useless cop of hers will never be able to protect her from me. In the past month, I could have snatched her away from him on nine or ten different occasions. He is no match for me.

As I move away from her house strolling like I belong in the neighborhood, I realize I must be more careful than I was in the department store today. Ashley almost saw my face. If she had, she would be dead.

CHAPTER 39

▼

Days are flying by both at work and home. At home wedding plans are going smoothly. Mom has all bookings confirmed. We discuss the menu for the wedding dinner. Mom's friend, Mona, is in charge of the meal and late evening menu.

Mom asks, "What is your opinion on a garden salad, a choice of pork tenderloin and/or chicken, roasted potatoes, a mixture of baby carrots and baby corn, steamed asparagus, and hot cheese buns for the dinner?"

"It sounds wonderful Mom. My mouth is watering just thinking about it."

"Mona and I spent a few hours in discussion, both on the food choice and cost. She has been so helpful to me."

"What will you offer for dessert?"

"We will have a choice. Strawberry cheesecake and/or chocolate mousse will be offered." She knows they are Sam's favorites.

"Knowing Sam he'll eat an entire strawberry cheesecake on his own. That man has such an appetite."

"I love every minute of it; when the two of you visit and Sam has a second helping. He doesn't carry extra weight around."

"I know, I was just joking. What are your plans for the late evening menu?"

"In the evening we will have hot hors d'oeuvre, a selection of cold meat, and a variety of cheese and crackers. The ladies from church are baking and donating the desserts for the evening. Mona organized that."

"It all sounds fantastic. Will the ladies from church be slighted if I donate money to your church organization?"

"Of course not, dear. It's very kind of you to make the offer. Mona would be more than pleased if you gave her the donation after the dinner. She has worked hard to organize everything."

"What about the flowers?"

"You remember Joan and Bob. They are great friends of ours and used to own the local flower shop."

"Yes. I do. Joan sang with you in the church choir."

"Anyway, they go south for the winter but will be back in time for Joan to help me with the flower selection."

Dad has the wine, cocktails, and both orchestras lined up. Two of his friends and two nephews have offered to tend the bar.

Mom states, "The string orchestra is from the city and you know that Dad called your friend Donna to play at the reception and dance."

I met Donna during my university days, and she has agreed to play for the evening dance. She is very attractive, with long, brown hair, deep brown eyes, and with a voice I love. The two of us shared an apartment for a couple of years, during the time I attended law school. She and her band can do pop, country, and jazz which should please everyone. Donna, her husband and two children now live in Abbotsford, British Columbia, but she is willing to come to Alberta to sing at my wedding. I'm so happy Dad and I thought of her, for the big day.

This morning Mom and I are going shopping for a wedding gown, while Sam and Dad check out a tuxedo rental.

Two weeks ago Pamela and I found a perfect maid of honor gown for her. I bought a fancy, but comfortable, pair of wedding shoes.

Mom promises the town's hair salon is excellent and booked the three of us for the morning of the wedding. I did receive a raised eyebrow from Pamela when I mentioned this, but no formal complaint.

My cousin, a professional photographer, is taking the wedding pictures free of charge as a gift to Sam and me. How wonderful of her to be so generous. I'm lucky Dad comes from a family of eight.

Mom and I drive to the first bridal shop, but don't find the perfect dress. We venture from shop, to shop, to shop. Mom wants fancy and I prefer plain. We can't find anything classy and in between.

All the time I'm shopping I am very aware of people around me. When I spot a man in a ball cap I freeze. Mom finally asks, "What is wrong with you Ashley? You are so jumpy."

I answer, "It's nothing. I'm just exhausted and I suggest we stop for a latte and a muffin."

Mom eagerly agrees and drops the subject of my anxiety. I keep forgetting that she is sixty-eight and might be tired. During our latte break, I decide to voice an idea that's been on my mind.

"Mom, I would be honored to be married in your wedding gown. Would you consider lending it to me?"

Before I can continue Mom is out of her chair grabbing me, "Of course, of course, what a wonderful idea. Oh thank you, thank you, my dear." Our affectionate display has the restaurant customers staring at us.

I ignore them and continue. "I may have to alter it. I think I'm slightly bigger across the bosom."

To which she replies, "That is because my bosom is at my knees."

I sit there with my mouth hanging open. Mom rarely makes comments like this. Then, I laugh until my stomach hurts.

When I get myself back in some semblance of control we decide that Sam and Dad have to pick up Mom's wedding gown tonight. Mom can't wait for tomorrow or next week. Besides, Mom says, it'll provide a grand opportunity for Dad and Sam to get to know each other better.

When we arrive home, Mom rushes in to tell Sam and Dad they are driving now to retrieve a wedding dress. They look at her with puzzled expressions. She ignores the expressions and Dad is warned that Sam is not to see the dress. Mom promises to have dinner prepared by their return. They leave promptly.

She advises that she has received two hundred and fifty-two positive replies to the invitations. Mom asks, "What plans do you have for decorating at the community hall where the reception is being held?"

"I was thinking that you can decide what decorations to use for the walls. If possible, have the color blue as part of the presentation. For table center pieces I would like floating candles. Pamela and I will assemble them and get them to you in advance. Someone will just need to add water. What do you think?"

"Sounds like a great idea to me."

We cook a ham, scalloped potatoes, and a vegetable salad. Mom brought two home made apple pies with her and we will serve one with dinner. Sam will gladly eat the other tomorrow.

He never stops complimenting Mom about her baking and often I tease him. My favorite expression is, "A man knows that the only way to a mother-in-law's heart is through complimenting her cooking and baking."

When Dad and Sam return, Mom and I forget dinner. We dash to my bedroom, leaving the guys to slice the meat and set the table. Mom helps me put on the dress. It fits perfectly, except I tell her it fits too much like a glove across the bosom. We assess the side seams and determine there is sufficient fabric to make the necessary alteration. I will take it to a nearby seamstress and then to a dry cleaner. We are pleased. The dress issue is settled.

The four of us enjoy dinner and discuss the events of the day. Sam has reserved a tuxedo. It has been a productive day.

On Monday, Edward Marlot calls to ask if I can find some time this afternoon to see him. We settle for a two o'clock meeting.

I puzzle, as to the reason Edward would wish to see me. We ended the Jaku-bitz case on good terms. He was pleased that the trial resulted in a guilty verdict.

At two, he comes into my office with a grim expression. He says, "Thank you, Ashley, for seeing me on such short notice."

"Unless I'm in the midst of a demanding trial, my time is flexible. So, it is not a problem today. What can I do for you?"

"How do I approach this? It's about Sam."

"My God, has something happened to him?" I am stunned, as if blind-sided. My heart is pounding in my ears.

He touches my arm. "Relax. I'm sorry for scaring you. I'm not good at this, but my visit is not due to an emergency situation."

My voice high pitched, I exclaim, "What is it then?"

"I am concerned about Sam's health. The brass is leaning heavily on him, because he is so sharp and never complains. I am sure you have noticed the number of Saturdays he works."

"I have noticed and we have talked about it. In addition to the increased assignments, he works many evenings on a research project assigned to him. Have you noticed something physically wrong with him? He hasn't complained to me."

"He was dizzy one day in my office and I badgered him about it until he admitted he saw a physician last week. He is suffering from high blood pressure. I think they called it hypertension."

"I'm embarrassed to admit that Sam hasn't spoken to me about his health. We have been busy with work, my stalker, and wedding preparations."

"I know. That's why I'm here. Sam related to me that he didn't confide in you, because your stalker has caused you enough stress. It's a typical response from that man."

"Thank you for sharing this with me. I will talk to Sam about this concern, but I won't mention that I heard it from you."

"Actually, I don't mind if you do mention where you heard it. Did Sam ever tell you he once saved my life?"

"No, he has never mentioned that. I know he cares for you and he often smiles when he relays pleasant experiences you two have shared. Things you have done together, such as fishing and over the top celebrating."

"Sam has a special place in my heart. We were partners for four years. On one case assignment we were staking out this scum bag we had been after for weeks. The scum bag had been warned and had taken to the roof. The jerk was set to shoot me from the rooftop. Sam spotted him, leaped, and pushed me out of the way. Sam took two bullets in his arm, which were directed at my head. I would do anything for that man." Edward is attempting to hold back tears.

I place my hand on his arm and say, "Sam did tell me about the gunshots to his arm, but not the circumstances surrounding them. He really is a hero. He is also very kind to and understanding of me. I'm glad that he chose you to give the toast to the groom. Now I truly understand why."

"As far as I'm concerned, you couldn't do better than Sam. I also believe that he is very fortunate to have found you."

"Thank you for saying that. And I agree about your comment regarding Sam. I have a first cousin who is a physician and I will call him today for a quick medical rundown on hypertension. I will confront Sam tonight. I probably have been a cause of the elevation in his blood pressure, because I realize how worried he is about me and my safety."

"Yes he is. Thank you for seeing me. Come, give me a hug. I have taken enough of your time."

"I really appreciate you coming to see me with this information. You are indeed what friendship is all about, and Sam is fortunate to have you."

We hug and Edward leaves. I immediately call my cousin Phil, Doctor Phil Kirklend, and leave him a message to call me this afternoon, if possible.

An hour later Phil returns my call, "Hello cousin Ashley, what's up with you? Do you need a blood test prior to marriage?"

"Thank you for calling back, and no, it's not about me. Sam has high blood pressure with resulting dizzy spells. What is happening and what is the treatment? What does high blood pressure mean in the long run?"

"I would first suggest that Sam make an appointment with his family physician. You should accompany him to the appointment. Write out your questions beforehand. Most causes of hypertension can be lowered by diet, exercise, and reduction of stress. If that doesn't result in reducing the blood pressure, then a regimen of medication can be ordered."

"What would happen if someone didn't seek medical treatment?" I ask, although I will drag him for follow-up if he doesn't agree to do so, on his own.

"Untreated hypertension will eventually result in a heart attack or stroke, with resulting paralyses, in most situations. It is what we call a cerebral vascular accident."

With fingers crossed, I ask, "If Sam doesn't have a family physician would you accept him as a patient?"

He hesitates than says, "I'm not currently taking on new patients. But for you, I will agree to see him if he calls to make the appointment."

"Thank you. You are a dear."

"See you at the wedding."

At home that evening, I ask Sam to join me in the great room. I have decided to broach his hypertension by being up-front with him. I wait until he's comfortable.

"You didn't tell me you were a hero."

"What do you mean?"

"Edward Marlot came to visit me today and shared your heroics."

"Oh. Didn't I mention it? It's no big deal. Do you have another case with Edward?"

I maintain eye contact and answer, "No. Edward came today because he is concerned about your health. He told me about your high blood pressure and dizzy spells. Why didn't you tell me Sam? You know, you and I can not enjoy a great relationship if we aren't honest with one another."

"You have plenty to worry about without adding my health concerns. I will blacken Edward's eyes tomorrow, when I see him. What an idiot running to you."

"I appreciated him coming to me. I called my cousin Phil, who is a physician and he said that untreated high blood pressure can lead to heart attacks or strokes. Sam, we must take care of this problem."

"I plan to. Now is not a good time."

"Phil said he'll accept you as a patient if you call and ask for an appointment. Who you choose to see is your decision but please see someone soon. I am willing to accompany you to the appointment, so that I understand the causes and treatments. Sam, I love you and need you around for a long, long, time."

"I'm sorry. I should have shared this with you. I don't have a physician and just saw whoever was available at the medical center, so I will call your cousin."

I'm not letting him off easy. I ask, "When will you call?"

"I'll call tomorrow. Just give me the name and phone number. You are such a pest, Ashley."

I ignore his comment. "Edward is such a charming fellow. We must have him over for dinner some night. What is his favorite meal?"

"When I was partnered with him on the beat all he ate was hot dogs." Sam laughs out loud, like this is a great joke.

"Find out will you? And since we are talking about your friends, how did Josh get the scar on his face?"

"When Josh was sixteen, his family went on vacation to California. One evening, he and his older brother walked down to the beach and a gang of thugs attacked them."

"I just hate hearing these stories. I shouldn't have asked."

"The story doesn't end there. They killed Josh's brother. Josh spent something like three weeks in the hospital after the brutal attack."

"Did they at least find the gang?"

"No one was ever charged. There are many unsolved gang killings in the States."

"Does the attack have something to do with why Josh joined the police force?"

"Oh yes. For years Josh took his vacation time to go to the same beach. He went looking for them. He knew it was a waste, but he had to try."

"I can understand because it's the way I feel about Gail's unsolved murder. Except in this case, I know you will find him."

"I certainly hope so and quickly."

"Meanwhile, come join me on the sofa. I need to lower your blood pressure."

"Best thing I heard all day."

CHAPTER 40

▼

Two weeks following my parents visit, Shelly gives the opening statement to the jury in the Brad Nedelton case. He is charged with sexually assaulting his daughter, Lois, for the past five years. Lois is now ten. Following a discussion with her friend Natalie, on sex and boys, Lois talked about her abuse to her mother, Shirley Nedelton. Mrs. Nedelton immediately confronted her husband who vehemently denied the accusation. She didn't believe him, notified the police and Brad was charged. For the prosecution, it had been an open and shut case.

We want and receive a quick start to the trial with few witnesses called for the prosecution. I have given Shelly Galeno total control of the trial and act only as an advisor.

During the five day trial many character witnesses have been called for the defendant. According to his twenty-five witnesses, Brad is in church every Sunday, and he is a gentle husband, a doting father, and friendly neighbor. To the witnesses he may seem to be all of these things, but he is in reality a child molester.

It was extremely difficult to place both Lois Nedelton and her mother on the stand. I noticed members of the jury attempting to hold back tears while they listened to their testimonies. Following their testimony and the physician's report on his examination of Lois, I inform Shelly that she will have her first win.

I go in early to listen to Shelly practice sections of her closing statement. At 8:30 she is prepared. We leave for the court room.

Judge Todd Price presides. He is the youngest judge in our courts. With his tall, slim build, and pitch black hair, blue eyes, and handsome face he looks more like a model than a judge. At times, because of his age, I have debated whether he understood the trial in its entirety. But the trial did run smoothly, so obviously I underestimated his ability.

Shelly completes her closing statement by 11:30 and Judge Price adjourns. We will reconvene at one in the afternoon.

The defendant's lawyer, Annette Coswin, will present her closing statement after lunch.

I have socialized with Annette and her husband in the past. Annette is in her mid-thirties, and is tall and slim, with a pretty face. She had blond hair and blue eyes. Annette has two children, a boy and a girl who are excellent hockey players in their levels. I met her in law school. After graduation she chose defense, Pamela corporate, and I prosecution.

Pamela meets me for a quick lunch in the Law Courts building's cafeteria. She is beaming and informs me of a new man in her life. She wants to bring him to the wedding. I reply with, "Absolutely, I'm dying to meet him." She is very excited about Perry Ondrick. He moved to Edmonton after being transferred by one of the large oil companies in Calgary. We speak further about him and the wedding. At 12:50 I have to rush away.

By three Annette has completed her closing statements. It is now in the hands of the jurors. Annette, Shelly, and I are almost knocked over by the news media. They are jockeying for positions to interview us when we leave the court room. I hate to think what will happen when a verdict is reached. When the media leave Shelly and I shake Annette's hand.

Back in my office I work on a recent case assignment. My opponent in court will be Marty Kroll. The new case involves a male elementary teacher accused of sexually assaulting one of his eight-year-old male students. There are now other students coming forward, swearing that they too, have been fondled by this teacher. This will be a front page news story.

It is despicable when children are involved in these types of situations. When I have back to back child molestation cases, I want to quit my job or ask Jim to assign me murder cases only. I have been working sexual assault cases for years and Jim wants me to continue, because most of the victims are female. I offer a lot of needed support to the victims and their families. The victims have related to me that they find it easier to talk to a female.

Sam picks me up at work and we decide to eat at our local Chinese restaurant. When our wine arrives I ask, "Are you getting cold feet?"

"No. Well sometimes I think about it. But honestly I think if you wear your Mom's wedding gown it will bring us good luck. Look how happy your parents are after all these years. The fact that I love you is never in question. What about you? Do you have any second thoughts?"

"No. I love you and have always wanted to marry and have children. How many children are we going to have Sam?"

There is dead silence. He asks, "Do you think I'll be a good father? It scares me. I suffered so much abuse as a child I sometimes wonder if I can be."

"You are one of the kindest men I know. You will be a wonderful father. Now, how many children do you want?"

"Oh yeah, I want four children, two girls and two boys." He is beaming.

"It sounds wonderful, although it doesn't work that way. We could end up with four girls."

Sam takes both my hands in his. "As long as they are healthy, I'm fine with four girls. Should we go home and practice making them?"

We do just that.

At two the next afternoon, Shelly and I are notified that after eight hours of deliberation a verdict has been reached and court will convene. The jury finds Brad Nedelton guilty on all charges of sexual assault.

When we leave the court room, Shelly and I are surrounded by reporters and camera men. Mr. Nedelton is a prominent citizen and thus the media attention. Following what seems like three hundred questions, I spot Marty Kroll passing by. When he stops for a moment to observe, a few of the reporters notice him and ask him questions about the teacher he's representing.

Marty gives me one of his false smiles and says, "Hey Ashley, guess we'll be facing each other in court. It has been a while."

I want to respond, "Yes, since you represented that sick bastard, Billie Chartrand." Instead I reply with, "Yes, it has."

By then Shelly and I have fielded enough questions and I advise the reporters that the press conference is over.

Thinking about it later I feel Marty purposely walked by to encourage the reporters to leave us and flock around him. After all, he thinks he is number one. Marty craves and lives on media attention. Well he can have it. I have no love for microphones being shoved in my face. These days, I'm more interested in getting married and having children than I am in climbing the ladder to the top.

One evening, as planned, Pamela picks me up at home. We go to a couple of hobby shops to select glass receptacles to hold the floating candles. We argue over the color and finally agree on Peacock Blue. I purchase matching ribbon to tie around the receptacle. We head for home with boxes of glassware, ribbon, and candles.

When we arrive I say to Sam, "Bring in the boxes from Pamela's car please. The two of us are going to prepare centerpieces this evening."

Sam grins at me because he didn't want to tie ribbons. He heads out the door, happy.

Pamela and I spread bundles of ribbon on the table, cut them in the appropriate lengths and start tying them around the rose bowl type glass receptacle. We place a candle in each bowl. After some time she becomes quiet. Her movements have slowed.

I ask her, "Are you bored? If you are we can stop. Sam and I can finish this on the weekend."

"I'm not bored at all. In fact I'm quite enjoying creating an attractive table piece for your wedding. How are you handling the loss of Gail these days?"

"It's still very difficult for me to accept that she is no longer around. I wish she was here to celebrate our wedding. It bothers me that we haven't caught the bastard who killed her. I just know he is the same low life who is tormenting me. I want to get my hands on him so badly, I can taste it. He has forced me into a life of fear. Even when I am with someone, including Sam, I'm aware of everyone around me. I can never relax. I'm afraid in my own home and jump at every sound."

She looks at me with compassion and says, "I wish there was something I could do. I feel so useless in this situation."

"There is nothing more you can do. I'm happy to get out of the house occasionally with you."

We complete our centerpiece project and she leaves for home. I remind her to call me when she arrives. After what happened to Gail I am constantly concerned for other people in my life.

Tomorrow afternoon Sam and I have a two o'clock appointment with Phil. So we discuss his symptoms and write out our questions. He is not looking forward to seeing the physician. He is restless in his sleep and both of us have another poor night's sleep.

At work the next morning, Shelly calls to ask if she can see me for a moment. I invite her down and tell her to take a seat. She seems uncomfortable and I ask, "What is the matter Shelly?"

"The office manager asked me to come see you. He said we have a close relationship and wanted me to tell you that two dozen roses arrived at the desk." She pauses and stares at me.

"What do two dozen roses have to do with me?"

"Maybe it has nothing to do with you. There is no name on the card signifying who is the recipient or the sender."

"What does the card say?" This is like pulling teeth and I don't like the uneasy feeling.

She hesitates and then answers, "The card says, "These blood roses are for you. One rose for each wound." They don't have to be your roses, right?"

"No, they don't, but I'm afraid they are. I thank you for telling me. Come, I will look at the card."

Shelly walks with me to the front desk. Karen is on the phones today and as we approach, I can see she is nervous.

"It's fine Karen. Show me where the card is. Did you touch it?"

"No, I didn't touch anything, Ms. Browne."

"Tell me what happened."

"At ten this morning this man walked in here and said the roses were for this department. He placed the vase with flowers on my desk, turned around and walked out. There was no name anywhere, so I called the office manager and he looked at the card."

"Was the card in an envelope?"

"No, it was exactly like it is right now." She points to it.

"Did Larry touch the card or vase?"

"No, Ms. Browne. No one has touched or moved the vase or card. It was so weird that I actually thought something was wrong. So I kept my hands off and made sure everyone else did as well."

"You are one smart person. Thank you."

Karen smiles at me. She has been with our department for years. She is in her late thirties, tall, with blond hair, and brown eyes. She is very efficient.

"Do you mind if we leave them right there for an hour or so? I will call the police and they will remove them."

"I don't mind. I will ensure no one touches them."

"Thank you." I thank Shelly and then storm down to the manager's office.

Janet has been Larry's secretary for many years. She is a tall lady, with dark brown hair, brown eyes, and a great sense of humor. She too is married, with a young family consisting of one girl, age nine and a boy, age six years. Janet has brought them to the children's Christmas party held in our building every year.

I ask her if Larry Bredly, the office manager, is in. She takes one look at my face and nods. I knock, walk in, and slam the door behind me. Larry looks at me and says, "Have a seat, Ashley."

"No. Thank you. Don't ever pull a stunt like this again." Larry attempts to say something.

"Shut up, Larry. Your responsibility as an office manager is to take care of your staff, not shuffle off this responsibility to some unsuspecting person. How dare you shirk your duties and have Shelly do your dirty work. I won't report you this time, but I do want you to apologize to her for putting her in an awkward situation. I'm calling the police and the roses will be removed from Karen's desk." I turn and exit, slamming the door behind me.

Janet is smiling and says, "Have a nice day, Ms. Browne."

"Thank you Janet. You have a nice day too." Gail had told me that Janet is an excellent worker and the two of them have taken in a movie occasionally. Janet's husband apparently hates to go to the theatre.

When I get to my office, I immediately call Sam. He answers, "Yes Ashley, I have not forgotten about the doctor's appointment."

"It's not that. It's that bastard. He sent me two dozen red roses with a card that said, "These blood roses are for you. One rose for each wound." I'm scared shitless. What am I to do?"

"If your office is open right now, close the door, lock it, and let no one in. Understand? No one comes in. I will be there in twenty minutes with a constable and a technician. Do you understand this, Ashley? Get up right now and lock your door."

I walk to the door and lock it. "Okay, the door is locked."

"Great honey, I'll see you in twenty minutes. Hang in there. I love you." Sam hangs up.

I sit in my chair staring out the window and notice the tall apartment block across the street. I stand up and close my drapes. Someone could be watching my every move. I can feel myself slipping into a cocoon.

When the knock comes I jump, and find myself still sitting in my chair staring at the drapes as I was twenty minutes ago. Sam says, "Open the door."

When I open it he takes one look at my face and hugs me close. We stand like that for what feels like hours; then Sam gently guides me back into the office and closes the door. He holds me close.

"The constable will follow through on the delivery man, and I have two men checking out the florist shops around here. He probably used a stolen credit card to pay for the flowers, and told the florist the message on the card is a private joke. He won't have touched anything, so there won't likely be any fingerprints, other than the flower shop staff and delivery man. He is getting bolder. Come, just relax in my arms. Let me hold you."

We sit in my chair. Sam holds me on his knee and I close my eyes. I don't want to think or move and realize I must snap out of this trance.

I am finding it difficult to breathe and say, "Can we please go outside for a minute, anywhere, because I'm suffocating."

"Sure. Reprogram your voice message and get your coat. Remember to lock your office. You are leaving here for the day. We will walk and later get some lunch. I will still be in time for my appointment with Phil."

When we enter the main office I notice that the roses are gone. I tell Karen I will not be back until tomorrow morning. She looks at me with an expression close to pity.

Phil is my dad's sister's son. Dad is one child in a family of eight so I have a total of twenty-four cousins. Sam is overwhelmed by the numbers. Phil is a small man with straight brown hair, brown eyes, and a slim build. What he lacks in looks he makes up for in kindness. He is known to have one of the greatest bedside manners in the country.

After we are seated, Phil asks Sam if he's okay with my being present. Sam nods and smiles at me.

The first question from Phil surprises both Sam and I. Phil asks, "I need a family history before we do a physical. Did your Mom or Dad suffer from high blood pressure?"

Sam is silent for a moment then confides in Phil, "Dr. Kirklend, my mom died of alcoholism and drug abuse approximately twelve years ago and if my dad is alive today, he is an alcoholic living on skid row. I never met my extended family, so basically I don't know anything about them. I was an only child, who suffered terrible abuse from my father."

"I am sorry, Sam."

Phil jots down Sam's history then does a physical assessment. He discovers Sam's blood pressure is elevated and orders blood tests, a urinalysis and an electrocardiogram for his heart. He wants these tests done immediately and tells Sam to take them at a laboratory and diagnostic center today. He informs us, "When the results are in I will give you a call and talk about lifestyle choices, exercise, diet, and stress relief. If these don't solve the problem, we'll look at a medication regimen. In the meantime, fire away with your questions."

He spends twenty more minutes with us and when we leave Sam is suitably impressed with the appointment. We get the blood test, urinalysis and electrocardiogram done. Four hours later we are on the way home.

I ask Sam, "Did you feel comfortable with Phil?"

"Yes. I found him to be very understanding and knowledgeable."

After dinner the phone rings and Sam answers. It goes dead as soon as Sam picks up. We both know it's him.

I look at Sam and say, "To hell with him tonight. Come lie down on the bed and I will do a neck and shoulder massage."

It is another night of restless sleep for both of us.

The next morning I answer my office phone and then hear the raspy voice say, "Did you enjoy the roses?" He follows this statement with a guttural evil sounding laugh. I slam the phone down and hold back a scream. I feel myself falling apart and grab Gail's picture. I hug it close.

My office door is closed and locked, my drapes are drawn. I sit in my chair hugging Gail's picture and staring at my phone. When it rings next I ignore it. The ringing seems to be coming from a distance.

I don't know how long I have been sitting at my desk when there is a knock on the door. I drag myself from my chair and say, "Yes?"

Shelly answers, "Can I see you for a minute?"

"Sure, just hold on for a second." I look in my mirror on my bookshelf and am shocked at my appearance. I look so drawn and pale. I unlock and open my door, inviting Shelly in.

She takes one look at my face and asks, "What is wrong? And don't say, "Nothing," because I won't believe you."

"I received another phone call in my office this morning. He asked about the roses."

"Honestly, how do you manage to remain sane? Please call Sam and have him pick you up. I will cover for you."

I look at her for a long time. I hear her repeat, "Please."

I dial Sam, who answers on the first ring and I hear the door close gently behind Shelly.

Sam asks, "What is happening?"

I reply, "He called me this morning to ask if I enjoyed the roses. I'm scared."

"Shit. Are you okay?"

"According to Shelly, I'm not. She thinks you should take me home. I'm so sorry for bothering you."

"Call me at any time. I will be there in twenty minutes. Stay in your office."

I call Shelly to thank her and let her know Sam is coming to pick me up. We discuss the few phone calls she must make for me. I inform her I have not received any word from Corporal Sherry Sparks about little Maggie and her father Mr. Clossete. He may be abusing her. I hope the corporal calls soon, because if she doesn't it's likely that no charges will be laid.

When Sam arrives, I let Toni know that I will be at home for the rest of the day and to call me if needed.

When we have settled on the sofa at home, Sam says, "I don't know how to approach this subject."

"Sam, you can talk to me about anything."

"Okay. Here goes. I think you may need some counseling." He pauses and takes a deep breath. "Now," and he holds his hands in a stop motion, "don't get mad, but you are really withdrawing lately and it scares me."

"Don't be silly, I'm fine. I knew I shouldn't have allowed Shelly to convince me to call you today. I could have stayed at work. Do you have to go back to work? What do you want for lunch?"

"I have to go back this afternoon. Are you saying you don't need any help?"

"That is precisely what I'm saying. Look, just because I over reacted a little today doesn't necessarily mean I'm insane."

"I didn't say you were insane. I'm saying that you need someone to talk to about your fear."

"Sam, I prefer talking to you. Really, it's true. Come, I'll be fine. Let me make you lunch before you go back to work."

After he leaves, I check the security system a few times and draw the blinds.

CHAPTER 41

▼

My wedding is twelve days away. I am excited and jittery. All plans have been finalized. I decided to take a one month vacation, two weeks before and two following the wedding.

The next twelve days will allow me to relax and assist Mom with any last minute details. Shelly Galeno is taking over the child molestation case, while I'm away. She believes I'm her mentor and Jim has encouraged our working relationship. I wish her well, remembering how uncertain I felt in my first two years as a prosecutor. She has a great attitude and kind heart. I assure her that should she feel the need; she is welcome to call me at home in the next two weeks.

Jim and I have given up on Logan Reid. I'm confident that Logan will not offer support to Shelly. While Jim appreciates her hard work and dedication, Logan views her as a competitor, a threat, and therefore he is a hindrance rather than of any help. When she approached me to discuss Logan I was honest with her and shared some of my experiences. I advised her to be cautious about requesting or accepting advice from him. I don't mention Logan's sexual advances.

Today, I feel antsy and I prowl the house. I stop occasionally to run on the spot. I desperately need to rid myself of this feeling of suffocation. I want to scream.

I rush into the bathroom, have a short shower, put on one of my jogging outfits, jogging shoes, a waist pack containing the pepper spray, and I'm out the door. I did those tasks quickly. A good or bad decision, I need to release some of my pent up frustration or I will explode.

In the past when I have read a book or watched a movie, I wondered why the main character would go directly into a danger zone. Now, I understand. Today, I feel if I don't run right now, I will lose my mind.

The sky is overcast and I wonder for a second if I should opt for my light rain jacket. Decision made I head for the park instead. I think that if I return to the house, I may not leave. I need this.

Randill Park has numerous jogging and bike trails that wind through dense bush and evergreen trees. Along the trails little clearings are dispersed throughout the park and are available for picnics.

I take the longer right trail. The traffic is light because many individuals have completed their jogs and are now commuting to or are at work. It is 9:30. I meet an elderly couple and we exchange greetings.

My thoughts are centered on the couple. I wonder how long they have been married. Do they have children, grandchildren? It is odd how the mind recognizes important factors that go along with the stages in our lives. Prior to meeting Sam, these thoughts would not have occurred to me.

A half hour later I'm on the return trail home and feeling wonderful. I think about our wedding. It is exciting that I, Ashley Browne, am getting married. I smile to myself.

Someone is running behind me. Jerked back to reality by a rush of adrenaline, I feel the resulting goose bumps on my arms. I can hear shoes gently slapping the pavement. Somehow I know I'm in trouble. My fear pushes me into a higher gear. I glance back quickly, and catch a glimpse of a man with a baseball hat pulled low. My heart is pounding against my chest wall and my breathing is rapid and shallow. I desperately plead for someone to come running down the path toward me. My prayer is not answered.

Up ahead the trail divides into three branches. The short cut to my home is to take the curve to the left. The man is gaining on me, as I move to the left path. One thing I do know is he's in great shape. On the other hand, I haven't been jogging for the past few months and have lost some of my edge.

Panting, I attempt to regain control. Perspiration is running down my face and into my eyes, making it difficult to see. My heart feels like it will burst out of my chest, followed by my lungs.

I hear the familiar, raspy voice, "Run Ashley, run."

It sounds like a roar and pushes me to a new speed. It is also more sinister sounding. My leg muscles are cramping; the result of a buildup of lactic acid. I see a shadow fall over my right shoulder. My God, he is that close.

"Run." He whispers again. I am dead.

I can't slow my pace to make an attempt to reach my can of pepper spray. Why in the hell was I not jogging with the can held in my hand? Too late now, there will be no next time for me.

Through the blur of my tears I suddenly see the end of the trail. I attempt to scream, but the result is a mild squeak. So close, I'm so close. As I burst into the street, I see a man walking his dog. The dog is barking at me and pulling on the leash. The man holds on tight.

He is staring at me and says, "What is wrong lady? Slow down and take a breath. Take a deep breath."

I am bent at the waist and gasping. I stop to take a breath. "A man, a man in the park was chasing me. He is extremely dangerous." I gasp hesitantly, taking a breath between each word.

"Come, I will walk you—" The man is stopped in mid sentence as his dog takes off, pulling the leash out of the man's hand. The dog, a German Sheppard, charges down the trail with the man running after him calling, "Rusty, Rusty stop. Rusty, stop right now!"

In desperation I try to shout, "Stop sir. Don't go into the park. The man is a psycho." But my warning comes out in a quiet squeak.

I hear the barking for another thirty seconds, then abruptly the sound stops. I hear the man cry out. I wait on the sidewalk terrified. Should I go after him or run home and call the police? I have my pepper spray, but no cell phone.

I decide to go after him. As I start running toward the trail I see the man returning. He carries his dog. There is blood everywhere and it's leaving a trail on the path. I can tell from a distance that the dog is dead.

The man is crying. He has blood smeared on his face and hands as he keeps repeating, "Why, why would someone do this?"

"I'm so sorry sir. What is your name?"

"My name is Ralph Mantle and my dog's name is Rusty."

"Mr. Mantle, I want you to come to my home. It's over there." I point out my house, which is visible from the park.

"Yes, I will come with you because I live a few blocks from here." The man is now crying openly.

When we reach the front yard, I ask him to lay the dog down on the grass. I observe that the animal's head is almost severed from the body. The stalker is definitely becoming more aggressive. I place my hand on his shoulder and apologize again.

My knees are weak and my calves bursting with pain from the cramping. I sit on the grass beside him and his dog.

He looks at me with tear filled eyes and asks, "Will you call my wife Polly at 555–1902 and tell her what happened."

"Absolutely, I'll do that for you. Why don't you come in and wash up?"

Ralph shakes his head, "Thanks for the offer, but for now I want to spend a few moments alone with Rusty."

I leave the man on the front yard talking to his dog. The first thing I do is call the police, and then I scrub my hands and face, as if by doing so I can erase this nightmare. When I phone Ralph's wife, I explain who I am and the present situation. I give her the address. She tells me she will be right over with a van, to pick up her husband and his dog.

Returning to the lawn, I suggest to Ralph he may want to wash up now, because his wife is coming over and he has blood smeared on his face. I give him directions to the bathroom. Ralph is back in five minutes and I can see he has been crying. Mr. Mantle is in his mid-sixties, medium height, and graying hair. He has a handsome face. We wait on the lawn for Polly to arrive. I feel so sad and guilty about his dog and offer support to Ralph.

Polly is a tall, slim, attractive woman, who I guess is in her mid-sixties. They hug. She helps Ralph place the dog on a thick blanket in the van. She informs me that Rusty has been with them for seven years. When her husband retired their son, Darryl, bought the puppy for him.

I get their address from Polly and inform them that the police will probably be around to interview them. I offer to pay for any funeral costs, but they will not hear of it. I feel so badly for them and later I will offer to buy them a puppy. I know it will not replace Rusty, but it may ease some of their pain. I will discuss it with Polly first.

Sam told me on Friday, that he has finally convinced the brass to open a case file on me, and to give him two corporals to do some research. He is too busy to do everything on his own time. They finally agreed to the request and he spent Friday evening compiling all the information on me into one file. The phone calls, letters, underground parking lot chase, the cut phone line and the damaged electrical power box, the stalking at the shopping center, the incident in our back yard, and the roses. We now have another to add to the file.

Alone in the house, I double check the security system and sit at the kitchen table, attempting to regain some degree of control. In recalling the nightmare, I realize the bastard was toying with me again. Near the end of the trail he could have reached out and pulled me down. It's obvious to me now, that this is still a game to him.

I call the police department again and tell them to hurry, because I'm petrified. The police dispatcher assures me someone is on their way. I'm leaning against the kitchen cupboard when my body starts to shake and I can't control it. Now that the adrenaline has decreased, my body is starting to react to the pounding it took. I slowly make it to a chair and sit down to wait for the police.

Constable Alana Warwick is at my door within ten minutes. She is now busy jotting notes in her small black notebook. Attempting to stay focused on the questions my eyes wander to the front door, expecting it to explode inward with Sam's presence. He will be angry.

I attempted to contact him both at his office and on his cell. I had no success.

Alana is petite for a police officer. She has intense, but kind, brown eyes and blond hair. The interview completed she rises and extends her hand. "Are you positive a patrol car outside is all you require at this time? We can station someone in the house until further investigation is completed."

"No, I am fine. Sergeant Sam Orlicky will be here shortly. I am positive the presence of a police patrol car out front will deter my stalker. Thanks again."

Alana has been very efficient, supportive, and professional.

After showing her out I again check the security system. In spite of having spent many years dealing with crime, it is amazing how these circumstances affect me now. It's an encompassing fear which is changing me, possibly forever. I can only wish that Sam catches him quickly.

I wander into the great room and literally fall into a chair. I shudder, as I realize how vulnerable I am to the maniac terrorizing me. He loves and feeds off my fear. I don't have the strength to continually put up a brave front. I feel myself sinking further.

People may think how ridiculous I was to go jogging alone. It may seem stupid to others, but somehow I have to maintain some semblance of normalcy, and a way of remaining sane. Jogging does this for me.

Right now I want to say to my tormentor, "Okay, I surrender. Come and get me." This thought surprises me. I have always been a fighter.

I jump, as I hear the scrape of the key in the front door. Suddenly the past four hours overwhelm me and I rush at Sam, to sob hysterically in his arms.

"Oh honey, I'm so sorry. We were on a stakeout and it couldn't be compromised. What happened? I have heard bits and pieces and also spoke briefly to Steve in the patrol car. We didn't go into details. I needed to be with you, just like this. I love you." He hugs me closer.

"He chased me in the park and like in the underground parking lot, he whispered my name in this raspy voice. He is becoming bolder. My God, Sam, he killed that nice couple's dog. Basically, he beheaded it. And again I feel responsible."

"Don't feel responsible, Ashley, because there is no way in which you are, truly. So you think it's the same man? Sorry, but I have to ask."

"I know it's the same bastard as the one in the underground parking lot incident. He wore the same cap. I'm positive the build of the man in the park is the same as Chartrand's. I can still feel those dead, evil, eyes penetrating my back in the court room. He is behind this, enjoying the control. Constable Warwick said they will investigate the crime scene and interview the dog owners."

"I need to fill you in on the case file we opened on you."

"Did you find something useful?"

"Yes, but it pisses me off because I have been badgering them about this for two months. Maybe today could have been prevented. But as you well know you could have avoided this threatening chase just by staying at home. Honey, you are playing with fire. You need to listen. Until we catch him, you have to stay close to me and home. Do you promise?"

"You can't possibly understand how frustrated I am being trapped like this. I had to do something. I was freaking out. Hell, I don't know maybe I was trying to prove to myself that the jerk could not keep me buried in my home. Please don't be angry with me right now. I can't handle it."

"I understand, believe me. Anyway, this is what is new. One of the investigators was able to gain valuable information from an old social work file. These are the facts on Billie Chartrand. He was born Cory Matlick. Cory suffered horrendous physical and psychological abuse from his alcoholic, drug addicted mother. As did his brother Matthew, who is one year younger than Billie."

I interrupt, stunned, "Billie has a brother?"

"Yes. The mother, Sharon Matlick, burned to death in a house fire caused by arson. The two sons escaped. The perpetrator who started the fire was never found. There was talk of the brothers setting fire to the house, but no one was ever charged. They were so young."

"My God, I can't believe this."

Sam takes a second than continues, "Cory was twelve at the time, his brother eleven. They were placed in an orphanage. The younger brother, Matthew, was adopted almost immediately. Cory, who we know as Billie, was not. He disappeared from a youth correction centre in Toronto at age fifteen. After that there is absolutely no paper trail."

"Did they locate any family members?"

"The corporal working the case can't find any connection between Chartrand and any family members and/or friends from the time he was fifteen, to the time he was captured for the kidnapping, sexual assault, and attempted murder here in the city."

Sam pauses for a second then continues, "It's like he ceased to exist. It is the oddest thing when you consider the age of internet and information sharing. He may have been in the States all this time. But where is he hiding now? Again, we have no sign of him although he may have grown a head of hair and a beard. He could also be wearing colored contacts lens. Another question we are considering as a lead is where does his money come from? You must have money to hire Marty Kroll, as your lawyer."

I'm excited about the information Sam's task force has been able to uncover.

"What about the brother? Is there any information there?"

"The family who adopted Matthew requested that all transactions be closed, and therefore all records are sealed. I doubt Chartrand would have sought his brother. Even if he had desired a family, I don't know how he would have located him. If they have connected, I would think the brother would have been at trial."

"I guess you're right about Chartrand locating his brother. But he is still playing with me. I believe he will not kill at a distance, like rigging my vehicle. For him it has to be up close and personal. Chartrand's desire is to see me suffer; pleading for mercy while he exercises his control."

I can't decide whether to share these feelings with Sam, but give in. "Tonight, just before you walked in; I wanted to fold up my tent and just lie down. I wanted to place an advertisement in the local paper saying, "Billie come and get me now." I have no fight left in me."

"Honey, you must stop entertaining such thoughts. I know it's easy for me to say. But hang in there with me. We will get the cunning bastard."

"We need to soon. Today in the park, I had a gut feeling he is close to losing control. Close to going for broke; going for, "the kill," is a better description."

"I agree with you. He keeps getting closer to you."

I comment, "Tomorrow night I want you to gather a few friends, to bring the rest of your clothing and furniture here. Close down your apartment."

"Are you sure about this? What will your parents say if I move in here?"

"I need to tell them about today. Actually, I plan to invite them here for a few days to keep me company. Then you are off next week, so they can return home if they wish. I'm falling apart and need almost constant support and protection."

"It's a great idea to invite your parents. And I will get Ted to help me tomorrow. That is, if his wife, Carmen, doesn't have thirty jobs for him to do after work."

"You know, I need to meet more of your friends."

"Tomorrow you will meet Ted and Carmen. You'll like them. Now, let's go out for dinner. I don't want to see you in hiding, when I'm available to be with you."

Sam grabs my hands and pulls me to my feet. I hug him close and can feel some of the tension leaving my body.

"Okay. I think it's your turn to buy, but my turn to select the restaurant." I smile at him although my heart is not in it.

Sam laughs, "Where to then; somewhere expensive?"

"I feel like eating Italian tonight. What do you think?"

"It sounds wonderful to me."

"I will call Mom and Dad when we return."

The dinner is not as tasty as usual, but I don't know whether to blame the chef or my frayed nerves. On the drive home, when we pass the park, Sam doesn't comment, but I think he notices me tense.

Trying to portray a normalcy I don't feel, I ask him if he knows the weather pattern in the Bahamas this week.

"I haven't heard about the weather. Hope your parents are still up." He mumbles.

I reach Mom and request that Dad pick up the other phone. I fill them in on today's incident. Dad is shouting with anger and Mom is crying. I ask them to visit me for a few days. Both agree immediately.

Mom asks, "Can we come tonight, dear?"

"Tomorrow morning will be fine Mom, because Sam is staying over tonight."

Surprisingly, both say, "Good."

I hang up and wonder how long this will go on? In my thirties and I need a sitter.

Sam and I spend a few minutes discussing Billie's brother. Who is he and does he have a role in this sick and deadly game?

We finally go to bed and spend time reassuring each other that I'm safe.

CHAPTER 42

▼

My parents arrive at four in the afternoon. They are very worried and anxious because they are late. Dad had a flat tire and some trouble changing it. They suggest that I accompany them home today.

I reply, "I would like to, but I must decline. Sam is moving his belongings to the house tonight; and I need to shop further for a few honeymoon things; and I have promised to be available to Shelly at work." The main reason, which I don't share, is that I intend to avoid tainting their home with this horror at any cost. I will not lead this monster to their home.

I inform my parents that I'm prepared to join them next Thursday, two days before the wedding. Pamela will arrive on the Friday, in time for the rehearsal.

The conversation stops when Sam arrives with a truck load of belongings. Ted and Carmen are with him. Ted is a corporal with the police department and Carmen is a registered nurse.

Carmen is of medium height and slim, with blond hair, and blue eyes. She has a pretty face and bright mind. Ted is tall, muscular, and handsome. Carmen tells me they have two sons, ages thirteen and ten, and a daughter, eight, who are currently visiting their grandmother.

Two trips later and they have Sam moved in. It's an event which should have me beaming, but I don't feel any joy. Mom and I cook enough spaghetti and meatballs to feed an army. The six of us sit around the table, with Ted and Carmen exaggerating stories of Sam's earlier years in the city.

They are a lovely couple with an over the top sense of humor. It makes us all laugh and distracts me from yesterday's horror. They leave at midnight, with a promise to see us at the wedding. They also suggest getting together on our return from the honeymoon. Sam thanks them again and promises to give them a call.

The next afternoon Constable Alana Warwick returns. This time she wishes to discuss the description of my stalker. She accepts my offer of an orange juice.

Constable Warwick asks, "Did you happen to see his hair?"

"No. The baseball cap is always pulled low. I think it's to shadow his face, rather than hide his hair. In any case, on all three encounters, at the shopping center, underground parking lot, and park, I caught just a glimpse of him."

"You stated yesterday that your assessment was of a tall man. Why did you assess him as tall?"

"On all three occasions I assessed him to be at least six feet tall by comparing him to objects beside him. For example, in the underground parking lot, I later compared his height to the van he was standing beside."

"What about the color of his skin?" Alana asks.

"Yesterday, I had difficulty focusing on what I noticed. Today, I recall that when in the shopping center I observed a flash of white skin. He is Caucasian. As stated, six feet tall and approximately one hundred and seventy-five pounds. He is in great physical shape. What did you find at the site where poor Rusty was killed?"

She hesitates for a moment than decides to share the information with me. "I found the weapon, a switch blade knife, covered in blood. We are hoping for a spot of the stalker's blood and/or a fingerprint from the knife or the dog's collar. But it takes time." She looks down at her note book.

"He terrorizes me and we wait." Now I know what my victims experience.

Constable Warwick stares at me and I see sympathy in her eyes. "I'm sorry, Ms. Browne."

"You can call me Ashley, and I'm the one who is sorry. It was a rude remark on my part, because I know it's not your fault."

"I understand. One more question please. How do you think the stalker knew you would be jogging there yesterday?"

I shudder and answer, "An interesting question you ask constable. Somehow I have avoided it because in all probability he was watching my house from the park. How else would he know?"

"I will request another patrol car for today. I'm certain it will receive high priority. Thank you for the information. By the way I spoke to the Mantles, but there is nothing of significance to report."

I see Alana Warwick to the door and she promises to keep in touch.

For a change, Sam is home early and the four of us enjoy a quiet dinner. We have discussions on the wedding, politics, and sports, but no one mentions what lays heaviest on all of our minds.

When we retire to the great room, Sam refers to Gail's murder. "All crime scene evidence results have been back for months, but we are no further ahead. No prints and no DNA available. Our monster is clever."

I say abruptly, "Well just find Chartrand and you have her murderer."

There is a prolonged silence. At last Sam speaks, "I'm not so positive anymore that it's Chartrand."

"What makes you think that?" I'm stunned.

"Maybe a cop's instinct. Where is he? No one has seen him. I have my snitches and I find it odd that we haven't even a sniff. Every cop in the country is looking for him and nothing. If he is responsible, he'd have to be around and someone would surely have seen him. I now wonder about his brother?"

"We have addressed a possible change in appearance for Chartrand, which means he could be living in the open. I can't see the brother being involved."

"Maybe that's true." Sam then turns to Dad and asks, "Do you know the background on Kevin? Is he an intelligent guy?"

All three of us just stare at Sam, than we talk all at once. I'm saying, "You can't be serious.", and Mom squeaks out a, "Kevin would never hurt Ashley.", and Dad, with his mouth gaping open finally says, "Do you think it is Kevin, for heaven's sake?"

Sam responds to all of us, "He has shown some weird behavior around Ashley."

My parent's heads whip around in my direction. Of course in the past I chose not to share my encounters with Kevin. I fill them in regarding his stalking behavior and include my threat of a restraining order.

Dad is fuming and Mom is totally silent. Then she exclaims, "My God, we may have introduced a monster into our daughter's life."

Sam responds, "Please, not so fast. It's just a hunch at this point."

I turn to Dad, "Where is he from and is he intelligent? I ask because our murderer is a very clever person."

"Kevin is from Ontario and yes, he is smart. Socially, we eventually found him to be aggressive. That is why we didn't pressure you about the relationship. By the way, he's not invited to the wedding."

"Interesting," is all Sam comments to Dad's information.

I say, "You know this nightmare has given me a headache. Let's talk about something pleasant."

Mom immediately shifts to the wedding. "Do you think there is sufficient selection for the evening lunch?"

Dad interrupts, saying, "You're not feeding the entire province." The argument is on between them.

Sam's expression tells me he's ready for sleep. Before excusing himself, he warns all of us against discussing Kevin with others. He then leaves for our bedroom. My parents and I chat for another hour.

Shelly calls the next afternoon. She tells me Marty Kroll called my office on Monday, wanting to speak to me and she informed him that I was away for a month. He shared with her that his client, the teacher accused of child molestation, is considering a plea bargain. But he said it could wait until my return. Apparently Logan suggested she proceed with negotiations, but she declined, preferring to leave the decision to me. I thank her for calling and reinforce the fact that I'm available should she need me again.

Mom and Dad leave the next day. It was pleasant having them. Sam is off tomorrow. I sarcastically think babysitting duties are over for my parents. A constant anger has moved into me.

I wave good-bye, but I continue to stand at the window long afterwards, as if frozen to the spot. This fiend is changing my character, creating an angry, paranoid, sarcastic, and a very frightened woman. I can't prevent myself from walking toward the patio doors, checking the locks and security system. I then perch on the sofa, staring into space, waiting for Sam's return. The patrol car is gone and I remain frightened, rooted to the sofa.

I know I need to snap out of this and decide to unpack Sam's boxes. We kept his favorite chair in the great room and put the remainder of the living room furniture downstairs in the family room. Sam sold his bedroom suite and dinette.

I check the security system again and then unpack. I put two boxes of books into the library and his compact discs into the entertainment center's CD stand. I shuffle things around in one of the bedroom dressers and free a shelf in the walk-in closet as well. I empty a box of briefs and socks into the dresser drawer and place a suitcase full of T-shirts on the shelf in the closet. Yesterday, we managed to find sufficient space to hang the majority of his clothes in the closet.

I should be happy, because Sam's moving in is a big event in my life. Stopping in front of the mirror I look at the reflection and am shocked at what I see. This is not like my usual face. It is gaunt with sunken cheeks, and prominent cheekbones. Large, black circles are under my eyes, a cloudy, almost vacant look emerges from my eyes, and a turned down mouth looks like it hasn't smiled in mouths. I try to recall the last time I was truly happy, and I can't remember an event in the past two months that brought me true joy.

I sit on my bed and think about what this monster has done to me. Later I rise and check the security system again. I am so depressed.

Suddenly, I'm exhausted. I can hardly move, but before I head for the sofa, I draw every drape. I check the security system one more time, lie down on the sofa and promptly fall asleep.

According to a wall clock the phone rings an hour later and its Sam letting me know he will be home in an hour. I haven't thought of what I would make for dinner, nor do I feel hungry. To put up a good front, I thaw two chicken breasts in the microwave and prepare them for the oven. I take out the rice and cut up fresh vegetables. I remind myself that Sam and I need to discuss his high blood pressure and plans for lowering it.

Following dinner Sam notices pamphlets I have placed on the kitchen counter. "Where did you get these?"

"When you went to the washroom at Phil's office, I picked them up. It's very interesting information on hypertension. If you aren't too tired, I would like to take time now to talk about some of the things."

"Sure honey, let's move to the sofa in the great room. I will grab a beer and get you a wine."

"Thanks, no wine for me tonight." Sam stops and looks at me and decides not to pursue the subject.

When we are comfortable on the sofa, I start with, "Sam, let us discuss exercise first. I know you move a lot at work, but the pamphlet says you should have sustained exercise, like riding a bike, using a tread mill, or jogging, at least three times a week. What about weight lifting? I know you did body building. Is there something you think you may like?"

"I have decided to join you jogging. It would be something we could do together. I also love to swim."

"That's wonderful. Swimming is a great exercise. There is a pool not far from here. You could buy a membership. Will you do that when we get back from the honeymoon?"

"Yes, I will. I plan to join you regularly as well."

"That will definitely please me. The diet isn't going to be as easy because I know you like adding salt to everything. It tells you here that you should avoid adding table salt to your meal. So I can cook with a little salt, but you shouldn't add the extra. How do you feel about that?"

"I hate it, but I'll try. What type of food do I avoid?"

"Things like bacon, ham, processed meats, canned soups, and salted peanuts. We will look at the salt or sodium content when we purchase food from now on. The pamphlet states you should eat more fish and chicken."

"There's nothing wrong with fish and chicken, as long as you throw in the occasional steak. Phil called about my results which were remarkably normal. He suggested an appointment with a community nutritionist. I'll do that, to take responsibility for my own health."

"You are a darling. I love you. As for the stress issue, I think once we catch whoever is tormenting me and they lower your work load, your blood pressure will slide back to normal levels."

"Glad you mentioned it, because I was talking to Edward today, and after our honeymoon the two of us are seeing the brass about our work loads. Edward is just as snowed under as I am."

"I believe our love will help us through these issues. We are fortunate to have each other and now that you are home with me, I'll get out of this funk I'm in."

"I hope so. It's just days away now and I am so looking forward to our wedding. It is our wedding, Ashley. It sounds like music in the air."

"I never knew you to be such a romantic. That last thought sounded like it should be part of a romantic poem."

Sam appears embarrassed at my comments and I tease him about it for a few minutes. We tickle each other and I win because he is extremely ticklish. We end up making love on the rug.

Sam later wants to watch a program on television. We spread out on the sofa and with Sam's arms around me, I fall asleep. We sleep on the sofa the remainder of the night, and it's the best sleep we have both had in some time.

CHAPTER 43

▼

This is the first time in our relationship that Sam and I have had more than two days off together. It is sad that I feel frightened that something awful is going to happen at our wedding. Having read up on the subject of depression, I know that thoughts of doom and foreboding can occur.

The phone call Mom received has scared me beyond anything I had thought possible. I think about it almost constantly, even if Sam has attempted to convince me it was a coincidence.

Pamela shares that when she suffered from a bout with depression, everything in her life became doom and gloom.

"I didn't know you suffered from depression. When was this?"

"When I broke up with Wayne, I went into a funk." He is a fellow she dated for three years.

"I didn't know that Pamela. You should have shared it with me. How did you feel at the time?"

"I felt that the walls were caving in on me. Yet, I didn't want to see anyone. I just withdrew from everyone and stayed in my home. I didn't even want to wash my hair."

"Did you miss work because of it?"

"No, because I took one month's vacation and saw a psychiatrist. Between seeing her and a medication regime, I was able to manage the symptoms. I eventually worked myself out of the depression."

"Thank you for sharing with me. I'm hoping to do just that." We say good-bye and hang up.

Sam's attempt to cheer me up does work. First, he decides to register both of us at the pool. On Sunday evening we grab our swimming suits and towels and head out. There aren't many people in the pool, because most have to work tomorrow and have not ventured out. Sam and I have a great time racing each other the length of the pool. He wins eight out of ten races.

On Monday, we go shopping for a gift for Pamela and Josh as a thank you for being the maid of honor and best man. We finally settle on gold cuff links for Josh, and marquis diamond earrings for Pamela. We have them gift wrapped.

As we leave the jewelry shop, Sam asks me. "Do you want to take in a movie or would you prefer to go home?"

I want the safety of my home, but realize that Sam doesn't need to suffer when he enjoys going to a movie. I say, "A movie is an excellent idea. I haven't gone to a movie theatre for years."

"What would you like to see?"

"Let's purchase a paper, Sam, and see what's playing. There's a drugstore over there."

We get the paper but notice that most movies listed center around violence. Although I'm aware that movies in the past ten or more years have become more violent; it never affected me before. Now I say to Sam, "I would prefer not to see one with a lot of brutality. Do you mind?"

"No. What do you think about this comedy? I heard it received great reviews."

"It sounds good to me. We'd better get moving because it starts in twenty minutes."

Sam pays for popcorn and sodas and then complains all the way to our seats. "It cost twelve dollars for four kernels of popcorn. Savor every bit, because I'm not buying any more."

I whisper, "Is that cost with or without the pop?"

Sam laughs and answers, "The twelve dollars is for the popcorn only."

During the movie I find myself occasionally checking around the darkened theatre for any movement that is unusual. Sam notices, grasps my hand and says, "Relax, enjoy the movie."

I try, but the past horrors are catching up to me in the darkened theatre. I find myself wishing for the movie to end, but make no suggestion to Sam that I want to leave now.

When the movie is finally over, I almost run from the crowded theatre. We stop at the local butcher shop and pick up two salmon steaks for dinner. While Sam prepares dinner, I put our wedding purchases in a bag destined for my parents. We enjoy dinner and make it an early night. Although Sam has told me he checked the security system, I do it again when he is in the bathroom.

On Wednesday afternoon the call finally comes. I have been waiting for it, somehow knowing he would call before our wedding. I am drawn to the phone, knowing I should ignore it, but afraid I may miss an important clue if it goes unanswered. We're chasing that needle in a haystack.

Sam is at the car wash getting one of the complete shine jobs to his car, which will be used for the wedding.

I answer, "Drop dead you bastard!"

The raspy voice laughs in that guttural tone, "Ashley that is not a proper lady-like response. Will you enjoy your wedding? Or better still, will you be alive for your wedding?" The line goes dead. I'm immediately angry with myself, because Sam requested that I keep the stalker on line as long as possible, in order to get a decent voice tracing. Sam will not be pleased.

I run to the kitchen to ensure Sam has locked the door. I must do something to keep my mind occupied. I decide to pack and pull out my suitcases. I pack one for the wedding and the other for the honeymoon. All my makeup, toiletries, and jewelry I put in a carryon case.

When Sam arrives, I admire the almost blinding shine on his car. I ask him if he needs help packing, but he declines. After dinner he does his thing, but I can't help but ask if he packed this article or that one, until finally he tells me to back off, because he has packed his own suitcase for twenty-five years. He then laughs, so I know he is not angry.

I have debated all evening whether I should share the phone call with him. I finally decide that after our conversation about trust, I should not be keeping any secrets. Also, something may be gained from the phone tap.

"While you were washing your car he called again. I wasn't going to tell you, but decided that would not be practicing my trust talk with you."

"I thought something was up because you have been more jumpy than usual tonight. Tell me every detail."

"I answered the phone, "Drop dead you bastard," and he informed me that it wasn't very ladylike of me. He told me to enjoy my wedding. Can you believe the monster telling me how I should behave? I could kill him right now." I stand up and stomp furiously.

Sam puts out his hand and gently pulls me over to the sofa. He says, "The interesting thing about the conversation is that he refers to our wedding. How would Chartrand know about our wedding?"

My mind races through possibilities and I see where Sam is going with this. "I see your point. There have been no announcements in the paper. Whoever it is must be close enough to us to have that information."

Sam has placed an arm around my shoulder and is holding me close. "Of our possibilities, who does know about our wedding?"

"Kevin would know because most people in town will be talking about it. Logan would have heard because I invited so many individuals from work. A lot of people using the Law Courts building regularly would know, because I haven't been around in any of the court rooms. Anyone could ask where I am, and the answer would be that I've taken time off to get married. The word would then travel quickly."

"It certainly leaves us with many people to consider. I don't like Chartrand as your stalker anymore. There are too many inconsistencies, when you look at all the evidence. Of course the big question is who do we look at now? I think we need to spend some time looking for Chartrand's brother. Maybe they connected and are now working together."

"That is a good idea. I'm so tired of being frightened. There is one more thing. The caller also said, "Will you be alive for your wedding?'"

"Oh crap, I'm so sorry I wasn't at home when you received the phone call. The day I catch this monster, I hope no one else is around because I'm going to beat him to a pulp. I mean that. They talk about police brutality, but until this very moment I have never experienced this type of anger against an individual, including my dad."

"Me too, I want to rip him apart. I want to find out what his fear is, because we all have a fear. I want to expose him to his fear, day after day, after day."

"I know you are sick of hearing this, but the case is at a standstill right now and we desperately need a break."

"We can't solve it tonight and we need to get some rest. Tomorrow is a big day. We should probably leave for Mom's around two. I will contact them in the morning, because they may need us to pick up something in the city."

"It sounds great honey, because I feel the need for some shut eye." We suffer another sleepless night.

CHAPTER 44

▼

The grand day has arrived. Today I become Ashley Orlicky. The last two days have been hectic with last minute decisions and a wedding rehearsal. The rehearsal went well, with Reverend Anderson making the occasional joke, to help put Sam at ease. Josh seems taken with Pamela and I wonder if Sam will tell him that Pamela's heart lies elsewhere.

Pamela and Josh arrived yesterday in time for the wedding rehearsal. Both are staying over at the house. Pamela's love is arriving later today and will stay there as well. Again, I feel badly for Sam, because he has no family present.

Mom and I have numerous phone and face to face contacts with Mona Komalski, who is in charge of the wedding dinner and lunch. I remember Mona from my teenage years. She is an attractive lady with dark hair, brown eyes, and a trim figure. We meet with her on Friday afternoon to finalize all menu plans. She is a beautiful person, with a great sense of humor.

We also meet with Joan and Bob to reassure them that their selection of flowers, baskets of lilies for the church, and small bouquets of roses with baby breath for the head table are acceptable. Orchids will be pinned on family members. Joan and Bob have aged well. I recognize them immediately. She has brown hair and hazel eyes, with an attractive face. Bob is handsome, of medium height, and loves to tease. Both are sun tanned from their stay in Arizona.

Dad booked rooms at a local motel for guests from out of town. As of last evening apparently there is not a hotel/motel room available, which is unusual in this town for mid-April.

Following a hearty breakfast we visit the salon, where I'm bombarded with questions from clientele coming to and leaving the shop. The wedding is the talk of the town.

One middle-aged lady with a tight perm comes up to me and says, "It's so nice to see you. I was pleased when your parents invited Ronald and me to the wedding. You will make a beautiful bride."

"Thank you. It is great to see you." I don't have a clue as to who this woman or her husband Ronald are. Mom tells me it is Mrs. Cook, who lives four doors down from my parent's home.

As we are leaving a former school friend of mine approaches me timidly. Her name is Sally Perlson and she married her childhood sweetheart at age eighteen. Mom shared with me earlier that Sally has six children, and her husband is mostly unemployed. I spend ten minutes talking to Sally and promise I will spend some time with her at the wedding reception.

Back home Mom and Pamela assist me with dressing. The gown looks lovely and both ladies keep repeating how beautiful I look. There is excitement in the room, and I am pleased that Mom and Pamela are here to share it with me. I'm missing Gail.

At one-thirty we are ready to leave for church. Dad states Sam has been ready since twelve-thirty and was pacing the floor, so he sent Sam, Josh, and Perry out for a ride. They will meet us at church. I am excited and looking forward to becoming Sam's wife.

The church is decorated with ribbons and flowers and filled with the smell of lilies. The pews are packed and the four piece string orchestra provides wonderful background music. The ceremony goes like clockwork and I hear the words, "You may kiss the bride." I am now, Mrs. Ashley Orlicky. It feels wonderful. As we exit the church there are countless family members and friends throwing confetti and rice. I am so happy.

We are on our way to the photo shoot, but everyone wants to chat with me. Sam grabs my hand and pulls me away from the crowd toward the wedding car parked in front of the church. Some of my cousins have decorated the car and a just married sign, hangs at the rear of the vehicle.

As Sam opens the back door for me, I gaze over the roof of the car. Lurking across the street, Kevin is taking pictures. He suddenly lowers the camera and I observe what I think is hate on his face. I don't acknowledge him, but quickly get into the car. Sam sits beside me. I'm so angry, I can't speak.

Sam is studying my face and gently squeezes my hand. He inquires, "What is wrong?"

I take a deep breath before answering, "Did you see that bastard taking pictures?"

"Who is taking pictures? What are you saying?" Sam is now whispering to me so Barry, my cousin, can't hear him. Barry is driving the wedding car.

"Kevin."

"Kevin was outside the church? I didn't see him."

"Actually, he was across the street taking pictures of us. I noticed him as I entered the car. It makes me so angry."

"The streets are common property. We legally can't prevent him from standing there. If this continues in the city, where he is staying outside our home, I could approach him for an official chat. We will be starting background checks on him when we return from our honeymoon."

"Oh, I'm sorry. Let's just concentrate on us for now."

"I agree, Mrs. Orlicky."

I whisper, "I love the sound of that and I love you. Maybe we should take a side trip to Mom's house? Are you interested?" I attempt to move onto his lap.

Sam laughs. "I didn't think I would ever hear myself say this, but no side trips. I was informed by your mom, I guess my mom now," Sam stops, his face turning red, "that it is photos at three-thirty sharp in the park."

I decide not to embarrass him further by mentioning the blushing. He is so pleased to be part of my parent's life.

My cousin takes the photos without a glitch at a local park. It's a bright and sunny day. She has us stand in front of beds of flowers with trees as a background. There is no wind to speak of, therefore my veil and everyone's hair remains intact. The wedding party and others' assembled, enjoy a few bottles of champagne and finger foods which Mom displays on a crisp, white, table cloth on a park bench

At 5:30 we arrive at the parish hall to greet the guests attending the dinner and dance. There are countless hand shakes, and of course a few sloppy kisses from the older gentlemen.

The dinner is wonderful. Mona has certainly outdone herself. I must remember to thank her, and Joan and Bob, during speeches. I'm too nervous and excited to eat much. Friends have shared with me that rarely does the bride remember all events of the day. My fondest memory will be of Sam calling my mother, "Mom." Edward does a wonderful toast to the groom and my uncle's toast to me is beautiful. Donna and I get an opportunity to chat and we catch up on some local gossip. Her singing and band are wonderful.

I do get the chance to talk further with Sally. I feel badly for her. Sally shares with me that she would like to leave her husband, but the thought of raising six children on her own is preventing her from following through. I discuss the services available to help her, and we promise to keep in touch. With my life in turmoil right now, I must try to remember to do just that.

A friend I haven't seen for two years is able to make it to our wedding. Barb and her husband Trevor retired in Hawaii, in their early thirties. Trevor was involved in a computer business, which he sold. Barb and I were friends in high school and got our first apartment together. She is petite and pretty, with black hair and deep, violet blue eyes. Trevor is handsome and loves hockey. He says he's surfing in Hawaii. Barb informs me they are thinking about returning to Canada to live. I hope they do, because a phone call will never replace the face to face interactions.

Sam and I say our good-byes and depart the hall at 2:30 in the morning. We stop at Mom and Dads for me to do a quick change from the wedding dress, and for Sam to leave his tuxedo. Dad has promised to return it for him. We leave a big thank you note to my parents, plus tickets for a Hawaii vacation for two.

Our bags are packed and in the car. We head to our honeymoon suite at a five star hotel in Edmonton.

Both of us are exhausted when we arrive, because it's now four. Sam suggests we need to stimulate our bodies by sharing a shower. He states, "It's what Sam has ordered, not the doctor."

He slowly removes my dress and slip, and then to my surprise he picks me up and lays me across the bed. He removes my nylons. To my delight he then proceeds to massage my feet. I may cry I'm so grateful. I moan, "The best wedding present imaginable." After a few minutes, I say, "Let me remove a few articles of clothing from you." With that I grab the zipper of his trousers. "How well I know you."

He grabs me and starts a slow trail of kisses over my face, neck, and breasts. I'm fighting with the buttons of his shirt when I remember an incident from my time at university. A friend of mine, Arlene, had grabbed this fellow's shirt in each hand, than pulled. I do the same now and buttons are flying around the room. Sam laughs with delight as he removes my bra and panties.

"Let's check out the shower, sweetheart." Sam moans.

"I'm more interested in checking you out, Mr. Orlicky." Holding hands we enter the large bathroom.

We set the temperature and spend some time soaping each other. We touch gently, lovingly, enjoying each other. I guide him into me. We are now both riding the wave and as we go under, Sam and I both cry out our love for each other.

We quickly towel dry after the shower and head for bed. We are exhausted. Sam is holding me in his arms and asks if I have any reserve energy.

I respond, "Not tonight Sam, I have a headache." We both chuckle and within seconds Sam is asleep. The next day at one in the afternoon, we leave for ten days in the Bahamas.

Sam booked a honeymoon suite in a five star hotel on the beach front. We arrive in time to view the sun set over the Atlantic Ocean from our bedroom balcony. As I take in the stunning, magnificent scene, all my troubles evaporate into the warm night air. It's unbelievable. This is the top of the world and I have the king of the hill standing with me, holding me tight.

The suite consists of a three room bathroom done with golden highlights, a living room, and a huge bedroom. The Jacuzzi is massive and Sam can't wait to jump in. The living room has a three piece white leather sectional, with lovely colored soft cushions scattered about the sofa. There is a gigantic entertainment centre with every electronic device imaginable. Sam will be in his glory. In one corner a dining suite overlooks the courtyard and beach area. It's a lovely view.

The bedroom is very impressive and the most luxurious. In the center of the room stands an enormous, circular, bed. It has a memory mattress, covered with white satin sheets, pillow cases, and plush, brightly colored, circular cushions are placed artfully on the bed. The furniture is oak with mirrored fronts on all the dressers and head of the bed. A large entertainment centre covers one of the bedroom walls. The walk-in closet is similar to mine at home.

On the bedroom balcony, Sam gently turns me in his arms and whispers, "Let's practice making those babies." This is a teasing statement, as Sam and I have decided to put off having children until my tormentor is caught. He has affected every aspect of our lives.

I gaze into his eyes, smile and say, "I have a surprise for you. I would like to model it, but need to unpack first."

"You do that while I unpack my luggage and order up some wine." Sam heads for the phone.

As I deposit my clothing in drawers and the closet, I locate the trunks Pamela bought Sam as a joke wedding present. They are bright red spandex. I display them to Sam and comment, "Only fair Sam. These are for you." I can't prevent myself from laughing out loud.

He appears shocked, his face turning red. Somewhat upset, he says, "You must be joking, Ashley. Where did you unearth those disgusting trunks? If I wear them you can kiss having children good-bye."

I laugh, "They are a joke gift from Pamela. She spotted and purchased them the day we went shopping."

I pause recalling the man stalking me. I quickly raise a hand signaling to Sam, I want no further discussion of the horrors we have faced over the past year. It is, after all, our honeymoon. Understanding, he walks across the room and holds me tight. Everything is soon forgotten.

A waiter brings a wonderful wine and two glasses. Included on his trolley is a basket of fruit from management. I enjoy some pineapple and coconut with my wine.

While Sam is taking a shower I put on my new negligee and immediately do a sexy dance when he enters the room. He has a towel wrapped around his waist. Sam dances toward me and says, "How sexy is that?" I move forward in a hurry and yank off his towel. He removes my negligee and carries me into the room with the Jacuzzi. We turn on the water and Sam gently places me in the Jacuzzi then joins me. Our lovemaking has never been better.

The ten days are heaven. We swim, lie on the beach, have drinks pool side, and in the evenings we have dinner out. We make love often, and I wish this dream would last forever.

Sam talks about what it was like to be raised in a loveless family.

I ask him, "Why haven't you sought the rest of your family? I'm referring to your extended family."

He looks at me then says, "My mom and dad's families must have known about the conditions I lived under, but never once did they come to visit or save me from my dad's brutality."

"Do you know where your parents were born?"

"My dad's family lived in Toronto and my mom's in a small town approximately eighty kilometers from Toronto."

"We can attempt to locate your mom's family. Maybe they never knew where your mother was residing."

"They could have looked for their daughter. My God, she was alone with that cruel bastard."

"I agree, but maybe they were poor or afraid to tackle the big city. Look at my parents when they come to the city. They only drive to certain stores, because Dad is now familiar with the road to get them there. You should give your grandparents the benefit of the doubt."

"I can understand what you are saying, but will never understand why people mistreat their children."

"I appreciate your comment. I see it often at work."

"It is difficult for me to discuss my life. Right now, I have no intention of looking for my past."

I decide to cheer up Sam and relate some funny stories about growing up in small town Alberta.

"My dad met my mom by bidding on her basket, which contained egg salad sandwiches, home made pickles, and carrot cake."

"What do you mean by, "her basket?" I never heard such crazy things before." He is looking at me as if I have grown an extra head.

"Years ago in our little town a woman, or I should say young girl, prepared a basket of home made goodies, and a man would bid on the basket during our Sunday fairs. It raised money for the church. Sometimes there would be three men bidding on the same basket."

"You are joking." He's laughing at me.

"No, I'm not. The man with the highest bid got the basket and sometimes, as in my mom's case, the girl would go out with the purchaser for a picnic."

Sam thinks I'm exaggerating or pulling his leg, because he has always lived in a city. We are getting to know and understand each other better during this quiet time.

Our departure day eventually arrives and it's time to face reality. We arrive back in Edmonton at two in the afternoon. As we exit customs, nine or ten reporters approach us.

One is holding today's local newspaper. The headline reads, "Prosecutor back from Honeymoon," with my picture beneath the caption. The reporters are firing questions at me, "Who was stalking you?"; "Why was a patrol car outside your house for days?"; "Are you in danger?"; "Was it someone you prosecuted?"; "Is it Billie Chartrand?"; "Will you receive further protection?"

The need to lie down and sob is overpowering. Sam stares at me and with a look of steel turns and informs the reporters to back off.

He states, "We have no comment at this time. Let us through please. I'm her husband, Sergeant Sam Orlicky. I promise tomorrow I'll have a statement for the press. Currently I don't appreciate you hounding my wife. Excuse us ladies and gentlemen. Thank you."

As we move forward a reporter reaches out and touches Sam's arm as if to detain him. Sam stops and glares at the reporter, who immediately steps back. Yes, my husband can protect me.

On the way to the airport for the Bahamas a friend of Sam's picked up his car at the hotel and took it to his home. Sam and I took a taxi to the airport. So we hail a taxi now and have him stop at a convenience store, because Sam is eager to get a newspaper. When we arrive home we huddle over the paper. The story discusses the chase in the park and the killing of the dog.

It refers to Billie Chartrand and the fact that I prosecuted him. The previous day's paper discussed Chartrand's escape. Sam is furious, "Who the hell talked about this to the press? I will kill the son of a bitch if I root out the culprit. Sorry for the language, honey. We have managed to keep this under wraps for months. Now someone wanted a headline. Damn it to hell. So you will suffer for it. The press will be all over us."

I interrupt, "Take it easy. Remember your high blood pressure, please. I can vouch for the Mantles. They promised not to discuss the chase in the park with the press or anyone other than the police. I trust them. I am annoyed with Pamela for not giving us a heads-up."

Sam looks at me with eyebrows raised and says, "How could she do that when we were in the Bahamas?"

"She could have contacted us at the hotel number I provided her prior to leaving. I asked her to call, if anything unusual happened. I asked her because Mom and Dad are traveling east, as you know, on a much needed vacation. A holiday they planned for the past two years."

"Who do you think talked to the press?"

"Well, it really leaves the people we work with because both groups knew about the chase in the park."

"I'm afraid it will push the psycho to make another move soon. They thrive on recognition in the news media and that fact scares me. Try contacting Pamela to see what she knows."

I call but her voice message comes on. I ask her to call me as soon as possible. We then listen to our messages which are numerous. Most are from family and friends thanking us for a great wedding celebration. There is no message from the stalker, but we didn't expect one. It appears he knows our every move.

Sam runs next door to collect our mail. He is concerned about further threatening letters. As predicted, a suspicious letter is among our stack of mail. Again on a single white sheet of paper made from newspaper clippings are the words, "You Die Soon. The Honeymoon Is Over." The envelope was mailed at the end of April. I want to cry but hold back the tears.

Sam handles it cautiously and then places the paper and envelope into a larger envelope. Chances of finding DNA and/or fingerprints on this letter are slim. I feel as if someone has dropped me down an elevator shaft and I stop suddenly. My stomach and heart are in my mouth. Feelings of anxiety quickly overtake me, and cast aside the feelings of joy experienced during our honeymoon. It feels as if we never left home. My tormentor made sure I would feel yanked back to reality on my return. I'm surprised he didn't meet me at the airport. I'm so angry, but do recognize I'm just wasting my energy. I'm at his complete mercy.

"Ashley, I must go to work tomorrow. If Carmen's free, can I ask her to come over tomorrow?"

"No. No more babysitters are needed for me. You said this is a top notch security system. I appreciate the demands at work are still there waiting for you. What could Carmen do to help in this situation? I will be fine. Can we go now to purchase groceries for the week? Then I will stay put and not leave the house." I realize I'm rambling and suddenly shut my mouth. To myself I think, *Yes, Ashley, you are a prisoner in your own home.* I'm a caged animal.

Sam is staring at me, but doesn't remark on my flight of ideas. Instead he says, "Great idea to get groceries now. I will just grab your car keys. I'll pick up my car later today."

While shopping Sam and I try to purchase foods low in sodium. We are top heavy with vegetables and fruit, along with fish, chicken, and extra lean beef. Sam stated emphatically that tofu is completely out of the question. We are back in an hour.

Sam calls a taxi and returns in an hour with his car.

There are no further phone calls. Following a light supper, we tune into the local television news station. Ten minutes later there is a thirty second news segment on me, with reference to Billie Chartrand. They have a picture of him on screen. That night, I wake up screaming with a nightmare. Sam is instantly awake and is holding me close. Shivering I ask for the hundredth time, "When does it end?"

As before, he has no answer. He holds me close and eventually I fall into a restless sleep.

On Thursday, Sam is late and doesn't arrive home until 7:30. His face is ashen and his hands are shaking slightly. I hurry to him and ask, "What's wrong Sam? You are so pale."

"Come sit in the great room."

When seated, he holds my hands and begins, "This morning we received a phone call from Alfred Anderly, a farmer east of the city. His son, Wayne, was hunting in a wooded area and stumbled upon a grave, which a wild animal had dug up. The grave was deep, but the animal was persistent."

Sam stops for a second and takes a deep breath. He continues, "Although we can't positively identify without DNA testing, I believe it is Billie Chartrand."

This is not what I had expected, and it feels like someone has punched me in the stomach. All the air escapes my lungs and I can't breathe. Suddenly, Sam is shaking me, yelling for me to take a deep breath. I can't and Sam gently slaps me across the face and I gulp in air from surprise. He then makes me deep breathe.

"Come on, breath in, blow out!"

When I regain normal breathing and some composure I ask, "How long Sam? How long has he been dead?"

I desperately want to hear three days, one week, even one month.

Sam replies, "For months, Ashley. From the condition of the body we think close to the time he escaped. He was shot once between the eyes and once in the heart. I don't have a lot of details."

"Why do you think it's him?" To myself I'm thinking, *Please let it be nothing but an educated guess.*

"Chartrand had a metal plate in his thigh. This was discovered when he was at the Remand Center. The man in the grave also has a metal plate"

"Who do you think murdered him?"

"Right now, I don't know for certain. We are speculating that it may be his brother, because who else would kill Billie? You or I didn't murder the bastard, although I would have liked to. I can't think of anyone else who would murder him. It's so important to get more background on Chartrand's movements over the years. Where in the hell did the bastard work? If he didn't work, how did he make his money? Did he rob banks, fence stolen jewelry, or paintings? Was he in touch with his brother over the years?"

"He had money before he was caught, because he was able to hire Marty. One thing we haven't discussed is drugs. He could have been a pusher. A drug lord could have murdered him."

Sam pauses. "You are right he may have had drug money. Before I was certain it was Chartrand stalking you, but if he's dead, obviously not. Recently, I thought your stalker might be Kevin. Nothing was gained so far from the phone tap."

"I'm terrified. Before we knew or thought we knew who was after me and that was bad enough. But now it's a whole new ball game. I'm terribly confused."

We both sit in silence for a few minutes. Sam reaches for me and holds me tightly. I can scarcely breathe. He whispers, "I love you so much. It tears me apart that I haven't caught whoever is doing this to you. I recognize you can't go on like this much longer. But I don't know where to turn. Tomorrow we are going to investigate Kevin further. Delve deeper into his background. I was hoping to do it today, but was snowed under after the discovery of the body. After all, Kevin, like Chartrand, is from Ontario and could be his brother."

There is a sudden creaking sound from the kitchen area and I jump. The reaction angers me, but I say nothing.

I tell Sam there is a roast chicken in the oven and it is time to eat dinner. His face tells me he is not into eating anymore than I. Recognizing I need to move about before I scream; I walk quickly to the kitchen and start serving the food. I hope this will use up some energy. We pick at our food but eat little.

It is a relief when the phone rings. It's Pamela. She apologizes for not telling me the news, but was down east and hadn't heard it. She was stunned when she arrived today and discovered the stories in the paper and on the television news.

Pamela asks, "What can I do?"

Realizing I need a friend right now I reply, "Well if you can spare a day from work can you come over tomorrow morning and spend the day? We can open some wedding gifts."

I look at Sam with a questioning look and he nods.

"My parents dropped the gifts off before they went on their trip east. The gifts are sitting right here. Sam doesn't mind. We will open some tonight. Tomorrow you and I will open the rest and leave them on display for Sam."

"I would be happy to keep you company Ashley, and open gifts. I hope we open a diamond or two."

Now I start speaking rapidly, "I must tell you Pamela that Sam believes they found Billie Chartrand, dead, murdered for some time."

"My God, who has been stalking you?"

"We don't know. It could be Chartrand's brother. I'm sharing this information with you so you can appreciate that it may be dangerous to come here. Remember, the stalker probably murdered Gail. I was so sure Chartrand killed her."

"Let the bastard try something with us. Anyway I have to go, my guy is here. See you early tomorrow, Ashley."

"Don't mention the Billie Chartrand news to anyone."

"I promise. Bye."

Sam is relieved that Pamela is coming over tomorrow. The stalker, who is terrorizing me, is also having a huge impact on Sam's life.

I ask Sam, "Are you sure you are okay with Pamela opening some of our wedding gifts with me?"

"Absolutely, I'm okay with it. I am so happy you will have company. Pamela will not necessarily be protecting you, but she will provide you with distraction. Just leave out the gifts with the cards beside them, so I know who they are from. I guess we need to send thank you cards, right?"

"Oh Sam, you are so cute. You surprise me every day and yes we will send out cards. I have time to do that. Actually, Pamela and I will leave the envelopes sealed, if the little cards are attached to the present. Many of the larger envelopes will have money in them."

Sam has a puzzled expression on his face. He says, "Are you joking? People give us money as a present?"

"Yes, we will open those together. I will list the gifts in a book with the senders name next to it."

"Man, I wish someone would have told me I could give money for a wedding present. Shit, I spent countless hours looking for a gift for weddings I attended in the past. The guys were probably laughing themselves sick."

"Sam, you are funny."

"Thank you, honey. Come let's open a few before we retire for the night."

The next morning Pamela arrives at eight just before Sam leaves for work. He jokes with her about the red spandex trunks He obviously feels more at ease with her.

Sam departs and Pamela and I enjoy opening gifts and jotting down the present and sender. We received six fancy toasters and I offer one to Pamela which she accepts. The gifts range from a beautiful painting, to a matching his and her towel set. We receive at least ten sets of sheets and pillow cases. Sam and I didn't choose a registry, because we were late in setting the wedding date.

I excuse myself mid-afternoon and phone my boss. I explain my present situation and request another two days, next Monday and Tuesday. He hesitates for a moment, then grants the request and asks for a meeting when I return next Wednesday. I thank him and hang up. I can understand his concern, because it is nearing the middle of May and I have been off one month now. If Logan is still as useless as before, then poor Shelly is overwhelmed.

Sam is home at five. I invite Pamela to join us for dinner, but she begs off as she has a dinner date. Of course, it's Friday night.

Sam and I spend a few hours looking through the gifts. He is overwhelmed by people's generosity. This type of sharing isn't something familiar to him. I have gathered all the wedding cards and we move to the sofa. I have my book ready to jot down the sender and amounts. Every time Sam opens a card he says, "My word can you believe this?" We have received many checks and cash. It's mounting.

When he reaches the card from Pamela, he is shocked, his eyes almost popping their sockets. "Ashley look, one, two, three, four, five, six, seven, eight, nine and one thousand dollars! Pamela gave us one thousand dollars."

"Yes, plus the five thousand dollar oil painting you liked so much. Didn't you realize it was from her?"

"No, I didn't. That is very generous of her."

At the end I add up the amount and it totals twenty-two thousand dollars, five thousand is from my mom and dad. Sam is like a little boy in a candy store, and I look at him and let him know how much I love him.

Sam later cooks ribs on the barbeque and I do rice and Chinese vegetables. It's a lovely warm evening, so we sit outdoors relaxing on the patio. We enjoy a glass of wine and sit there until the evening cools off.

Sam states, "I hate to bring this up, but one of my investigators found the reason for Kevin's departure from an Ontario teaching position. There was a stalking charge brought against him by his ex-wife. Did you know he had been married?"

I'm shocked and my face must show it. "No. He never mentioned it to me or my parents."

"Anyway, his ex-wife put a restraining order on him. There was no evidence of any physical abuse or assault later."

"Sam, I threatened him with a restraining order. Now I know why he became furious. Shit, he could be the one. The height is right anyway."

"Monday I am bringing Kevin into the interrogation room. If he shouts, "lawyer," then maybe he does have something to hide."

Sam sighs and then continues, "But for this weekend Ashley, this is our time. No more evil interrupting our space. Let's go try for twins."

We smile at each other.

CHAPTER 45

▼

The time has arrived Ashley, no more fun and games. No further court dramas, media circuses, and the holier than thou attitude for you. It is my desire, no my right to watch you squirm, and beg for your life. The game has been fun, rewarding, and therapeutic for me.

My sick, stupid, stubborn, and greedy brother did not heed my warning, would not leave me alone. First, I suffered the many years of blackmail and paid the psycho probably a total of half a million dollars.

Then he was begging for my help, when he was caught.

I recall the very first telephone call so many years ago. I was in my apartment when the phone rang at eleven in the evening. Looking at the clock, I remember thinking who in the hell is phoning me at this hour.

I bark, "Hello."

"Hello Matthew, this is Cory." I recall at the time that I thought this is a nightmare and I will wake shortly.

Stunned I say, "There is no one by the name of Matthew here."

"Listen Matt, don't screw with me. I have a very long gun with many notches and would rather not add your fucking name to it."

"I am not screwing with you. I am not Matt or Matthew. You have the wrong number."

I'm about to hang up the phone when his chilling voice, very menacing says, "Matthew, I will give you three seconds then I am visiting the local newspaper tomorrow. Do you understand me? One, two—"

"Yes," I mumble.

"Good. I am glad because I don't want to kill you. Here is what you'll do for me, by tomorrow afternoon at five. You will place in an envelope ten thousand dollars in unmarked twenty dollar bills."

"You're crazy. I am not giving you a cent, much less ten thousand dollars."

"Death will not come quickly to you Matthew, if you don't follow my directions." This is delivered to me in a very threatening manner. "It will be very slow and painful. Do you understand?"

Cory stops to let that sink in and then continues, "At precisely five in the afternoon you will shove this envelope underneath your front door, with a corner sticking into the hallway. I will pick it up immediately. Don't cross me Matthew or you are fucking dead."

My voice shaking, I ask, "Do you need my address?"

In the chilling voice my brother states, "No, I know where you live. In fact, I know everything about you."

The line goes dead and after all those years this is my welcome to my long lost brother. A brother, I had hoped never to see again.

Eighteen months later, I receive the second phone call from Cory, who is now answering to the alias of Tom Breton. This time he demands fifteen thousand dollars.

I beg him, "Cory, I can't continue paying you these large sums of money. This has to stop."

"Matthew, listen closely, very closely. You left me in the fucking orphanage to rot, while you enjoyed the good life."

I interrupt, "Believe me, my life wasn't wonderful."

"Shut the fuck up!" He screams, "What did I do over those years? I killed that slut of a Mommy of ours fourteen times, but she keeps reappearing no matter where I go. Here in Canada or in the states, selling her body in the streets. I did this killing for you, as well as for myself, so you owe me little brother, big time."

I am stunned, speechless, and wonder where do I go with this? I ask, "What do you mean Cory, when you say you have killed Mommy fourteen times?"

"Just what I said and she deserved it every time Matthew, after what she put us through. Do you remember the fucking pain and humiliation? Now back to the money. I want it at five, just like the last time."

I can't let the topic slide. "Look, Cory, Mommy died when we set the house on fire. She burned to a crisp. You were there for Christ sake, you know she died!"

"Yes, I know, but somehow the bitch keeps showing up again and again. I have to keep killing her. Remember to leave the money. See you brother."

I remember sitting far into the night thinking how screwed up Cory was; crisscrossing North America killing women who must look like Mommy. Obviously, he is picking the women off the street, probably mostly hookers.

I can taste the pain from my childhood. I don't recall a time when I was not faced with pain or an all consuming fear. I remember the guilt initially felt when it was Cory's turn to suffer. Later on, I would be happy, smiling in the darkness that she was beating on him, not me. I feel the all consuming anger building up, until I'm in a rage.

Cory's blackmail continues for years. He was constantly changing his name, until he answered to Billie Chartrand. This last time he called from a jail cell asking for help, because he had been charged with kidnapping, sexual assault, and attempted murder.

When he escaped I contemplated taking over his role in life. I decided it would be exciting and challenging. Certainly it was most profitable with no further blackmail. Besides, it was simple to carry out. I could still live my present life and get away with murder.

The stupid psycho called me shortly after his escape, as I knew he would, "Hey brother, I'm sure you heard about my escape. Killed the one pig, but hear the other lived. I just need ten grand to help me on my way."

"Do I call you Billie or Cory?"

"Matthew, with you it's always Cory."

"Well Cory, I would like to meet with you somewhere."

Suddenly, his voice sounds very angry. He asks, "Are you shitting me? What the fuck for?"

"I thought for old time sake, like a reunion, just you and me. We can share a few beers. You can fill me in as to what happened to you after we split, and I can tell you about my adopted parents."

"No need Matthew. After you left I spent most of my time in one of those teenage detention homes. I then escaped and lived on the fucking streets until I found you. Now brother, the detention center was something. One of the gay guards there came to our room nightly. He grabbed my ass out of bed and then dragged me kicking and screaming to the bathroom. I became his bitch. Don't have to explain to you, what fucking happened then."

I attempt to sound sympathetic and say, "That is a tough story, Cory."

"You bet your ass, while you lived the life of luxury. I used to think about meeting up with you a lot."

"Hell Cory, I just want to share a few beers."

Cory's voice becomes hard, "You will bring the money because if you double-cross me, you are stone, cold, dead." He speaks the last three words slowly with long pauses between each.

I didn't think it would be so easy. "Sure brother, I will bring the ten grand, plus the beer."

"Where do we meet?"

I convince him to meet me outside a wooded farm area at night. I explain I can't take a chance being seen with him. If I'm picked up I tell Cory, his source of money dries up. He falls for it. Cory is too hungry for the money, and is self confident he can take me out quickly if things go wrong. I am counting on surprise.

It was painless because from the first second of our meeting, Cory, continually whined about how I got all the breaks. Mommy had beat on him more. I was the one adopted after her death. I received an education. I made the money, and on, and on, and on. I could not listen to the whining and decided to quickly relieve his misery.

It was very straightforward to me. Bang a bullet between the eyes, then bang, a bullet in the heart. My years as a member of the Gun Club proved beneficial. Of course, I didn't use my registered guns.

There was shock in his eyes when I pulled out the gun, then a hint of a smile as I pulled the trigger. A smile, perhaps, because he thought I had dropped to his level?

No Billie, I am much, much, more intelligent. This is a game to me, while with you it was a lifestyle. You were a psycho, and I am not.

His blackmail over the years cost me a lot of money. But our hatred for our mommy bound us together. Yes, we did kill her so many years ago. Cory and I could no longer tolerate the abuse. We talked many nights when she was out about how to kill the bitch. Cory wanted to use a knife and make her cry out in pain. I convinced him to agree with my suggestion. We would burn her to death, thereby leaving less evidence. We waited for her to pass out drunk one night and torched the house.

It was my suggestion to wait until the fire had destroyed a large portion of the house, before we flung open the front door screaming, "Our mommy is in there!" But of course it was too late to save her.

We were covered with soot; our clothes smelled of acrid smoke; and we had inhaled some of it. The cops never suspected us. That night was the last I saw of Cory for many years. Cory never did explain how he located me, because of course I carry my adoptive parent's name.

My adopted parents were kind and generous enough, but after the fire I no longer cared about love. Was what our mother dished out to Cory and I called love? If it was I wanted none of it. Occasionally, I do wonder what love feels like, but have managed fine without it.

Power is what I have always sought and craved. With power comes control, and control is the greatest aphrodisiac in the world. Like, "Hey, Billie, you bastard, black-mail me," bang between the eyes, control.

Ashley you may be one of the up and coming prosecutors, but right now I completely control you. No one, not even you, would argue with that. I have forced you to your home. You are afraid to leave even to the corner store to purchase a carton of milk. But still you will be a greater fighter than Billie and Gail.

Your friend, Gail, was a disappointment. She was just too easy. In fact she was no fun at all. Oh she begged for mercy, but I needed to slash her arms to imitate Billie. It worked. Imagine the slashes on Sheila Kuzew's arms represented the number of kills for Billie.

Ashley, the reason for Gail's death was to hurt and control you. In addition it was so successful it proves to me that you will be easy to get to.

I understand you have completely gone underground, but I will prove it is impossible to run and hide from me. Soon you will die. The game is over. It is payback time.

CHAPTER 46

▼

Sam and I have a wonderful weekend together, relaxing and enjoying each other's company. It has been a while since we've had an opportunity to do this. Shopping is part of our agenda.

On Saturday afternoon Sam suggests we visit a few furniture stores. I'm interested in a bedroom suite and he wants a sixty inch plasma television.

Our first stop is at a very exclusive furniture store, and of course the suite I love is ten thousand dollars.

Sam comments, "Ashley, ten thousand dollars for somewhere to lay you head. It's ludicrous."

I look at him and attempt to explain the need for something this beautiful and comfortable. "You lay your head down at least six hours every day. You need comfort. Don't forget this lovely dresser and chiffonier. Look at the mirror."

"I am looking and I see a beautiful blond that in seconds will be down on the ten thousand dollar bed."

Obviously Sam isn't listening or if he is, doesn't care for my rationale. I say, "Be serious for a minute okay?" I suddenly feel closed in and want out of the store. I see a man with a baseball cap outside the large front window, and feel the perspiration rolling down my back. I don't want Sam to see my fear increasing, so I turn my back.

"Okay, if you like it we should buy it. I really do think it's beautiful. A lot of drawer space as well. I'm truly behind purchasing it."

"Well, we can leave it for now. But we do have the money from the wedding sitting in the bank."

"Is it my turn now?"

"Yes, let's go and look at some televisions now." I can't wait another minute to leave the building and head straight for the front door, at a fast clip.

One hour later Sam and I are proud owners of a sixty inch plasma television, with all the bells and whistles. He's so happy, it's comical. They have promised to deliver the television on Thursday next week. I can feel my fear decreasing, as we leave the crowds and head for the safety of our home.

Sam makes reference to my stalker late Saturday evening.

"Our artist will use his computer program to place a head of hair on Chartrand. We are hoping by doing so we can match him to his brother. It may be someone one of us will recognize."

I feel so depressed and frightened, I don't want to discuss my stalker, but know he needs to talk about it.

"That's a great idea."

"The judge couldn't be convinced to subpoena the adoption papers on Matthew Matlick, who is Billie's brother. I will continue to apply pressure. It may not assist us, but we need to cover every angle."

"When are you bringing in Kevin?"

"Monday afternoon."

"The more I concentrate on the characteristics of Kevin, the greater the possibility that he could be my stalker. He certainly was controlling, even to the point of selecting a movie without consulting me and arguing about which restaurant we would meet at for dinner. I realize it's minor but one usually wants to start a relationship with the best foot forward. In addition, Kevin, made reference to my work, that it was demanding too much of my time and attention. Can you imagine that?"

"Now that I know you, no I can't. There goes any need for me to be jealous of Kevin. Seriously, I feel we are close. Hang in there honey."

"I'm trying but each day I feel myself slipping deeper into depression. Every sound, movement, and accidental touch sends my heart pounding and takes my breath away. At times I stop breathing because of my fear and end up holding my breath. When I become dizzy it reminds me to breathe. I probably do need counseling."

"Actually, I remember the same thing happening to me as a young child, as I lay under a thin blanket, trying to lie perfectly still when my dad came home drunk."

"I know. Come here, I need to give you a hug."

"It's okay. This is about you not me. Sorry, I even mentioned it."

Sunday afternoon Mom and Dad call from the east coast. When I answer, Mom asks, "How is Mrs. Orlicky doing this morning?"

"Great Mom, everything is fine. What about you and Dad? Are you two having a grand time?"

"Yes and we thank both of you for the vacation tickets to Hawaii. Dad and I can hardly wait to take that trip. How is Sam doing?"

"He goes back to work tomorrow." I'm hoping she will not notice the fact I haven't included myself in the statement.

"Have you received more phone calls?"

"No, Mom I have not." I think to myself, *I must change the subject quickly.*

"Mom, what have you seen on your trip east?"

"We took many pictures dear, but I guess our favorite was Quebec City. And we enjoyed Toronto. There is so much to enjoy in that city. We took in a NHL hockey game. Dad wants to say hi."

Dad and I chat for a few minutes then we hang up. They are heading back to Alberta on Wednesday. Dad gives me their itinerary until then. I'm glad I didn't have to lie to Mom, because she asked about the telephone calls, not letters.

Sunday evening we enjoy some television, while stuffing ourselves with popcorn. Sam makes reference to the twelve dollars he paid for four kernels of popcorn at the movie theatre. We share a laugh.

At eleven, Sam suggests it's time for some shut eye and I agree. For two hours I watch him sleep. Occasionally, I find myself staring at the open bedroom door, as if expecting my tormentor to walk in. Eventually, I fall asleep.

CHAPTER 47

▼

It is Monday morning and Sam has left for work. He tells me to hang in. The phone rings early. I hate to answer it, but call display tells me it is work.

Shelly Galeno is calling, because Logan has been making sexual advances to her. Shelly says, "On Thursday last week he came into my office and said how attractive I was, that I looked hot and he was the man who possessed the remedy to fix me. I told him to get the hell out of my office, which he eventually did."

"I assume that didn't stop him."

I feel as if I'm suffering from information overload. What is wrong with me?

"No, on Friday he was back in my office and grabbed me. I became very angry and demanded he stop this behavior, but to no avail." She stops here and there is a long silence.

I cry out, "Oh my God, Shelly, did he touch you?"

Meekly she says, "No, not sexually, except he pushed me away from my door when I attempted to escape my office."

"Logan is such a jerk. Has he been back to your office?"

"No, but he cornered me in the office supply room; shut the door and would not let me leave. He said some pretty disgusting things to me. What do you suggest I do?"

I feel so guilty, because I could have prevented this by going to Jim myself, when Logan had grabbed me.

"See Jim immediately and tell him everything. Tell him I will talk to him on Wednesday, about a similar incident that happened to me. I'm so sorry, Shelly, for not doing so earlier."

"It's okay, as long as you support me later."

"That will not be a problem for me. Not only did he try a similar tactic with me, but he is useless at work."

"I have one more thing to tell you. Marty Kroll spoke to me this morning and is very anxious to speak to you, about a plea bargain with the school teacher he is representing."

"Yes, I remember he had called before the wedding, but I believe you said he agreed to wait for my return."

"I told Marty you were not in today, but he seemed very much in a hurry to speak to you. What should I do?"

"Do you mind calling him back and telling him that I will be there on Wednesday? I will see him at that time." We discuss the current case and hang up.

To keep my mind occupied I start by sorting through the wedding gifts, placing them according to gifts to return, gifts to keep, and gifts to share. The keep gifts, I stash in appropriate cupboards. The return gifts will have to wait until Sam or Pamela can accompany me to the stores. I want to cry because the bastard has truly forced me to stay within my home. Choking back the tears, I put a CD in the stereo and turn up the volume.

I sit at the kitchen table with a blank sheet of paper in front of me. My objective is to list recent men in my life who would have cause, or what they interpret, as reason to despise me and ultimately cause me harm. Sam has asked me to do this, and I know it's to keep my mind occupied.

I now accept that if my stalker is not captured soon, he will kill me. Somehow I can sense the game is nearly over. Torture will be a big part of his game. I die a little inside every time Gail comes to mind. She suffered so much because of me. It's now my turn, and I'm scared shitless.

Sam or someone needs to identify my tormentor soon, because I'm losing control. There are scores of fears inside of me. Lately it seems difficult to breathe. I'm afraid to sleep at night without a light. Even with Sam beside me I appreciate how quickly his life and mine can be extinguished. Have I not listened to countless women who were asleep in their own bed, only to have a molester wake them to a live nightmare? That will not happen to me.

When I shower, Sam must accompany me to the bathroom. When the water is running over me I can visualize a knife to the back or hands around my neck squeezing. No amount of coaxing from Sam, about my locking the bathroom door, calms me.

When Sam leaves the house I'm petrified and must be constantly moving. If I don't, I often sit and stare at the kitchen door knob expecting it to silently turn. I check the security system at least twenty times a day. I find it difficult to relax.

A creaking sound from the house or click of the furnace will have me bolting from the chair. I admit that the CD suggestion from Sam has helped. Even glancing out the window freaks me out. My stalker may be out there with high powered binoculars, watching my every move from the park across the way. My home has become a darkened dungeon, because I often have all blinds and drapes drawn.

I'm afraid to and am prohibited from doing the simplest of tasks: to get groceries; to shop for new clothes or shoes; or to take in our dry cleaning. My yard is off limits to me. I am prevented from checking my trees, to assess how they have survived the winter. By the time Sam arrives home and we eat, it's too late and he's tired.

Driving is out, work is out, entertainment is out, and visiting is out. My only companion is fear and it is rapidly destroying me.

My stalker has managed to limit my contact with family. I am frightened for my folks, so I tell them things are fine. Visits from my parents are discouraged, because I will not have them lay down their life for me. Nor will I visit them, to draw attention to the important role they play in my life. Gail suffered and lost her life because of her association with me.

This fear has replaced many of my positive emotions and what remains is an all encompassing terror. Terror is driving a wedge between Sam and me as well. In recent days, I'm experiencing difficulty in expressing love of any kind. Of course, Sam, senses this and our lovemaking is suffering.

The fact is that if someone were to ask me if I was capable of murder today, my answer is yes. I feel like I have nothing to lose and hate my tormentor beyond anything I ever imagined.

I stare at the blank paper in front of me. I wander over to the security system to check it. I then return to the paper. The first name I jot down on the paper is Billie Chartrand. For many reasons, I believe he is the key to the puzzle. The only problem is that there are too many pieces missing. From day one in the courtroom the sensation was there that his eyes were attempting to rip my soul from my body. He will definitely be my number one pick, if the police can not prove through DNA, that the body discovered is his. Lack of forensic evidence in this mystery is the problem. My tormentor is intelligent. There is no doubt about that.

From Chartrand my mind immediately jumps to his brother. Who and where is this mystery brother? Did he attend Billie's trial? The psychiatrist did refer to Chartrand's intelligence. Is his brother as brilliant? Does this man even have a role in this mystery?

Third on my list is Kevin. Prior to the recent discovery of his marriage and subsequent divorce, I had felt Kevin was annoying but not dangerous. Today, I mark a star beside his name. The stalking charge laid against him by his ex-wife concerns me. It will be interesting to hear about his reaction during the meeting with Sam this afternoon. He certainly is a control freak. Kevin has remained interested in me. He was there taking pictures at my wedding.

I add Logan to my list. There have been increased vibes of uneasiness about him. Since day one on the job, I observed his total lack of respect for women. He despises me not only for the recent episode in my office, but because of my position in the department. Logan honestly believes he will one day be the chief crown prosecutor. My stalker's walk seemed familiar, when he left the department store that day.

Over the past year, I have been conscious of the animosity toward me of other sexual assault predators I prosecuted, but not to the point of hatred. This assessment would include Lott and Jakubitz, who now sits in a federal penitentiary in Prince Albert, Saskatchewan.

I am thinking further about my list when the door bell rings. I leap out of my chair in fear, and slide my piece of paper into a drawer.

To my surprise, when I check the side window, I find Marty Kroll standing there, briefcase in hand. Obviously he didn't receive Shelly's call. I stare at him. Marty is busy glancing at his watch.

I shut off the security system and open the door. "Hi Ashley, I desperately need to discuss a plea bargain for my client. I don't wish to negotiate a plea with Shelly Galeno."

I am not totally comfortable, but decide I can get rid of him quickly.

"Marty, didn't you receive a call from Shelly saying I will meet with you on Wednesday?"

"No, I didn't. I promise I will not be long."

I open the door wider and lead Marty into the kitchen. I say, "Okay, I will get a quick coffee for you, than I must leave for a 1:30 appointment. We can set a time for Wednesday, when I am back in my office."

As I reach into the cupboard for a cup, I hear this raspy voice directly behind me, "Ashley, don't lie."

I think I will convulse. The cup falls suddenly from my nerveless fingers and smashes into pieces on the floor. Fear rips through me, as I slowly turn around. Nightmares have now become reality.

Marty is sitting at the kitchen table, gun in hand. I lean against the counter to keep myself upright. My voice trembling, I say, "I don't understand, Marty."

This statement is the truth because the last person I would suspect is Marty.

"No, few people do. Although my brother Billie, if he was alive, would understand why I'm here. Sadly, he is dead. But you and the police are aware of that fact. The fact that it was me who killed him will remain our little secret, Ashley."

"Don't do this." I can't keep the plea from my voice.

Pointing the gun in the direction of my head he commands, "Sit."

I hesitate and Marty leaps from his chair, knocking it to the floor. He rushes at me and strikes out, his fist connecting with my check bone. I hear a loud cracking sound, throughout my head and the resulting pain leaves me faint and nauseated. Marty is not done.

The next blow from a backhand across my lower jaw, snaps my head to the side and I fall to the floor. He picks me up and smashes me in the mouth, so hard I feel teeth sliding down my throat. During the beating, Marty, keeps shouting, "Take that Mommy!" over and over. His eyes are opened wide and glazed over, and he is breathing rapidly, almost hyperventilating.

My mind is screaming, *Please, no more! I can't take anymore!*

He finally reaches down and grabs my hair. He drags me to a chair. My world is spinning and I know I will vomit soon. I attempt deep breathing, but the pain in my jaw makes it difficult to breathe and blood is now pouring from my nose. I know I should attempt to stop it, but am afraid to move. I just let it drip down my shirt and onto the table.

Marty grabs a box of tissue from the counter, and throws it in my direction. "Here, clean your face. It's a mess."

I press a hand full of Kleenex to the bridge of my nose, trying to stop the flow of blood. Tilting my head back, I realize the blood is now coming from my mouth as well.

Death stares at me from across the table. I must concentrate on escape. The key for now is to keep him talking.

"When did you discover Billie was your brother?" It hurts so much to talk and I'm now swallowing my own blood.

"Ashley, Ashley, I will fill you in, but death still awaits you. Don't attempt to stall what is inevitable."

He sits there saying nothing further, but his eyes are glued to my face.

I look at Marty and the more I stare at him the more he resembles his brother. They have the same dead, evil eyes, and Marty now wears the sneer Billie wore throughout the trial. It sends a shiver through my body.

He looks at me and says, "You do look so like Mommy. She made us call her that you know. Just like Mommy, with your long, blond hair, and blue eyes, and the way you walk. I remember the first time I laid eyes on you; the overwhelming hatred I experienced. I wanted to kill you right then and there. But it is well worth the wait. Didn't you see the similarities between Billie's last victim and you?"

"No, and I still don't." The pain and fear are threatening to render me completely helpless. I must maintain consciousness and somehow escape this mad man. The bleeding has slowed somewhat.

"Billie confided to me how much emotional pain was relieved as he carved up the Kuzew girl. Mommy was getting her due. You see as the eldest, Billie, took more hits. He had so many scars to prove it. One day she grabbed a broom handle and whacked him so hard she broke his thigh. Mommy would place sharp knives under our finger nails, when she was drunk or spaced out on hashish. To this day I can hear Billie screaming."

"My God, that is terrible. But Marty, I'm not your mommy. Look at me please. I'm Ashley."

Marty pauses for a moment, as if he didn't hear me and then, "You know the bastard blackmailed me for years. He kept popping up like a Jack-in-the-box." He is staring at me, as if he wants me to ask.

I whisper, "What about?"

"We killed our mommy in a fire. We burned her right up by torching the house." Marty snaps his fingers. "Just like that and she was toast." He laughs the same sick way he had on the phone. "She deserved much more, the filthy bitch. Cory wanted to torture her first."

"Look at me. I'm not your mother." I decide to go for it. "You want an excuse for your behavior, so you pretend I'm your mother. We can get you professional help. Don't do this." The energy used to plead has left me nearly unconscious.

"Oh yes, you bitch, prancing in front of the jurors getting the men to vote guilty. You are no different than Mommy. She used her beauty to get drug money."

"I'm different from your mommy. I have never hurt you. Tell me. When have I hurt you?"

"I need a release from this pounding in my head before it explodes." He suddenly stops speaking, then continues, "It hurts so much." A pause, then he says, "Your husband is getting too close to finding me."

It's becoming more difficult to speak, much less clearly.

"For the pain in your head you can use the strong analgesic in the medicine cabinet, that Sam used when he hurt his ankle."

Suddenly he shouts, "Look at this knife, look at it!" Marty is now waving the knife in front of my face. The gun is in his other hand. As I glance toward the kitchen door, he places the silencer of the gun between my eyes. I feel the cold steel. I stop breathing. Sweat is sliding down both sides of my face and my whole body is trembling.

"Yes, Mommy you do know the fear. I can smell it. The fear of awakening in the morning, of going to bed at night, of fixing meals, or walking too loudly, or too softly. I never knew when your heavy hand would explode on the side of my head, or when I would feel the excruciating pain because you twisted my arm behind my back. It's payback time, you bitch."

As Marty rants, I try to measure the distance from my chair to the door and his distance from me, as he circles the table.

When he stops for a second I ask, "Why did you agree to represent him at trial?" Anything, just keep him talking.

Marty stares at me, then answers, "Because he threatened to notify the press about the two of us killing Mommy. Of course I couldn't let that happen."

"Did Cory want to kill me?" By now I am having great difficulty even whispering; the pain in my mouth and jaw are so severe. I am pinching my nose hoping to completely stop the flow of blood.

"Of course he did, probably as much as me. One day in court he wrote on a paper, "Should we kill her right now?" Yes, my brother hated you."

No wonder I felt so much evil in the courtroom during Billie's trial. There were two of them filled with this hatred for me.

"Why did you kill Gail? You knew her and what a kind person she was. It was such a senseless killing."

He is looking at me with pride. He answers, "I just wanted to bring, Ms. Know It All, down a peg or two. You bitch. You really thought you were so much brighter than me. Look at us now. Who is the winner here, Ashley?"

I'm thinking, *What a sick man, a psycho.* Hoping to keep him occupied, I ask, "Did you call the newspaper about your chase in the park?"

He roars, "Yes!" Suddenly Marty is back beside me, "Put your arm on the table, flat. Now!" he screams. The knife slashes across my right forearm and blood quickly replaces the knives edge as Marty whips it away. The feeling initially is a burning sensation then the pain takes over. Before I can fully register what is happening to me, he slashes again and again.

I am screaming in pain and terror. Someone save me from this madman. Sam, where are you?

"Mommy, you look frightened. Did you ever think about my fear, my pain, and need for love? No, I don't think so."

"Please Marty, let me go." I sob. "I have never hurt you or Billie. I'm not your mommy.

"Oh you would appreciate being released. Did you release Billie at trial?"

I realize Marty is drifting back and forth. My arms are bleeding profusely and I know I must make a move soon. I wish Sam and I had known about the black-mail money Billie was living on. If we had, I believe we would have thought of Marty as a possible suspect. He is very intelligent, with loads of money. Even the remark he made to me after Billie's escape makes sense to me now. It all makes sense when you have the pieces to the puzzle. It's too late, I am going to die.

Marty starts again, "My brother tracked me down years ago to blackmail me. I was also his ace in the hole if he ever required legal help. When charged with the rape he called and begged me to see him in prison. How could I refuse? He was my brother. Over a two hour conversation he shared his life with me. I knew immediately he was my older brother. We kept our relationship a secret, because I didn't want the world to know I had a psycho for a brother. When he escaped from prison he contacted me and I was eager to meet with him."

He pauses and looks around as if lost in another world.

He continues, "I had a plan. I could commit murder and never be a suspect. I set a date, time and the place being off a secluded farm road outside the city. We exchanged pleasantries, then I shot him between the eyes."

He waves the gun and then places it between my eyes, "Bang!"

I scream and Marty smiles. I have soiled my pants.

I feel myself losing a grip on reality. Seconds elapse and I whisper, "How could you do that to your brother?"

"Easy, Cory meant nothing to me. We shared a house, not a home, from birth to eleven years. There were no playful memories, shared little boy secrets, love, only abuse and sadness. I was left with one emotion, hate. Can you feel the hatred, Mommy?"

"I can understand your hatred of your mother but I have always respected you, Marty." At this moment I hate him as much as I'm sure he hated his mother. The strength of this emotion is totally new to me.

He sighs, "Sure you did, Ashley. It's people like you who make the monsters of the world." Suddenly he is shouting and pounding his fist on the table. "Someone has to stop them, punish them!"

"How did you get into Gail's house? Did she let you in?" I am now slurring my speech as I feel my life slipping away.

"No. When she was in the library one day, I went into her room and searched her purse. I stole her keys and made copies of them. I then watched her room from the main desk, and when she left for the washroom, I slipped into her office and replaced the keys. The girls at your front desk are always so helpful and friendly. They never asked what I was doing on the floor. After all, I have business meetings there often. I waited in her bedroom closet for her."

I feel so nauseous, so helpless, and so very weak.

He pauses, "Same applies to your cell phone when I cut your phone line. My presence in your office area was never questioned." Suddenly Marty jumps to his feet and his face is red and vicious looking. "Listen you little whore, enough talking. It is time for you to feel the pain now!" With that he slices me again and again.

I'm now throwing up and failing quickly. I recognize it is now or never. Waiting until he rounds the far end of the table, I push back my chair and bolt, bent over at the waist, for the door.

I feel the bullet miss my head and implode in the door frame. Then I sense the knife entering my back with brutal force. My last split-second thought is of Sam. Then total darkness.

CHAPTER 48

───────────── ▼ ─────────────

When I attempt to open my eyelids, they feel weighted down as if leaded. Hearing voices in the background I want to reach out to touch; to have human contact. My mind commands my arm to lift, but it remains flat on the bed. Where am I? Then the nightmare rolls in and I feel agitated, restless, and want to scream. There is an overwhelming fear. But a voice I recognize high above me tells me to relax, let go, and sleep. With these words of reassurance, I feel a rush of warmth flow through me and I drift off.

The first voice I truly remember hearing is my mother's, "Dad, she is trying to open her eyes. Ashley, Dad and I are here. We love you."

"Mom is he in jail?" The effort needed to speak seems to drain me of all strength. I do not remember her answer. I drift in and out of this nightmare, remembering Sam, Mom, Dad, Pamela, Shelly, Jim, and many others. The pain at times is severe, and I hear myself whimpering.

The doctor seems to have a brisk demeanor. This is followed by the kind words of a nurse.

I remember asking Dad about Sam, "Where is Sam?" I whisper these words because I can't open my mouth for some reason.

Dad leans over and answers, "Sam is fine. He is at work, busy with follow-up."

After some time, I manage to whisper, "I remember him being here."

"Yes, Sam has been here, sometimes for hours. He comes as often as he can. This has been hard on him. Mom and I are very impressed with your husband. We love him. He has been very kind and drives us back and forth to the hospital. We are staying at your home. You remember your mom's friend, Vi. She is taking care of our place. Vi is your mom's church buddy. She's the one with the very pretty face and great sense of humor."

"How am I, Dad?"

I don't remember his response. My need for information is great, because during my periods of consciousness I am beginning to feel fear, as it takes over my waking moments as well.

The next time I open my eyes the sun is streaming into the room and the sun beam seems to give me strength.

With great difficulty I ask my parents, "What happened?" Just thinking about Marty causes feelings of restlessness, and I am aware of Mom's hand resting gently on my shoulder.

With a great deal of emotion, Dad responds, "Sam killed that bastard in self-defense, Ashley. He put a bullet between his eyes. Oh, I wish I could have been there."

I hear Mom taking a deep breath and speaking sternly to my Dad, "Barry, this is not the time to have this conversation. Ashley, close your eyes and sleep."

"Mom, I want to know what happened." It takes me what seems like an hour to speak these few words.

Dad continues, "Well, as you fell to the floor from the bastard knifing you, Sam came charging in through the front door. Marty grabbed his pistol from the table and pointed it toward Sam. Exactly at that moment Sam pulled his trigger and shot him right between the eyes."

I can't believe he was my tormentor all those months. I ask, "Is Marty dead?"

"Yes. Poor Sam saw you covered in blood with only the handle of a knife sticking out of your back. He said he wanted to empty his gun into Marty. Sam thought it would be a payback of sorts, for you and Gail. Instead, he ran to your side and called an ambulance."

My eyes sweep the room. I look at Mom, "What about me? How am I? I need to know because there are things I can't remember."

Mom answers, "They did three hours of life saving surgery on you. Sam managed to reach us on the coast and we were here in hours. Your prognosis is for a slow, but full recovery. That was three days ago. This is great news, Ashley. Try not to think about it now. Just rest; it's what you need. Sam tells us it is months since you slept well."

Later after yet another sleep I awaken and do remember my conversation with Mom and Dad. I see Mom standing beside my bed and I ask, "When will I be able to go home?"

I desperately want to hear her say tomorrow.

"You will remain in hospital for a least another three or four days. You lost so much blood. Your jaw is also wired which is why you are having difficulty speaking. Of course you have a lot of pain."

I whisper, "I see."

Mom says, "You have to give yourself time to heal dear. You can't rush these things."

"Mom, I'm afraid." I barely whisper.

"What did you say?"

"Nothing, it's okay." I feel embarrassed.

Mom then continues, "Dad and I are planning to stay with you when you are discharged from hospital. That way Sam can continue to work and not worry about your physical care at home." Mom gently rubs my forehead.

"Why did Sam come home?"

I should add and save my life but my mouth hurts too much. I can feel where my teeth are missing.

"Sam had the technician using a computer program to add a head of hair to a composite of Billie. When completed, Sam felt he recognized a few similarities to someone he knew. Ten minutes later it came to him and Sam had one of the investigators hunt up a picture of Marty Kroll. The technician then removed Marty's mustache and as Sam explained, "Bingo, the rest is history." He is upset that he didn't figure this out earlier."

"Mom, I feel dumb letting Marty into our home. I never suspected him. I disliked him, but" I need to stop to take in a breath, "I didn't think him capable of such heinous acts as torturing and murdering Gail."

"I know dear, but remember nothing is your fault."

The surgeon visits the next morning. I ask, "Will I have scars on my arms?" I remember Sheila Kuzew and how conscious she was of her knife scars. I haven't seen mine because they are bandaged.

"Mrs. Orlicky, at this time you need to rest and help your body heal those wounds and your jaw." He examines me and promptly leaves without answering me. I'm disappointed, but say nothing.

After the surgeon and nurse leave, I realize I'm alone. I feel the fear overtake me. The trembling starts in my hands and spreads throughout my body. I'm in a panic, when I hear a voice ask, "How are you, Ashley?"

It's my boss, Jim. I have never been so happy to see him.

"Come here and sit beside my bed." I can't prevent myself from adding, "Can I hold your hand?"

He doesn't look at me but instead he glances around the room, perhaps for help.

I clarify, "I'm so afraid, just let me hold your hand."

Jim clasps my hand in his and I see large tears rolling down his checks and so much compassion in his eyes. I squeeze his hand harder and slowly the fear subsides. If he notices the increase in pressure, he doesn't acknowledge it.

"Thank you for doing this. How is work holding up?"

Jim looks more comfortable with this subject and says, "We are extremely busy; I will not lie to you. With all the gang related killings we are having difficulty keeping up. But don't concern yourself with work, instead concentrate on getting well."

"Is Shelly managing my case load?"

"Yes, she is and she is doing a fine job. You did a fantastic job of training her and thank you for that. I have fired Logan and we are in the process of hiring another prosecutor. Ashley, take as long as you need, just get well again. Your job is waiting for you whenever you are ready to return. That can be in six months or two years. You are impossible to replace."

"Thank you Jim. And please pass along a thank you to all the folks at work for the many flowers and well wishes."

As he rises to leave he must notice the look of horror that crosses my face. He asks, "Do you want me to stay with you or call a nurse?"

"Yes. Call a nurse, because I know how busy you are. Thank you." He presses the call button.

The nurse arrives and I ask if she knows where my parents or husband are right now, because my visitor is about to leave.

She is about to answer when Sam walks in and I start to sob. The nurse and Jim leave and Sam holds me gently in his arms.

"What is wrong? Why are you crying?"

I look into his eyes and sobbing say, "I'm so afraid, Sam. I know Marty is dead, but I'm still frightened. Am I crazy, Sam?"

"No honey, it will take time. I will make sure someone is always with you. Your parents, Pamela, Shelly, your other friends or mine, and of course me, will sit here beside you."

"Thank you."

"I will ask for a cot to sleep here at night, until you come home. I love you so much."

I reach for and hold his hand. "I love you too. Thank you for saving my life."

"I wish I could have been there an hour earlier. You look exhausted honey, close your eyes. Someone will be here when you wake up."

The love in Sam's eyes eases my fear and I sleep.

In the morning I awake and Pamela is sitting beside me. It must be time for my pain pill, because when I attempt a smile my whole face screams out in pain. I ring for the nurse.

Pamela leans close and consoles me, "It is fine if you don't talk, I have a lot to say."

I whisper, "What does my face look like? No one gives me a mirror. I will be up to the bathroom this afternoon."

"Why Ashley, your facial features consist of two deep blue eyes, high cheek bones, and a luscious mouth. Your face is framed by long, beautiful, blond hair. These are your permanent features."

I must be looking confused, because Pamela stops for a second and then continues, "Temporarily you have two black eyes, a huge bump on you left forehead, which knocked you unconscious when you hit the corner of the lower cupboard on your way down to the floor. The right side of your face has all the colors of the rainbow. You have, let me see, seven stitches running from your lip to jaw line. From what I can tell you have three teeth missing."

I can't laugh, because I have too much pain, but manage to say, "Please don't make me laugh."

"Okay. Now I will tell you. I have never seen you look so beautiful. Do you know why I say that?"

"No." I whisper.

"Because you are alive my friend and many of us waiting during your surgery didn't know if you would make it. So rest Ashley, you look beautiful to all of us."

The nurse arrives with my analgesic and I sleep. Pamela holds my hand.

True to his word, I'm not left alone while in the hospital. It is heart warming to realize how many wonderful relatives and friends I have, who offer me comfort and what I perceive as protection.

E P I L O G U E

▼

Eight months have passed and I'm stronger each day. When I arrived home from hospital, I was shocked and pleasantly surprised to see that Sam had purchased and organized the ten thousand dollar bedroom suite. The room looked magnificent. He had transferred all our belongings into the new drawers. He had his friend, Ken, take the old furniture to my parent's place.

Mom and Dad visit often. They are currently down for a weekend. My parents keep reminding us about their grandchildren.

Mom teases Sam, "Dad and I want to hear the patter of little feet soon. We are not getting younger."

The expression on Sam's face is priceless; somewhere between embarrassment and surprise at his mother-in-law's comment. Sam's reply surprises me, "Soon. We are constantly working at it."

Mom laughs and then Dad says, "Actually, it's almost time to go to bed."

Sam and I have discussed having children and we agree it is important to wait until I have regained control of my life.

We have discussed the possibility of my opening a small private practice some day. Maybe it's time to move away from the years of dealing with the rapists and child molesters. To date, I don't know if it's possible to give up my career as a prosecutor. When I hear the foreman of the jury say, "Guilty," I feel my heart beat faster for justice. Sam keeps reminding me there is more to life than being a prosecutor. Shelly has also expressed an interest in joining my practice, if I choose that route.

Sam and I have grown closer since the attack. He encourages me to discuss my fears, which still linger. I have found a psychiatrist, who I see weekly to help me overcome my obsessive-compulsive behavior. I no longer check the security system every fifteen minutes, during my waking hours.

We have spent time discussing Sam's grandparents on his mother's side. I have convinced him to visit the place of his mother's birth and to take me with him. His blood pressure has stabilized and is controlled with his lifestyle changes.

Daily, Sam shares his inner strength with me. Today, I'm able to shop for groceries on my own.

One day I hope to return to my morning jog in the park. But I haven't reached that stage yet. Sam does jog with me, mostly on Sunday afternoons. We visited the Mantles and they were delighted with the German shepherd puppy we bought them. Ralph named the puppy, Rusty.

My friends, in particular Pamela and Shelly come over regularly. Pamela's relationship with Perry is still going strong. There may be wedding bells in the near future. Shelly shares that work is pleasant with Logan gone. They have hired another prosecutor to replace him. The three of us shop on a Saturday or have lunch on Sunday. Once a month Sam and I pick up Gail's mom, and the three of us visit Gail's grave. I feel her smiling down on us.

I would not have believed it possible, if someone had told me prior to these horrific events entering my life, that I could be totally dominated, and controlled by another individual. But that is what Marty did by terrorizing me. He filled me with fear and I occasionally still need to fight back the feelings I experienced. But now I am able to control my reaction to it.

My parents told me Kevin Manguard has moved back to Ontario. Apparently he came to the hospital wanting to visit me, but Sam had left word for Kevin to be excluded from my visitor list.

Dad brings me back to the present by asking if we have picked out names for his future grandchildren.

Sam responds, "Of course, Tyler, Barry, Samuel for a boy and Cymbre, Lucille, Gail, for a girl."

My parents and Sam smile at me. I am on the road to recovery.

978-0-595-48926-8
0-595-48926-5

Printed in the United States
109677LV00004B/73-87/P